# heartwaves

A GREYFIN BAY NOVEL

ANITA KELLY

ISBN 978-1-7372298-4-1



Cover photograph by Jordan Steranka.

# content warnings

While containing plenty of joy, *Heartwaves* also tackles many weighty topics, including:

- grief from recent death of a close friend
- PTSD from a random act of violence, including triggers on page
- malicious property damage
- mentions of past cheating
- illness of a parent, but no parent dies on page (nor is any dog harmed)

Polyamory/non-monogamy is also discussed, along with queer life in small American towns. While I always aim to explore my characters' experiences with complicated topics as true to those characters as I can, everyone's experiences are different. Please take care if any of these subjects are impactful to you.

*For Melinda*
*Romancelandia will always miss you*

# one

THE FIRST TIME Mae Kellerman saw the ocean, she screamed.

At least, her parents had always described the memory as such: a long howl, torn from their toddler's chest at the first crash of a wave. Accompanied by vicious kicks into Mae's mother's stomach, a pounding at shoulders her parents first interpreted as fear. And so Jodi Dupont-Kellerman had hugged her toddler tighter, shielding her bonneted head from the wind with a hand, until her husband Felix suggested they try putting baby Mae's feet down in the sand.

And the moment they hit, Mae was off. Running in the half-sideways, mostly-drunk way of toddlers toward the green-blue of the Atlantic.

Her howl turned more shrill, chubby fists rising in the air, until gradually, Jodi and Felix understood it was a cry of wonder. One Mae kept up the entire time Felix lifted her through the shallows of the waves, the sound refusing to leave Mae's body no matter how Jodi and Felix tried to calm her. Until, eventually, laughing and holding palms over their ears, they walked away from the sand back to their old Subaru, to give Mae's growing lungs a rest.

Forty years later, Mae gazed at a different ocean and rather felt like screaming again. Until her lungs once more wore themselves out. Until the waves told her what to do.

Instead, she sipped too-hot green tea from a paper cup.

And glanced back, again, at the building behind her. Wide slats of worn, dark wood ran up both stories, like a saloon in an old Western. Like it was weathered half by sea salt, half by tumbleweed.

A faded red and white sign hung in its picture window, above a chipped sill covered in dust.

*For Sale by Owner*

*503-555-9032*

Mae's eyes flicked back toward Main Street. It was rare on the Oregon Coast, a shoreline almost completely protected by state law, to have a commercial strip so close to the sea. She studied the small café across the way where she'd acquired this green tea, the waves of the Pacific visible behind it. To the left, a kiosk for whale watching tours. Just past that, a set of wide, concrete steps, leading down to the shore. Mist rose off the sand as the morning warmed, burning off the wet damp of night. Revealing more of the cliffs that stood at either end of the beach: lichen-covered brackets for both the shallow bay and the town that hugged it.

She wasn't supposed to be here.

She was supposed to be in Newport, at the very least, visiting her parents before heading back home. She was supposed to be in Portland. She had to return to work tomorrow at the community center after almost two weeks away.

She turned and rested her back against the railing of the

porch. Stared again at the smudged window and the dark space beyond. An emptiness, waiting to be made bright.

Mae dug her phone out of her pocket.

She'd had time, these last two weeks, to scream.

It was time for something new.

A rough, deep voice picked up on the third ring.

"Dell."

Mae's pulse jumped at the brief, monosyllabic greeting. Was that a name?

"Hi." She cleared her throat, standing straighter, as if the person on the other end of the line could see her. "I'm calling about the vacant storefront? On Main Street?"

Silence.

Mae had dialed before she could think too hard. Figured it wouldn't hurt to at least get some information. Had also figured procuring it wouldn't be a terribly difficult thing to do. But as the silence on the other end of the line stretched, she got her wits about her, and retrieved her customer service voice to properly continue the conversation.

"Sorry, let me start that again. My name is Mae Kellerman, and I'm standing in front of this storefront for sale, here at the end of Main Street in Greyfin Bay. Next to the bar."

Mae had never spent much time in Greyfin Bay before yesterday. It was south of the towns on the northern coast that were an easy day drive from Portland. A small blip along the way to Newport when she drove down to visit Jodi and Felix.

But as she'd stood on the sidewalk of Main Street last night, the ocean at her back, Jesús's ashes now churning in its depths, she'd looked at the strip of darkened storefronts buffeted by the foothills of the Coastal Range behind them, and something about it had made her pause. Actually take it in, for perhaps the first time.

Maybe everything simply looked a little different, after you'd lost someone.

A world-weary sigh rattled in Mae's ear.

"What do you want with it?"

"Well, I'd love to take a look at it. Hear the listing price."

"No. What do you plan on doing with it?"

Mae frowned. Dell's voice was throwing her off. Not only because he sounded so annoyed at being asked about the property he was purportedly, according to the red and white sign, trying to sell.

But because the gravel of that voice, the deep timbre, was the exact kind of voice that had always made Mae's skin hot and tight. Like a smoky pull of whiskey, settling low in her stomach. Even without having any idea what this person looked like, Mae felt a flash of out-of-place desire, an irrational wish for him to ask her to strip off her clothes.

She blinked. *Customer service voice, Mae.* Like a grown, competent human with a shocking amount of money to burn.

An amount of money that allowed her to finally answer—

"A bookstore."

Another beat of silence. During which Mae tilted her chin at herself in the dark window, commanding her reflection to not feel embarrassed about voicing her and Becks's old dream out loud.

She had told herself last night that it was silly. That the storefront, when she'd first aimlessly stumbled upon it, had prompted ancient memories to bloom inside her head at all. Such unexpected visitors, so funny next to her empty, out-of-body grief, that Mae must have smiled deliriously to herself and that dusty window in the darkness for twenty minutes.

It had been a long time since she'd thought about Becks.

And maybe it was still self-indulgent. Standing here again now, in the light of day, calling this grumpy, sexy-voiced person. Still somehow contemplating the idea.

But maybe it wasn't silly. Maybe it was, in fact, remarkably easy to imagine that empty room beyond her reflection filled with bookshelves. With tables and displays and pride flags and an antique lamp on that sturdy counter, and maybe a map of the Oregon Coast behind it, and—

"You think," Dell drawled, "Greyfin Bay has enough of a draw to sustain a bookstore. All year round."

"Yes," she answered, with confidence. A confidence she might not have fully felt, say, ten minutes ago, but which she felt in every ounce of her being after listening to this stranger talk to her like she was a fool. The old dreams and new ideas that had gathered in her head overnight, half conscious as she attempted to sleep in the backseat of her car, began to unspool.

"I was thinking it could also be a coffee shop. Surely residents need caffeine twelve months of the year in addition to books."

It had been high on her and Becks's list, back in the day. A hissing espresso bar on top of a grand mahogany counter had, obviously, been a necessary component of their fantasy store.

"Ginger's is right across the street."

Mae glanced again at the café where she'd gotten her tea. She wanted to point out that Ginger's only seemed to offer drip coffee that probably came in a pre-ground bag and Lipton tea packets, and she was confident Greyfin Bay, as small of a town as it was, could use a latte or two. But she didn't press her luck, in the chance she somehow sound eager about putting the small town café across the street out of business.

Which, for the record, she was not. Lipton wasn't bad.

"I was also considering"—Mae looked up at the second story and set her jaw—"that part of the building could be fashioned into a queer community center. Which, unlike Ginger's, I'm pretty sure Greyfin Bay doesn't already have."

Because maybe Mae couldn't go back to the community center that had been her home for so long. That had been her home with Jesús. Maybe it would still be irresponsible, leaving the life in Portland she'd worked so hard to build. But maybe her old dream with Becks would be less selfish if she could continue social work here, too. Maybe—

There were so many maybes, suddenly, in this old building.

Jesús had loved this town. Had specified the beach behind her for the spreading of his ashes.

Maybe Jesús had led Mae to Greyfin Bay on purpose.

Which was normally the kind of fate-tinged bullshit Mae didn't believe in, but a desperation filled her chest just then, quick and hot as lightning. An aching, yearning sensation that threatened to burst out of her skin. The world had been tilted, strange, slightly out of her grasp ever since Jesús left, and she wanted to grab onto something—wanted to punch through this old door and dance in the middle of the dirty floorboards—until she could set it to rights. Until she could hold reality in her hands again. Going back to the city didn't even make *sense*. What was left for her in the city other than her friends? And she knew she'd never lose her friends. She was so burnt out, and starting new, taking Jesús's money and doing something *fully hers*, like he had told her to, something she could build from the ground up—

Jesús's voice, raspy and tired and sure in his hospital bed, broke into her brain once more.

*I know that woman hurt you.*

*I want you to trust the world again.*

Mae found herself short of breath.

"And I'd have a strong online presence, for both sales and virtual events and—"

"Where are you from?"

The question, asked like a slap, broke Mae abruptly out of her reverie.

Mae, to be clear, was as white as a white person in Oregon could be, but her brain still rankled at the concept of the question.

"Where am I *from*?"

Another aggrieved sigh.

"Where do you live? Currently."

Mae inhaled, a premonition of what this condescending, arousing voice would think of her answer creeping over her skin.

"Portland. But I—"

"No."

And he hung up.

Mae pulled her phone away to frown at it.

Well. Okay. So, fuck that.

She was in the process of dialing again when a low chuckle rang out behind her.

Mae turned. A butch-looking white woman stood on the street, leaning against the wooden railing of the ramp that accompanied the porch.

"That Dell McCleary?"

The woman lifted her chin toward Mae's phone. Which Mae stared back down at, blood still simmering.

"Yeah," she said after a moment. "I think so. Yes."

"Didn't go so well, I reckon."

Mae considered what her comfort level with this woman should be. She looked to be in her forties or fifties, likely just a bit older than Mae. Her hair was short and silvery gray, mouth curved in a smirk that Mae suspected was semi-permanent. She wore a corduroy jacket over a Henley, jeans and worn boots.

Meeting butch-looking older white women like this in small towns was always a gamble, in Mae's experience. Either they were gay as hell or had no idea they looked gay as hell and, disappointingly, actually believed drag queens reading to children signaled the downfall of the world.

"It did not," Mae answered.

The maybe-very-gay, maybe-very-not woman ambled around the ramp to walk onto the porch. She leaned her back against the rail next to Mae, folded her arms across her chest.

"Dell can be a cranky son of a gun. Real stingy about who he sells to. Particularly with commercial properties."

Ah. So Dell wasn't only the owner of this building, then; he dealt in real estate. Somehow, this only made Mae even more irritated. A goddamn *professional* had hung up on her.

"To be fair to him, though," the woman continued, "I think some folks have put him through the wringer, so he's cautious. Just wants what's best for this town. What would you do with it?"

"A bookstore," Mae answered again. And then, deciding again to go for it, see where she ranked with *this* townsperson: "And a queer community center."

"Huh."

In their reflections, Mae watched the woman raise an eyebrow.

But then she turned toward Mae. And the smirk grew into what Mae ascertained to be a full-blown butch smile.

"That's a hell of an idea," she said.

Mae smiled back, feeling all at once a bit more like herself. A bit more right.

"I'm Liv." The woman held out a weathered hand, which Mae gladly shook. "I run the IGA, over on Hastings." Liv tilted her head toward Ginger's. "We actually have the best coffee in town."

"Mae Kellerman." Based on the vibe Mae was getting from Liv, she decided to throw in her pronouns, too, which she often used as a sort of *hey, I'm queer* Bat-Signal. Or, depending on the person, a *fuck you, I'm queer* declaration. "She/they. It's nice to meet you, Liv."

"Likewise, darlin'. Maybe I'll see you around."

Before Liv turned to walk down the ramp, she threw Mae one more smirk. One that almost felt a touch flirtatious. And as with any time a butch had thrown Mae the tiniest bit of attention, Mae blushed.

Maybe she was still overheated from that asshole's voice.

"Hey, Mae," Liv called from the sidewalk a moment later. "Give Dell hell, all right?"

Mae's own lips twitched as she nodded.

"I will."

With a brief two-fingered salute, Liv ambled off. Mae watched her go before turning back to the storefront.

Jesús's money might provide the means.

But giving hell was something Mae Kellerman was capable of all on her own.

She unlocked her phone.

Unsurprisingly, Dell sent her to voicemail.

So she hung up. And dialed again. And again.

Until eventually, she said this at the beep.

"Hey Dell, it's Mae Kellerman again. I just wanted you to know that I'm going to keep calling until you at least agree to come down here and tell me no to my face. Because I've got nothing else to do today, and I'm stubborn as hell. So I'll be here, waiting, whenever you're ready."

And then Mae walked back to her car, parked on a side street. She grabbed a couple of blankets from the hatchback —one for her ass, one for her lap—and rummaged around in the backseat until she found the paperback she'd been carrying around all week. It was an old Tessa Dare, one she'd somehow never read. She hadn't found time to crack it open until now, but she'd figured if there was anyone who could make her smile in the hollow absence of Jesús's laughter, it would be Tessa Dare.

She walked back to 12 Main Street and plunked herself on the ground in front of the door. Settled in. Took another sip of her tea.

Opened her phone one more time.

She almost texted the group chat. But in the deepest parts of herself, the parts she vowed to never let Dell McCleary see, she was still too fragile, too still-tilted and unsure to share the dream with everyone.

She brought up Vik's name instead.

*Serious question*, she typed. *How would we feel about me moving to the coast and opening a queer ass bookstore?*

She bit her lip before turning the phone face down on the wooden slats of the porch.

And then Mae rested her sore back against the door, and she began to read.

# two

DELL RUBBED a hand over his face and looked out the kitchen window. A scrub jay landed on the bigleaf maple in the yard before flitting off into the hills.

That *fucking* storefront.

Crosby nosed at Dell's hand, excited for the possibility of a ramble, as Dell crossed the room.

"Not now, Cros."

With a ruffle of Crosby's amber fur, Dell settled onto the bench by the door to pull on his boots.

He hadn't wanted the Main Street storefront from the beginning. That was the best part of working for himself now, his whole purpose: he only bought, managed, and sold the properties he wanted to. Which, these days, mostly consisted of tracts of land, old non-commercial structures, pieces of the community he could help preserve. Selling only to the folks and the occasional non-profit who actually gave a damn about this place. Who were here to stay.

A small fight, in his own way, against the Californians and foreign investors who had bought up real estate by the fistful, often in cash, over the last two decades. Who had helped make his own previous career so lucrative, while changing the landscape of the communities who actually had history in the places where out-of-towners sought a profit.

But then Cara had come to him two years ago.

She'd decided to cut the losses of owning a crumbling brick and mortar storefront in a tiny town and take her pet supply business fully online. Dell had gotten to know Cara—at least, better than he got to know most people, these days—what with needing the very supplies she sold for Crosby (golden retriever), Stills (German shepherd mix), and Nash (some lab-pittie mix). So when Cara said she only trusted Dell, knew he'd sell the storefront to someone who deserved it, well. He'd had a hard time saying no.

Only problem was no one had ever deserved it. Even the ones Dell had taken a chance on over the last two years had pulled out at various stages in the laborious process of selling a commercial property, usually when they'd realized how many repairs the old building actually needed. All of which was evidence as to why he shouldn't be pulling on his shoes or grabbing his car keys right now.

Reason said he should have blocked Mae Kellerman's number hours ago. Particularly after she'd texted him a photo of her sneakers forty-five minutes ago, legs stretched out across the porch of 12 Main, the squat shape of Ginger's and the waves of Greyfin Beach visible behind them. Accompanied by the words: *I dunno, seems like a pretty good view for a bookshop to me.*

It was bold, texting a photo of your legs—and the words "I dunno"—to a stranger.

Dell should not have liked it. Just as he should not have liked that voicemail.

Which he didn't. For the record. Like either of those things.

And he would have ignored them, would have deleted and blocked, if both of those things hadn't made him believe her. That she would, in fact, sit in front of 12 Main Street all day. And the residents of Greyfin Bay would have things to say about that. He'd already gotten one text from Liv Gallagher—*there's a gal on your porch down here, Dell, in case you haven't heard*—which, as much as he liked Liv, he found even more irritating than Mae Kellerman's sneakers.

And on a Luca day, too. The first Luca day in three fucking months.

Dell would be damned if some Portlander ruined a Luca day.

He reasoned with himself, as he climbed into his truck and began the bumpy ride down his August-dry dusty drive, that he hadn't allowed Mae Kellerman to disrupt his routines. He'd still spent the morning in his workshop, prepped a few custom orders, printed and taped their shipping labels. Which—shit, he'd left on the kitchen table.

With a sigh, he braked halfway down the road and turned around in Freddy Hampton's driveway.

A pain in the fucking ass, was what 12 Main Street was.

But all he had to do today was drop off these orders—which he grabbed off the kitchen table before climbing back into the truck—at the post office. No pressing real estate duties today, other than saying no to Mae Kellerman's face, which he was more than capable of, before he could head north to Luca's.

He couldn't find a parking spot on Main Street, because it was August, and of course he couldn't, but he drove by and saw her there before he turned onto Klamath to park up the hill.

Sitting exactly where she'd promised. Head tucked over a book.

Dell huffed out a breath as he yanked on the parking brake.

It would have been impossible to miss her, even if he hadn't been looking. She had a head of bubblegum pink hair. Because of course she did.

He reminded himself, as he walked toward Main Street, that he was a mere two hours away from Luca Yaeger. From Luca Yaeger's thighs, to be specific. He just had to get Mae Kellerman off his porch, and he could once again touch Luca's shoulders.

And it all would have been much easier, if she hadn't been crying when he reached her.

If she hadn't, confusingly, at the same time, been smiling.

She stood as soon as he approached, clutching her book to her chest, and said through her tears: "Don't you just love a mass market paperback?"

And, well. Dell, quite frankly, had no answer to that.

Instead, he said, "Why are you crying?"

Because he had expected a stubborn-as-hell pain-in-the-ass. He had not expected a large, soft, crying person with pink hair smiling up at him like she'd just seen the resurrection.

"Because," she said, "romance is always rewarding when the people are good *to* each other, but it's the best when they're good *for* each other. And Tessa Dare's people are always *so* good for each other."

Mae hugged the book even tighter to her not insignificant breasts and shook her body a little, embracing the paperback in the kind of hug with which you greeted a long-lost relative at the airport.

All at once, she stilled, her smile turning to a frown as she scowled directly at him.

"The people of Greyfin Bay deserve access to Tessa Dare, Dell McCleary."

He scowled back. He had never said they didn't.

Even if he had no idea who Tessa Dare was.

He also did not want to know how Mae knew his last name.

"Oh, Mae Kellerman, by the way." She held out a hand before he could respond, chin held high. "She/they pronouns."

Dell massaged the bridge of his nose.

He never quite understood *she/they*, if he was honest, or any similar combination he'd mostly seen on folks' online profiles. There had to be one Mae preferred. Dell was a person who liked to get things right. He wished people would just tell him what they wanted.

Not that it mattered to him, what Mae Kellerman wanted. Whether she secretly wished he would use *they*.

He did not reach for her hand.

Which he was aware was a dick move. But maybe if he was a dick, she would leave faster.

"Yeah." Mae's arm flopped back to her side. "Thought so."

"I never said Greyfin Bay doesn't deserve a bookshop."

"Greyfin Bay doesn't even have a library. The closest one is in Lincoln City."

"I am aware," he said tightly, meeting her renewed scowl. Nothing like a Portlander spouting information to him about his own town, as if he didn't know.

It reminded him of the moment on the phone that had irked him the most. The haughtiness in her voice when she'd said she was *pretty sure* Greyfin Bay didn't have a queer community center, either.

He'd only gritted his teeth, unwilling to have that fight with a stranger, especially first thing in the morning. But he'd *wanted* to ask why the hell she was so confident about that. Sure, she'd likely driven by fewer rainbow flags on her way through town than she normally did in whatever neighborhood in Portland she hailed from. More *Trump Won* flags in their stead.

But that didn't mean there weren't queer people here. That they weren't able to take care of themselves.

There were queer people everywhere.

"What this place *does* deserve," Dell made himself continue, "is a business that won't fail within six months. Run by someone who actually plans to stay longer than those six months, no matter what."

Mae might have been more stubborn than some, but he'd seen her type before. Had received similar pleas from Portlanders, from ex-Silicon Valley types, taken by the beautiful moodiness of the rocky Northwest shores, the mists of the Coastal Range hills. Taken by a whim to relocate here, to swing the small town life, start that small business they'd always dreamed of.

Except that's what it always was: a whim, soon dissolved in the realities of that small town, small business life. Harder and less idyllic than it appeared in Hallmark movies.

"Cool." Mae rested her hands on her hips, one fist still clutching her book. "Super awesome how you're judging my personal ethics and business skills right off the bat here."

Dell sighed.

"What is your connection to Greyfin Bay, Mae Kellerman?"

It was quick. Gone in a flash as her eyes turned stormy and determined.

But for a half second, Dell saw it. An uncertainty, veering on panic.

"My best friend just died." Her voice wavered on the last word, and Dell did his best to not wince. The knowledge that Mae might be on the verge of tears again, in a real way now, kicked Dell in the chest. And brought home how ridiculous it was that he was even still talking to her. He did not need to know that Mae Kellerman's best friend had just passed away. He didn't need to know anything about this person at all.

Even if those stormy eyes were a fascinating shade of blue, almost gray. Almost like the waves that crashed into the sea, just beyond their shoulders.

"He wanted his ashes left here. He cared about this beach. And he left me a mission, before he left, along with a shit ton of money, and..." Mae swallowed, pausing to breathe. But she never once broke eye contact, which, like that voicemail, some part of Dell admired. "And I just know, now that this is in my head as what that mission could be, I won't be able to let it go."

"And that shit ton of money he left is how you plan to pay for it."

She swallowed again. "Maybe."

"Well, I'll tell you right there, banks don't love that." Dell scratched at his beard. "Big gifts of money might be nice for a cash offer or a down payment, but if you need a loan, they'll need to see your credit, make sure you have savings beyond a lucky windfall."

Mae's eyes narrowed.

"One, my credit is excellent. Two, I would be able to figure out exactly how I'll swing it if you just tell me the asking price. Being as that was all I was ever looking for here."

And Dell could have told her. Could have thrown out a number. Couldn't explain why exactly he didn't.

Except for the fact that Mae Kellerman—with her eyelashes still clumped together from her tears, the pastel sweetness of her hair almost matching the splotches of color that had appeared on the tops of her pale breasts, visible under her half-zipped sweatshirt, the pink inching toward her neck as they'd talked—was, inexplicably and against Dell's will, making his belly stir.

He decided to blame it on today being a Luca day. That the light in those blue-gray eyes, the dimple that'd appeared in her plump left cheek when she'd smiled only pulled at his skin because he already had sex on the brain. Sure, Mae's body type was one that always pleased him, that largely matched his own—wide, soft, ample—except even wider, even softer in all the curves he lacked, in the swell of her breasts, the ellipses of her hips.

It was the opposite of Luca's. But Dell had always had a plethora of types. When he allowed himself to look.

He cleared his throat.

"Listen—"

"Aren't there legal rules here? Isn't it discrimination if you refuse to sell to me without legitimate cause?"

"Well." Dell couldn't help his grin. "As a real estate agent, yes. But owners of property can really do whatever the hell they want if they choose to sell on their own." He stuck his hands in his back pockets, shrugged his shoulders. "And I happen to be the owner of this establishment."

"This establishment," Mae repeated, deadpan. "That

you've clearly been letting languish. Collecting cobwebs. Marring the downtown of the place you purport to care about."

Dell frowned. Sure, he didn't give Cara's old place a sparkling cleaning job every month or anything, but he wouldn't say 12 Main Street *marred—*

"Give me a price, Dell."

And like that, Dell's frown threatened to slip back into a grin. This was the voice he'd expected to hear on this porch. Free, now, of tears and wavers. Straightforward. A little pissed off. Using his first name like they knew each other, like they were on equal footing here.

All of which only made the hair on the back of his neck prickle even further.

But fuck it. He had places to be. Time to wrap this up.

"A million dollars."

Mae's eyes darted toward the storefront's picture window, teeth biting her pillowy bottom lip. As if to say, *for this*?

He had a retort ready for whatever she was about to say. Sure, he'd purchased it from Cara for slightly less. But if anything, a million for a Main Street commercial property with an ocean view was an undersell in real estate these days, no matter how crumbling. Even in Greyfin Bay.

But to Mae's credit, she didn't flinch. Didn't protest. Only looked back at Dell and said, "And you won't let me see inside."

"Got places to be today."

She narrowed her eyes at him once more.

A silence stretched, during which the fallacy of lingering this long with Mae Kellerman settled good and deep in his bones. He'd meant to say no and leave. And he was going to do that. Now.

He'd just started to turn when she spoke.

"Give me a month."

He raised an eyebrow.

"I need to wrap up things back in Portland. But I assume we can handle any paperwork that's needed over email."

Dell huffed out a laugh.

"I don't believe I agreed to sell to you."

Mae leaned down to pick up her bag, along with a pizza box from Greyfin Pizza Junction.

She gave him a look as she brushed past him, a look that Dell, decidedly, did not feel in his toes.

"I'll be back in a month."

Dell, again, rubbed a hand over his face.

He'd gotten Mae Kellerman off his porch.

But somehow, he'd just lost a game he hadn't even known he'd been playing.

Dell only picked up his phone again after he'd successfully dropped off the packages at the post office. Swiping open the screen as he climbed back into his truck, he half expected to see another message from Mae. But there was nothing.

Which was good. Obviously.

He tapped over to the earlier text from Liv, the one stating he had a gal on his porch. Which he only opened because he had to text her about the dogs anyway.

*no comment*, he replied.

He only added the next thing because he knew Liv would hate misgendering someone.

*Although I'm not sure she'd consider herself a gal. she/they pronouns, just fyi*

Of course, as soon as he pressed send, he knew he'd stepped his foot in it.

*HA!!!!!* Liv texted back immediately. *so you DID talk to them!!*

*And I consider gal gender neutral*

*you're a fine gal yourself, Dell McCleary*

And even though Dell truly did not want to be texting with Liv about Mae Kellerman at all, he felt himself snort.

For one second, he contemplated texting back, *thanks?*

But he shook his head at himself. The question mark would be disingenuous. He knew Liv meant it as a compliment. Knew a good chunk of him had accepted it as one, too. That it had made a small flutter rise up in his chest.

He shook his head again, about to type what he'd actually meant to text in the first place when Liv kept going.

*I don't know, Dell, I like this one*

*They could be good for the place*

Dell stared at those texts for longer than he should have.

And then he did the most sensible thing he'd done all day, and ignored them.

*You can still take care of CSNY tonight, right?*

*yeah,* Liv responded. *But don't be surprised if Young is missing when you get back*

Dell smirked. Liv had been hounding him for years to add a Young to his Crosby, Stills, and Nash. When he saw a collie mix pop up on the Instagram of his favorite coastal shelter six months ago, he couldn't say no.

Of course, Young had taken to Liv like honey on a vine.

*Thanks, Liv*

*Any time. Tell Luca I said hey*

Even though Dell never explicitly told Liv, whenever he asked her to take care of the dogs, that he was going to see Luca. But she always knew anyway.

Heat danced up the back of his neck as he chucked the phone onto the passenger seat and threw the truck into gear.

Luca opened the door with a grin.

"Hey."

He stepped back to let Dell inside the cabin. Dell sucked in a breath before crossing the threshold.

"Hey."

He'd shaved his head again, which he often did during a longer fishing jaunt. Easier upkeep, Dell supposed, although he liked when Luca was on land for longer, too. When he let his dark hair grow out into its curls.

But shaved-head Luca always focused Dell's attention on his dark eyes, the way that grin cracked open his tanned face, the dimples hidden in his cheeks, in a way that felt sharper. More immediate. Harder to escape.

"Want a beer?" Luca asked as they walked into the kitchen, the same way he always did, and Dell nodded, taking the offered can from Luca's hand, like he always did. The beauty of a routine.

And the moment the hops landed on his tongue, Dell was able to relax. To push Mae Kellerman—and any and everything else—away. To ground himself here, in Luca's cabin.

It was a true cabin, Luca's place, essentially one large room divided into a kitchen and a living space, a bed tucked into a corner. All cocooned in warm cedar, Dell's favorite choice of lumber. Nestled in a quiet hillside close to the beach, almost every window offered views of the churning surf. Sometimes, Dell wasn't sure if he was more enamored with Luca or Luca's cabin.

"How was Alaska?" he asked.

Luca shrugged, cracking open his own beer. "You know. Long. Exhausting."

Dell watched him. The way his throat bobbed as he took a sip. The way the warmth that had been in his eyes cooled as he stared away from Dell, out the window toward the ocean.

And there it was, the rub Dell increasingly tried not to feel, every time. His and Luca's arrangement was simple. Physical. Once a month, on the months Luca was in town. It worked out for both of them, their own dedicated solitudes. They'd connected on an app, had liked the experience and decided to keep it going. Romance hadn't quite ever been involved. Dell, especially, had wanted it that way. Demanded it that way.

It wasn't fair of him, he knew, to have any other demands—any other possible wants—now.

Still, after two years of pre-sex small talk, the occasional post-sex endorphin-fueled confessions, Dell had learned some stuff about the guy. That, for instance, he had some feelings about the months-long trips to Alaska he and his family often had to take, like most Oregon commercial fishermen, to make ends meet. That Luca, Dell was pretty sure, didn't love being a fisherman at all.

But Dell also knew, from the set of Luca's shoulders, the rigidness of his jawline, that *You know. Long. Exhausting* was all Dell was going to get out of him about the last three months of his life.

Which was, again, the arrangement.

Dell moved on to his next standard question.

"How's book stuff?"

And Luca still stared out the window, but his mouth curved, body relaxing when he replied, like he almost always did: "You know. Shitty."

Dell smiled into his next sip of beer. The other thing he knew about Luca Yaeger—the most intriguing thing of all—was that he was writing a book. That most likely, he would much rather spend his days writing that book than being in a fishing boat. It was a fantasy novel, and he'd been trying to get an agent for it, but that was all Dell knew. All he'd likely ever get.

But Dell loved that grin Luca gave him every time he asked about it anyway.

"How's stuff with you?" Luca asked next. Dell shrugged before he answered, taking another long draw from his can.

In truth, Dell loved a good Oregon IPA. Always had, since the day he'd moved here in his twenties. He never kept any at the house, though. Tried to not keep any alcohol in the house at all. Something about drinking alone always left him feeling...off. A bit more melancholy than expected, each time he'd tried. And it always fucked with his sleep, which was good and fucked to begin with.

Drinking a beer with Luca in Luca's cabin, though. That always felt good.

He loved the shared taste of it in their mouths.

"All right," he answered. And then, inexplicably, he said, "Someone new wants to buy the Main Street property."

Luca turned toward him, quirking a brow. "Yeah?"

"Yeah. Some Portlander with pink hair."

And Luca's grin deepened, a spark firing in those damn dark eyes as he took a pull from his own can.

"Tell me more, Portlander."

Dell sighed, heat simmering in his gut at that look. Luca was the only one who got to give him shit about the fact that he was once a Portlander, too, a fact Dell tried to not spread around. Okay, Liv gave him shit for it, too, but—he was never going back, and that was what mattered.

"Fuck you."

Luca bit the side of his lip.

"You really hate that property."

"I really, really do."

"I dunno." Luca shrugged one shoulder, taking another sip of beer, still grinning. Still giving Dell that look. Luca knew exactly what that look did to him. "Maybe you should just fucking sell it."

Well, fine. Dell slammed his can on the counter. And for the first time in three months, he grabbed Luca Yaeger by his belt loops and kissed him on the mouth.

# *three*

HER HOUSEPLANTS WERE what did her in.

Mae stared at her favorite pothos, cascading over her favorite (now empty) bookshelf, and picked up her phone.

*please come help*

Vik texted back immediately.

*on my way, sugar*

And Mae couldn't make herself do anything but keep staring at her pothos, sinking, again, into the memory of that last day with Jesús, when they'd spread his ashes in the waves. When they'd laughed at the awkwardness of it; when the wind had whipped her hair as her friends slowly departed. Until it had just been her, and the ocean, and a tiny town Jesús had loved.

Mae had spent the last three weeks boxing up her office and her apartment. Whispering goodbye to her life in Portland, the life she knew she had loved so deeply.

But sometimes, these last few weeks, it felt like she'd never fully left that beach at all.

A knock sounded at the door, startling her back to Southeast Portland and her domain of half-packed boxes:

disorienting rooms composed entirely of cardboard and memories.

"Hey." Vik's thick brows were furrowed in concern. They stepped forward, wrapping Mae into an embrace, and Mae barely held herself back from kissing their black curls. Vik had always been a hugger, but their squeezes had gotten tighter, more lingering as Mae's departure date loomed. Mae wanted to write a thank you card for each one. "What's up?"

"My plants."

Mae disentangled from Vik's limbs before tears arrived.

"Goddammit." Vik released a long sigh, forehead unfurrowing as they understood. "I've been dreading this day ever since you sent that damn text."

"I know," Mae said, plopping back down on her favorite armchair. "I know. But I can't take all of them—"

"Of course you can't."

Vik pushed aside piles of junk on the couch.

"And maybe if you could just—"

"Mae, I can*not* take your plants. Jackson has told me, multiple times, that if I bring a single one more home he'll divorce me."

Now Mae sighed.

"I know."

"You could ask someone else. Ozzy or Ben or—"

"No one's as good of a plant parent as you."

Vik breathed out before reaching their arm across the couch to take Mae's hand.

"Only you."

Buying houseplants together was one of Mae's very favorite parts of her friendship with Vik, although she had lots of favorite parts. She understood Jackson's feelings. They had been buying too many plants together for at least ten years. Had officially run out of room in both of their homes for more somewhere around Obama's second term.

Mae did not want to leave a single one.

But the plan was to only take what she could pack in the car when she returned to Greyfin Bay, in a week. Everything else would be put in storage until she had her living situation more fully sussed out.

Having an actual garden—her own borrowed square of soil to plant and weed and love—had always been one of the biggest features of Mae's daydreams. And part of her mourned for the fact that buying 12 Main Street, as incredible of a venture as it might possibly be, wouldn't satisfy that particular longing.

Although maybe there was a small plot of land behind the building that Mae hadn't been able to see, since Dell McCleary hadn't let her look. Maybe, next to the trash cans, she could find a spot to grow cucumbers and peppers and snap peas and cosmos and dahlias.

Actually...

Something she *could* do, right away, perhaps the very first thing she could do, was use some of Jesús's money to buy one of those enormous ceramic planters for the porch of the store, the ones that cost hundreds of dollars that Mae had never been able to afford. She could research the best container plants that would survive the climate of the coast, maybe a combination of—

Vik dropped Mae's hand with a gasp.

"You're doing it. You're picturing all the plants you're going to get without me." Vik shook their head. "You little ho."

"I wasn't! Well, I was just thinking about—"

"About something you can do at your store." Vik smiled,

their gentlest, most affectionate one. "I know that look by now, Mae."

Mae could feel it then. That she'd been smiling, without consciously thinking about it. A smile that faded as she looked Vik in the eye.

"Tell me again," she whispered. "That I'm not making a massive mistake."

Vik was the only one she'd asked this of, the only person to whom she'd expressed any doubt.

The reactions of her friends, when she'd called them all to brunch after returning from Greyfin Bay, had been mixed.

"Ew," Theo had said immediately. Ozzy had clocked him on the arm.

But Mae had only burst into laughter at Theo's down-turned lips, the honest confusion in his eyes. Had continued laughing when he'd turned to Ozzy and said, "What? I'm sorry, babe; you know I love a day trip to the coast, but *living*? In Greyfin Bay?"

Because bless Theo Pham for not being afraid to voice the question that entered Mae's own head at least once a day.

"Do they even have any gay bars on the coast?" Theo asked, turning back to Mae.

"Oh!" Mae smiled, giggles still burning in her throat, somewhat deliriously.

But everything had felt slightly delirious, really, since Jesús died.

"They just opened one in Astoria!"

Theo tilted his head.

"And how far is Astoria from Greyfin Bay?"

The giggles finally disappeared. Mae messed with the hem of her skirt.

"About three hours."

"Theo," Ozzy said. "We hardly even go to bars anymore."

"I know, I know." Theo waved off his partner. "We're boring as shit now. But..." He looked Mae in the eye. "I love you, Mae. Honestly, it sounds brave as fuck. And we all know you'd create an incredible space. I just promised myself a long time ago that I wouldn't live somewhere where there weren't at least places I could go to feel safe when I needed them. And I can't lie and say it doesn't make me nervous, watching you do this. Especially right now."

The rest of the table laid in wait, watching Theo and Mae.

A lump rose in Mae's throat, as sudden and true as the laughter.

"I know," she whispered. Because she did. And she knew Theo knew. He'd been raised in a small town in Georgia; their connection to the South was one of Mae's favorite things about their friendship. He knew the realities of being queer in a small town.

And they all knew how conservatives had weaponized the fear of queerness, of transness, over the last few years. How effective it had been. How effective it had always been.

How it made every fear in the back of every queer and trans person's own mind stand on edge. Especially in places where they didn't have as much strength in numbers. Places like Greyfin Bay.

"But maybe," Mae continued, "that makes doing something like this more important than ever."

Because she knew, in that moment, just as she'd known the second she'd talked to Dell McCleary: she couldn't show those prickles of fear about this. She was upending her entire life. She had to be all in.

And to perhaps everyone's surprise, Theo's eyes had turned wet as he turned away, blinking.

"Okay, girl," he'd said, and Theo's *girls* were always gender neutral, so Mae and Vik never took offense, "I love you so much, and I still kind of hate it, but okay."

And Ozzy had wrapped his arm around Theo's shoulder, the deep brown of his knuckles brushing briefly against the light brown of Theo's forearm, before he looked at Mae and asked, "What do you need?"

Mae rested her head against Vik's wrist now as Vik answered, as Mae knew they would: "You're not making a massive mistake." Vik was likely only saying it because they knew Mae needed them to say it, but it helped either way.

Vik shrugged.

"In all honesty? Even if it doesn't work out? I'm jealous as shit about it. If I didn't have Jackson, you know I'd be down there every weekend helping you paint the walls and buy lighting fixtures."

"Lighting fixtures," Mae sighed dreamily.

"Fucking lighting fixtures!" Vik huffed in annoyance. "You're gonna buy lighting fixtures *and* new plants without me."

"I'm going to text you photos of every single one before I make any decisions."

"Good," Vik said. Before sighing again. "No, you should probably make some decisions without me. This is your store, Mae. You need to make it your own."

"And I'm not..." Mae swallowed, physically willing herself to not apologize for needing this affirmation from Vik one more time. "I'm not a horrible person for even considering this. For using Jesús's money this way."

Technically, it was mostly Steve's money.

Steve, love of Jesús's life, had been both a workaholic

and the inheritor of generational wealth. The lone true business gay of their group.

And he had died of a heart attack, four months before Jesús's body gave up, too.

*"That's the beauty of it,"* Jesús had said in the hospital that last day he'd been lucid, when Mae had protested his hints that this wealth would now be passed on to her. *"It's Steve's money, really. I'm just the lucky fairy"*—he had tried to do a saucy wink after he said *fairy*, but the tubes running to his nose had restricted his facial movement—*"who gets to distribute it."*

"Mae. Fuck no, you're not a horrible person for following a dream you've had since you were nineteen."

Mae stared at the ceiling.

Vik sighed once more and squeezed her hand harder.

"Mae," they said again. "I know you're so used to it, giving so much of your energy away, but...you do know that living your own dream is queer resistance, too, right? Letting yourself be happy, doing what feels right for *you*, is queer joy. And queer joy is always a revolution."

Mae knew they were right. The community center had always been Jesús's dream. Their fearless leader. She had been along for the ride, had felt purpose along with all the hard parts, but...it wasn't the same, without him singing in the office next to hers. It never would be.

And she knew. That Jesús had specifically told her to be selfish.

*"What I need to implore,"* Jesús had said, voice growing ever hoarser, *"Mae, my darling, is that the money is for you. I'm choosing to give it to you, and dios mio, Mae, if you just give it back to the center, or donate it all away—"*

He had shaken a finger before dropping his hand back to the bed. His head lolled toward her, the tough guy act he'd been trying to enforce fading away. Replaced by a warm, tired look of only love that Mae wanted to both run away from and treasure in her heart forever. She wished she could've saved it in a locket, a physical thing she could return to, over and over, until her own last days.

*I want you to trust the world again.*

"Yeah," she whispered now. "I know."

"And anyway," Vik continued, "We know you're going to stock that bookstore to the gills with queer shit, which is its own kind of social work in and of itself, really."

Mae laughed through the pressure in her sinuses.

"I was thinking of putting a huge trans flag right in the window. Just really putting it all out there for any passersby."

"The mid-Oregon coast won't know what hit it."

"I'm sure there are other storefronts on the coast with trans flags, though," Mae added after a minute. "Even if I don't know where they all are, yet."

Vik nudged Mae's foot with their own.

"Yeah," they said softly. "But having another one never hurts."

Mae finally turned away from the ceiling, rolling her neck to smile at Vik.

"Yeah," she said, equally as soft. "That's true."

Vik's mouth morphed into a grim line.

"And you're sure this Dell person isn't going to screw you over?"

Mae broke eye contact to stare back at the pothos, using all of her concentration on not letting heat flare up her neck.

Dell still refused to sell Mae the building outright. But he'd begrudgingly agreed to lease it to her, for a time.

A compromise.

A compromise that, if she let herself think on it too long, still pissed her off.

"Yeah," Mae said, and she couldn't tell if it was a lie or forced optimism. "It'll be okay."

She should be grateful he had compromised at all. That she was still going to be able to move into 12 Main Street. That this perhaps unhinged plan still had legs.

It was simply that Mae had never had the opportunity before to *own* something. She had spent most of the last two decades alternately dreaming about owning a house and making jokes with her fellow forever-renter friends about how they would never be able to actually accomplish such a thing.

Unless a loved one died, and unexpectedly left you three-quarters of a million dollars.

And maybe Mae *should* finally buy a fucking house. Tell Dell to go fuck himself. She could keep working at the community center she loved, and grow the garden she'd always dreamed of. It was hard, on her days of doubt, to understand why the hell she *wasn't* doing that.

Yet...

"I felt him next to me." She looked at Vik again. "When I was in Greyfin Bay. I felt *me* there, next to me. I won't let Dell McCleary take that away."

Because wasn't that what Jesús had taught her, when she was finding her bearings at the center? Trying to figure out the best ways to connect their clients with the health care and housing and *support* they needed? Like any progress in this world, advancement came with stumbling blocks. With thinking you finally had something, before another asshole came along and took part of it away. Made it exponentially harder to grab, whether through bureaucracy or bigotry, just because they could.

So maybe Mae had suddenly inherited $750,000—an amount of zeroes that still felt surreal, that made the whole world feel different—and still couldn't fully own what she wanted. Because she was from a place someone else didn't like. Because she had pink hair, maybe. Because even if she was richer than she had ever dared to imagine, Dell McCleary still had more power.

There was always someone with more power.

But she wouldn't let this one win this time.

"Still. If he *tries*..." Vik narrowed their eyes and pulled away to extract their phone from their bag. "You *sure* this guy isn't on Instagram? I can't believe I can't even stalk him."

Mae tried to laugh, but it got stuck somewhere in her throat.

"I swear, if I ever find his profile, I'll send it to you straight away."

Even Vik didn't need to know how hard Mae had tried to find it herself. How often she'd replayed their brief in-person interaction in her head.

So *what* if Dell happened to be one of the most attractive people she'd ever seen. She'd known it was him as soon as he'd stepped onto the porch that day, instinct confirmed when he'd opened his mouth and that voice unfurled. As deep and sexy as his body—big and burly, the kind of body that was soft and solid all at once: a belly made for his thick, folded arms to rest upon perfectly. The kind of body Mae wanted to climb like a tree, if her own body was more adept at climbing trees. That sandy beard she could practically feel on her skin the moment she'd let herself truly look at it. Closed-off brown eyes she wanted to see lit with laughter.

Except no, no she didn't.

Because who *cared.*

She didn't care in the least about his eyes or his beard or the fact that, in the flashes of her memories of that day, she was pretty sure his nails had been painted. But maybe she'd made it up. Maybe the thick fingers accompanying his thick body hadn't been adorned with a surprising shade of deep purple at all.

It didn't matter, if true, that it was the exact sort of surprise Mae had always been most drawn to.

God, *fuck* Dell McCleary.

"I only have one other thing I've been wanting to say."

Mae actually jumped a little, turning back toward Vik.

Vik raised an eyebrow.

"You alright there?"

"Yeah."

Mae was pretty sure her pothos believed her, about how fucking *pissed* she was about that guy.

She wasn't so sure about Vik. Who wouldn't relax that damn eyebrow.

"What else were you going to say, Vik?" Mae waved a hand, imploring Vik to get on with it.

Vik shifted on the couch, throwing Mae one last suspicious look before staring at the dark screen of Mae's TV.

"Well. There's, you know, the fact of how horribly I'm going to miss you, which is"—Vik shook their head—"a conversation for another time, and mostly one I need to have with myself and my therapist, but."

They looked back at Mae, the smile returned to their lips, if a bit more bittersweet.

"Mae, you should let go of this community center idea. Above the shop."

Mae opened her mouth. Closed it.

Having an adjoining queer community center on the second floor of the bookshop had continued to be part of her pitch—to her friends, that day at brunch; to Dell, in their terse email exchanges. It wouldn't be a full-time, multi-pronged center like the one here, like what Jesús had built, but...

"Queer joy is enough," Vik whispered.

Because Vik knew. That the look they'd apparently begun to recognize on Mae's face, the smiles that grew when she had a new idea—that look was never about the second floor.

"Play with your books a while." Vik smiled again. "It's enough, Mae." They turned their gaze to Mae's pothos. "It's enough."

Three days later, before signing the papers for her new storage unit, Mae put every houseplant onto the sidewalk outside of her apartment except one—a Chinese money plant that had started as a transplant from one of Vik's, held in her favorite teal planter. It took ten trips, along with an extra, tired, frustrated trip to find where the hell she'd packed a clean piece of paper and a Sharpie with which to scribble: *FREE.* Frazzled and running late, she stuck the note under a fishbone cactus.

When she returned two hours later, storage unit secured, extra boxes from U-Haul tucked under an arm, every plant was gone.

And when she walked into her apartment two minutes after that, for the first time since she'd moved in years before, it no longer felt like home.

She stood for an extra minute to absorb the shock of it.

Until she whispered, "It's enough." And she picked up the packing tape once more.

# four

DELL BLEW OUT A BREATH, trying to calm his bouncing knee. Told himself, one more time, that it made sense to meet Mae here, at this brewery in Pacific City, instead of in Greyfin Bay. One, because he had to get lumber up in Tillamook today anyway, so it was on the way. Mostly. Two, because he liked this brewery. The view of the cape from its windows made him feel calm, and he normally felt okay, having a beer here, and—whatever. He could make whatever damn choices he wanted.

Mae Kellerman had already made far too many decisions without his consent over the last month. It was time he started pulling in the reins.

He still couldn't quite discern how exactly he'd gotten himself in this situation in the first place. Sitting in Pacific City, stabbing into his Ahi poke bowl, lease paperwork sitting on the seat next to him.

She had just been so *persistent*. Emailing a copy of her credit report. Her registration for a small business course, not in Portland, but at Oregon Coast Community College down in Newport, set to start three days from now. Fucking PowerPoints with her plans for the shop. Each email always finishing with, *I'll be back in town by the first of September.*

And Dell had always looked forward to the first of September, too. When the kids went back to school. When the air turned cooler. When the crowds started to go away, at least during the weekdays, and he could breathe easier.

"Mr. McCleary."

Mae swept into the booth across from him.

No, this September, he wasn't breathing easier at all.

"Just Dell, please." He had always hated *mister*; something about it itched at the inside of his brain in the most irritating way possible. And the last thing Dell needed at this moment was further irritation.

She looked better, somehow, than he remembered, and he had been telling himself over the last several weeks that his memory had been overblowing it. But the Mae Kellerman across from him had well-rested eyes, giving a sharpness to her stare that felt even more lethal than the looks she'd leveled him with a month ago. Her pink hair seemed freshly touched up, a Valentine's Day concoction from the roots to the tips, pulled into a neat yet elegantly tousled bun. Flyaways were pinned away from her face with tiny pastel barrettes adorned with glittery stars.

She wore a faded Decemberists T-shirt and a thick, copper-colored cardigan. The cozy fall aesthetic of her body shouldn't have worked with the rainbow unicorn flavor of her hair, but somehow...it did.

She nestled her fingers together, resting them atop the table.

An awkward beat of silence transpired that only made Dell respect her more for not making a move to break it.

He shoved a menu her way.

"The beer here's good, if you're interested."

"Yes," she said, voice clipped. "I've been here before. But I'm good."

All right, then. After another sip of his pale ale, he slid the folder with the contract across the table. She promptly opened it and started reading, even though nothing in it had changed from their last email.

He laid a key next to his beer as she read.

"You're angry at me," he couldn't help but note. He didn't know why it mattered, why he said it out loud. He was pissed at her, too. She'd been a real pain in his ass, a pain that he knew, with every click of the pen she'd taken out of her bag, was only going to get worse.

Mae's nostrils flared.

"This is a business transaction," she said, voice even. "My emotions do not matter here."

Dell kept looking at her. At the freckles visible on her nose as she bent over the paperwork, her long eyelashes against her pale cheeks, how they started dark and ended light, almost translucent, at the tips. Her blunt, unadorned fingernails, the thin gold necklace that swung underneath the ripped collar of her T-shirt, hiding its pendant against her skin.

He broke the stare when she flipped to the third page, forcing his gaze instead to the surf outside the window.

"It's not personal," he said. Mae snorted. Something curled in his gut at the sound, at the fire of the person he'd met four weeks ago breaking through the ice wall she'd shown up with today.

"I think you should look up the meaning of that word, McCleary. Considering you are literally not selling me this property because of who I am."

"That's not—" Dell cut himself off with a slight shake of

his head. "A year," he said, confirming the conciliatory nature of his deal out loud. Most commercial leases required much longer terms than a single year. "This lease is good for a year. If you're still here, if your business is up and running in a year and you still have the means to buy, the property will be yours."

Mae exhaled slowly through her nose.

"Six months," she said.

Jesus Christ. "The lease"—he shoved his poke bowl to the side, tapped the paperwork between them—"is for a year. I maintain my position that this isn't personal, Kellerman, but I'm not changing this paperwork for you."

Her lips thinned.

*Six months.* God, they'd gone over this a hundred times.

"We're still going 50/50 on all TMI?" she asked after a lengthy pause.

Dell didn't hold back his sigh. He knew Mae's lawyer had already double checked all of the details last week. Because he'd received approximately twenty emails from Mae and Mae's lawyer, checking all the details, last week.

And the 50/50 deal on all taxes, maintenance, and insurance was still a point he wasn't fully certain on, so he didn't appreciate being pushed on it. Most landlords made business tenants responsible for TMI on their own, but he'd decided, in a fit of foolishness, that helping Mae out with the technicalities and the repairs—and there would be a lot of repairs—was both an olive branch for not selling her the building outright and his own penance to the town for letting the Main Street property languish for so long.

It was possible the reason he was doing this entire venture at all was because that comment Mae had made —*marring the downtown of the place you purport to care about* —had stuck in his craw.

Still, the reminder of the fact that he was willingly tying himself further to this thing—and that Mae refused to be grateful for it—grated his already inflamed nerves.

"And I have first right of refusal?"

He let another sigh fly.

"I wouldn't sell the place out from under you."

"I don't know you." Finally, Mae lifted her eyes to his. Those blue-gray irises were a winter storm. "I don't know anything about what you would do."

He fisted his hands on his thighs beneath the table and stared back out the window.

"You have first right of refusal and you know you do. You know what's in that contract. I don't know why you're prolonging this."

"You're right."

And while Dell refused to look at her again, he could hear how she pressed her fancy pen into the paper with extra vengeance, how she flipped through the final pages and moved on to the second copy with sudden efficiency. Could feel her fire, burning across the table between them, punching further into his stomach.

When she reached the final signature, she pushed his copy of the contract across the table and stood from the booth before he could double check it.

She folded the key neatly into her fist.

"I'll be seeing you in six months," she said, and walked out of the restaurant.

Mae stood in front of 12 Main Street and hugged Vik's *pilea peperomioides* to her side.

"Would you look at that, Becks," she whispered to herself.

And felt, immediately, conflicted. As she had every time her mind had drifted to Becks over the last month. That old, familiar ghost of guilt haunting her shoulders once more.

Mae Kellerman and Becks Holloway had dreamed of opening a bookstore together when they were young and in love. But Mae hadn't talked to Becks in over twenty years. Or, more accurately, Becks hadn't talked to Mae. Maybe Becks wouldn't care for the fact that Mae was, of all things, pursuing their old dream, without her.

Or, again, more accurately—Becks most likely wouldn't care at all.

But there were other people who would.

Mae shook her head. Attempted to calm the fluttering in her chest.

"Would you look at that, Jesús," she tried.

And just as immediately, she felt him. His smile, that day in the hospital. The shake of his head back at her.

It was possible Greyfin Bay—something in the ocean air—made Mae a suddenly spiritual person.

*Try again*, he said. *That wasn't what I told you.*

She took a deep, shaky breath.

"Would you look at that, Mae Kellerman," she whispered.

Jesús thumped her on the back.

She stepped up to the porch, removed the key from her pocket, and stepped inside.

She walked to the center of the room. Placed the Chinese money plant in its pretty teal planter next to her feet. Let the overpacked tote bags on her shoulders slide to the floorboards.

There was a lot to do.

Her car was packed to the very brim with things to unload, including cleaning supplies and a new air mattress. She needed to go grocery shopping. She needed to double check that her website and social media, which Vik had helped her design but which she'd felt cautious about launching before actually acquiring the keys, were ready to go. She needed to do...so many things.

But first...

Mae closed her eyes. Made herself forget Dell McCleary: his assessing brown eyes, his thick, tanned forearms full of sandy hair.

His ownership of this building.

Mae let herself sink into the bubble of hope Jesús Herrera-Baptiste had spent his whole life living in. She turned, and she looked, and she let herself believe this was hers.

It would never be Powell's, but the room was big, large enough for bookshelves and tables and a reading area in the corner. She walked toward the door, feeling along the wall until she located the light switch. Even though she wasn't certain Dell had called the electric company yet, another reason why she wanted to be solely in charge of—

The light flicked on, and Mae twirled back toward the room.

A gorgeous, dusty light fixture of dangling glass filled the room with a golden glow. The walls were painted a shade of mauve that Mae couldn't tell, at first glance in proper lighting, whether she hated or weirdly loved.

But it was the floor Mae took in now, the slightly uneven planks of hardwood that shone faintly in the light. Like the walls, Mae could see the ghosts of the storefront's former occupants: where rugs must have been; the criss-crossing scratches of dogs' nails where they hadn't. Mae slipped off her sneakers, ran her socked toes along every abandoned inch.

She'd learned about 12 Main Street's former life as a pet store through her texting with Liv. And what a delightful thing to learn. A place where animals had felt at home felt like a place books would be at home, too.

She decided she rather liked the scratches in the wood. They added character. And sure, the floor did seem to sort of *swoop* downward here, but Mae found herself enjoying that, too: a fun little surprise for her feet.

And then there was the best thing of all, the thing she had only glimpsed through the window last time: a massive, elegant counter built into the back of the room. Mae ran a finger along the dust. Stepped behind it, picturing the extra merchandise that could fit in all its drawers and cubby holes. She'd read up on all the farmers' markets that existed within a hundred mile radius, made a list of local vendors who might want to sell their wares in the shop. There was one in Lincoln City that ran through September. Maybe she'd stop by tomorrow, pick up some fresh flowers to put on this counter. She'd be the only one to see them, for now, but as one of her personal heroes, Miley Cyrus, had taught her, she could buy herself flowers.

She peeked into the tiny bathroom, the office, both a tangle of abandoned shelving; she inspected the main room from each corner.

It was only slowly filling in, what it would end up actually looking like. She knew it would be hard. Not only because of whatever harsh realities the inspectors she'd scheduled would tell her this week; not just because she still had a world of knowledge to learn about running a small business. But because it would be hers, and Jesús's, and Steve's, and it would be loudly queer in this sleepy small town on the coast where people might not want her —her fat queer body or her fat queer ideas.

*I want you to trust the world again.*

Mae closed her eyes and opened them, over and over again.

And what she truly knew, more than anything, was that some people in this sleepy small town, some people that might only be passing through, one day—those unknown friends *would* want a space like this. Might not just want it, but *need* it.

She hauled in more things from her car. Her small toolbox, for a hammer and some nails. The things she'd need for tonight. Moved around the bags in her trunk until she got to the collapsed foot ladder. Back inside 12 Main Street, she emptied one of the tote bags until she found the flags.

Leaving it all on the ground for now, she picked up a flashlight and some cleaning supplies first. She'd made a pact with herself, weeks ago, that she'd take her time with all of this. Every single step. If she was going to do this, she was going to do it right.

Thirty minutes later, the front picture window was wiped clean, the casing and the sills dusted. And Mae, for now, would continue on in privacy, protected from the eyes of Main Street through colorful sashes both soft and bold.

She stepped outside to snap a picture for Vik.

And then she locked the door and dug her phone out of her bag. Ignoring her notifications, she opened Jesús Herrera-Baptiste's final playlist one more time.

She turned the volume all the way up. Placed the phone on the floor and pressed Play.

And as at Jesús's death party, the first track made her laugh out loud.

She supposed she should have introduced herself to her neighbors before blasting Ricky Martin's "La Copa de la Vida," the official song of the 1998 World Cup. But really, if they were going to have to get to know Mae and Jesús anyway, this was the way to do it.

Mae contemplated getting more things from her car, or figuring out how to get upstairs, where she planned to sleep. But you couldn't listen to 1998 Ricky Martin without shimmying at least a little.

And so Mae danced around the room she intended to make hers, to Ricky and then "Jumpin' Jumpin'" by Destiny's Child, which, naturally, followed as the second track, laughing softly to herself and feeling Jesús in the room with her all the while. Even if she didn't truly believe in spirits lingering. Even if she knew he was gone.

Jesús's death party playlist had been perfectly him, a mix of tracks from both his favorite queens like Bey and Taylor and his Latine kings: Don Omar, Marc Anthony, Manuel Turizo. And here and there, his favorite showtunes.

Jesús had shared the playlist at the same time he'd transferred his powers of attorney to Mae, after Steve's heart attack. Like he knew. That he would tell his own body to let go, soon. To be with his corazón again.

She might not have truly believed in an afterlife herself, but Mae was somehow able to hold onto the hope of it, for them.

The playlist was exactly one hour long. *"One hour of talking about how great I was! Make sure there's lots of candy. Maybe some sparklers. And then you can all go get drunk or do whatever you want. Although it would mean a lot if you drank some piña coladas at Tropicale for me, if the mood struck you.*

*Stick some googly eyes on the pineapples and pretend it's my spirit."*

And they had, later. Stuck googly eyes on the pineapples.

And by god, they *did* feel like his spirit.

Until Alexei had eventually peeled the silly eyes from his, hiding them away inside his palm before he'd said in his quietly commanding way: "Okay. Go find Steve, now."

And the patio of Tropicale had gone quiet, filled with that almost happy, reverent version of deeply sad.

Mae felt close to the same now. She had felt the distance, with every mile she'd rolled further from Portland earlier today. How far away she was now from her people. How truly alone she was, here in this empty storefront. But the music helped her inch closer to almost-happy. The music helped her be almost fully there.

And just as at the death party, it was when Judy appeared that things really got swinging.

All of their friends had been busy hugging, eating all of Jesús's favorite snacks, laughing as they tried not to cry during the first twenty minutes of the party, held in the auditorium at the center. But when Judy Garland came in with "The Trolley Song," somehow everyone started moving at once. As if they were all in St. Louis, Jesús at the front of the line, urging them to hop onboard.

They didn't *dance*, exactly, as much as they escaped their grief for a moment to jump inside a musical instead, as Jesús would have wanted them to: arms outstretched, swinging each other by the elbows, dramatically singing along, swooning with hands held over hearts.

Mae was just as into it here, alone in Greyfin Bay. She fisted her hands in front of her neck, leaned her head back and closed her eyes as she spun. She threw off her sweater, shimmied out of her skirt. She always felt most comfortable when she was as close to naked as possible. She sang out loud to the ceiling of her future bookshop about how grand it was for Judy just then, holding his hand 'til the end of the line, feeling every clang clang clang and zip zip zip and—

A throat cleared, and Mae twirled toward the door.

# *five*

MAE'S EYES popped open as she stumbled. She clutched at her chest, face aflame as Judy Garland faded and Janet Jackson's "Together Again" began playing from the phone on the floor.

"What," she gritted out, "are you doing here?"

Dell worked to keep his face blank.

He had not meant to interrupt her dance session. Had not meant to witness her...like this, body in motion, inside a private moment. Her skirt, along with the copper cardigan, had been abandoned on the floor, leaving every curve of her thighs, her ass, her hips and her belly on display in her leggings and threadbare T-shirt. The loss of the cardigan exposed the fact that one of her pale arms was inked with tattoos, covering almost every inch of skin he could see from wrist to sleeve: a mosaic of intricate black linework interspersed with spots of brightly colored flowers.

Dell was increasingly disturbed at how many facts he was amassing about Mae Kellerman.

"It seems rather fast," he said slowly, "to have already forgotten I own the place."

Mae yanked her phone off the floor, cutting off Janet. The silence that followed felt profound.

"I'm pretty sure," she said after a long moment, still staring at her phone, "that landlords have to give notice before entering a property with a tenant. I'm like, super good at being a renter. I know these things."

She crossed her arms atop her belly. Dell could see, even from across the room, before she tucked them away under her armpits, that her hands were shaking.

He had embarrassed her. Hadn't meant to do that, either.

Even if he knew he had watched for longer than he should have. She clearly hadn't heard him come in, hadn't seen him lingering in the doorway, watching her dance to "The Trolley Song," mouth open in silent laughter whenever she hadn't been singing along.

Dell couldn't quite remember the last time he'd let himself move like that. Be...*silly,* like that, even when alone.

He cleared his throat again and shifted from the doorway, focusing back on the moment at hand.

"And *I'm* pretty sure you wouldn't qualify as a tenant yet, considering you left the restaurant before giving me your security deposit."

Mae's arms dropped, cheeks flushing an even deeper shade of rose as she turned to grab one of her bags. As she searched, Dell's eyes roamed the rest of the space. His stomach sank when he spotted the air mattress.

"I'm sorry," Mae said as she walked the envelope to him, avoiding eye contact all the while. "I meant to give it to you."

He folded the envelope into his back pocket without checking it. The deposit was now the least of his worries.

"I was also curious where you're planning on staying. I meant to ask, before you stormed off."

Mae frowned, annoyance overtaking the discomfort on her face.

"Why does it matter to you?"

"I just wanted to make sure you didn't have the hare-brained idea of staying *here*."

Mae eyed him warily. Dell liked having the attention of those sea-churn eyes again.

Wait. Dammit. No, he didn't.

A terrible idea. This had been a terrible idea from the start.

Finally, Mae looked away again, clutching her elbows as she muttered, "*Hare-brained* is probably not a very politically correct phrase."

For fuck's sake.

"And *that*," he said, "is why I don't sell to Portlanders. If you're concerned about being PC around here, you're going to have a hell of a rude awakening."

"Oh, fuck you," Mae snapped, whipping her face toward his, nose wrinkled in distaste. Dell forcibly told his body to calm down—to stop reacting to that *fuck you* like it was a come-on—as she stepped toward him. "Hold your condescension for me, Dell McCleary. I was making a joke because I was uncomfortable. I don't even like the term politically correct! But you're making me feel uncomfortable on purpose, with your..." She waved a hand toward him. "Your big crossed arms and your..." Dell's pulse ticked up as she glared, his mind torn between wanting to laugh and—*dammit*—wanting to grab her by the waist. "Your face," she eventually fumbled to finish. "Yes, I'm planning on staying here, all right? Because I want to. Because I'm all in on this place, and I don't care if it needs repairs, or if you think I don't belong here. Please, make your jokes about how annoying and woke Portlanders are, as if we're not all as fucking human as anyone in Greyfin Bay. I'm planning on being a pain in your ass either way for the next six months, so please, might as well get it all out now."

Dell breathed in and out, deep and slow, before he spoke again.

"The pipes," he said, "are fucked. You have no plumbing. You can't stay here."

Mae visibly deflated.

"Oh," she said, voice small as she turned, scratching her forehead. "Okay." And then, after a pause: "Got it."

Dell stood still as she gathered her bags. Resisted the urge to reach out to her as she looked around the space, scratching her forehead again. As she searched for her keys, tossed her cardigan over her shoulder. As she barreled toward him, determination once more steeled over her features.

"Please," she said when she was in front of him. "Move."

And Dell truly should move. He shouldn't care about the exhaustion hiding behind the steel in her voice.

"Where are you going to go?"

"I'll find a hotel. I'm not completely incompetent. Please, get out of my way."

Dell frowned.

She was a tenant. A tenant who had just promised, out loud, to be a pain in his ass. She'd be gone in a few months anyway, disappointed and disillusioned, the money she'd inherited from her friend wasted on a town that couldn't bring her a profit.

Also: the only lodging that might actually have vacancy

was The Fin Inn, a dilapidated motel next to a weed store on the northern edge of town.

He grabbed a bag from Mae's hand.

"You're staying with me."

"What?" Her incredulous voice asked the question to his back, as he was already turned toward the door.

"Not with me, technically," he clarified from the porch, motioning her outside. "But on my property. I have an ADU. An accessory dwelling unit. It's fully furnished."

She only stared at him, jaw slightly dropped. Her pink hair glowed under the light from the chandelier.

"It's a private space," he said, voice now as exhausted as hers. He had no idea why he was trying to sell this to her. "You can pretend I'm not even there."

Mae didn't move.

"It's late," he said.

Finally, she shook her head, muttering under her breath as she adjusted the tote bags on her shoulder.

"It's late," she echoed as she brushed past him. "That's the only reason I'm agreeing to this. I'll find another place tomorrow."

He remained silent as he clicked off the light and locked the door.

When he turned, his eyes caught on the flags in the window. As they had when he'd walked up. Being that they were impossible to miss: a trans flag and a progress pride, both huge. Even now, with the internal lights off, the haze from the streetlamp outside Freddy's next door caught their colors through the glass.

Mae was glaring at him, arms crossed over her chest again—daring him to say something—when he tore his eyes from the window. He held up his hands.

"I'm not saying shit," he said. Even if his chest had filled with a barrage of complicated things when he'd first seen them. Even if he actually had a lot to say about those flags, here. Put up by Mae Kellerman her first night in town.

And when she finally turned, walking down the porch, Dell found himself, as he had from the start around Mae, immediately breaking his own promises.

"I like them," he said to her back, his voice quiet as they walked through the chill of an early Greyfin Bay September evening, toward her car and his truck, and the place in the hills he called home.

Mae gripped the steering wheel as she followed Dell's truck up a steep, narrow gravel lane. *Dumb.* Dumb, dumb, dumb. It was dumb she hadn't thought about plumbing. She'd thought about heating and cooling, electrical, wifi, all things she could work out the first week. But somehow she hadn't thought about plumbing, and of course Dell McCleary had to show up *just* to point it out to her.

It was even dumber that she was currently following his truck up this obvious murder lane in the dark. But fully furnished, free lodging was, unfortunately, a highly logical option to accept. Even as she hated that, less than one day into the first truly solo adventure of her life, she was already leaning on someone else for support.

And that someone else was *Dell.*

She squinted into the dark as they rounded a curve.

She rarely drove at night in Portland these days; if she met friends in the evening she preferred to take public transit or a rideshare. Although more often than not, especially since the split with Eden, she was simply at home once the sky turned dark, reading a romance novel and tending to her plants.

But as she followed her headlights under the canopy of firs that lined Dell's road, a deep, visceral memory began to slash away her frustration and embarrassment. Replaced instead by the feeling of driving among the pine trees of the Carolinas past sundown, screaming along to mix CDs. Speeding below the maples and ashes of Madison with Becks a few years later. Blood humming with pent-up dreams, Becks's foot always just a little too heavy on the gas.

Dell's truck swung a right, his brake lights haloing in Mae's retinas as he came to a stop. She pulled up next to him, trying to blink away the nostalgia: the remembrance of a sensation she'd forgotten she loved.

Dell's door slammed shut. With a shake of her head, Mae released her seatbelt.

And then she leaned forward and released a quiet curse.

Of course. Of course Dell McCleary's house was a fucking masterpiece.

She could only see glimpses: the flash of what their headlights revealed before they cut their engines, the narrow window of illumination from the spotlight at the side of the house. But she could tell it was a modern build. A sloped roof, sharp lines and angles similar to what developers knocked over old bungalows to build in Portland on the regular these days. Except while those houses in Portland were usually painted in stark contrasts—whites and blacks, navy and glass—Dell's home was all natural wood, befitting of the Coastal Range foothills it was nestled against.

Mae wrestled her tote bags back over her shoulder. The quiet-but-loud noises of the coastal countryside at night—

insects and toads and, even from here, the distant ambient rush of the ocean—settled into her system, both comforting and unnerving as she stared blankly at the suitcases in her trunk, struggling to remember which one contained her toothbrush.

Dell reached past her shoulder and grabbed one at random before she could figure it out.

Closing the trunk and biting her tongue, she followed him as he walked away from the drive. The flashlight from his phone led them along a neatly manicured stone walkway behind the house, until a minute later, another spotlight clicked on.

Holy hell.

Dell rustled with his keys before opening the door to the ADU. He pushed her suitcase inside, flicking on the lights before he turned.

"You coming inside?"

Mae snapped her mouth shut and did as asked.

Dell's ADU matched the beauty of the main house, just smaller in scale: a slanted roof over warm wood and clean glass. And as Mae stepped past Dell into the heart of it, the structure became even more remarkable.

No doubt the space was small, but it was designed and decorated impeccably. A wall divided the narrow galley kitchen and dining area from the living space. Dell parked Mae's suitcase by the bed that hugged the wall. Walked past the bookshelves that lay at the head of the bed to click on another light in the bathroom, hidden neatly behind those bookshelves. Everything was suffused in warm autumn colors, like one of Taylor Swift's pandemic albums: the art on the walls, the shelves, the Pendleton blanket folded neatly at the foot of the bed.

The Pendleton blanket that probably cost more than Mae's old rent.

Even if...she could probably afford Pendleton blankets too, now. At least if she managed her business plan well. She kept forgetting she had money now. She felt like she'd probably always keep forgetting.

"This is..." *Fucking gorgeous*. But Mae was having trouble translating words from her brain to her mouth.

Dell stuffed his hands in his pockets.

"I built it for my mom," he said. "She's getting older, and she's been alone since my stepdad died, but..." His shoulders lifted as his eyes scanned the space. "Haven't been able to fully convince her yet."

He *built* this.

Of course he did.

He built this for his *mom*.

Words finally tumbled from her tongue.

"This is the Airbnb of my fucking dreams."

A wry smile tugged beneath Dell's beard.

"I actually did try that, for a while. As evil as the empire is, it felt like what I should do." His shoulders lifted again as he rubbed his jaw. "Turns out I wasn't the friendliest host."

Mae laughed before she could stop herself. Dell's eyes met hers, a spark of self-deprecating amusement accompanying his grin.

And what in the hell? It was entirely too cozy in here, and Mae and Dell did not...share self-deprecating smiles. She was definitely, fully pissed at this fine specimen of a human. This practical stranger who kept derailing her plans. Who had looked at her, until this very moment, like she was small.

And maybe she couldn't stop thinking about his nails, which she had been able to observe, up close and personal this time, at the restaurant. They were painted a metallic shade of pale yellow now. Maybe she couldn't stop thinking about his *I like them* comment about her pride flags. Said in a different tone than she'd heard from him before, a low vibration that had settled in her toes. Which had been confusing at the time, being that she was busy being pissed at him. As aforementioned.

Was Dell McCleary gay? Queer? An ally?

But it shouldn't matter. It *didn't* matter.

Because she also remembered his comment about her having *a hell of a rude awakening* in this place. Like because she wasn't from here, she had to be some naive, leftie joke.

Dell McCleary was still just another asshole. Just one with pretty hands and a pretty house.

Mae turned to place her things against the wall.

"I'll start looking for another place tomorrow. But thank you."

"I'm happy to have the space used." He moved past her toward the door, tapping a smart thermometer on the wall with a thick knuckle. "Adjust the temperature however you want. Text if you need anything." He tugged a key off his key ring, placed it on the table next to the door.

Mae stared at the Pendleton blanket instead of his face.

"Thank you," she said again. Because Jodi and Felix had raised her to be polite. Because she had learned, through a decade of queer social work, that you often couldn't get the things you wanted without keeping your cool.

With a nod, Dell closed the door behind him, leaving her alone in a space that was almost confusingly wonderful and inviting. A space she had to admit was worlds more comforting than an empty building.

A space that could only be made better, she thought, by all of the plants she had left behind.

# six

MAE WAS awoken by a high-pitched bark.

Clutching a blanket, she blinked at an alarm clock on a bookshelf in a room that was not her own.

In another blink, reality permeated.

Mae's head fell back against the pillows as she stared at the ceiling. She shouldn't have been so surprised by a few barking dogs. Lord knew Portland was a city practically composed of barking dogs. She'd had to eventually leave the first apartment she'd lived in, after she'd moved from Brooklyn years ago, because the dog next door never shut up.

Still. Even a familiar noise could be unsettling when you were in an unexpected place.

Mae knew Greyfin Bay itself wasn't unexpected, even if the bed she slept in was. But she was reminded in that moment how different it was, waking up in a new place when you weren't just on vacation. When it wasn't actually an Airbnb.

When you had abruptly decided to carve yourself a new home.

But it didn't feel like home.

At least not yet.

Early morning sun shone through the wide windows that took up the opposite wall. Mae gave herself exactly five minutes to look at the misty forest beyond the glass, the gnarled yet sturdy trees—the crinkled grays and the deep greens—and let it weigh on her chest.

She lived here.

She was on the coast, without an end date.

She lived here.

For five minutes, Mae let her new reality sit there on her ribs, more terrifying than freeing. And then she got up and shoved it away. She ignored how the tiny house she was currently occupying was even more charming in the daylight. She ignored the truth that she had slept better in Dell McCleary's guest bed than she had in weeks, months even. A fact that seemed almost impossible in the face of the mountain of uncertainties, of futures she could only hope for instead of predict—a coastal range of anxiety—that composed her new life. But somehow, under Dell's Pendleton blanket, she had slept like the dead.

She pulled clothes for the day out of a suitcase, unplugged her phone from the charger, washed her face, and steadfastly ignored the fantastic array of mugs she discovered in the kitchen. The kitchen meant for Dell's mother.

Today would be a coffee day, she decided, grabbing her laptop bag. She was normally a tea drinker, but some days required extra fortitude.

She contemplated revisiting Ginger's, the café across the street from her store.

"*My store,*" she repeated out loud to herself in a whisper.

It felt different, now that she had the keys. Now that she'd danced inside of it.

She wanted to make acquaintances with the employees of Ginger's, and the bar next door, all of her new neighbors. But there was someone else she wanted to see first. Someone who had promised she actually brewed the best coffee in town.

Renewed by having a plan, she swung her bags over her shoulder, locking the door of the tiny home behind her.

The sound of heavy wheels rolling over gravel rumbled up to meet her as she walked the short path back to her car. She wasn't fully prepared to make conversation with Dell again this early in the morning, so she rushed to open her car door before Dell opened his.

And she almost would have made it, too, if she hadn't been interrupted by a dog headbutting her thigh.

"Well, hello there." She held out a hand for the panting, amber-haired pup to smell before she crouched down to give them a proper ruffle behind their ears.

"Crosby," Dell's goosebump-inducing voice called. "And Nash—dammit."

And then there were two.

Mae's grin grew as she extended her pets to the new dog, their broad, solid body covered in mostly gray fur but for the white on its chest and three of its paws. One of its ears appeared to have been mostly torn away at some point, or perhaps it was a birth defect. Either way, barking wake-up call or not, the soul in their eyes wrapped around Mae's heart at once.

"Nash, Cros, come on, give them some space."

Mae stood, facing Dell, who—

Who stood with his hands on his hips, wearing a faded University of Michigan T-shirt, darkened with sweat at the collar, and black athletic shorts that were just short enough on his thick legs to look indecent.

Just short enough to reveal that Dell McCleary had a thigh tattoo. What looked to be the roots of a tree, spread out beneath his sandy leg hair.

Mae blinked her gaze away from Dell's thigh to his face and found that she had absolutely nothing to say.

"Sorry," he said. "Hope the others didn't wake you up this morning. Young's still relatively new around here. Barks every time a bird flies too close to the house."

Dell's hair was damp with sweat, too. He wiped the back of his wrist over his forehead. His T-shirt clung to his belly in the most perfect of ways. A way that made Mae want to lift up the cotton and dig her fingers in.

"Gotta go," she eventually got out.

Dell nodded as he stepped back. Whistling for his dogs, he headed toward the house before he paused, turning toward where Mae still stood frozen.

"Hey. You need a recommendation for a plumber?"

"Oh, no." Finally finding her voice, Mae waved her phone, which she'd been clutching in her hand. "I already asked Liv for all her preferred contractors two weeks ago."

Dell frowned, staring into the treeline.

"Who'd she say for plumbing?"

Mae consulted the list she'd copied into her notes app.

"Art Greenwood."

Dell harrumphed in seemingly reluctant agreement.

"Send me the estimate," he said after a beat. And then he turned and took his sweaty ass self into his gorgeous house.

Mae huffed as she got into her car, picturing Dell scowling down at Art Greenwood's estimate, that dangerously attractive face coloring her dream with disdain.

The IGA on Hastings was easy to find after all the studying of Greyfin Bay Mae had done over the last month, which was a good thing, considering her cell service was absolute shit out here. Google Maps had said "no thank you" when she'd attempted to call it into service for reassurance.

But she'd found the IGA anyway. And she was attempting to take that as a good sign.

The moment she spotted Liv, though, and Liv spotted her back—a wide, crooked grin splitting open her face—a muscle in Mae's gut she hadn't even known she'd been clenching let go.

She had confirmed Liv's queerness in one of their very first text exchanges, three weeks ago.

*My wife would've loved to have your store,* Liv had said. *She was a huge reader.*

Mae had sat at the edge of her couch, surrounded by half-packed boxes, both grateful for the text and regretful for the past tense of it. Both for Liv and for herself, that she couldn't magically open the bookstore in time for Liv's wife. She'd bit her lip, wondering how to best ask follow-up questions.

But Liv had plowed ahead before Mae had to figure it out.

*She's been gone five years now but I still talk to her all the time like a lunatic*

*Cancer's a bitch, but we got more time than a lot of folks. You don't need to say nothin*

*Did Dell sell to ya yet?*

Liv stood next to the three self-checkout stations. There were two regular checkouts next to them, the number *1* currently lit. A bored-looking teen leaned against the till, checking her fingernails.

The relief Mae felt in her bones heading toward Liv didn't only have to do with Liv's support of the store, although that helped. Mostly, it emphasized how much Mae had needed to start her day this way: in the company of another queer person.

At least...another for-sure queer person who didn't scowl at her.

"Mae Kellerman." Damn, Liv's smile truly was beautiful. "You made it."

"Sure did. I'm here about some coffee."

"Let me show you the ropes." Liv waved a hand, leading Mae to a coffee station outside a small office. She leaned against the doorframe as Mae got to work.

"I heard about your flags."

Mae blinked. *She* had practically forgotten about her flags until just then. "You did?"

Liv smirked. "Turns out some rumors about small towns are true. Word travels fast. Especially when you're one of the known village queers."

Yes, Mae was irrevocably glad for Liv's existence.

She also felt a tad queasy.

"And what was...the tone of the traveling word about my flags?"

Liv threw Mae a knowing glance before shrugging.

"You know. Although I heard it first from Olive Young, who was so excited she was practically vibrating. You'll meet Olive soon enough. She's Greyfin Bay's loudest ally. I don't think she's been as excited since Obergefell."

Mae laughed into the steam of her coffee.

"Oh dang," she said after her first sip. "That's good."

"You're damn right it's good."

Mae turned, leaning against the coffee station to stare out at the rest of the store.

"All right," she said, blowing on her cup. "Who are the other major players of Greyfin Bay I should know about?"

"Well, hey." Liv's grin sparkled in her eyes as she gestured subtly with her chin toward an old man in a well-worn baseball cap, approaching one of the self-checkouts. "This'll be relevant to you. Brooks, man in the baseball hat? He's a published author. Been writing full-time for years. But he uses a pen name. One he's never shared with *anyone.* We have no idea who he really is."

Mae's mouth hung open in both shock and glee, this incredible tidbit and the first glugs of coffee-strong caffeine kicking her brain awake.

She itched to dig out her phone, call together a brunch for her friends to dissect this juicy mystery, which was the exact kind of not-truly-consequential hot goss they thrived on. Theo was their resident master detective; he would somehow be able to google-wormhole his way to answers.

And then Mae remembered she couldn't call for a gossip brunch.

She lived here now.

Her mouth snapped shut. She murmured a response to Liv that she hoped indicated her intrigue. She'd still share with the group text chain. Gossip dissected via group chat was still a good time.

Liv interrupted her thoughts with a snort. "I'll be right back."

Mae watched Liv assist Brooks while he gestured and scowled at the screen in front of him. A minute later, Liv returned, crossing her arms as she leaned against the coffee counter at Mae's side.

"He always uses self-checkout because he doesn't want

to talk to any of us. And every single time, he does something that requires him to talk to us even *more*." She clucked her tongue. "I love that cranky bastard. Oh, and here comes Ashley. She works over at the wildlife refuge."

A trim, dark-haired woman in a khaki U.S. Fish and Wildlife Service uniform walked over to grab herself a cup of coffee. It was a problematic thing, sometimes, but Mae had always had a thing about a woman in a uniform.

"Mornin', Liv."

"Ashley, meet Mae Kellerman. They're gonna open a bookstore in that empty property on Main Street."

"The one by Freddy's? No kidding." Ashley smiled, showcasing perfectly white teeth, before holding out a light brown hand. Mae forced herself to not shiver as she shook it. "That sounds great. There are some folks in this town who could do with some more readin'."

"That's what I'm sayin'," Liv agreed.

The introductions were quick and steady after that: Archer, who worked at the steelhead hatchery up the river; Kehlani, who worked at the spa and resort down 101; Malachi, a chef at one of the local seafood restaurants; and Jett, a local mechanic. With each one, Mae's recollection from her own distant upbringing was affirmed anew.

The grocery store, *especially* if it served good coffee, was the heartbeat of a small town.

Liv introduced Mae the same way each time, without hesitation—*They're gonna open up a bookstore on Main Street*—and each time, a small hit of dopamine buzzed down Mae's veins. There were days she felt more *she* than *they*, and vice versa. But she'd finally found peace when she'd accepted that pronouns were just words for her. She didn't mind when people used *she* or *her*, especially when they were used by her closest loved ones. People she knew already saw her, understood her, as being more than just one thing. Someone a bit further down the spectrum, on a sliding scale.

Still. She loved when a stranger, someone she was just beginning to know, used *they*.

When they gave her that space to be something different.

"And here comes Taylor. Taylor Nguyen." Liv's voice shifted to something softer. Mae glanced over to see something in her eyes shift, too. Concern. A flash of worry. "I have to talk to her for a bit. But hey, you can meet Lanh, the sharpest Pokémon Go player in town."

Liv crouched toward the floor as the woman and young boy made their way to the coffee station.

"Hey, Lanh. This is Mae. They're new in town. Think you could show them some of your Pokémon while I chat with your auntie?"

Lanh didn't look away from the tablet in front of him. But after a small beat, he replied with a monotone, "Okay."

Liv stood and stepped aside to talk with Taylor, and Mae gamely took her place. Mae's body was still sore from the hard labor of moving out of her apartment, and the crouch made her wince, but in a good way. A stretch that reminded you your body was still alive and needed to move.

"What's your favorite Pokémon, Lanh?"

Lanh didn't hesitate. "Arceus. Legendary Pokémon." He was a cute kid, with dark hair shaved close to his head and serious black eyes. She estimated he was six or seven.

"I always liked Bulbasaur," Mae said. "Any of the grass types, really."

Lanh swiped at the screen.

"Fire types're better."

"Fair." Mae shrugged. "I still like the grass types, though."

Lanh gave a quiet grunt and captured a Golbat.

Mae squatted like that for five minutes more, watching Lanh battle, until Liv and Taylor returned.

"Thanks for keeping him company," Taylor said with a kind smile. "I'm Taylor." With effort, Mae stood and shook Taylor's hand.

"Will you have some Pokémon books at your new store?" Taylor grinned down at Lanh. Mae made a mental note to make the Pokémon section as extensive as possible.

"Absolutely. Maybe Lanh can give me some pointers on the essentials."

"We can't wait. Thanks again, Liv."

And as Liv and Taylor shared another hug, exchanging goodbyes, a small hit of optimism struck Mae in the sternum.

*We can't wait.*

Mae was starting to say her own goodbye, not wanting to take up too much more of Liv's time on the clock, when Liv put a hand on her arm.

"Hey," she said. "How're things going with Dell so far?"

Mae paused. It felt...weird, sharing that they were somehow almost living together at the moment. She didn't want Liv reading too much into it; didn't want Liv giving Dell a hard time about it.

She settled for, "Okay."

Liv searched her eyes for a minute before she nodded.

"I still want you to give him hell, but now that you're actually here...you should also know he's been through some shit." She shrugged, monitoring the self-checkouts. "Probably not my place to share, but if y'all are working together...don't give up on him, all right?"

Mae didn't know what to say.

But she trusted Liv inherently. So she settled, again, for, "Okay." And after a second, "Thanks."

And then she did say goodbye, and in lieu of fully processing that exchange, focused instead on memorizing the layout of her new grocery store.

The morning went by quickly from there. She drove to a nursery outside Lincoln City to buy two huge ceramic planters, sapphire blue and beautiful, along with enough plants and soil to make Vik proud and her own previous sense of fiscal responsibility horrified.

She hauled the planters to either side of the front door back at 12 Main, filled them with fall daisies. Discovered that there *was* a small space behind the building, abutting an alley and a listing back deck, where she could perhaps put a raised bed or two. Inside, she tackled the office, dirt under her fingernails, Jesús's death party playlist blasting from her phone. She tossed broken furniture through the back door onto said deck, shoved things into piles and against walls, filled one of the trash bags she'd purchased at the IGA, then two.

She dusted and sprayed and organized and danced until her back ached.

And then the first inspector arrived.

She took notes for over an hour, nodding like she understood half the things they were saying. When they left, she collapsed into the one functional chair she'd discovered in the office. Rested her forehead on the wood of what she assumed was Cara's old desk, which she'd decided to keep.

"One thing at a time," she said out loud, everything she needed to fix swirling in her head. "One thing at a time."

And after a few more slow breaths, she picked up her

laptop, locked the front door, and went to visit her new neighbors at the Greyfin Tavern.

The bar was dark inside, the kind of bar Mae had never felt fully comfortable in unless there were rainbow flags in the windows, which there decidedly weren't here. But she braved the walk through the room anyway, greeting the sole bartender with a smile.

"Hey." She held out a hand, which the bearded white man shook with a small smile in return. "I'm Mae Kellerman. I'm opening up a bookstore right next to you here, in Cara's old place."

And the smile fell. Replaced by a dead-eyed stare that hit Mae like a block of lead.

Well. Mae had known this, right? That not everyone was going to be as welcoming as Liv Gallagher and her friends. It was...unfortunate that one of those possibly-not-excited-about-Mae's-flags-in-the-window people was Mae's new neighbor. But the day had probably been going too smoothly. A small stumble was inevitable.

The bartender, who had not introduced himself in return, rested his palms on the edge of the bar. Mae contemplated leaving, her face flushing against her will in the face of the man's stare. But no. She couldn't let someone chase her away on her first full day in town.

"I'm going to do some work for a little bit. Is there table service, or should I order here?"

The bartender stared a minute more, a small crease building between his brows until he turned away. His hair was dark, his beard sharper and suddenly infinitely less attractive than Dell's. Which was...an extremely irrational thought to be having at that moment.

"Sit wherever you want." He slapped a towel across his shoulder as he walked away.

Mae found a booth near the kitchen. She texted Vik, trying to calm her pulse. *You ready?*

The bartender dropped a menu onto the table.

Mae perused the smudged plastic. The fare was what she'd expected. She ordered a BLT and refused to further contemplate the hard set of the man's jaw.

She opened her laptop, connected her airpods. Squeezed her fingers to calm their shake. And when Vik's face appeared on her screen a few minutes later, Mae tried to pretend her eyes didn't momentarily fill with relief.

"My Vik."

"My Mae. How is life in Greyfin Bay thus far?"

"It's..."

Maybe she was sitting in a room with someone who hated her, someone who would always be just a wall away. Maybe she hadn't truly had to experience that feeling in a long time. But Mae thought of the work she'd just put into that shop on the other side of this wall. She thought of Liv's smile, the locals who had greeted her kindly this morning.

*We can't wait.*

Her eyes tracked over the top of her laptop to the small window in the front of the building. Where, even from the back of the room, she could make out the waves. An ocean bigger than Mae's flags, bigger than anyone else's feelings about them.

"It's good," she said.

And then they filled each other in: Mae's new plants; the new vocabulary she'd just learned from the inspector; a hike Jackson had taken with Ben and Alexei and almost died on. Mae never quite forgot where she was, but with each little story, she felt closer to home. The one that lived inside herself.

"Okay, Kellerman," Vik said. "You ready to do this?"

"Yeah." Mae bit her lip. "I am."

"I'm going to make the website live. You got the graphic I sent you for Instagram?"

Mae nodded, bringing up the *Coming Soon* graphic Vik had made using the photo Mae had sent them yesterday: the front window of 12 Main Street from the sidewalk, pride flags lit from within.

"Sweet. Go publish that shit."

Mae tweaked the caption she'd been brainstorming in her head for weeks while Vik typed away on their end, a lock of curly hair falling over their forehead.

"It's live," Vik said with a smile, flicking the curl away. It promptly fell exactly where it had been.

Mae clicked *Share.*

"It's live," she echoed.

Bay Books was live.

Vik and Mae had deliberated over the name for a week. Mae knew it was simple, that it would likely be only one of many Bay Books out there in the world. But simple was easy to remember.

And what really sold them was the fact that, while the window would display those words, their friends agreed they would always read it as *Bae Books*. A name Mae thought would make Jesús laugh, his head knocked back, hands coming together in a single clap, like he used to do when he was especially pleased.

"You're a business owner, babe."

"I mean..." Mae thought of the incorporation paperwork she was still waiting to get approved, of the small business class she hadn't even started yet, the list of repairs the inspector had just given her.

"It's on the internet now," Vik said. "And the internet, future generations forgive us, is forever."

Mae navigated to baybooksoregon.com. And while she'd already seen the drafts Vik had sent her, she still gasped when it loaded.

"Vik, it looks so good."

"It does," Vik agreed. "It's gonna be so great, Mae."

For the length of the rest of their call, Mae let herself believe them.

It was late by the time Mae returned to Dell's property. Between putting more elbow grease into cleaning, scheduling a bevy of contractors, and completing Vik's emailed list of marketing tasks, finding another place to stay had somehow slipped Mae's mind.

She meant to go straight to the ADU, to shower and collapse with a book. But the golden light coming from Dell's front porch—along with the strums of an acoustic guitar—pulled her like a moth to a flame.

The porch looked over a short yard that tumbled into the forested hills beyond. One of the dogs she'd met this morning, the golden retriever she thought was named Crosby, lifted his head to give her a single bark as she stood at the base of the stairs. Dell's voice, low and rumbly, the words just audible, paused mid-verse.

"Oh, come on," Mae accidentally said into the silence.

Dell lifted his head, fingers frozen on the frets.

"What?" he finally asked.

"You're all..." She flailed her hands. It was like Dell McCleary was following some textbook titled *Cliché Ways to Turn Mae Kellerman On*. And he was following it to a T. "Iron and fucking Wine over here."

Dell stared some more.

"I was playing Fleet Foxes."

"I know you were! Oh, fuck you."

Flustered with herself for even walking over here in the first place, Mae turned to leave.

But at the last second, she pivoted on her heel.

"We launched our website and socials today. Bay Books. You should follow us."

"Bold," Dell muttered, turning back to his guitar with a small, derisive shake of his head. Mae steeled herself for the points he was surely about to make about launching marketing before a single bookshelf was installed.

But all he said was, "Who's *we*?"

Mae blinked, mind still preparing rebuttals about how people would love following renovations online, about the importance of building a following before opening day.

"What?"

"You said '*we* launched our website.' Who's we?"

Mae hesitated.

"Me and my graphic designer." It was the truth, technically. Conveniently, it also sounded more professional than *me and my one friend who believes I can do this.*

Dell only grunted, staring across the deck into the trees.

For some reason, Mae kept talking.

"Our Instagram's @baybooks.oregon. If you want to look us up."

Dell looked back down, plucking some strings.

"That's okay. I'm out of space anyway."

Now Mae was the one who prolonged her stare. "Space?"

"I only follow a couple hundred people," Dell said, almost absently, his focus clearly returning to the instrument in his lap. "Strict personal policy."

At that, Mae's words ran out.

She stared another minute until she thought, *Enough.* Time to stop thinking about Dell's thighs and listening to his guitar.

Time to get to work.

Bae Books and Bae Books only. All in.

She turned with purpose and walked toward the little structure in the woods where she slept almost too well.

# seven

DELL RAN his favorite hand plane over the western edge of Minnesota, and he thought about Luca's ears.

It was 7:15 a.m.; his coffee was still hot. And inside his workshop today, all he had to focus on was finishing this cherry cutting board of the North Star State. He'd offered bigger pieces, when he started his online shop, but shipping them was a pain in the ass. And while the geography-based cutting boards seemed like a pedestrian thing to offer at first, he found he liked the tiny details of each custom request. Making sure, for instance, that he got all the strange grooves of Minnesota's border with Ontario correct, the angle of its eastern shore with Lake Superior just right. He only offered natural grain cuts, liked seeing where the lines and whorls happened to line up with whatever requests the customers had made. Here, a star in Fatima and Naeem's hometown, St. Cloud.

Dell especially liked working on Midwestern states, ones that reminded him of his own hometown in the Upper Peninsula of Michigan. He had never been to St. Cloud, but he'd driven across to Duluth plenty of times as a kid. He blew a patch of dust off the curve he'd just been working on. There was still a fair amount of sanding to do before he got to carving that star, followed by Fatima and Naeem's names, but that was okay. Almost everything was okay when Dell was in his workshop.

His mind drifted when he was alone with the smell and feel of cherry, cedar, walnut under his hands. There were topics it drifted to most often: memories of his mom in the garage-turned-workshop of his childhood home in the UP, where she first taught him the basics of woodworking when he was in middle school. The sugar maple that took up the view from the window in that garage, above Mom's sanding table. The way the light filtered in at different seasons of the year.

The noises Luca Yaeger allowed himself to make, sometimes, when Dell touched him.

Yesterday had been another Luca day. And while the sex had been more rigorous than normal, Luca seemed more absent than usual, after. Wasn't up for talking at all. Luca never kicked Dell out, let him stay the night. Dell likely wouldn't have kept up the arrangement so long, honestly—it would have all felt different—if he wasn't able to sleep off the endorphins next to Luca. If Luca didn't make him a strong cup of coffee the next morning.

And while there typically wasn't a lot of talking done, especially over that cup of coffee, sometimes there were moments. And so Dell had tried to keep his eyes open for as long as possible last night, on the gut instinct that Luca had things he probably needed to talk about with someone. But when Dell finally gave in and drifted off, Luca was still wide awake next to him, stone still and silent, staring at the ceiling.

Dell knew it was ironic, or at the very least unfair that it bothered him a bit, now. That he'd thought, in the throes of it—in the rougher way Luca held his good shoulder, pushed his thumbs into Dell's hips until it hurt, in the way he wanted Dell deeper in his mouth than he'd ever been able to take before, that extra round...

The noises Luca let himself make.

Dell knew it was on him, that he'd thought it'd all meant something. Dell himself had let go more than he usually did, following Luca's lead. Releasing sounds of his own that he rather regretted now. Biting those ears, sticking out from his still-shaved head, repeatedly, among other things. Which he didn't regret at all. Either way, by the time it was over, Dell felt strung out and half wild.

And Luca had reverted to a statue. Leaving Dell to realize that whatever had just transpired between them hadn't been a furthering of a connection at all. At least, not intentionally.

Luca just had things he had to fuck out of his system.

Which shouldn't bother Dell because when they first met, Dell had used Luca to fuck the darkness out of his system, too. So it was fine. It wasn't Luca's fault that Dell was more stable these days. That his heart, against his will, was apparently deciding other things.

Dell picked up a sander, and he let his mind drift from Luca Yaeger's body to his own. The muscles and stretches of skin that were most sore from last night, the joints he always stressed most when he was focused in his workshop: more reminders that he was alive. That he was living.

The aches in his left shoulder and left thigh. Never quite gone, just like the scar tissue. But more healed now, less noticeable with each month that passed. Whispers instead of a shout.

Dell finished Fatima and Naeem's cutting board,

cleaned it and stained it, left it to dry. He stretched out his back before making sure power tools were turned off and unplugged. Back in the main house, he checked his email, let the dogs out once more. Picked up the two orders he'd finished yesterday, ready for the post office.

Let his mind drift until he thought about barely anything at all.

A woodworking session almost always ended this way. He wasn't sure how he'd be functioning without them.

For the entire bumpy drive down his road, Dell knew peace.

And then he passed 12 Main Street.

He gritted his teeth as he kept driving, determined to take care of the post office first this time.

Even if he knew he'd inevitably stop on the way back.

Dell couldn't seem to stop himself from driving past 12 Main Street at least once a day, these last three weeks. He told himself it was mostly to double check that those flags hadn't inspired someone to smash the window in.

He couldn't stop thinking about that woman in California. The one who had been shot to death in her store a few years ago because of the rainbow flag she'd hung in the window.

Every time he drove by 12 Main Street to see everything intact, he breathed a sigh of relief.

For Mae. For the town. For himself.

And the days he didn't just drive by, but pulled over to stop in? Well, he did have a vested interest in this thing. The invoices Mae had been forwarding him almost nonstop weren't easily forgettable. The plumbing repair price tag had been the most jaw-dropping, although hiring Eli Zalasky to update the electrical throughout the building had cost a pretty penny, too. Just this week, the price of hiring the Gutierrez boys to update the front porch ramp and stairs, along with the crumbling back deck, had almost doubled when they'd discovered more boards on the verge of rot than anticipated.

They had still been working out back yesterday. It made sense to stop again today, Dell told himself as he pulled into a rare spot on Main Street, to check on the progress. Mae was holding up her end of the deal in paying for half of all the work, but still, Dell hadn't sunk this amount of money into a project since he'd built the ADU. He needed to verify the quality of the work.

"Dell McCleary," Mae said with a smile when he walked through the front door, which Mae had recently painted bright turquoise. "Wait'll you see. My back porch is fucking *gorgeous* now. Oh, and you should meet Gemma."

This had been happening more and more, each time he stopped by. Mae greeting him with a smile instead of a glare. He couldn't pinpoint exactly when the switch happened, but it made him uneasier with every single occurrence. He thought, maybe, Mae was simply lonely. He'd learned by now that her parents lived down in Newport, which had intrigued him, but still, Mae had moved to Greyfin Bay on her own. And while she was apparently friendly with Liv, Liv was a busier person than Dell. It was clear Mae was bursting with things to say about this old building, and Dell—somehow—seemed to most often be the person around to hear them.

"Gemma's starting work on the murals."

"Howdy." Gemma, a wiry person with a mullet and an enormous amount of hardware in their ears, stepped forward to shake Dell's hand.

They had a good grip. And they were definitely not from Greyfin Bay. Dell attempted to not scowl at them.

"Murals?" He pointed the question back to Mae.

"Of course. The main one will be back here." Mae turned and spread her arms toward the back wall behind the counter, where Gemma had returned to rolling a layer of primer over Cara's old hideous paint. "And then a small one over in the children's section." Mae pointed to an alcove near the bathroom. "It's going to be a whale reading a book." She grinned up at him.

"Obviously."

"Obviously." All Mae's gesturing couldn't help but bring Dell's attention to her arms, which were fully exposed today, as she wore an old Myrtle Beach T-shirt whose sleeves had been cut off along with its collar. Mae, Dell had learned, hated collars. And her dislike of sleeves today proved that the tattoos wrapping around her left arm did, indeed, stretch all the way to her shoulder. While her right arm remained bare of anything but the occasional freckle.

"Why not a single one on that arm?" Dell blurted the question before he could stop himself. The question had been in his brain for weeks now; it was inevitable it'd escape at some point.

"Huh?" Mae looked up from where she'd been examining some sketches spread across the counter.

Annoyed with himself, he gestured toward her bare arm. "Your tattoos."

"Oh." Mae's mouth slid into a grin again. "I like being incongruous. Come on, look at the back porch."

And she turned, as if the statement—*I like being incongruous*—was nothing.

Dell swallowed a curse and followed her through the office to the back door.

And damn if the porch wasn't a thing of beauty now. A somewhat private beauty back here, which was always

Dell's favorite kind. It felt particularly special, somehow, that it was hidden just steps from Main Street. And—

"How in the hell did you have time to find *more* plants? The stain must have hardly dried yet."

"Jonny said it'd be good after twenty-four hours! Which..." Mae crossed her arms and squinted into the distance. "It almost was, when I came back from the nursery this morning."

Dell rubbed his forehead, staring at the raised beds set in the gravel just beneath them, the planters that lined the railing. "You know we're heading into winter, right? That half of this shit will die by spring?"

Mae turned without answering.

"I'm going to go see if Gemma needs help."

"Hey." Dell stopped her retreat with a hand on her shoulder. Her bare, tattooed shoulder.

A shoulder that was soft, and smooth, and a jolt to Dell's calloused hand. He dropped it immediately.

"Where'd you find Gemma?"

Mae breathed slowly in and out of her nose, a sign that Dell was truly pissing her off. Dell had learned this well by now, too.

"They live in Yachats. I've been following their work for a long time. I tapped them for these murals over a month ago, before I even signed your paperwork. These kinds of decisions are all mine, you know. We're starting to move past the repairs now."

Dell held up his hands.

"Fine. You're right."

And she was. Dell had never stipulated having any say over how she decorated or ran the shop itself. And maybe he *had* assumed too quickly that Gemma must have been a friend from Portland. Maybe he was relieved Mae had found an artist from the coast, even if they weren't from Greyfin Bay. Not that he would ever say it.

But Mae paused before going inside, as if waiting for him to extrapolate anyway.

"Andy's going to start work on the water damage upstairs tomorrow," she said eventually, all shades of her smiles of ten minutes ago firmly gone. "Said the roof overall looks good for now, but I might need to replace it in a few years."

Dell stuffed his hands in pockets. "Good," he said, and she stepped back inside without any further salutations.

Dell gave it a moment before following. He tried not to dwell too much in that office, which Mae had fashioned into her own unique workspace in no time: pastel-colored knick knacks and office supplies on the desk; framed posters on the wall arranged just so, the contents of which pulled Dell toward Mae Kellerman in a way that made him even more uneasy than her smiles. There were book covers he didn't know, mostly old school romance ones, and a bunch of paintings of plants.

But some of the national parks posters were the same ones he had in his own home. Concert posters for some of the same shows he had gone to, too, once upon a time.

Dell put his head down and walked back into the main room.

He should leave, now. He'd gotten the daily update. He felt especially uncomfortable with Gemma there, whether that was unfair to them or not. Any time there had been other contractors around during his previous visits, they were folks he knew. Folks who helped reassure him that this whole business would turn out okay if they were sinking their time into it, too. He still doubted a bookshop would last in Greyfin Bay, especially one as loud and proud as Mae Kellerman's. But fixing up the building would be penance for the time he had let it lapse, a punched-out tooth in the otherwise healthy enough maw of Main Street. The repairs would let him sell it at a higher price point to the next investor who came around.

But the smell of freshly cut wood from the Gutierrez boys's work lingered in his senses.

He stared at the walls, the ones yet untouched by Gemma's work. They weren't dusty anymore; Mae had cleaned everything in the space in a frankly remarkable manner within the first week she was here, even if the continued repairs shook fresh debris into the building daily. Mae just went ahead and cleaned that up, too.

The walls were still Cara's horrifying shade of paint, that had taught Dell purple could be depressing. He knew Mae planned to cover them all up with a light, fanciful wallpaper; she had shown him the different designs she was struggling to choose between just earlier this week. As if Dell would have opinions on hipster wallpaper.

She had eventually shoved her hands in her hair with a half scream and instructed him to leave, muttering something about asking Vik again. Even though she had been the one to ask his opinion in the first place.

Something about the scent of fresh cedar, though, made him contemplate, for the first time, what would be in front of that wallpaper.

"Hey," he said. "Where are you getting your bookshelves?"

Mae turned from where she stood behind the counter, at the computer she'd set up at its far end, next to the window. A vase of flowers sat next to the monitor. Every time Dell had stopped in, from the first week, there had been fresh flowers. She had a custom keyboard, round keys in a gradient of pinks. It was so damn cute—especially when she was standing there next to it, matching her hair and her flowers—that Dell could barely stand to look at it.

As she stared at him, Dell realized what else felt off about the shop today. The music was different. Every other time he'd been in here, Mae had been playing the same bizarre mix she'd been listening to that first day, of reggaeton and Judy Garland and nineties pop. Dell couldn't remember the last time he'd heard so much Destiny's Child.

Maybe Mae was letting Gemma control the music today. It was some shit he'd never heard before. He was irrationally grumpy about it.

"You don't even know how much time I've spent looking into bookshelves," Mae finally said. She turned back to her monitor before mumbling, "Apparently real bookshelves are more expensive than all my IKEA Billys. I..." She bit her lip, a move Dell absolutely did not track with his gut. "I am a little overwhelmed about the bookshelves."

Dell's mouth parted in surprise.

Mae, from what Dell could ascertain, had been spending upwards of twelve hours a day in this building, and this was the first time he'd ever heard her admit to being overwhelmed.

"They have to be perfect," she went on, turning away from the computer, voice increasing in volume as she stretched her forearms across the counter. "You know? The bookshelves will set the whole vibe. I just—"

"Want me to build them?"

It had seemed a logical ask, five minutes ago when the idea popped into his head. Mae needed bookshelves; Dell knew how to build them.

But he knew, from the way her jaw dropped, those

Pacific-Ocean-in-the-Pacific-Northwest eyes going wide, that this was going to be a thing.

"You...can build bookshelves?"

He sighed, crossing his arms and looking back at the walls.

"I spend every morning in my workshop at the back of the house building shit out of wood. I built the structure you're currently sleeping in. Yes, I can build bookshelves."

Even though, to be more accurate about it, Dell hadn't built anything as big as a bookshelf—as big as enough bookshelves to fill a whole bookstore—in a long time.

It was one of the simplest constructions you could make, but still, the scale of it excited him, in the same way that the opposite—carving tiny decorative details into a cutting board—excited him. A good piece of woodworking was always a balance of function and art, and building something that could help support a business, used by the town—for however many months the place lasted, anyway...

It wasn't his mom's ADU, nowhere near as complex as that, but it would be good. Having a bigger project again. Routine was good for his brain, but if things got *too* routine, shit could get dark again, sometimes. In a muted, sneaky way.

He could feel Mae's stare against the side of his face as the silence stretched.

"Sometimes you work out," she said.

Dell turned. "What?"

She cleared her throat, jerking back toward the computer. "You said you spend every morning in the workshop. But sometimes you go somewhere and come back all..." She waved a hand, leaning in even closer to the screen. "Sweaty."

Dell huffed a confused laugh. Yeah, a couple times a week, he made it a habit to run on the beach with the dogs before retreating to the workshop. Well, with all the dogs except Young, whom he still didn't quite trust to stay with the pack. He felt most at home within the foothills, but he never wanted to forget—to stop appreciating—that he lived by the ocean, too.

Anyway, he didn't know what that had to do with bookshelves.

"If you don't want me building your bookshelves, Mae, that's fine. It was just an offer."

Her fingers paused above her pink keyboard.

"Could I send you some of the ones I've been looking at? See if you'd be up for the designs?"

"That'd be a good place to start, yeah. But I can do anything."

"What's your going rate?"

His rate? He scratched at his beard. Contemplated what to tell her. He'd been planning on just doing it for his own personal enjoyment. And he didn't need money. But he understood Mae's desire to be taken seriously as a businessperson.

"Cost of materials," he eventually said with a shrug.

"That's it?"

"Wood's pretty damn expensive these days."

"I know. I just got the Gutierrezes's invoice."

She kept staring at him.

He shrugged again. He wasn't going to beg to make the damn bookshelves if she didn't want him to.

Eventually, she bit her lip again. Her eyes softened when she asked, "Could I come with you to look at lumber?"

Dell's mouth opened and closed. That...was a reasonable request, he supposed; Mae should obviously pick out the kind of wood she wanted. But damn if that didn't sound like some kind of seduction to Dell's ears.

Going to the lumberyard was Dell's private time.

Even though...admittedly, almost everything he did was his private time, but whatever, it was fucking different.

"Okay," he eventually said, the single word stumbling awkwardly out of his mouth.

Mae smiled at him again. Her dimple punctuated her left cheek like an exclamation point. "Thank you," she said.

And before Dell could stutter any more about this now-strange situation he had somehow gotten himself into, he left.

# eight

"WHY DO you go all the way to Tillamook to buy lumber? Newport has to have some options."

Dell glanced in his rearview mirror before backing out of the drive.

The real answer was that the employees at the lumberyard outside Tillamook never gave Dell shit about his nails. An employee at the place in Newport had, once. And even though, in general, Dell didn't find Tillamook a necessarily more welcoming place than Newport—like any city, even on the coast, he preferred to simply avoid it when he could—he had learned you could never fully trust the way any place anywhere would treat you. So he stuck to the places that worked. Let go of the ones that didn't.

"I like the place in Tillamook."

Mae grunted.

They'd only been in the truck for five minutes, but Mae's grumpiness was apparent. Dell tried to ignore it. Just like he tried to ignore his awareness that this was the first time she'd ever ridden in his truck. That he was closer to her, now, than he generally let himself be for any serious amount of time. That she'd be close enough to smell and touch for the next hour.

"I want to say something you're going to give me shit for," she said five minutes later, once he'd navigated onto 101.

He glanced over to find her glaring at him.

And here he was, thinking her grumpiness might actually equate to a peaceful drive.

"Well," he said. "With an intro like that—"

"I would *kill* for a matcha latte right now."

It was then Dell realized Mae hadn't been glaring at him at all, but at the travel coffee mug he'd been sipping from. Dell huffed out a breath.

"You have to get used to living without things like matcha lattes here. Unless you make them yourself."

"One, I knew you would say that."

"Then why did you—"

"And two, I don't *want* to make them myself." Mae's voice stretched into an actual whine that Dell would pay good money to never have to hear again. "They never taste as good."

"There's a Starbucks in Lincoln City you can always drive to, if you want one so bad."

"That's the thing, though." Mae sat straighter in the passenger seat, sounding abruptly more awake. "Why do matcha lattes have to be a city thing? How come people in Greyfin Bay can't enjoy some matcha? Why do I have to drive to Lincoln City for a treat?"

Dell rubbed a hand over his forehead.

"You know you moved here on purpose, right? You knew there wouldn't be matcha in Greyfin Bay. It feels like you're baiting me into a fight here."

"I know." Mae groaned, closing her eyes. "I'm just...so fucking tired."

And Dell knew she was. He was goddamn impressed with how much she had accomplished at the shop already. Today was the first day since he'd offered to build the bookshelves six days ago that she'd actually had enough time to venture to the lumberyard with him. She'd been busy supervising Gemma's murals and Andy's work on the water damage upstairs and Bay Heating and Cooling, whom she'd hired to update the HVAC systems.

It was irritating, how impressed he was.

Her voice retreated to a pout again. "I want a treat."

"What you're telling me," Dell said slowly, "is that I'm going to have to stop at the Starbucks when we drive through Lincoln City."

"Oh, absolutely." Mae opened her eyes. "If they make it weak and I have to ask them to put more matcha in it, will you push me out of the truck?"

"Possibly."

And when Mae's head rolled toward him with a lazy smile, well, that was a touch too close to flirtation for Dell. The mixed messages between the two of them were starting to give him a headache. Jesus. He couldn't believe he was taking her to the lumberyard. And listening to her city whines as he did it.

He placed his right hand at the top of the wheel and focused on the road.

She smelled like something bright and sharp. Like lemon but not quite. Grapefruit, maybe.

"It makes it more special, sometimes," he found himself saying, some minutes later. And when he felt her eyes on him again: "Having to go out of your way for something."

He shrugged. "It...makes it kind of a fun thing, when I drive to Lincoln City for a matcha latte."

The truck was quiet for a minute before Mae inevitably asked, "You like matcha lattes?"

"I'm allowed to like matcha lattes."

And Dell could hear the smile in Mae's voice when she said, "That you are."

"This is better than the lighting aisle," Mae breathed an hour later. "It smells so fucking good."

Dell made a small hum of agreement as he scanned the stacks. And like he kept doing, each time Mae said something nonsensical, even though he knew he should just let it go, he asked, "The lighting aisle?"

"At Lowe's. The best place in the world. Well, other than the plant store. And my favorite dive karaoke bar."

Dell released a shudder at even the idea of a Portland dive karaoke bar.

"So not actually the best place in the world, then."

"Oh, shut it." But it wasn't even said with much heat. Dell told himself he didn't find that somewhat disappointing.

But he bit back a smile when he heard her mumble, "I bet you love the lighting aisle, too."

Ignoring that—so what if he did?—he led them around a corner to his favorite spot.

"Here." He nodded to the shelves in front of them. "This is all their remainders and reclaimed. Leftovers, odd sizes, things that don't fit elsewhere. Stuff recycled from somewhere else. I normally get wood for my pieces from somewhere in this corner. Probably not the best place to get what we actually need for your shelves, since we'll need enough for consistency. But you can look around and tell me if there's anything that speaks to you."

The corner of remainders at the lumberyard wasn't *his* very best place. That would be his house, followed by Luca's cabin, followed by the stretch of sand at the state park up the road from Greyfin Bay where he took his morning runs, more rugged and less crowded than Greyfin Beach.

Still, this corner of the world was up there.

Mae leaned down, picked up a square chunk of reclaimed cedar to examine it.

"Your pieces? You mean the things you make in your workshop?"

As Dell made another hum of assent, a glint of gold caught his eye. Leaning down to the bottom shelves had finally knocked the chain she always wore free from the confines of her T-shirt. It was possible he'd spent an embarrassing amount of time wondering what kind of pendant hung from that chain, always locked away underneath fabric, resting on top of her skin.

He saw now that there were actually several pendants, all tiny, all gold, knocking against each other in a petite bundle. It was difficult to make out what they were, they were so small and intricate, and he needed to stop staring at her chest, like, pronto, but if he could only shift an inch closer—

Flowers. The pendants were, of course, flowers.

"What kind of things do you make?" Mae, blessedly, was still examining the block of cedar.

Dell shrugged, blinking away.

"Small things easy to ship, these days. The question is" —he lifted a board of red oak—"What's your plan for the shelves? I'd imagine you want them pretty uniform. Do you want them painted? Stained?"

Mae bit her lip.

"I was originally thinking they'd be all white. I want the store to look bright and clean, you know? But now that you're making them, and we're here..." She placed the hunk of cedar back on the shelf. She took a minute before she spoke again. "This is all so beautiful. I don't think I want to paint them anymore. Just show the natural wood, you know? And maybe they don't have to all be uniform, either."

Dell nodded. He liked the sound of that.

He liked the sound of that a lot.

"How thick were you picturing the shelves themselves?" he asked, already plotting.

"Maybe..." Dell determined he should just stop looking at Mae at this point. Being that she was clearly going to be chomping on that damn lower lip for the entirety of the trip. Being that her eyes lighting up over reclaimed wood was too much for him to handle just then. "Not super thick on the shelves themselves, but maybe we could get some of these thicker reclaimed pieces for floating shelves that I could put on the wall next to the counter? To display cards or candles or whatever other merchandise we'll feature. Or to display picture books in the children's area."

*Things we'll feature.* Most of the time, Mae used the singular when talking about the shop. *I'll put the children's area over here.* But sometimes she slipped into the *we*. And Dell always wondered what that meant, exactly. Who the *we* entailed.

Because he was pretty sure her graphic designer friend back in Portland wasn't planning on moving to Greyfin Bay any time soon.

"I like that," he said out loud this time. Floating shelves with reclaimed wood were always, in his opinion, a good idea. He liked picturing 12 Main Street full of natural wood. Maybe it would offset the hipster wallpaper enough that the rest of Greyfin Bay wouldn't hate it, either.

In the end, they grabbed a variety of remainder and reclaimed pieces, for either floating shelves or Dell's own projects; he'd keep track of the receipts. After lusting after some mahogany for a while, Mae ended up choosing a gorgeous knotty alder for the actual bookshelves. She'd truly been sold when a worker who happened to amble by told her it was more sustainable than other hardwoods, being more abundantly in supply, especially in western Oregon. At which her eyes had gone wide in gratitude. "Oh, good. Oh damn, I wasn't even thinking about that." And then, to Dell, eyes serious: "I'm not setting out to have some, like, ancient redwood kind of shelving in my store, you know? I don't want any part of that shit."

To which Dell found himself laughing.

"George is right," he assured her. "Alder's a sustainable choice."

"Perfect," she said, eyes steeling in resolve. "Let's go spend a shit ton of Jesús's money on some alder."

"Can I ask you a question?" Mae asked an hour later as they headed south on 101, the bed of Dell's truck full of red alder and remainders.

Dell was in the middle of muttering, "You're gonna ask me anyway," when Mae said over him: "Freddy Hampton."

Dell glanced her way.

"My neighbor. Owns the bar. What about him?"

"He's your *neighbor*?"

"Well." Dell raised a shoulder. "So much as I have neighbors. He lives down the road."

Mae mumbled an unintelligible something under her breath.

"Has he ever seemed...homophobic to you?"

Dell frowned as he thought it over.

"Not really. At least...not outwardly, I guess, to me." By which he meant, Freddy had never given him shit about his nails. But then again, Dell didn't interact with the man much. A dark bar on Main Street that had to be half filled with tourists most of the year wasn't Dell's idea of a good time. And other than a passing wave out the truck window, he didn't talk much with the other folks who lived along his road. It was possible Freddy had never gotten a good look at Dell's nails. "But I've learned to never fully trust anyone I haven't at least shared a meal with. And I've never broken bread with Freddy Hampton, so."

He shrugged when he felt Mae staring at him.

"He do something to you?"

She shook her head, breaking her stare.

"I mean...if you count *giving off vibes that he really fucking hates the flags in my window* as doing something, yeah."

Dell blew out a breath. He tried to figure out what to say to that, but found he didn't have anything. If there was anyone who was going to change a person's views on something like that, it wasn't a Portlander with pink hair who liked being incongruous. That was just the truth of things. And Dell simply didn't have any interest in talking to bigots, so he wasn't going to sit Freddy down to parse out his views, either.

Unfortunate his bar was right next door, though.

"If he threatens you," he eventually said, "let me know."

Mae rolled her eyes. "I don't need you to protect me, you big burly man. I was just...curious."

Dell frowned deeper at that. *Big burly man*. He didn't like her thinking of him that way. He was big, yeah. But the rest rubbed him in all the wrong directions.

"I wasn't protecting you," he said, a bite in his voice he couldn't hold back. "I just like to know who the assholes are."

They stared out the windshield in silence. Dell was about to turn up the music when she spoke again.

"Speaking of assholes. I have to talk about the candy store."

Somehow, a surprised laugh huffed out of him.

Sometimes, people were so hateful, all you could do was laugh.

"Oh, yeah. The Millers. They are ugly people."

"Thank you." Mae threw up her hands. "But they own a *candy store*. It just..."

"Feels wrong?"

"Yes! I fucking love candy! I live on *the coast* now. I should be able to get some salt water taffy if the mood strikes me without being assaulted with a *God made two genders* sign!"

"They switch up the signs, sometimes." Dell's smirk grew. "I never step foot in the place, to be clear. But Liv sends me an update when they put up a new one."

"I should ask Liv to add me to that chat. Except—no." Mae shook her head, voice sobering. "I wouldn't be able to handle it."

Dell took a slow breath through his nose.

"Living here," he said slowly, "requires you being able to handle it."

He wasn't trying to start a fight. He wasn't trying to be an asshole. He was just trying to tell the truth.

Mae Kellerman had gotten him excited about red alder bookshelves. If she couldn't handle the Millers, she wouldn't last even a few months, let alone the year he was holding her to for the lease.

And Dell wasn't ready to be proven right just yet.

But Mae only looked out the window.

"I'm too tired to argue with you about that," she said after a minute.

And, well. Dell wouldn't let that break his heart.

"I'm thinking I should set up out back," he said.

Mae glanced back at him. "What?"

"Out back, behind the shop. On that nice deck the Gutierrez boys built for you. Probably makes the most sense for me to build the shelves there."

"Oh." Mae stared out the windshield again. "Whatever works best for you."

Dell rubbed a hand along his jaw, contemplating.

"I'll have to bring over a bunch of my equipment, but... it'd probably be better than having to transport the shelves from home and risk them getting damaged on the way."

"And you think it'll all be safe back there?"

Dell almost made an annoyed comment about Greyfin Bay not being Portland, but somehow he stopped his tongue. He understood the concern. Mae had just paid a pretty chunk of change for the wood in Dell's truck bed. He'd be nervous, too. But—

"It'll be safe." And then, "I'll be able to start on Friday. Got an appointment in McMinnville tomorrow."

He didn't tell her that the appointment he drove all the way to McMinnville for was his monthly manicure and pedicure.

A ritual almost as sacred to him as his monthly date with Luca.

Maybe more.

"That's fine," Mae said, voice increasingly soft. After a minute, she added, "I really...I really appreciate you doing this."

Dell shifted in his seat. Adjusted his hands on the wheel. He didn't know how to process the vulnerability in her voice. It made it feel like...like he was offering more than he was. Like she was offering something in return.

Something he wasn't entirely sure of the shape of. Or if it was something he wanted in the first place.

"Sure," he managed, after a possibly awkward amount of time.

They rode the rest of the way to Greyfin Bay in silence.

Three days later, Dell hummed as he refilled his mug with coffee in the kitchen.

He still wasn't quite sure if building the bookshelves on site was the most efficient option, but the weather had been beautiful, these past few days. Cool and crisp, but still with a surprising, lingering summer warmth at the peak of the day. Good days to spend on a deck, working with your hands.

As he'd suspected, there was something satisfying about coming back to furniture, to large scale work. Mae had requested small cabinets be built into the bottom of each shelf to hide extra stock; he thought he might integrate even a small bit of carving into their doors. Function and art. Solid pieces of woodworking.

Mae, meanwhile, plugged away at putting up the wallpaper while he worked outside. He had to admit, the pattern was classier looking than he'd expected. A mostly white background with subtle gold accents and an occasional sage-colored leaf. It would look good, Dell thought, next to the bookshelves. The wood warm, the walls clean.

"Well. Just wait until you see what I have planned for the bathroom," Mae had said with a wiggle of her eyebrows, when he'd ill-advisedly decided to give the walls a compliment.

It had altered his daily routine, spending most of the day on Main Street instead of at his house, but it'd been okay. Good, even. It was peaceful in the quiet of the shop's back deck, in the muted world of his headphones and the whir of his circular saw.

He took a sip of his coffee, tapping awake the laptop that lived on a side table just off the kitchen. He'd spent the morning back in his workshop with one of the pieces of reclaimed wood they'd brought back from Tillamook for floating shelves; it only required some sanding and prep for the wall mount. Maybe he'd install it today before he got back to work on the larger shelves. Might be exciting for Mae, to actually get something on the walls.

Opening his emails, there was only junk on the personal and real estate side, and one custom order from the online shop. He'd make time to fit that in over the weekend. Shutting the laptop, he took an extra second to rub the velvety pittie head of Nash, who had wandered over to rest his jowls on Dell's thigh.

The dogs had been a touch clingier, confused at Dell's days away from home.

"We'll go on a run tomorrow morning, all right, boy?" he murmured, giving Nash's head another pet, taking another sip of coffee, before moving to stand.

And that was when the shots rang out.

# nine

MAE CLUTCHED the neck of the bottle of champagne, standing on Dell's deck, staring at her reflection in the sliding glass door in front of her.

It was October first.

She'd officially been in Greyfin Bay for a month.

It had been, simultaneously, the longest and shortest month of her life.

And now that she'd reached this anniversary, now that she was allowing herself the first day of complete rest since she'd moved here...

She'd been running on almost complete adrenaline for thirty days. Had accomplished more than she'd even hoped for at this point. She had swung by the IGA last night just before it closed to grab this champagne, in anticipation of being lazy and triumphant today.

But when she woke a few hours ago, she'd only felt melancholy.

She'd dwelled in those unproductive feelings for a while, until she found herself here. In front of Dell's sliding glass door.

The only other person she truly knew in this town was Liv, and even that was still a developing friendship. The only other people she knew on the coast were her parents and the folks in her small business class at the community college in Newport. And while she'd loved getting to know her classmates—people young and old, from all walks of life, with such diverse goals and dreams, such a different experience from undergrad—Mae was still, on the whole, more alone than she'd perhaps ever been.

Even the messages in the group chat had started to make less sense. Stories Mae hadn't been there to witness, to fully understand. Vik still reached out regularly, but the others already felt so far away. The list of everything she missed from the city had started to become a physical ache, a quiet pain constantly present.

So she'd taken to spilling all of her thoughts to Dell.

Dell was just...always there.

Mae knew, logically, that Dell was likely only interested in monitoring how his property was coming along. Because she acknowledged, begrudgingly, that it was still his property. But if he *truly* hated listening to her talk, she could only imagine he would eventually stop walking through the door.

It was possible her landlord—her landlord twice over, really—had somehow become her closest friend here.

And his land, nestled in the foothills, her safest space.

No matter how hard she'd tried to ignore him. No matter how she'd pretended, in the beginning, that she was looking for another place to stay.

And his truck was still in the drive, so she knew he was here. Even if he hadn't answered her first knock on the door that led to his workshop, on the other side of the house. Mae had still never actually been inside Dell's house, but she'd gotten a peek one night a week or so ago, when Liv had come out of the workshop door as Mae was returning home. "I take care of the dogs when Dell visits...a friend," Liv had said with a smirk, which was impossible to not interpret as Dell having a fuck buddy. Which, well. Good for Dell. The idea hadn't made Mae's thighs clench at all.

Point was, his non-answer at the workshop door had made her come around here, to the deck. The deck where he played his quiet guitar with his rumbly voice.

She readjusted the champagne bottle in her hand, taking a deep breath before she knocked again. She'd already tried once, softly, nervously, but to no avail. Maybe he was watching her through the glass from the other side of the room right now, purposely ignoring her. All she could see was her own reflection, the misty morning behind her. She hadn't asked for permission to come over. Maybe it really was silly, asking Dell McCleary to share a mimosa with her.

Whatever. Whether he ignored her or laughed at her, she hadn't let Dell slow her down yet. She'd ask, and then retreat to the ADU to commence her celebratory day of rest by herself. Which was just fine. She was fine. There was no reason for her palms to be sweaty, for her pulse to be hammering in her throat.

With forced confidence, she raised her fist and rapped her knuckles against the glass once more.

A moment of silence rang out afterward, too loud in her own ears. A sign she had perhaps knocked too aggressively this time, her nerves flipping a switch and overcompensating.

But it had worked. Because this time, only one more short second went by before the glass door was yanked open so fast and hard that she jumped, worried Dell had thrown it right off the rails.

And then Dell himself appeared, and Mae jumped back again, the look on his face throwing every alarm in her brain before he even opened his mouth.

But then he did.

"Get. Out. Of my house!"

Mae clutched the champagne bottle harder, opening her mouth to stutter a reply.

Dell's entire body was a storm, unlike anything she'd ever seen before. His eyes were wide but strangely unfocused, cheeks red, a wall of empty rage. His chest heaved.

"I just—"

"*Get out!*" The yell was so deep, so guttural, as if Dell had put every ounce of his diaphragm into it, that Mae felt an odd, terrified desire to laugh. It was as if he was playing a part in a historical action movie, a Viking preparing his troops for battle.

Except Dell didn't act. Normally hardly betrayed any emotions at all. Other than quiet disgruntlement. Bemused acceptance.

They were both large people. She had never felt small in his presence, until now. Suddenly, every bit of her size felt too soft, every bit of his too hard.

"*Get out of my house!*"

He raised an arm, and—

Something crashed onto the deck beside her. In a daze, she saw shards of a ceramic mug scattered around her feet. They looked similar, she thought, to the mugs in her own cabinets back in the ADU. The mugs she'd been using to drink her tea.

But no. They weren't actually her cabinets. They weren't her mugs.

This wasn't her safe space at all.

She realized she couldn't breathe. Dark spots blinked into the corners of her vision.

She ran.

She ran until she reached the door to the ADU. She realized she was still clutching the bottle of champagne, the wire cage covering the cork digging into her palms. She deposited it on the kitchen counter and grabbed her bag, yanked her keys from the hook next to the door.

Her fingers shook as she opened her car, as she struggled to insert the key into the ignition. Her eyes kept darting out the dash, waiting for Dell to appear around the corner. To crush his fists into her hood. One day, she thought, another half-delirious giggle fighting to make its way out of her throat, she'd get a new fancy car where you simply had to press a button to go. Where it could practically drive for you.

*Honey,* Jesús drawled in her ear. *Why haven't you bought yourself one of those already? My inheritance is* languishing *over here.*

With an actual, startled laugh, Mae reversed out of her spot, hands gripping the wheel as she navigated away from Dell's house in the hills. It was only when she reached 101 again that she realized she had no idea where she was going.

Glancing in her mirrors to ensure no one was behind her, she shifted to park. And finally, just for a second, she closed her eyes.

What the *fuck* had just happened?

Mae had been threatened before. At the height of Trump's campaign to demonize Portland, when the Proud Boys had terrorized the streets, there had been some protests outside the community center. For a while, it had been a bit scary going to work. Even without white nationalists, though, there were occasionally folks who actually needed the center, who were in the midst of a mental health breakdown, traumatized and stuck in crisis mode, who lashed out instead of retreating.

The more Mae's heart rate calmed, the more her own brain returned to stasis, she realized Dell's face had looked almost exactly like that. Like someone stuck in crisis.

But as with every other time Mae had felt fear, that knowledge—that maybe something was wrong, something that had nothing to do with Mae—didn't make her own hummingbird heartbeat any less frightened. Hadn't made the moment any less disorienting in her memory.

Flexing her fingers away from the wheel, she opened her eyes and reached for her phone.

Her first instinct was to call Vik. But she took another breath, and scrolled to a different number instead.

"Hey. Hey Liv, I know you might be working, or busy, and this is random but..." Mae glanced at the time on the dash. "Could you maybe meet me for brunch?"

Dell didn't know how long it took to return to reality.

He never did.

When his vision started to clear, when his skin prickled with cool air, flowing in through the still-open sliding glass door, he doubled over, stomach immediately swamped with nausea. He managed, a second later, to close the door, stumble toward the bathroom. The cold porcelain of the toilet felt good against his forehead, which was clammy and hot, even though he knew he shouldn't actually be putting his face on the toilet. He needed to take a shower. He was so tired.

He needed to figure out what had just happened.

One second he was at his computer. And then...and then he was here.

He thought he remembered Mae. Mae had been outside. But as soon as he thought it, his mind questioned itself. Had it been Mae, or someone else?

Had anyone been outside at all?

Were they still there now?

Panic rose in his throat, and a rush of bile flooded into the porcelain. He blinked wetness from his eyes, unsure if it was sweat or tears. Had he locked the door? Were the dogs safe? He had to make sure the dogs were safe.

Numbly, he forced himself to stand, to toss some water at his face, in his mouth. Crosby was there, right there, staring at him from the doorframe of the bathroom. Good. That was good.

He spotted Nash next, not far behind, his concerned pittie eyes staring right at him. Young sat by the kitchen island, tail thumping the floor, ears back. She whined, cowering the tiniest bit when Dell approached, and he hated himself. He left her alone, muttering curses as he searched for Stills. Eventually, he found her exactly where he should have expected her: down the hall, on her bed right outside the door to his workshop, sound asleep.

Feet heavy, he returned to the living room. The nausea had receded, but the dizziness lingered, a distant ache he knew was an incoming headache that would last for at least a day. The deep exhaustion began to permeate. He sank onto the couch and put his head in his hands.

He tried to remember. He always tried to remember, even if he knew it was useless, right after. He needed to know if it was Mae. If he'd done something to Mae.

He forced himself to lift his head, look around, try to ground his five senses. He could smell...the lingering scent of his coffee, the ever present smell of the dogs. He could see, across the room, through the glass door—

The broken pieces of Lauren's mug, smashed across the planks of the deck.

"*Fuck,*" he said, louder, clearer, punching a fist into a cushion.

And then he took a heaving breath. He didn't know what to do. No, no, he did. All he wanted to do was sleep, but he'd promised her he'd always call.

He found his phone. Returned to the couch.

And he called his mom.

"Dell? Is everything okay, honey?" Concern laced Georgia's voice already. It always did, whenever he called her outside of his regular call schedule, every Sunday afternoon. Dell couldn't remember what day it was. But he knew it wasn't a Sunday.

"I..." He cleared his throat, blinking more dampness out of his eyes. "It happened again."

"Okay. That's okay, Dell, honey. Where are you? Are you safe?"

"Yeah. I'm at home." Dell closed his eyes. "No one else is here. Everything's fine. I...I don't know what happened."

"That's okay," Georgia repeated, voice soft. "I'm here with you."

A few quiet seconds ticked by. Dell breathed. In, out. In, out.

"Was there a loud sound?" Georgia asked eventually.

"I think so. Must've been." He swallowed. "I think... maybe...Mae was here. Maybe Mae just knocked. I don't know."

As soon as he said it, though, he could picture it. Mae knocking on the glass as hard as she could. She was loud about everything. He breathed out.

"But she's not there now?"

"No. I don't know. They might be at the ADU. I just...I just came to and called you."

"Okay. I'm so glad you called me."

"I broke one of Lauren's mugs."

"Oh, *hon*." The sympathy in Georgia's voice practically reverberated across the line. Just as he knew it would. He felt blood rush to his cheeks anyway.

He was embarrassed he'd said it.

He was embarrassed he hadn't been able to make himself go outside and collect the broken pieces first, before he had to call his mom. That he'd broken the mug at all.

"Have you reached out to her recently?"

"No."

He wasn't sure Lauren would like to hear from him anyway; he'd never seen much good come from reaching out to exes. And either way, Lauren was from Before.

"It wasn't the only mug of hers you have left, was it?" There was a twinge of desperation to Georgia's voice, one he could tell she regretted from the way she cleared her throat after she asked it. The corner of his mouth twitched, a hint of relief opening up in his chest.

His mom knew Lauren was in the past, respected it. She just couldn't say goodbye to good pieces of art.

"No. Although most of the rest are at your spot."

This was how he'd always referred to the ADU. *Your spot.*

"It rather sounds like it's Mae's spot, now."

Dell held in a groan. Georgia had known Mae had moved in the week it happened. It had been the most interesting thing he'd had to report during their Sunday afternoon chats for months. Even if he knew she'd give him shit about it. He had made some resolutions, after the incident. One of which was to call his mom more. To tell her things. To keep her close, even if she refused to leave Michigan.

It was probably the best resolution he'd ever kept.

"That's temporary."

"Maybe it shouldn't be."

"Mom."

An airy, Midwestern mom noise was her only response.

"I just...I don't know what happened." Dell returned to the moment at hand. Sometimes he was able to talk it out. "Maybe they just knocked at the door and it took me by surprise, but it's been three years. That shouldn't be enough to trigger me anymore. Unless they were outside shooting off fireworks or something—"

Dell stopped himself short. He knew setting off fireworks at ten in the morning without giving him notice wasn't *actually* a logical thing for Mae to do. Then again, this was Mae they were talking about. Dell could never quite predict what she would do.

But no. He shook his head at himself. He didn't know what had happened, but whatever it was, if Mae had been involved, Dell knew she hadn't deserved it. That he'd probably scared the shit out of her.

Dell's stomach clenched into a stone.

"It's been so long since I've had a trigger," he eventually mumbled into the phone.

"Well," Georgia said slowly, "it is getting close, you know. October 4th is just around the corner."

Dell froze, momentarily stunned.

And then he blew out a hard breath.

Fuck.

"Did you forget?" Georgia asked when Dell didn't respond, her voice so soft Dell could barely hear her. "That the anniversary was coming up?"

Dell rubbed a hand over his face. "Yeah."

"Well," she said, diplomatically. "I think that's good. Must mean it doesn't have as much of a hold on you anymore."

"Except—" Dell hung his head. "My body clearly remembered something."

"Yeah," Georgia said, whispery soft again. "Yeah, hon. I know."

Even after three years, it was hard for Dell to accept. That his body remembered that night better than his brain did. That it obviously kept remembering it, even when he thought he was doing better.

He knew, he understood, had learned in therapy that PTSD was more physiological than anything, that the brain held trauma in its deepest, instinctual recesses that preceded rational thought.

But it was still fucking hard to accept.

"Tell me what you had for breakfast today," Georgia said after a minute. "Tell me what you're working on in the shop."

And so he told her about his toast and about Mae's bookshelves, about a new creamer he'd been indulging in for his coffee, about the Minnesota cutting board and how he had to take Young for her next round of vaccines at the vet tomorrow. "Good," Georgia said for each one. "Good."

And when he knew his hands had stopped shaking, he was able to say goodbye.

"I love you, Dell. I'll check in tomorrow, all right?"

Dell didn't want her to have to check in. Dell didn't want his mom to worry about him at all. He wanted her to paint watercolors in the backyard and make her own mugs on the pottery wheel in the garage. He wanted her to move to Oregon.

"Thanks, Mom."

"And Dell, honey...have you told Mae? About your PTSD?"

Dell frowned.

"No. I hardly know them, really."

A small pause.

"Well," Georgia said carefully, "if this Mae is living on your property...and I know you wouldn't let someone on your property you didn't trust, Dell, so you must know them somewhat...you gotta tell them."

Dell stared out the glass doors.

"I'll talk to you tomorrow, Mom."

"Okay, hon."

"Love you."

He left the phone on the couch, and went outside and cleaned up Lauren's broken mug.

And then he paced for a while.

His brain was already hyper focusing on what he knew to be true: while the trigger was over, that night three years ago would visit him again, over the next week or so, in his dreams. More than usual. He'd remain shaky and half conscious for a while, unable to grasp the comfort of his routines.

And now that his mom was off the line, he just felt...alone.

He didn't want to talk to anyone else. He could not imagine telling Mae about the incident, even though...if he *had* thrown a mug at her, or done who knew what else... fuck, Georgia was right. He'd have to tell her *something*, but he couldn't think about that right now.

He wanted...

He wanted to be held. For just a few minutes.

Which was funny, because in the first year after the incident, he could barely stand to be touched at all, even when he wasn't being actively triggered. He wasn't sure when or how it had graduated to this. Needing another body next to his.

It wouldn't even have to be anyone he knew. Did he wish it was Luca's? Sure, because he knew what Luca's body next to his felt like. Knew it would be familiar and warm and comforting.

But he also knew he couldn't ask Luca. That wasn't what they had going.

He wished there was a service you could call. *Would like the heat and pressure of a body next to mine for approximately ten minutes. No other touching required. Would prefer no speaking.*

And then he saw them. Crosby and Nash, right next to Young, who still cowered by the kitchen island.

Slowly, he lowered himself to his knees. Patted his thighs.

"Hey, guys," he said, voice hoarse. "C'mere."

Nash reached him first, his cool nose rubbing against Dell's beard, his eyes searching Dell's. When Dell slid all the way down to the floor, Nash immediately lay with him, snug against his stomach. Crosby rested nearby, not flush against Nash—Crosby preferred a bit of space—but close enough that he could keep his eyes on Dell, that Dell could reach out a hand and rub his soft, golden head.

After a minute, Young followed, walking around Dell to

curl up at his back. Dell focused on the warmth of Nash and Young against him, on the sound of the dogs' breathing and the wind rustling through the trees outside.

It wasn't exactly what Dell wanted.

But it was enough.

# *ten*

MAE LEANED against her car and pulled her coat closer around her neck.

Shelly's Café was up the road from downtown Greyfin Bay, at the edge of the long, marshy inlet that held the national wildlife refuge. The small restaurant's gravel parking lot sat next to a wide, open expanse of reeds and seagrasses, and the unimpeded breeze cut through Mae's clothes, whipped her hair around her face. It was quiet, other than the wind and the caws and songs of the birds that the refuge helped protect.

Until a crunch of gravel announced the arrival of Liv's Volvo.

"Hey, Mae." Both Liv's voice and her smile seemed softer than normal. Maybe because it had been clear on the phone, how pathetic and alone Mae was feeling. "Let's head inside."

Shelly's was warm and humid. The sweet and salty smell of breakfast food was cut through the middle by the bitter scent of coffee. Mae's joints finally began to relax as soon as they crossed the threshold.

"Thanks again for meeting me," Mae said as she flipped open a menu. "And for bringing me here."

"Haven't been here before, I take it?" Liv pushed her menu to the side, like she didn't need it. Mae smiled at the idea of Liv already knowing her Shelly's order. Liv seemed like the sort of person who was born to be a regular.

"No." It was close to 101, but not directly off it; Mae still mostly only knew the places she'd driven by before. And she hadn't honestly been driving many places other than Dell's house, 12 Main Street, and Oregon Coast Community College.

"Hmm." Liv crossed her arms, rested them atop the table. Like she had thoughts about Mae not knowing about Shelly's.

But the server returned before she could share them.

Mae ordered the french toast; Liv ordered an omelet and coffee. Mae took a sip of her water and glanced around at the decor. Like a lot of places on the coast, it seemed trapped somewhere between making an attempt to modernize—the logo and design of the menu had seemed new, current—while mostly being stuck in the 1970s. But the wood-paneled walls, the old picture frames comforted her. She liked being in a place that Liv Gallagher trusted.

"So. Something happen with Dell?"

Mae blinked back at her. She hadn't mentioned Dell on the phone, but it made sense that Liv would guess it. What other connections did Mae have here, after all?

"Yeah." Mae breathed out, wondering if being here at all, processing this with Liv, was a betrayal to Dell.

"C'mon, go ahead and spill it." Liv made a brief gesturing motion. "You look like you've seen a ghost, Kellerman."

Mae's lips parted.

"That's it," she said. "That's exactly what it looked like."

Their server returned with Liv's coffee. Liv stirred in two sugars, spoon clacking against the inside of the mug as she raised an eyebrow at Mae.

"Sorry." Mae shook her head, clearing some of the cobwebs. "So, today is my one month anniversary of moving here."

Liv's mouth tilted at the corner.

"Has it been a month already? Congratulations, darlin'."

Mae felt a rush of a half laugh escape her throat, a smile curve her cheeks. She thought Liv was maybe making fun of her, a little. Or maybe she wasn't, but suddenly Mae wanted to be made fun of. For making such a big deal out of thirty measly days. There were so many things she wanted to be able to laugh about.

"Yeah. So, I went over to Dell's, to see if...he wanted to celebrate with me." A blush crept up Mae's cheeks; she stared at the tabletop to avoid Liv's eyes. "And he didn't answer at the workshop door, where you were the other day, so I walked around and knocked on the sliding door by the deck. But after I knocked, he came out and he..." Mae bit her lip. "He was so angry, and yelled, and threw this mug at me, and..."

Mae leaned back in her chair and met Liv's eyes again.

"When you just said that, about seeing a ghost, I realized that's exactly what he looked like. I could tell he wasn't himself, but it was still...disconcerting."

Liv leaned back too, bringing her crossed arms to her chest. A serious crease lined her forehead.

"And what happened then?"

"Oh, I ran away," Mae said with a shrug. "And then I called you."

Liv nodded, thinking this over. "Right. Good call there."

"Was it, though?" Mae turned her head to look out the window, which looked over the wetlands. "Do you think he's okay?"

Liv released a small puff of air.

"I think it says something about you that a person throws a heavy object at your head and you're here wondering if *they're* okay, but..." She leaned forward again. "Listen, Mae. It's not my place to reveal Dell's confidences, all right?"

Mae quickly shook her head again.

"No, of course not; that's not why I—"

Liv held up a hand. "I know. I know. But if you're living up there—and I do think it's a hell of a thing, that Dell McCleary is allowing you to live on his property—then you should know that something awful happened to him before he moved here."

And Mae remembered, then. Liv telling her, that first day at the IGA, that Dell had been through something. But—

"Wait." Mae frowned as the extra detail Liv had just mentioned slotted into her brain. "When'd he move here?"

Now that she thought about it, the fact that his mom lived elsewhere, that he didn't seem to have any family around, already signaled that maybe his roots weren't directly from here. But he *seemed* like such a local that she'd never really considered it, the fact that he could've lived somewhere else.

Liv took a sip of her coffee.

"Few years ago now. Three, I think. Give or take."

Mae's jaw hung open until she snapped it shut. It made sense, when she thought about it. Lord knew the ADU looked brand new. So did his house. Had he built that, too? Three years ago?

"Where did he move from?" She knew she was contradicting herself, being a nosy Nancy, but couldn't stop the question from escaping.

"Where does anyone move here from?" Liv brought the mug to her lips again. "Portland. Same as you." And then, after a second's consideration, "Well, at least he wasn't from California."

Mae's mouth unhinged again.

"Dell is from *Portland?*"

Liv laughed at Mae's expression.

"And let me tell you, he fucking *hates* it when you give him a hard time about it. One of my life's greatest pleasures. Except..." A frown passed over her features before she sobered back to neutral. "Maybe it shouldn't be. Because like I said, some bad shit happened to him there before he left. Even I don't know the full details. I doubt even Luca knows the full details. But I know it was bad. There's a reason he doesn't like the city. As opposed to, you know"—Liv waved a hand again—"most of the assholes around here who just want to be assholes."

Mae clutched her plastic water glass, trying to wrap her head around all this.

"Who's Luca?"

Liv winced. "Ah, shit. I'm really saying more than I should, here. I thought you might know..." She held up her hands. "Nevermind. Please don't tell Dell I mentioned him. Luca's not the point here. What is—"

And then their food arrived.

There were fresh pears sliced on top of her french toast, and between that and Liv's cursing—Mae always felt more comfortable being with someone she knew she could curse around—Mae almost wanted to cry in gratitude.

Once she got over the fact that Dell was from *Portland*. What neighborhood had he lived in? God, he'd probably had some gorgeous house on the west side. Or Westmoreland, maybe, Sellwood. No, that'd be too hip for him. She had so many fucking questions.

"What is important," Liv continued as she reached for the hot sauce at the end of the table, "is that I believe Dell might have a fair bit of PTSD, and I'm only telling you this because if you're living five yards away from him, you should know. Think loud noises bother him. He always takes the dogs to somewhere in the middle of the woods on the Fourth of July. New Year's, too, I believe."

"So he was in the middle of a trigger," Mae said, mostly to herself, trying to push Portland to the side for now. And *shit*, she'd done it with her over-enthusiastic knocking. "I think I already almost knew that. I worked with people in crisis, sometimes, back in Portland. I was a social worker."

"'Course you were," Liv said easily, before shoveling in some of her omelet. And then, "Man, Nova really would've loved you."

Mae looked up from her French toast. "Nova?"

"My wife."

"Oh." Mae was still navigating how to do this. Talk out loud about the dead. Eventually, she decided to go for honesty. "That makes me feel really good."

Liv smiled back at her. "It should."

They ate in silence for a few minutes. Mae's mind drifted back to Dell. How she was still a little shaken, a little pissed at him, even if it hadn't been his fault. How she was worried about him. If he was coming down okay.

"So about this month that you've been here now," Liv

said when Mae was halfway through her French toast. She looked up to see Liv waving a fork at her. "How's that been going for you?"

"With the store, you mean?"

Liv shrugged. "Sure."

"Great." Mae smiled, and without being able to stop herself, launched into a monologue about the shelves Dell was making, and the work the Gutierrez boys had done, and Gemma's murals, and how the heating and plumbing even worked now. How many followers she'd gained on social media. Liv chewed and drank coffee and listened, with a politely amused look on her face.

"So anyway," Mae finished. "I'm feeling really good about it all. I actually can't believe how it's all coming together already."

Liv took another slow, assessing sip of coffee before she spoke again. Mae distinctly felt like she was about to be graded on a presentation. And even though she'd worked really hard on it, the outlook wasn't good.

"You talk much to Marty yet?"

"Marty?"

"Martinez. Head of the Small Business Association."

"Oh!" Mae smiled in recognition. "I've emailed him a few times, actually." See? She knew stuff. She was doing her homework. Literally, emailing Austin Martinez had been part of her OCCC homework, but she wasn't going to tell Liv that.

"About that." Liv adjusted her mug on the table until its handle was just so. "Marty never checks his emails."

"But..." Mae tilted her head. "He's the president of the Small Business Association."

"Yeah, and he can barely turn on a computer. You have to email Olive if you want anything to actually get done. Or, no, I shouldn't say that. Marty gets stuff done. But if you want your emails read, you gotta send them to Olive."

Mae wracked her brain for a second.

"Olive Young. She's the treasurer. And the woman who's real pumped about my gay flags."

Liv shot her a finger gun. Mae's chest puffed with the approval.

"What small business does she run again?"

"An antique store slash kitschy odds and ends place. Called This and That, right on Nehalem, behind the hardware store."

"*Ohh*," Mae said in recognition. "Right."

"Yeah. Most of her customers are conservative old ladies, while she's like, the most radical person here. It's a weird existence she lives, that Olive, but I don't question it."

"But she's good at checking her email. As...the treasurer."

Liv lifted a shoulder. "That's what I'm saying."

"Huh. Okay. Thanks for the intel."

"Sure. But actually." Liv pushed her plate aside, leaning forward on her forearms again. "What I'm really trying to say is, maybe you have to cool it on the emails."

"Do you also have intel on my Gmail?"

"I just mean you've been here for a month. And the town's barely seen you."

"Hey, that's not true." Mae stuck out her lower lip. "I go to the IGA all the time."

Liv laughed. "And I appreciate the business. But even *I* don't see you that much. You're like—" Liv zigzagged a finger through the air. "Zoom, zoom. In and out. You haven't stopped to get a coffee since that first day."

Mae heaved a dramatic sigh.

"I have to admit to you now that...I don't actually love coffee that much."

Liv rolled her eyes.

"One of those tea queers, are you?"

Mae honked out a laugh that felt so real, so genuinely sparked from her gut that it almost left her breathless. "I am."

"Regardless. What I'm saying is...you have to *talk* to people, Mae. I'm sure you're doing all kinds of networking online, and you've met some contractors. But if you really want the trust of Greyfin Bay, you have to be present in person."

"There's just been so much to do at the shop. To get 12 Main Street ready."

"I know. I drive by there at night and see the lights on behind those flags all the time. I'm sure you're working yourself to the bone. Just..." Liv took another sip of coffee. "Say hi, sometimes."

The server stopped by to freshen up Liv's mug. A thread of anxiety needled into Mae's stomach as she attempted to take Liv's words seriously.

"Okay," she said. "Okay. But...what if people don't *want* me to say hi? I know..." She thought of some of the nastier comments on her social media posts, the ones she tried to delete and block out of her mind as soon as she saw them. The Millers and their hateful candy store. "I know some people aren't thrilled about my presence."

Liv made a neutral noise.

"Some people aren't thrilled about my presence, either, but they've had to put up with me for fifty-odd years anyway."

"So you are, in fact, born and raised Greyfin Bay?"

Liv gave a smug tilt of her head as she sipped her coffee. "Born and raised."

"Was Nova, too?"

Liv placed the mug down on the table, did her finicky adjusting game with the handle again. "No. Nova was..." She cleared her throat. "Canadian."

A shocked guffaw exited Mae's mouth.

"Liv," she said. "You fell in love with a Canadian? Damn. That's sexy."

Liv smirked, still staring at her mug.

"Gave up socialized health care for me, for this place. If that ain't love, I don't know what is."

Mae wanted to know more about Nova, about her and Liv's love affair, but she wasn't sure how much Liv would divulge. And she was still feeling vulnerable, even if the French toast had helped. So she went with the selfish ask, the pathetic cry for help.

"And you and Nova...living here, being married here, you didn't feel..."

Mae trailed off, letting the silence fill in the words she assumed Liv understood. *Lonely. Unsafe. Angry.*

Finally, Liv looked at her.

"Look. It's not always easy, no, but I venture it's not always easy anywhere. Some folks are plain ugly people, like the Millers. You have to learn to just live with that, or the mad will eat you right up. A majority of folks here, though...they might disagree with you on what feel like pretty important things, but they've just been surrounded by different viewpoints from you their whole lives, and that's a hard thing to change. They're decent underneath. Something connects you when you know your grandaddies went fishing together. They'd come rescue me if I needed help, as I would them. I try to remember that. At least..."

Liv frowned, squinting into the distance.

"It used to matter, anyway, your grandaddies fishing together. Things have been different with some folks since Trump. Bein' mean takes precedence, now. It's more popular, powerful, to show your ugliness on the outside." She swirled her coffee, staring into its depths. "But it still matters to some folks. And you've got your spatterings of Olive Youngs. And then...then you find your people. And there *are* your people."

Mae was trying to take Liv's words to heart. Trying to adjust her mind so the mad wouldn't eat her up. Adjust to a life, a future, where she had to survive here.

But the thought came to her immediately, unbidden, at Liv's last sentence.

*I* did *find my people.*

*And then I left them.*

After a few seconds went by, Liv must have taken Mae's silence for doubt, because she went on.

"You got me, obviously, and I'm important. And then there's Freya, who owns Greyfin Winery, just up those hills a bit"—Liv gestured out the window—"who's almost as old and almost as much of a dyke as me. Down the road, there's a bartender at a brewery outside Lincoln City who's as flamboyant as Fred Astaire."

A smile cracked across Mae's face, easing the ache of her fading group chat.

"So you're saying the queers have the alcohol industry of the central coast locked down."

"Not quite," Liv said. "But we do have a bit of a history there, as a community."

"For better or worse," Mae agreed. When the queer bar was the only place in town you could be yourself for a good century or two, it had an effect on things.

Now that Mae thought about it, even Liv's IGA—through a door to a separate little room at the back—was the only place in town you could buy hard liquor.

"For better or worse," Liv agreed.

"Hey." Mae brightened. "At least I'm adding books to the mix!"

Liv cracked her own grin. "And thank Christ for that. If we were at the brewery right now instead of Shelly's, I'd cheers the hell out of that."

Mae smiled down at the table.

"But you know," Liv said after a moment, voice serious again, "truth is, I know it's easier for me, living here, because my roots are here. My family's here, and they've always supported me. I mean"—she tilted her head again, raised a shoulder— "my siblings have spread out a bit, but enough of my kin are still here. To ground me, make me feel safe, you know? I imagine what you're doing—and doing it as loudly as you are with those flags, and bless you for that—has to be a lot lonelier, and a lot braver. Whereas for me..."

Liv leaned back, casting her eyes toward the window, drumming her fingers on the table.

"I have the keys to my parents' place, the house where I grew up. It's sitting empty at the moment, but I own it. And so I always know that, even if the Millers took over the entire town council—hell, even if a civil war breaks out across this whole country—I could go bunker down in my mama's kitchen if they came for me." Another one-shouldered shrug. "I think I'd be all right, if it came down to it, dying there."

"Jesus." Mae blinked. "That got dark fast."

"Well," Liv said. "We're living in dark times. There are a lot more angry men with guns in this county than there are me. I have to make my peace with that reality somehow."

Mae stared over Liv's shoulder, where a pastry case sat by the front counter.

"I think," she said slowly, "if I get my store to the place I want it to be...I think I'd be good dying there, too."

A sad smile tilted Liv's mouth.

"There you go," she said.

Mae pictured it, for just a second. The righteous revolution coming for her. She hoped she'd have enough time to put on Jesús's death party playlist. She hoped she'd go out dancing.

"And hell," Liv said, breaking Mae's morbid reverie, "sometimes, if I'm really feeling wild, I'll take myself on a trip up to Seaside or Astoria. More and more places up north these days to be loud and proud, if I want to be."

Mae grinned again, putting the revolution behind her.

"I'd love to be invited on one of those trips, one day."

Liv raised a brow.

"Show your face in town a little more, and I'll think about it."

Mae put a hand across her heart.

"I promise to make you proud, Liv."

Liv reached into the back pocket of her jeans for her wallet.

"See that you do."

After waving goodbye to Liv, Mae drove back to 101, turned south.

And then she kept on driving. Past 12 Main Street and

Ginger's, past Freddy's and the hardware store. The Millers' candy shop and the tourist shop next to it, the one full of whale stuffed animals and baskets of polished agate. Greyfin Pizza Junction and The Bay Diner.

Country songs by artists she didn't know filtered by on the radio; it was the only music station that came in here. It had slowly grown on her, the guitars and strong voices and nostalgic melodies. A nostalgia, perhaps, for a world outside of her orbit, for places she had never touched. But sometimes the sweetness of the feeling was enough.

Without fully thinking about it, Mae kept listening to songs about small towns and driving along the coast, the cliffs and the forests and, the further south she drove, the dunes. Toward Newport. Toward Jodi and Felix.

*Enough of my kin are still here. To ground me, make me feel safe, you know?*

Unlike Liv's roots, Mae's parents had only moved to the Oregon Coast a few years ago. Once Mae had left North Carolina for college in Wisconsin all those years ago, Jodi and Felix had drifted, too, as Felix picked up guest university teaching spots: to Massachusetts, as Felix had long dreamed of moonlighting as a New England professor, to St. Louis and Austin. Until finally, they both retired, and decided, somewhat to Mae's surprise, on fucking Newport, Oregon.

"We're ready to be lazy!" Jodi had explained with glee, throwing her hands in the air. They'd apparently been researching senior living communities around the country for years. And their apartment in Newport—on the fourth floor, with a balcony facing the ocean—was close enough to their only child that it was easy to visit without breathing over her shoulder.

And then here Mae was, breathing over their shoulder instead.

"Hey, Mom," she said into the phone once she'd reached their parking lot. "I happened to be in town and I was just wondering..." She looked out the windshield of her car to the waves in the distance.

Was Dell okay?

Maybe the dogs were taking care of him.

What were the people who had taken her and Jesús's jobs at the center doing right now?

She missed the dogs she used to see in her neighborhood. She always made up little stories about their owners.

She hoped her old favorite baristas were well.

She missed the bus.

She'd planned, on the drive down here, to collapse on her parents' couch and have a little cry. She'd been wanting to have a little cry ever since Dell yelled at her and threw a mug at her head.

But now that she was here—

"Would you like to take a walk on the beach with me?" came out of her mouth instead.

"Oh!" Shuffling in the background. "You're here? Right now?"

"Yeah. In the parking lot. Sorry for the complete lack of notice."

"No, no, it's fine! I'm just down here getting a drink with Phoebe. Here, let me go upstairs and get your father."

Mae smiled. Phoebe was her mother's favorite gossip partner.

"No rush at all, Mom, seriously. You can finish your drink. I'll just be sitting on the bench out front; you can come meet me whenever."

"What a wonderful little surprise. Okay, see you soon, Mae."

And Mae had just settled on that bench, had just taken in a good deep breath, when it was whisked out of her again with a hug from Felix.

"Mae! I know you didn't move to the coast *just* for surprise visits to your folks, but I have to say, this is working out splendidly for us."

"Hi, Dad." He was wearing a cardigan buttoned over a blue button-up and khakis. In other words, what he had worn almost every day of her life.

"I hear we're taking a stroll on the beach?" He turned toward the path to the sand, mobility cane in hand, already walking away when Jodi jogged out of the doors behind them.

"You two!" she yelled. "Always running off without me."

"Hey, Mom." Mae slid an arm around her waist as they walked, an in-motion half hug.

"What brings you here in the middle of the day on a non-class day?" Jodi asked. Mae had taken to having dinner with Jodi and Felix every Thursday, after her business class.

"It's my one month anniversary of being in Greyfin Bay. Thought I'd take the day off to celebrate."

"How lovely," Jodi said.

Mae didn't respond.

She bent over to take off her shoes instead. Balled her socks inside, rolled up the hem of her linen pants.

She stood, wiggling her toes in the sand. She thought, *that's better*.

It was funny. She had pictured, as she'd packed box after box in her apartment, morning walks on the beach. Sunrises and sunsets.

But in practice, her feet had barely touched the sand at all over the last thirty days. The ocean had still settled under her skin in a way she'd never been able to experience before—the constant awareness of it, subtly saturating her senses—but it simultaneously became easier to ignore.

She looked at the water in front of them, and couldn't quite picture the last time she'd truly seen it.

"I can't believe we both live here now," she murmured as they moved closer to the waves. It was chilly out, even colder the nearer to the water they moved, but nobody complained. "Next to the ocean, I mean."

Felix let out of a hum. "You always loved it so much," he said, voice fond.

"So you've told me."

They walked along the waterline.

Mae wondered why she'd asked Felix and Jodi to walk with her. What she wanted to tell them. Why she was truly here, on the coast, at all.

She wanted the walk to soothe her. To tell her how small and unimportant and weightless she was, like the ocean always used to make her feel.

But god, why was she *here?*

She came to a sudden stop. She stared at a partially crushed clam shell.

"Mom," she said. "What if I don't actually know what the hell I'm doing?"

"Oh, honey." Jodi put an arm around Mae's shoulder. "None of us do."

"That can't possibly be true."

Jodi shrugged.

"Maybe. But as an example, twenty years ago, I didn't know Newport, Oregon even existed. Wouldn't have guessed I'd be retired here."

She looked at Mae.

"But now that I'm here? I'm pretty glad life worked out this way."

"Yeah."

"Sometimes you just have to go where life takes you. I've always been proud of you for doing that."

It was true that Mae had moved a fair amount in her life. From North Carolina to Wisconsin, from Wisconsin to a brief stint in Brooklyn, from Brooklyn to Portland, and now to Greyfin Bay. She should understand these little aches. The love you still held for those you moved away from. For those who moved away from you. She had chosen this.

Mae stared at the ocean. And feeling suddenly like a small child, she blurted, "I miss Jesús." Her vision blurred. "Steve, too. I miss them so much."

Quietly, Jodi pulled Mae into her. Mae shuddered into her mother's shoulder.

Because it wasn't just the little aches. It wasn't just Greyfin Bay.

None of it was Jesús. Someone who had known and loved every part of her.

"Why did he have to go, too?"

"I don't know, honey," Jodi whispered into her hair. "I don't know." And then, "We never do. We just have to keep going on, for them."

"I know." Mae pulled away, embarrassed. She wiped at her eyes. "I know."

It was what Jesús would have said, too.

But knowing that wasn't the same as actually hearing him say it. She was so lucky to have two healthy parents, alive and loving and here, right next to her.

Yet even they didn't fill the Jesús-sized hole inside of

her. She wanted his arms around her. His laugh and his rough cheek against hers.

And she couldn't have it. Ever again.

They kept going. Mae and Jodi and Felix walked until the wind grew too cold, and they turned for the slow walk back home.

# eleven

DELL DUG his fingertips into a sheet of sandpaper and focused on the irritating sensation, each tiny prick of skin.

He just needed to finish a bookshelf.

He had taken the rest of the day off yesterday, mostly drifting in and out of consciousness in bed with the dogs. He was still exhausted, his whole body one strange ache: neck tight, muscles sore, as if he'd run a marathon. But if he didn't get back to work today—well, he might be useless today, too. But it'd be worse if he didn't try.

Most of the pieces of red alder were already cut and shaped; all he needed to do now was assembly. He just needed to build a fucking bookshelf, one of the easiest things a person could do. And he was almost there, with the first one. Almost there.

The door to the back deck opened behind him. Dell closed his eyes before he turned.

"Mae."

She leaned against the doorframe, arms crossed. It was hard to read her face. She wore an incredibly fuzzy purple sweater, a turquoise skirt. She looked like a muppet.

"Dell."

He ran a hand through his hair, trying to calm the shake in his fingers. He'd been preparing for this, what he would say. He hadn't seen her again yesterday, even if he kept looking out the window, watching to see if her car had returned to the drive. It hadn't until late, until the sun had gone down. His chest had finally unclenched when he'd seen her headlights coming up the road, sweeping across the corner of his living room.

And when the hell had that happened? He'd spent three years at the top of that hill precisely so that he could be alone. And there he'd been, unsettled without Mae's car parked next to his.

"Did I hurt you?" he blurted. It wasn't how he'd planned to start, but it was what he needed to know most. Even if, with relief, he noted that her face wasn't bruised, cut anywhere.

She kept her stare level. He felt comforted somehow that she was looking at him at all. That he hadn't freaked her out enough to be unable to hold his gaze.

"No," she said. "But you scared me."

He swallowed. "I'm sorry, Mae. I wasn't myself."

"I know," she said. She was so...calm. A very calm muppet.

And then she added, "I knocked. Loudly. On the glass. I'm sorry for that, too."

Dell let out a breath. That had been his best guess, but it helped to have it confirmed.

"You shouldn't have to be sorry for knocking."

It was a miracle, he now realized, that this hadn't happened earlier. He had told her, when she'd first moved in, to text if she needed anything, but he should have been clearer.

She merely raised a shoulder.

"Still."

She was being so understanding. *Too* understanding. Like she already knew there was something wrong with him.

He couldn't believe, at this point, years later, he couldn't survive a fucking knock on the door.

*But,* the rational part of his brain said, *when was the last time someone knocked on your door?*

He'd given Liv a key, once he knew the Luca situation would be an ongoing thing. She always let herself in quietly through the workshop door. There had been that miserable month he'd attempted to be an Airbnb host, when his awareness of other people on the property had always been on high alert, but that felt like forever ago. And other than that...

Other than that, Dell had never had any visitors.

Until Mae.

"Something fucked up happened to me," he forced out. "A while ago. So I'm susceptible to triggers now when I get surprised. Which I should have told you when you moved in. That's on me."

Mae only nodded. But her eyes appeared to soften.

Her eyes, Dell realized now, seemed puffier than usual. Like she'd had trouble sleeping, too. He frowned.

"Is there anything I can do?" she asked. "To help you now, or in the future?"

"No. I'm usually...slower. At getting things done, afterward. But I'm almost done with this one." He gestured to the bookshelf behind him. "Want me to install it when it's ready?"

"The Gutierrez boys are coming back today to fix some

of the floorboards inside," Mae said. "But once the floor is no longer a tripping hazard...absolutely."

"All right." Dell scratched his head. He should just let it go, but—"You're not pissed at me? I know I threw a fucking mug, Mae. You should be pissed at me."

Mae had been pissed at him for—god, how long had she been here now? A month? It felt longer. Either way, she'd been pissed at him every step of the way for weeks, and now he had done something actually worthy of her ire, and she...what, pitied him? It turned his fucking stomach.

"Oh, I was," she said easily, and shit, he could've kissed her for that.

Which...was not what he should be thinking, right now. Or ever.

"But"—she shrugged again, just as easily—"now I'm not."

He released a half laugh. He didn't know what else to do. God. If only his body could switch gears so freely.

"Let me know if you need anything," she said. And then, looking toward the sky, "It's getting colder out here."

He didn't reply. Cold was good. Cold kept his senses awake.

Even if cold also made his shoulder sore. Made the sinew of his thigh ache louder than in the summer.

She'd turned to go back inside when he asked, "Why did you knock?"

A month, and she hadn't knocked on his door until yesterday.

She paused on the threshold, back to him. Her hair was up today in the high bun she often wore it in, soft tendrils that didn't quite reach whispering over her exposed neck. The longer she stood frozen there, the longer he couldn't stop staring at them. Something stirred in his half asleep body. This feeling that had been stealing over him more and more, whenever Mae closed her mouth long enough for it to grow. An awareness of what the creamy skin on that neck would feel like under his mouth. How easily his body would curve around the back of hers.

"I was going to invite you over for a mimosa."

It took a second for her words to penetrate through his mind fog.

An obvious second too long, because she said, "It was silly," stepping inside and closing the door before he could respond.

The next morning, Dell plunked a bottle of champagne onto the counter.

Mae blinked away from the computer screen.

He lifted his other hand and placed a bottle of orange juice next to the champagne.

"I'm going to finish a bookshelf today," he said, voice gruff. His face looked just as rough as it had yesterday, eyes just as bloodshot. Any time she'd peeked her head outside after their morning conversation, he'd been puttering around the back deck, muttering to himself.

"The Gutierrez boys going to be done with the floors today?"

Mae moved her stare from Dell's face to the champagne.

"Yeah. They only have two more boards to replace. Said they'd be done by noon."

Dell grunted. "Good." He turned to look at the room. "Where do you want it?"

Mae blinked again. "The bookshelf?"

"Yeah. Walls are done over there, yeah?" He gestured to his right.

Finally forcing herself to snap out of it, Mae stood, walking around the counter. "Yeah." She only had a bit more wallpapering to do on the opposite wall. "I was thinking the first shelf could go..." She walked toward the door, pivoting on her heel in front of the window. "Here."

Dell moved to her side. Grunted again. Stepped forward, withdrawing a stud finder and a tape measure from the bag stretched across his chest. Mae watched him take his measurements, the movement of his shoulders underneath his flannel. She should be excited to get back to the computer. She was about to press *Submit* on her first official book order. But yet...

Dell took a pencil from his bag and made a mark on her new beautiful wallpaper.

"Hey!" She stepped forward with a frown. Dell made another mark.

He walked away without another word, until he paused by the counter.

"When it's up," he said, nodding toward the champagne, "we'll do that."

And he was gone.

Mae put the champagne and OJ in the small fridge she'd installed in the office. The Gutierrez boys finished the floor. She submitted her book order.

Something changed inside her, once she did.

Somehow, every uncertainty that had risen to the surface two days ago about her existence in this town, every bit of grief she'd cried into the sand next to her parents—it all felt lighter. It all felt a bit more okay, when she remembered books.

Getting to buy books and sell books. Getting to exist alongside them.

When she remembered books, she remembered this would all be worth it.

Thinking of her conversation with Liv, she decided to finally try The Bay Diner for lunch. To say hi to someone new. It was mediocre, but the waitress was nice to her, even when Mae introduced who she was, so she counted it as a win.

And when she returned, her bookshop had a bookshelf.

"Oh my god." Her bag dropped off her shoulder to the floor.

Dell turned. And for a second, he smiled. Just the slight twitch of his lips that Mae had come to learn was a Dell smile. His eyes, a bit brighter than they had been in days.

And then, like that, it was all gone as he frowned.

"Uh." He hugged his elbows across his belly. "I hope it's okay. I realize, now, that I should have waited for you before I actually put the screws in."

Silently, Mae walked to the shelf, firmly secured against the wall. She ran a hand over the smooth wood, almost soft in the lack of varnish. After a minute, she squatted down to run her fingertips over the detail Dell had carved into the center of each low cabinet door: little flowing waves.

She stood. Turned.

"I have a bookshelf," she said. The smile tugged its way back to Dell's mouth.

"With more to come," he said.

"With more to come!" she shouted, like a dam suddenly bursting. She bounced on the balls of her feet, cupping her cheeks with her palms. "Oh my god." She twirled back to the shelf. "Okay." She forced herself to stop bouncing, to think of her floor plan. "I'm going to put local interest stuff here. Guidebooks and travel and non-fiction. History. Kids' books about whales and seashells and clams. And then!"

Mae twirled again.

"Right where you are."

She stepped forward. Dell raised a brow, retreating just before she collided with his chest.

"Right here." Mae spread out her arms. "A beautiful table for new releases. And a rug. I want a gorgeous rug, running all the way from here"—she skipped to the counter—"to here. Oh my god." She covered her mouth with a hand before dropping it. "The floors are done. I have a bookshelf."

She restrained herself—barely—from launching her body at the beautiful burly person in front of her and shaking his shoulders. Didn't he see?

"I can get the rug and the table now. *Right now*. That's what I'm going to do." She took a breath, her day suddenly, brilliantly reconfigured in her head. "I'm going to go see Olive."

Dell nodded.

"Her store's got a dumb name for the quality of the stuff she's got in there," he said. "Well, some of the stuff. It's a good idea."

Mae stared at Dell a moment more. All of the doubts, all of the sadness of the past few days felt ever further away.

"Sorry I can't do mimosas right now," she said after a beat. "I'm too full of adrenaline."

Dell nodded again. "Me too."

Mae laughed.

"This is you full of adrenaline?"

Dell's smile grew as he rubbed a hand over his face.

"Very tired but full of adrenaline, yeah." He looked over at the shelf, stuffing his hands in his pockets. "It looks good." And then, looking back at Mae, "Maybe we meet back up in a few hours. For the champagne."

"Yeah." Mae smiled back. "I like that plan."

"All right," Dell said, voice still gruff, but lighter, somehow. "See you soon."

And then he walked past her into the office, until she heard the back door slam, followed, soon, by the familiar whir of one of his power tools.

She knew exactly what he looked like back there, by now: safety glasses, a light sheen of sweat on his brow. Forearms on display, T-shirt stretched across his wide shoulders. Perhaps a bit of sawdust in his beard.

It didn't affect her at all.

Mae shook her head, grabbed her bag and her keys. She was still smiling when she locked the front door behind her, turning to walk down Main Street, ready again to say hi.

Olive Young recognized Mae the minute she walked into This and That.

"Mae Kellerman!" Olive whipped a tea towel she'd been examining onto the massive counter in front of her. "Owner of Greyfin Bay's new bookstore. Am I right?"

*Finally*, Mae thought, trying to tamp down the enthusiasm of her grin so as to not appear as manic as she felt. *I've met one of them.*

Olive Young, with her graying hair swept into a bun behind a flowing, floral headwrap, her vintage glasses hanging around her neck on a chain, and a voice so loud and distinctive you could sense her personality within a single sentence, finally filled the void of *quirky townsperson* Mae had been conditioned to believe existed in small towns through an adulthood of romance novels and Hallmark movies.

Even though Mae, in childhood, had herself lived in a small town, and could only remember a lot of tired people who weren't very quirky at all.

Still, she was glad to meet Olive.

"You knew my full name," Mae said. "Impressive."

Olive navigated around the three-sided counter in the center of the room to reach Mae with a handshake.

"A gal like you moving to town is memorable." Olive perched the glasses back on her nose to give Mae a better look.

"Actually," Mae said, still a little high on bookshelf adrenaline, "I don't really identify as a gal."

"Ah. Nonbinary, then?"

Mae shrugged. "Whatever you want to call it. I'm good with she or they pronouns."

Olive flicked herself in the forehead.

"Gotcha. Got it locked away in my noggin now."

Mae realized, while holding in a laugh, that she recognized Olive's distinctive accent.

"Olive," she said, "Are you from—"

"Jersey?" Olive stood taller, put her hands on her hips. "Sure am."

"What brought you out here?"

"Oh, you know." Olive deflated a touch, rolling her eyes and flopping a hand in the air. "A man. Didn't last forever, but he gave me my babies and this store, so I can't complain. Are you an East Coast defector, too? Well, not that I should say I'm a *defector*." Olive winced, rolling on before Mae had a chance to answer. "Still go back every year around the holidays for a few weeks, but I'm pretty well settled here now, y'know? This place sticks its claws in ya."

"Yeah. I never lived in Jersey, but I did spend a year in Brooklyn, a long time ago."

"Well, of course you did."

"Couldn't quite afford it, I'm afraid."

"Of course you couldn't! And Jersey's just as bad these days!" Olive threw up a hand. "And the taxes! Out of control, absolutely out of control. Don't even get me started. Anyway, anyway, come on in, Mae Kellerman."

This and That was both dark and warm, so full of things that daylight from the street hardly made its way inside, but this reality was offset by the abundance of lamps, lit from all corners of the room. Their golden light highlighted the stacks of bookshelves and end tables, the velvet chairs and the plastic milk crates full of old records, photographs, postcards. Glass vases rested on every available surface, some full of seashells, others, buttons.

It reminded Mae of her old favorite thrift stores on Hawthorne Boulevard, except a touch less vintage, more heavy on old lady, coastal kitsch.

She was in love.

"Olive. This place is incredible."

Olive's face brightened. "Why, thank you. I do rather like it myself. Is there something you're looking for, or did you just stop by to say hi?"

"Both. I really should have stopped by to say hi earlier. So, hi!"

She waved, even though they were standing three feet from each other, and Olive laughed.

"Oh, I knew I would like you. What you looking for, then?"

"A table." Mae glanced around the shop. "And...you don't by chance sell any rugs?"

"I do, actually, but I don't always keep 'em out front. Too easy of access for kids' sticky fingers and their grownups' spilled coffee. Here, follow me."

Mae followed Olive through the narrow pathways of the store until they reached a door in the back corner. After a bit of fiddling with a jingling key ring, Olive opened it up, and Mae held in a gasp as she walked through.

The room was much bigger than she had expected, almost as big as the main room. And *almost* as cluttered, if less purposefully cozy.

"Store everything in here that's not quite ready for the floor yet," Olive said, fists on her hips again, "or that I don't trust to be on the floor. The rugs are way there in the back, but if there are any tables here that look promising too, let me know."

Distantly, the bell above the front door jingled.

"You just feel free to look around, all right? Make yourself at home. Let me know if you need anything."

Mae didn't waste any time in exploring.

None of the tables matched exactly what she was picturing—something heavy, circular, easy to wander around while anchoring the front of the shop—but magically, she fell in love with the first rug she saw.

It looked about the perfect length, full of turquoise and pinks, faded just the right amount.

It was perfect.

She took a slow walk around the main store while Olive chatted with her other customer; she tried to hold in her excitement. None of the tables out here quite met her exact dream either, but she discovered a little sea-green console table that would be *perfect* for the shop's bathroom, the last part of Mae's remodel plans she had yet to truly tackle. But she had a vision, and this table was a good start.

"I have a delivery boy who can get these over to you early next week, if that works," Olive said as she rung Mae up, and Mae's elation deflated, just a bit.

"Oh." She had walked here, not fully thinking through this part. "I was hoping to at least bring the rug over today. There's no rush on the table. Maybe I can bring my car around—"

"You know what?" Olive slapped Mae's receipt onto the counter. A grin curved the corner of her mouth. "12 Main Street ain't so far away. Think you and me could manage it?"

Mae looked around. "I wouldn't want to make you leave the shop unattended."

"Please." Olive waved a hand once more. "It's a Thursday in October, Mae. You're the most exciting thing that's going to happen to me today."

And that was how Mae found herself struggling with one end of a rolled up rug while Olive led them down Main Street.

Olive was walking backwards and seemed hardly winded.

"Olive," Mae panted. "This rug is *heavy*. Are you secretly ripped under that sweater?"

"Of course I am," Olive answered, sounding offended. "I spend half my days moving furniture around. Old furniture, the kind that's not made of particle board. Why wouldn't I be ripped? Sixty-somethings can be ripped, you know. Hey, Cara! Cara, do you know who this is?"

Olive came to an abrupt halt, and Mae almost dropped her end of the rug. Again.

Good god, they weren't even to the bigots' candy store yet. Her arms were going to be Jell-O for the rest of the day.

"I don't believe I do," the short Black woman Olive had stopped to talk to said.

"This here is Mae Kellerman. They're the one who's moving into your old shop!"

Cara turned to look at Mae. "No shit," she said, and Mae liked her immediately.

"Yeah!" Olive enthused. "We're taking this rug over there right now. Want to get an early look at the bookstore?"

"It's still really a work in progress—" Mae attempted to interrupt.

"Hell yeah, I do." Cara ambled to Mae's side. "You need help here?"

And before Mae could answer, Cara was tugging up their end of the rug, and Olive was on the move again.

"It's a great space, eh?" Cara asked Mae as they walked. "I miss it, sometimes, but it made sense to go online."

"Yeah," Mae breathed. God, there was just nowhere good to grab ahold of this thing. "Thanks for leaving it for me, I guess?"

Cara snorted. "You're welcome. Although I suppose we should all be thanking Dell. If he's letting you have it, he must really believe in you."

"Well—" Mae felt herself flush, even more so than she already was. "He's not letting me have it, exactly. He's letting me lease it, with conditions. Even though I *wanted* to buy it outright."

Now both Cara and Olive laughed. "Sounds about right," Cara said. "Still, my statement stands. Hey, Freddy!"

she shouted at the bar as they passed it, even though Freddy wasn't actually anywhere to be seen. "Miss being next to that bastard," she said with affection, and Mae felt a streak of...something, that Cara and Freddy had apparently gotten along.

But then she stopped caring, because they were passing Freddy's, and that meant—finally—they were here.

After fishing her keys from her bag, the three of them stumbled through the door.

"Holy smokes!" Cara dropped their end of the rug onto the floor without fanfare. "Look at that mural!"

"What mur—oh, wow!" Olive turned, dropping her end with a similar *thud*, and they walked in tandem to admire Gemma's work behind the counter. "Bay Books!" Olive shouted. "Would you look at that!"

Cara crossed her arms, looking down at the floor with a crease in her brow.

"Hold on a minute," she said, walking a few steps away from the counter this way, then that way. "These floorboards aren't sticking up anymore."

"The Gutierrez boys fixed them this week." Mae wiped a forearm across her sweaty brow.

"You mean you're opening this place back up without any tripping hazards?" Cara let out a disbelieving puff of air. "You're gonna make me look bad."

"The floor still dips a bunch over there," Mae said brightly, pointing toward the back of the room, "if that helps." Multiple contractors at this point had assured her this little quirk was fine.

Cara's face broke into a grin. "You know, it does."

"Oh, this bookshelf is pretty." Olive glided over to the newly installed shelf, sniffing the air as she did. "And it smells like fresh wood? Was this custom made?"

"Yeah. Dell's making all the shelves."

Olive turned.

"Dell makes bookshelves?"

"Yeah, he has a whole woodworking shop at his house. They're good, right?"

Now Cara turned.

"Dell has a woodshop at his house?"

"You've seen his house?"

Mae glanced between Olive and Cara, standing shoulder to shoulder in front of her. She sensed she should not disclose that she kind of lived there.

"...yeah."

"I've heard it's gorgeous," Olive said.

"Yeah, Liv's the only one he ever lets visit. Which"—Cara tilted her lips in a gesture of non-judgment—"he's a smart man. If I had to choose one person in this town to share my secrets with, I'd choose Liv, too."

"Hey!" Olive said in offense. And then, a second later, shoulders dropping: "Yeah, I would, too."

"So the rug," Mae said, turning away. She wasn't out of breath anymore, but her face still felt hot. "Want to help me position it?"

"Oh, sure," Olive said, already on the move. "Now, you'll want to get a floor protector underneath here, and I don't sell those, but let's see how she looks." The rug was already half unfurled toward the counter before she'd even finished her sentence. Within another minute or two, after some adjustments from Mae and Cara, she stood back up, dusting off her hands. "Well, would you look at that. It's perfect."

Mae backed up until her butt hit the pride flag in the front window. She covered her mouth with her hands, shaking her head as she took in the whole view.

"*Perfect*," she agreed.

"I'll have Dustin bring that console over to ya in a few days, all right?"

"Of course. No rush at all."

"And hey, if you can't find that other table you're looking for in my place, there's a great flea down in Florence in a few weeks. I get a bunch of inventory from them each year. You should check it out."

"I will. Thanks, Olive. And thanks for your help too, Cara," Mae added as both older women made their way to the door.

"Sure thing," Cara said. "This was a treat. You have an opening day in mind yet?"

Mae blinked. *Opening day.* As Cara would say: holy smokes.

"There's a lot to do, and I'm still waiting on my license. But...I'm hoping to be open before the holidays."

Both Cara and Olive's faces lit up.

"That would be fantastic!" Olive gushed. "More local businesses to support during holiday shopping is always a great thing. Let us know if the SBA can do anything to help get the word out when you do have a launch date, okay?"

Mae nodded, heart racing. She felt Jesús behind her, jumping up and down, palms pressing down on her shoulders.

"Yeah," she said. "I will."

# *twelve*

SLOWLY BUT STEADILY, Dell had been recovering.

The nighttime flashbacks had lessened; he was almost —almost—able to sleep through a regular night. Regular meaning whatever semblance of restless half sleep he'd maintained ever since the break-in.

The mind fog was getting better, too; getting that bookshelf installed that morning had helped him more than he'd likely ever be able to admit to Mae.

But it was when he walked back into 12 Main Street later that night after a few hours of rest at home and Mae looked up with a smile brighter than he thought he'd ever seen before—somehow, that lifted the last of the heaviness right off his shoulders.

And that was when he knew, truly, that he was in trouble.

"Am I glad to see you!" she said, bouncing off her chair behind the counter. "That champagne has been whispering to me for hours. Look! At! My! Rug!"

She spread-eagled her arms, twirling around on—Dell

looked down to see—yes, a rug, stretching through the center of the room.

"Isn't it beautiful?"

"It's nice," Dell admitted. "The light colors might be hard to clean, but—"

"Nope!" Mae flounced over and booped him on the nose with the pad of a finger. "Nope, I am not going to let you take away from this feeling! The colors help the room feel spacious and light and airy!"

"Yes," Dell said, stifling a chuckle despite himself. He couldn't quite remember the last time he'd been booped on the nose. "Light and airy. That is what I meant to say."

"That's right it is." Mae beamed at him before skipping into the office, emerging a minute later with the OJ and champagne. "Plus," she called over her shoulder as she retreated once more, "I think I had an unexpected soft open today."

She returned holding two mugs.

"Yeah?" Dell stepped forward to open the juice.

"Yeah. Olive and Cara were here. They gave a thorough inspection."

Dell gave a soft huff of laughter, pouring juice into one of the mugs. "I bet they did."

Mae tilted her head, giving Dell a thorough inspection of his own as she twisted the cage off the champagne top.

"Do you not tell people you do woodworking?"

Dell's brows raised in surprise before he shrugged.

"Why would I?"

"Um," she said in disbelief, crinkling away the foil. "Because it's awesome?"

Before Dell could reply, she'd propped the bottle against her hip, releasing the cork with a *pop*. She laughed as the carbonated liquid streamed over her fingers. "Whoopsidaisies."

Dell also couldn't remember the last time he'd heard anyone say *whoopsidaisies* out loud.

"How much do you want?" she asked after she'd wiped up the spilled champagne with a nearby towel. She tilted the bottle over Dell's mug.

"That's okay." Dell slid the mug closer to himself. "I don't need any."

Mae stared at him. "You don't want champagne?" And then, shaking her head at herself, "Sorry if you don't drink. I didn't know."

"No, I..." Dell scratched his brow. "I drink sometimes. But it can fuck with my sleep, and my sleep's already pretty fucked after a trigger, so." He shrugged. "Always best to play it safe. You should have as much as you want, though."

Mae stared at him a moment more.

"Good," she said, finally averting her eyes. "Because I always want champagne." And she filled her own mug to the brim.

"If you only drink the juice," she added, "and I only drink the bubbles, it's kind of like we're just doing...deconstructed mimosas. Together. Whatever," she replied to Dell's snort. "We're also drinking them after six p.m., but I'm just saying, it counts."

"Sure."

"So what else do you make in your woodshop anyway? Other than bookshelves."

After a moment's contemplation, Dell retrieved his phone from his back pocket. Opened up to his Etsy and handed it over. Figured it was easier than talking.

Mae brought the screen close to her face as she scrolled.

"Dell," she said. "This stuff is...beautiful."

Dell plucked the phone back, even as Mae made a sound of protest.

"Thanks." He said it sincerely. He worked hard on his shit.

Even if he sighed a second later, understanding that now Cara and Olive—and so, the rest of the town—would likely soon know about his shit. It wasn't that he didn't want Greyfin Bay to know he had an Etsy; Tim at the post office certainly already knew. It was just, the less people had to talk to him about, the better. Real estate was clear cut, easy to discuss.

Having a woodworking Etsy where the listed items tended to skew more artistic than rustic...well, Dell knew that would result in the same kind of glances some folks gave his fingernails. It was tiring, was all.

"Anyway." He turned with his mug, taking a step away from the counter. "Let's try out this rug, then." And with only a small grunt, he lowered himself to the floor.

"Hell. Yes."

He'd planned only on sitting, but Mae stretched herself on her back, swiping her arms and legs like she was making a snow angel.

"I give it an A," she said after a minute. At which point Dell realized he was sitting there like a creep, staring at her, so he shifted onto his back until he was staring at the ceiling, too. "Mind if I put on some music to appreciate the rug to?"

"Go for it," he said.

A few moments later, Mae placed her phone on the rug between them. Maggie Rogers poured through its tiny speakers, and Dell suppressed a grin.

"So," he said, halfway through the song. "Why books?"

Maybe it was the high of finishing the bookshelf, or the

admiration for how quickly Mae was bringing this place together. Maybe it was residual guilt from throwing a mug at her. Or it was just Maggie, and the fact that they were both lying on a rug together, a strangely intimate affair.

Regardless of the reason, Dell felt a need to start making an effort. Not just through bookshelves, but with words, which were a hell of a lot harder.

"Huh?"

Dell cleared his throat.

"You have this supposed blank check from your friend who passed away. Why a bookstore?"

Mae's phone transitioned to a song he didn't know.

"You really want my *why books are special* speech?"

"I mean." Dell shrugged against the floorboards. "I'm building you bookshelves. At this point I kind of feel like I deserve it."

Mae released a small laugh.

"God, it just feels so trite to say it all out loud. Like, who *doesn't* think books are special? I'm fucking boring, really."

Dell knew both of those points deserved a solid rebuttal. But he was still pretty damn tired, from the last week, from life, and so his efforts to converse here only went so far.

"Tell me anyway," he said instead.

She fell quiet for a time. But eventually, after a long breath, she started.

"I grew up in a small town in the mountains of North Carolina. Even in my oldest memories, I remember feeling too big for it. My body, which has always been big, and in every other way, too. It was a decent place, more diverse than Greyfin Bay. But books let me explore new places, you know? Taught me how much bigger the world was than the Carolina mountains. That felt so important to me. Books honestly helped me want to wake up each day."

A pause.

"And as an adult...being a social worker was hard. My relationships haven't always been great. Escaping into romance books helped me feel like...things could be okay. And...when the world is so awful." Mae sighed. "I don't know. Sometimes it feels like books are the only things that keep me from being full of rage just...all the time."

A whole song went by until Dell said, "Yeah."

"So." Mae took a loud, deep breath in and out. "I guess that's pretty much it. I can't make the world any less shitty, but I can stock some good books written by people who are smarter than me, I can stock books where people are good and kind to each other, and maybe that's...doing something."

"It is," Dell agreed. Mae went quiet again, as if she'd said her piece. None of which had felt very trite to Dell at all. He almost opened his mouth and told her how he felt the same way when he was able to save a piece of land. When he was able to preserve an inch of this town. Like he was doing something.

"So," Mae said eventually, picking at the sleeve of her cardigan. "That's why."

And then another thought occurred to him altogether.

"I...have a friend," Dell said slowly. He swallowed. "He's writing a book. A fantasy book."

And then he paused, because what the fuck was he doing?

"Have you read it?" Mae asked after a moment.

And for half a second, Dell's heart broke, picturing an alternate universe where Luca trusted Dell enough to let him read his book. Where Dell had been different from the beginning, more open. Where they could've gotten to a place where Dell would be brave enough to tell Luca he wanted to.

But he could only shake his head and stare at the ceiling.

"No. But I was just thinking...maybe you'll sell it here, one day."

"Yeah." Dell could hear the smile in Mae's voice. "I'd like that."

And then she shifted up on an elbow, casting Dell a wry grin.

"Wait. One day? As in, you think this bookshop will still be around months and years from now? What happened to me abandoning this place the second it gets hard?"

Dell raised a brow in her direction, even if she was right. He was slipping up.

"Haven't changed my mind. Jury's still out. I was just engaging in some hopeful thinking, I suppose."

Mae took another sip from her mug of champagne before collapsing back onto the ground.

"Well," she said. "I suppose I'll take it."

Dell leaned forward to drink more of his OJ before settling back again. Damn, lying on this hard floor felt confusingly good for his back.

Mae's phone shuffled through two more songs. Dell was almost starting to feel zen, close to a nap, when Mae spoke again.

"Can I tell you the other part?"

"The other part?"

"Of why I wanted to open a bookstore."

Right. Dell blinked himself awake. "Sure."

Another slight pause. Sometimes it felt like Mae physically held herself back before every sentence she ever said to Dell. At least, any sentence that mattered, any sentence that wasn't about repairs to the shop, that wasn't just to give him shit.

But they eventually always toppled out anyway, because Mae simply wasn't very good, in the end, at holding herself back.

"The first person I ever loved was this woman Becks. We dated through college, and don't laugh, but we worked together. At...Blockbuster."

And dammit, but Dell did laugh.

"I'm old enough to remember, yes."

Mae laughed a little too when she said, "And even more embarrassing, we both secretly loved it."

"Working at Blockbuster?"

"Yeah. She knew way more about movies than I did, and she was *great* at talking about them with customers. She was super charming, could relate to almost anyone who walked through the door. And even though I was going to school for social work, I found the business side...weirdly soothing? I loved everything about inventory, checking the movies in and putting them back in their designated sections, and I *loved* rearranging the New Releases wall every week. Counting the till at the end of the night. I don't know; it was all satisfying."

"Okay," Dell said, a hint of a question mark in his voice.

"Anyway, so sometimes we dreamed about dropping out of school and starting our own store, where she could handle the customer service and I'd handle the back end. Except it was clear even then that the movie rental business was going downhill, so...we dreamed up a bookstore. Selling something I, at least, loved even more than movies."

"Ah."

"We would spend entire nights talking about our future

store, writing out plans. I even contemplated switching my major to business a few times, even though by the time we were really in the thick of our daydreams it probably would've been too late anyway; we were almost seniors. Looking back, I probably got so invested in the idea as a way of ignoring the impending real world, where I knew I'd have to get a job that didn't just involve restocking DVDs every day. And, well, because I was in love with Becks."

"Right."

"Except." A sigh. "Then I fucked it all up."

Dell waited, until Mae let the next set of words tumble free.

"I...cheated on her."

Huh. That wasn't where Dell had expected the story to go at all.

He sensed he had to say something here, that Mae needed a push for this one. Her voice had almost warbled on the last word; her shame practically vibrated in the air above them.

"And there went the bookstore dream, I imagine."

"Yeah." Another sigh. "There was this guy in one of my classes, beginning of senior year, and..." From the corner of his eye, Dell saw Mae cover her face with her hands. "We worked together on this big project and...he loved all the same music I loved. Invited me to some shows. And there were a lot of things about me and Becks that weren't perfect. The bookstore dream was probably the one thing that still really brought me joy when we were together, and in my head, at the time, the fact that me and this dude loved all the same bands made me feel like he...saw me, understood me in this way that felt so important and deep but—"

Mae flung her arms away from her face with a loud groan.

"Oh my god, this is so embarrassing. I can't believe I'm telling you this. Guess what; liking the same music as someone else isn't actually that deep! Dude was kind of a douche, actually! But even if I did want to have a fling with him, I should've broken up with Becks *first*. God. I was such an asshole. I've never really forgiven myself for it."

"I don't know." Dell shifted his shoulders against the rug in a shrug. "It sounds like a pretty typical thing to do in your early twenties, if you ask me." Part of him laughed inside his head, though, swiftly aborting his half-formed plans of sharing his thoughts about those concert posters in her office. "Your brain makes some deeply embarrassing decisions in your early twenties."

"I don't know." Dell sensed her frown as her words echoed his. "I think you can do dumb stuff without hurting other people."

"You *can*," Dell agreed. "But hurting other people does tend to be a pretty common consequence."

Mae sighed. "Yeah."

Something was different, Dell realized all at once, about this whole night. Like the moment they'd lain on the floor, their different perspectives made the atmosphere shift, too. Mae, full of regret for years gone by, seemed infinitely softer.

From the moment Dell had met her, she'd been full of bluster. Ever since she'd moved here, she made twenty decisions a day about the shop with aplomb. But right now, she was only...human. Familiar.

After a minute, he asked, "Have you told Becks? About Bay Books?"

"Oh, god no," Mae said without hesitation. "That was years ago."

Dell didn't hold back his grin this time. He knew it was difficult to accept the contradictions within yourself. He wondered if Mae knew how obvious they sounded, though, out loud.

"I've thought about it, though," she added after a minute, voice quiet. "Sometimes. I *did* decide to make this store for me and Jesús. But...it was Becks I thought about, when I first saw the For Sale sign."

Silence settled between them again. Another song went by, and another. Mae got up to refill her mug; she lay back down again. Dell contemplated asking more about Jesús. More about what else went through her head, exactly, when she saw his For Sale sign.

But he found he liked listening to music with her. Resting in the quiet but not quiet space of it.

So he kept his mouth shut.

Until, abruptly, he didn't.

"The longest relationship I ever had was with a woman named Lauren." The words were out of his mouth before he could fully think them through, half a surprise to himself.

It was just...Mae was still beating herself up about some dumbass mistake she'd made twenty years ago. He felt he owed her something in return, something to help even out the vulnerability.

"Yeah?"

"Yeah." Dell cleared his throat. "We were together a little over two years. Before I moved out here. I—"

"Oh!" Mae popped her head up. Dell couldn't look at her; he had to focus straight ahead at the ceiling if he was going to talk about Lauren. But he could sense Mae's hair in his peripheral vision, the excitement in her voice evident. "Is this when you moved to Greyfin Bay...from *Portland*?"

Dell only let out a weary sigh. He opened his mouth to reply, but a punch to his shoulder took him by surprise before he could.

"Jesus!" He laughed, rubbing his arm. "Ow, Mae."

"Oh, you are *fine*. I can't believe you're refusing to sell me this building because I moved here from the same fucking place you did!"

"It's—" He shook his head, suddenly immensely tired, the way he felt whenever he thought about Portland. "For the record, I am not *from* Portland. I'm *from* the UP. I only lived in Portland for a little while." Or fifteen years. Whatever. Mae didn't need to know every detail.

"Michigan?"

"Yeah. My mom's still there."

Mae released a small *hm*, head dropping back to the rug.

"And I'm not refusing to sell you the building, I'm just giving myself some insurance. I compromised with you. I'm not the bogeyman here."

Another, far more skeptical *hm*.

"Anyway." Dell rolled his eyes. "Lauren was a good person. But...I left her after that thing that happened to me, before I moved to Greyfin Bay."

"Oh."

And Dell could feel it, that his head was clearer than it had been yesterday, when they'd first talked about this. It felt more embarrassing, childish now to keep using a vague euphemism—*that thing that happened to me*—instead of just fucking saying it. Why was he still holding it back from Mae, from anyone? He should be better. Able to use his words. They were there, right now, clear in his head. Why couldn't he just say it?

*A stranger broke into my house in the middle of the night, while I was sleeping. They took the randomest things. They had a gun. I was shot two times but somehow survived. Nobody caught them or knows why it happened. I can't remember what they looked like.*

But he'd already said *that thing that happened to me* instead, so the moment had passed. Again.

Dell stretched his fingers over his belly, tried to keep himself from fidgeting.

"We were already starting to drift apart a bit. I think she'd been pissed for a while that we weren't living together. I couldn't tell you why we weren't, other than me being stubborn, but anyway. I just felt like a different person, after. Needed to get away. And Lauren loved her job in the city with the parks department; it was meaningful to her. I couldn't take her away from that. But..."

He winced. God, he really did rarely think about Lauren. He didn't have a lot of guilt about it, how easy it'd been to leave Portland behind. How much of that portion of his life simply became a blur. Bringing Lauren back up hurt, though. Lauren hadn't deserved the home invasion—the effects of it—any more than he had.

"I know it was shitty. Not letting her help me through it. It was probably rough for her, just a really shitty way to leave someone, but what's done is done. I think she and Georgia kept in touch, though, at least for a while. I felt a little better, knowing that."

"Georgia?"

"My mom."

"Oh."

"My mom was an artist and an art teacher her whole

life; she always dabbled in whatever medium she could get her hands on to try, but she loved pottery and sculpture the most, and Lauren did, too. Lauren had a wheel in her basement, made some beautiful stuff. The mugs in the ADU were made by her. And the mug I, uh, threw at you."

"Those are from her? Dang. Those are beautiful. And you broke one of them! I'm so sorry, Dell."

Dell huffed. "Considering I almost gave you a concussion with that mug, I don't think you have much to be sorry about, Mae."

"Well. I still am."

"Anyway." Dell lifted a shoulder. "Sometimes we hurt people."

"Yeah," Mae said, quiet. She sighed, just as soft. "Sometimes we do."

An old Caamp song shuffled onto Mae's playlist next. Dell smiled. This playlist had been so different from the one she played most often at the shop, the one full of Destiny's Child and reggaeton. He wondered which playlist was actually most Mae.

And then it came to him.

"That playlist you're playing all the time in here. Is that Jesús's?"

"Yeah," she answered without questioning the swift change in topic. "His death party playlist. So Georgia still lives in the UP?"

All right, then. Guess she was ready to open up about Becks, but not Jesús. Which was no skin off Dell's back. Why was he wanting to ask all these things anyway?

Because the jury *was* still out. It was possible Mae was crafting a fine store, a place he'd like to hang out in, something Main Street even possibly *needed*. Not just a bookshop, but a bookshop made by Mae. A store where people would know they were welcome, with certainty, in a way no place else on Main Street offered.

But none of that changed the financial reality of owning a small business in Greyfin Bay.

Mae would likely still be back in Portland in a year.

"Yeah," he said.

"And she's still refusing your request to move from the UP to Greyfin Bay?"

Dell sighed. "Yeah."

"I always wanted to visit," Mae said after a moment. "I went to school in Madison, but never made it up."

"A Badger, huh?"

"Yeah. And you're a Wolverine?"

"Never actually went to college, but my mom was."

"What brought you out west?"

Dell rubbed a hand over his face.

"Well, now it's time for my story of dumbass things you do in your early twenties, I suppose." He trailed off, though, having a hard time pushing the words out. Probably because, if he rarely thought about Lauren, he *really* barely thought about Naomi. It truly felt, sometimes, like he was a whole other person. He barely recognized that other kid.

"Moved out here for a girl," he finally forced himself to say, just as Mae was pouring herself more champagne. He watched her lips twitch into a smirk.

"You and Olive," she said.

"What?"

"Nothing. Didn't last, I take it?"

"Not even a month." He found himself smiling at the ceiling as Mae resumed her position on the floor. Or, rather, she returned to the floor, but he was pretty sure her position had shifted. That she was closer now. He could smell grapefruits.

"But you stayed. In the big evil *Portland*." And before Dell could even roll his eyes again, she retracted the tease. "Sorry. I should stop giving you shit. Something fucked up happened to you there. I get it. I mean, as much as I can. I just mean I'll stop." A pause. "Unless you don't sell me the building. Then I'll keep giving you shit forever."

Dell's mouth curved even deeper.

"I'd be disappointed, at this point," he admitted out loud, perhaps foolishly, "if you didn't." He added a minute later, his grin finally sobering, "But yeah, I stayed, because Oregon sucked me in. I'll always stand by the UP being one of the most beautiful places on earth, and it was honestly a great place to grow up. But the Northwest felt like home real fast. I know Georgia would love it, too."

He stared at what he now considered his corner of the chandelier.

"And look. I don't hate everyone who's from Portland. Okay? But...you're far enough south here that a lot of the locals? They don't just hate Portland. They hate the *north coast* because they think it's too much like Portland."

"I know," she said softly.

"I know you do. But..." But what? What was he trying to say here? Blending in with the locals had never been hard for Dell because, well, he mostly didn't give a shit, especially that first year, about anything other than his house and his dogs and getting to see the ocean. But he also didn't have pink hair and a full sleeve of tattoos. He had never been interested in opening a shop on Main Street. "You have to watch out for yourself," he finished.

"I know," she said again.

And that was officially enough Portland talk for Dell for, oh, the next year or so. He pushed himself off the ground with a grunt.

"I think you're missing out," he said as he refilled his own mug. "Orange juice is delicious."

Mae wrinkled her nose. It was fucking cute, and Dell cursed himself for being upright enough to see it. "Too acidic."

Dell paused with his mug halfway to his mouth. "Mae. You're drinking champagne. It's basically like acid with bubbles."

"Yeah," Mae said pointedly, lifting her mug. "*Bubbles.* Changes the whole game."

Dell shook his head as he dropped to the floor again. At the last second, he switched to lie on his stomach.

"Oh yeah," he groaned into the rug. "That's the ticket."

"Good call," Mae said, heaving herself around. "I should switch this business up, too. Oh damn. That *is* good."

Dell's grin returned, until he realized they'd made a grave mistake.

Because instead of staring at the ceiling, they were now...staring at each other. Cheeks pressed into the floor.

For what could've been a few seconds or a few minutes, those blue-gray eyes stared back at him. And yeah. At that moment, Mae Kellerman definitely felt soft.

Their matching grins slowly faded. Mae's pink lips parted, ever so gently. She had a small age spot, or perhaps a birthmark, above her left eyebrow. There was a pimple growing on her chin. Dell's fingertips tingled at his sides as if they could sense it, what her skin would feel like.

Everything seemed to go very still.

And then Mae's eyelashes fluttered closed. Dell released a silent breath.

He stared at her light-at-the-tips eyelashes and said, "Is your hair always pink?"

Things were starting to leave Dell's mouth way too

easily. He wondered if it was possible to get a contact high from someone else's champagne. Wait, no, that didn't make sense.

It was possible he wasn't thinking clearly after all.

"Like, is the pink hair your thing? Or do you switch it up?"

Mae's eyes remained closed, but she smiled.

"It's been my thing for a while, yeah. Few years. I'm totally fucking up my hair doing it, but I'm kind of attached now. *Ugh*, I'm gonna have to find a new stylist here. And a dentist. And...everything."

"That tends to happen when you move."

"I know, but I've been so focused on the shop, I haven't thought about a lot else."

*Because it'll make it easier, then, to leave,* part of Dell's brain thought. That part wasn't at all surprised that Mae hadn't put down firmer roots for herself yet. Wasn't surprised that Mae had never left Dell's ADU. Found a place other than 12 Main Street to make her home, for real.

But another part of Dell's brain, looser and louder just then, sort of wanted to punch that first part in the face.

Because maybe Dell didn't want Mae to leave the ADU anyway.

"I don't think Doug does coloring. He's Greyfin Bay's sole stylist, by the way. Although I think he prefers the term barber."

"Does Doug work on your beard?"

"Yeah."

"Hm. I should thank him sometime. It's a good beard."

Maybe Mae's a little drunk, he thought. It was too dangerous to think any further than that.

"God, what time is it?" he babbled. "It feels like it's midnight but it's probably like, nine."

Mae laughed. What a thing. Watching someone laugh with their eyes closed. "Story of my life," she said. And then, "I can't believe I told you about Becks."

"I think you think Becks is a bigger story than it is."

"You just never expect it, you know? You never expect to be a bad person."

Dell only sighed. It made dust from the rug tickle his nose. "Mae."

"I hate knowing that she hates me. That she's probably always hated me, ever since, and I deserve it."

"Not to bruise your ego," Dell said, "but this was what, twenty years ago? I bet you Becks has probably moved on, Mae. She's okay."

"No, I know she is." Mae frowned, nose crinkling the tiniest bit. "She's married. I know she's fine, but it doesn't change—" And then her whole face crinkled, and she turned it away, facing the front window instead of Dell. He stared at the mop of her pink hair, his mouth parting in disappointment.

"Hey." Awkwardly, ridiculously, he shuffled his stomach over the rug like a worm. Hesitating only a second, he reached a hand out to rest on her shoulder. Let it trail down her back, the warm fabric of her cardigan, before it came to rest on the rug next to her. "Mae. It's okay."

"Maybe the fact that I'm opening a store without her would only make her hate me more."

"I don't know," Dell said. "I don't think so. I think..." Dell thought back to his own past partners, the things he wished for them, whether things had ended well or not. "I think it might make her happy but in a...bittersweet way, maybe. A complicated way. But that's how life is most of the time. And anyway, you're not *really* opening the store for her. I've never met Becks, never knew Jesús, but I've seen how happy this all makes you. Just you."

A long pause. Dell weighed the pros and cons of touching her sweater again.

"Will you still be this nice to me when we're upright again?"

Dell chuckled. "Can't guarantee it."

"I can," Mae said quietly. "I think maybe you've always been nice."

Dell was quiet.

"It's kind of funny," she said after a few minutes, voice different, far away sounding. "Books inspired me to get out of the small town I grew up in. And here I am, over twenty years later. And books have brought me back to another one." And then, before he could respond: "Will you let me sell some of your stuff in the shop? Some of the things from your online store?"

Dell groaned. God, he didn't feel like thinking about his woodworking right now. He didn't feel like thinking about anything.

"Dunno." His own eyelids drooped irrevocably toward the floor. "I should probably check on the dogs. Mae," he murmured, "can you drive us home?"

"What?" Mae laughed, and fuck, Dell was glad to hear it. "Why can't you? Dell, you've only been chugging orange juice for the last two hours. More orange juice than a grown man should probably consume, really."

"A *person*"—and Dell knew he wasn't drunk, but he was tired enough to slur his words anyway—"can drink however much orange juice they want."

"Well, *I've* almost consumed an entire bottle of champagne, so no, I cannot drive us home."

"S'okay," Dell said to the rug. "I live here now." And then, "I've been sleeping like shit."

Mae was quiet. Until she said, "Do you have trouble sleeping after a trigger? Or just all the time?"

"Yeah," he mumbled. "And yeah."

Another minute passed by. Dell was almost fully unconscious.

And then. A set of fingers, in his hair.

"I'm sorry," Mae whispered, voice close.

Dell wasn't sure if Mae was apologizing for causing the trigger, or just for the pathetic state of his circadian rhythms in general. Either way, who gave a shit, because Mae's fingers felt incredible.

They stretched through the short strands of his hair, repetitive, soothing, before they dug in a little deeper, massaging his scalp.

Dell groaned out loud into the rug. It was possible he was drooling.

"Fuck," he mumbled. "Feels so good."

He was cocooned in the scent of grapefruit: sharp and clean.

"Yeah?" Mae's voice was so feather soft he almost wasn't sure he actually heard it, or if he was just making things up. Maybe he was making this all up. Maybe he'd lost his whole entire mind.

"Yeah. Never stop."

He couldn't quite say if she followed the instruction. Because somewhere in the next sixty seconds or so, Dell fell the fuck asleep.

# thirteen

AS IT TURNED OUT, falling asleep on a hard floor barely cushioned by a thin rug hadn't been the best of ideas for two forty-somethings. Both Mae and Dell hobbled to their vehicles early the next morning with matching scowls, returning to Dell's home on the hill as the sun was rising, the morning mist rising off the beach. Later, Mae would laugh at the memory of the two of them stumbling out of the bookstore in the dark, grumpy as hell and in pain, but at the time, all Mae wanted was a hot shower and the soft comfort of a bed.

Dell's truck had left the gravel drive again sometime later, but Mae stayed holed up in the ADU for the rest of the day. Once she was more awake, she opened her laptop, placed more orders for the shop. Finished an assignment for class, did her required check-in on the message board. When her brain was done with working, she sat at the tiny kitchen table, sipping tea out of one of Lauren's mugs. Staring out into Dell's landscaping, the trees beyond, the ocean she knew lay beyond that.

And she thought about Dell's dark eyes, boring into her own as they looked at each other across the floor. How his voice turned even deeper, even scrapier, when he was tired. The warmth of his scalp under her fingertips.

Shit.

Mae covered her face with her hands and breathed in, deep and slow. Her back still ached, but her headache had finally fully receded. She knew champagne always gave her wicked hangovers, especially cheap stuff that shouldn't even be called champagne, but...it had felt like a good idea, at the time.

Dell had talked about making dumbass decisions in your twenties, but the more her irrefutable crush on her landlord solidified, Mae couldn't help but think that maybe dumbass decisions never truly went away.

Part of her itched to get back to the shop and work away this distraction until she could fully compartmentalize. Tuck whatever fantasies she had about Dell McCleary neatly away.

The other part of her...it was immature, but she couldn't stop thinking about how this was exactly the kind of hot dish that Jesús Herrera-Baptiste would have absolutely shivered with delight to learn all about. She wished he was here. She wished he could make her laugh. About Dell. About how proud he was of her. About all of it. God, Jesús would love Olive.

It occurred to her, though, after a while, that there was someone else who would love to gossip about Dell, too. Mae just hadn't talked to him in what felt like a long time.

Mae grabbed her phone off the table, searching for Theo's name in her messages.

They had never conversed much in one-on-one texting, even before Mae left Portland; Theo was the kind of friend you connected with in person when you were together, so instantly and importantly that it somehow sustained all the stretches of silence in between. She contemplated sending him one of the pictures of Dell she'd surreptitiously taken over the past few weeks: at the lumberyard; working on the bookshelves. She was positive Theo would have things! to! say, honey!

*I miss you,* she ended up typing instead.

Something healed in her when it only took Theo, a notorious erratic texter, five minutes to reply. *Mae Bae* 💓

*miss you too*

*when can we come see your store?*

Mae bit her lip, heart warming even more at the fact that he wanted to come. That he wasn't still mad at her for leaving.

She tried to not think about it, the idea of her friends here, in Greyfin Bay. She wanted it too badly. It felt foolish, somehow, wanting it. Like she was failing Liv. Proving Dell right.

*Soon* 💞, she texted back.

While she had her screen up, she navigated to Instagram to check on Bay Books's account. She frowned at a spattering of new comments on her most recent post from yesterday. It was a simple post, Dell's installed bookshelf to the right, the trans flag in the front window visible to the left. *It is ON,* she'd typed in the caption.

For some reason, this had inspired her fellow humans and/or bots to say:

*Go back to Epstein Island*

*Greyfin Bay needs to remain safe for our children*

*k*ll yrself*

And for half a second, as happened every time, Mae almost deleted the whole post. She almost deleted the whole account. She almost planned what she'd say to Dell as she packed her bags and forgot this entire fucking venture.

But then the half second passed, and she deleted the comments. Blocked the users. Tossed her phone back on the table and stood, grabbing a pint of Ben & Jerry's from the freezer. She breathed out a sigh of relief when the first bite hit her tongue.

Her phone buzzed.

With trepidation, she picked it up. And burst out laughing in relief as she read the text from Vik. Jackson had apparently been trying to get into bread making, and it was *not* going well.

Mae responded while she wandered into her bedroom-slash-living room, and then she tossed the phone onto the foot of the bed, resolving to keep it there, face down in time out. She drifted instead toward the shelves that lined the back wall, ice cream carton still in hand. Something about this particular night tugged her there, a pull underneath her sternum that made her stop and really look.

She had brought a random collection of paperbacks from Portland, stuffing them into every nook and cranny of the car: behind her suitcases in the trunk, underneath the seats, tucked next to her *pilea peperomioides*. It had been frivolous, she knew, bringing along books when she barely had room in her little Kia for actual essentials. But what kind of reader moved to the coast to start a bookstore without at least a few of their own favorites?

Some she'd read before, some multiple times; a few were volumes from favorite authors she hadn't gotten around to yet. There was Ann Patchett and Akwaeke Emezi; Alexis Hall and Talia Hibbert. Kate Clayborn, Gabriel García

Márquez. Cat Sebastian, Olivia Dade. Kacen Callender and Jonny Garza Villa.

She contemplated the shelf.

She knew it was a bad idea.

But she picked up a Lisa Kleypas anyway.

Damn that Lisa. Damn her to hell.

Of course Mae had ruined whatever semblance of rest she'd gained the day before, staying up entirely too late inside the ridiculous, wonderful world of historical romance. But whatever, maybe she could fuck up her sleep as much as Dell's in solidarity.

No, that probably wasn't a good idea. Grand gestures for a person who was likely already seeing someone else weren't a good idea, either, but dammit, Kleypas was in her *brain.*

And fine, maybe a morning beverage wasn't the grandest of gestures. But when Mae finally blinked awake after the fifteenth snooze of her alarm and the idea needled into her mind, she felt good about it anyway.

With each mile she drove to Lincoln City with tired eyes, though, she was more and more grateful she *had* picked up the mass market paperback last night, in a way that had nothing at all to do with Dell McCleary, but everything to do with the way she still felt wrapped in its magic this morning. The absolute blessing of that feeling.

That feeling was why she was here.

She had to keep remembering why she was here.

An hour later, she approached Dell on the back porch of 12 Main Street, hands hidden behind her back. She smiled when she saw him, bent at the waist, the whir of his power sander echoing through the alley. It was a Saturday; he didn't need to be here. But somehow she knew he would be anyway.

"Hey." Dell straightened with a frown once he noticed her, pushing his safety glasses into his hair. "Where have you been? You normally—"

His voice cut off as Mae shoved the matcha latte into his hand.

"Good morning," she said. "Thought you deserved one of these."

Dell stared down at the green froth in his cup.

"I'll be out for a bit today," Mae added. "I'm heading down the coast to pick up some candles and soap made by a woman near Newport that I'm going to sell in the shop."

"Okay," Dell said, still staring at the cup in his hand.

Mae contemplated saying *thank you, for the other night*, or *thank you, for...everything*, or something else silly and romance novel-influenced, but the rational part of her brain knew nothing else truly needed to be said. So she turned to head inside, until Dell said, "Mae," and she paused.

"I should have this next bookshelf done soon," he said.

Mae smiled. "That's amazing, Dell."

"Thanks for the matcha."

"Thanks for the bookshelves."

And when he finally lifted his head and smiled back at her, she opened the door to the office and stepped inside before she could linger any longer in the moment than she should.

Mae clapped in delight when Antonio knocked on the back door on Monday morning.

"Antonio! My favorite person."

"Bet you tell Kat the same thing." Antonio quirked an eyebrow at her as he dumped his armful of packages onto the counter. Mae gasped.

"I would never."

She totally told Kat the same thing.

And Cooper.

"All right, you're all set for today," Antonio said as he scanned the last package. Because Bae Books was beginning to receive so much actual merchandise, *all set for today* was officially a thing delivery drivers said to Mae. "You have a good day."

"You too!" she called to his back as he retreated to his UPS truck, idling at the edge of the alley. She really did love Antonio. And Kat, her FedEx driver. And Cooper, her mail carrier for USPS. They were all, each and every one of them, her favorite people in Greyfin Bay. Well, after Liv.

She actually squealed when she opened the boxes Antonio had brought her today. She FaceTimed Vik immediately.

"Vik!" she screamed into the phone, flipping the screen to show the goods on the countertop. "Your stickers came! And your cards! And they are *so good*."

"Show me the whale with glasses better," Vik instructed, laughter in their voice.

"Oh, the whale with glasses is top tier, Vik." Shuffling through the stacks of Vik-designed merchandise on the counter, she brought the sticker of the whale reading a book, propped on a sea rock, closer to the phone. In the corner of Mae's screen, Vik's head dropped back as they laughed.

"This is the finest work I have ever done. Thank you for this, Mae, seriously."

"Thank *you.* Oh man. I need...vessels."

"Vessels?"

"Yeah, to put all this stuff in, on the counter." Mae's mind was whirring. "I need...so many vessels."

"You're really doing it, Mae."

"Yeah. I should go. I bet you Olive has some good vessels."

"Olive's the one with the antique shop? From Jersey?"

"Yeah. Oh wait, I didn't even ask how you are. I'm sorry. I'm the worst."

"You're not the worst, and I'm good. Just plodding through work that is *way* more boring than whales with reading glasses, so this has seriously made my day. And hey, give me a little tour before you go. Things look way different from the last time you video called."

And so Mae walked Vik on a slow sweep of the room, watching Vik's dark curls in the corner of her screen, their smile and their own glasses they used while they worked, more than she looked at anything else.

"I miss you," Mae said when she was done, standing in the middle of the rug.

"Miss you, Mae. All right, I should get going, too. Send me pics when you have all my shit in vessels."

"Will do."

Mae smiled down at her phone when they'd hung up.

And then she brought up her messages, and scrolled until she found Ben.

*I miss you,* she typed. Because she'd decided, after texting Theo, that this would be her new thing. Maybe their relationships would never be exactly the same, with Mae here, with all of them still there. But she could tell her friends, as much as possible, that she missed them.

Dell walked into the room before she could see if Ben replied.

"Hey." He held a small stack of mail in his hands. "Cooper came by, too."

"Sweet." She stuffed her phone in her pocket and walked behind the counter while Dell began to peruse the stickers and postcards. Most of the mail she received was junk, all kinds of banks and contractors reaching out to a new business about loans and services, but seeing mail addressed to Bay Books or to Mae Kellerman at 12 Main Street still brought a flutter of disbelief to her chest.

"Oh my god."

Dell looked up as she held a single envelope, the rest of the flyers dropping out of her hands.

"What is it?"

"I hope..." Instantly, outrageously nervous, Mae ripped open the envelope. Maybe it was nothing. Maybe it was a rejection because she'd filled out the application wrong, or because she was from Portland, and she knew her flags had caused friction at town council meetings. Maybe—

Mae read the words on the page and looked back at Dell in awe.

"It's my business license," she said faintly. "Greyfin Bay approved my license."

Dell only smiled back, that slight lift of his mouth. That small shine in his eyes.

"That's great, Mae."

"It's not just *great*; it's—" She looked back down at the paper in her hands. It was *it*. The last official approval she needed to become a small business owner. To make Bay

Books real. She could open the shop tomorrow, if she wanted to.

"Dell?"

"Yeah?"

"I'm going to ask you something, and you should definitely feel free to say no."

Dell put the postcards he'd been examining back on the counter, eyes turning cautious.

"Okay."

"Can I hug you? I just...*really* need to hug someone right now. But I can always go hug Freddy instead."

Dell's mouth twerked back up.

"Think he'd let you?"

"Hell no. But I'd find someone."

"Yeah, Mae. You can hug me."

And so Mae flew around the counter, and into Dell's soft stomach, and it was...exactly as she had known it would be, the first time she saw him. Maybe she couldn't have predicted the exact feel of his arms wrapping around her back, but her face in his shoulder, their bodies pressed together, the way it made everything inside her feel warm and quiet and safe—that was all exactly right. Like she'd already hugged him a hundred times before. He smelled like sawdust and sweat and Greyfin Bay.

She pulled back before, once again, she let herself linger too long.

"I need to buy a frame for that. And vessels." She twirled and ran into the office, grabbing her bag off the desk.

"Next bookshelf will be done in a couple hours!" Dell called to her running form as she sped through the shop.

"Amazing! You're amazing!" Mae called back. "Lock the door behind me, will you?"

And she was gone, again, down Main Street, to find her next missing pieces.

With Mae's help, Dell pushed the second bookshelf upright.

"You want this one flush against the other? Or you want a slight gap in between?"

Mae walked behind him, examining the space, biting the tip of her thumb. NSYNC'S "Bye Bye Bye" played from the death party playlist.

"Flush," she decided.

So Dell pushed the bookshelf flush with the first, returning a moment later with a stud finder and a drill, a pencil between his teeth. And while Mae knew she wasn't truly needed for this part, she kept standing there anyway, watching his shoulders and his hands once more make his measurements and drill his holes, double checking the alignment of both bookshelves twenty times, until he finally stepped back.

"Amazing," she said. "You're amazing."

"What's going in this one?"

"Non-fiction." She'd start general fiction in the next one. And then, on the other side of the room, her favorites: romance and children's.

"Oh shit," she said suddenly, rushing back behind the counter, clicking off the playlist just in time.

"Why do you always do that?"

Mae looked at Dell after she'd shuffled to something new. He motioned toward her phone.

"You always run over to turn off this playlist after NSYNC's done."

"It's just..." Mae looked away again, clicking the

computer awake. "The last song on Jesús's death party playlist. I can't listen to it."

She could sense Dell processing this as a second ticked by, then two. Until—

"That's right. The death party playlist. So...*this* is what you played at Jesús's funeral."

Mae shook her head decisively.

"No, at his death party. He had a funeral, too, at his church, but Alexei took care of that part. I don't fuck with church."

"So he had a funeral and a death party."

"Correct."

"And...you played 'Bye Bye Bye' at the death party. And...'The Trolley Song.'"

"Jesús played it, technically. He made the playlist, before he died. I just pressed the buttons."

Mae glanced over again when she felt Dell's stare. His arms were crossed over his belly, head tilted.

"Okay. So why can't you listen to the last song?"

"Because." Her eyes darted back to the keyboard. "It's just...Jesús being rude."

Another pause.

"Why don't you take it off the playlist?"

"Because." A lump formed in Mae's throat. How annoying, on such a triumphant day. And anyway, wasn't it obvious? "Jesús made it." Changing the playlist in any way would be like breaking her own heart.

Dell made a small, gentle sound that Mae took to mean he understood.

But as more seconds ticked by, and Dell didn't move from his position in the middle of the room, Mae was forced to look at him again.

He had turned, scratching the back of his head. Mae

sensed a mood shift in the air around him, like Dell was gearing up to say something. Her body tensed.

"Liv'll be coming around again tonight to watch the dogs," he finally said, staring straight ahead at the shelves. "Just FYI."

Ah. Mae swallowed. Hugged her arms to herself. Chose her words carefully.

"Another date with your...friend?"

Dell's hand fell to his side. "Yeah."

"Tell him I said hi," Mae said, after a moment. Dell turned to look at her again then. "I want to know all the local authors in the area."

A beat passed, his face unreadable before he said, "Yeah." He turned back to the wall. "I will."

And if Mae hadn't already suspected what this *friend* meant to Dell, it was cemented, right then, when color seeped into Dell's cheeks: a deep, delicious red.

Mae had never seen Dell blush before.

It made her chest ache.

"I can look after the dogs, you know," she said as she returned to the computer. "If you don't want to bother Liv. I think they know me well enough now."

"Yeah," Dell said, and she purposely avoided looking at him again, reading anything into the slight warble of his voice before he cleared his throat. "You're right. Next time."

"Next time," she echoed, and something tugged inside her throat, sharp and embarrassing.

It was good, she reasoned after Dell left without another word. Good to remember that Dell's heart was already occupied. She had plenty to do anyway. Each day, Mae had more and more merchandise to organize, to label with her new label maker, to track in her new inventory management system. Her own little Blockbuster, in the middle of the Oregon coast.

She logged into her email, and she opened her newest book order. She restarted Jesús's playlist. She was halfway to compartmentalizing already.

And when she unearthed one of Kennedy Remington's candles to burn while she worked, she would've told anyone who stopped by that she was testing out product. That it had nothing at all to do with eliminating the scent of sawdust, lingering in every corner of Bay Books.

# fourteen

"JESUS FUCK." Luca's breath escaped in heavy gusts. Dell dropped his head, rested his forehead between Luca's shoulder blades. "Dell, that was so good. What the fuck."

Dell brushed his lips over Luca's tacky skin.

"It's always good," he said, struggling to get his own breathing under control.

"I know, but—" Luca made an unintelligible noise. Dell smiled. Luca was loquacious tonight. Lighter. "Whatever that was, thank you for it. Fuck. I think I needed that."

Dell had broken routine. There had been no beer tonight, no small talk by the kitchen island. When Luca had opened his door, Dell had simply stepped in, taking Luca's face in his hands, Luca's lips in his teeth, pressing forward until Luca's back hit the kitchen counter.

Luca hadn't seemed to mind.

"Me too." Dell planted a last kiss in the small of Luca's back as he pushed himself to standing. "Be right back."

After he'd cleaned himself in the bathroom, after he'd returned with an extra towel for Luca, he arranged himself on the mattress again, an arm behind his head.

Luca, to Dell's pleasure, shifted himself over until his face was within nuzzling distance of Dell's breast. Dell wrapped his other arm around Luca's back, welcoming him closer.

After a few minutes of comfortable, pulse-calming silence, Dell said, "This is kind of a weird ask. But would you mind playing with my hair?"

Luca didn't move, but he smiled against Dell's skin, pale against his own tanned face.

"Play with your hair?"

Dell was too sex-drunk to even be self-conscious.

"Yeah. Like, scratch my head."

Luca laughed a little before he adjusted himself enough to reach up a hand, fingers sifting into Dell's sandy hair.

"You really don't have a lot to play with here, you know."

"I know, but just—" And then Luca's fingers curled, his short nails making work of Dell's scalp. Dell sighed in contentment, eyes drifting closed. "Yeah. That's good."

"Hard to believe we've fucked this many times," Luca said after a minute, "and I'm still learning your kinks."

"Not a kink," Dell murmured, but shit, it felt so good, maybe it was. "Just feels good." And then, "Thank you."

Luca was quiet another minute, fingers continuing to do their thing, before he murmured back, "You're welcome."

And maybe if Dell hadn't been so tired, maybe if he was a better person, maybe if he had taken even a second to get his brain functioning better, he would have stopped the night there. Fallen asleep to a scalp massage, Luca's body heat at his side.

Instead, for absolutely inexplicable reasons, he opened his mouth again.

"I think I'm developing feelings for Mae."

Luca's fingers stilled in Dell's hair. As they very well should have.

"And Mae is..."

Holy hell. What was Dell doing?

He swallowed, caught between an awkward laugh and a flush of embarrassment. In his mind, everyone within a sixty mile radius now knew who Mae was. But Luca did keep to himself. Like Dell. Or, like Dell used to.

"The person who's renting out the shop, on Main Street."

"Ah." Luca's fingers retreated from his head. Dell winced at the loss. "The Portlander?"

"Yeah." And after an excruciating moment of silence, "Sorry. I don't know why I told you that."

Luca flopped onto his back. Dell wanted him close again, didn't want to talk like this, both staring separately at the ceiling, like it was some big serious thing.

"They said to tell you hi." Jesus Christ, every sentence that came out of Dell's mouth was worse than the last. "They're looking forward to carrying your book one day, in their bookstore."

Silence. Until, strained, Luca asked, "You told Mae about my book?"

"I'm sorry," Dell said immediately, squeezing his eyes shut. "I'm sorry. I don't know what the fuck I'm doing."

And for one irrational second, he felt a hot, flashing bolt of anger at Mae. If Mae hadn't crashed into his world, if she hadn't been so persistent. Maybe he and Luca could have started to build something different. Maybe everything about this moment could be different.

But just as quickly, it faded, the anger switching on himself. It was on him that he'd negotiated with Mae

Kellerman in the first place. That he'd never kicked her out of his ADU.

Because the truth was, in some private part of himself, Dell had liked her from the start.

"It's okay," Luca said, but the way he barely said it, a half whisper, Dell didn't know if it was.

A long, painful stretch transpired until Luca said, "So," voice back to normal, hitting Dell like a punch to the gut. "Was this a goodbye fuck?"

"No."

"I mean, it was a fucking great one, if so. Good job on that."

Dell turned on his side, feeling frantic at the odd timbre of Luca's voice, needing to feel Luca's shoulder against his chest.

"Luca. No. Doesn't have anything to do with us. I just..." Dell rubbed his forehead. This could *not* be the last time he saw Luca. That hadn't been the plan at all. "Sorry. I know we don't share shit like this. Nothing's even happened between me and them. They'll probably be back in Portland in a few months anyway. Don't know why I said it."

Luca looked at him. His eyes seemed sad. *Fuck.*

"It's okay, Dell," he said after a minute, sounding more like himself. "We're not...beholden to each other. You know that. It's okay." And then, breaking eye contact to stare at the ceiling again, "They're opening a bookstore?"

"Yeah."

Luca made a small sound of approval in his throat. "Cool."

His hair was really starting to grow in now, a thick layer of fuzz. He was beautiful.

"I know I'm a pathetic bastard," Dell said a few minutes

later. The space between them had grown more comfortable again by degrees, but Dell knew he had fucked it up, that it wasn't the same. "But can you put your hands back in my hair again?"

And thank fuck, Luca actually laughed a little.

"Yeah, Dell." He turned toward him, pushing Dell's body back down. Dell could've cried in relief at the pressure of Luca's body over his again, at the return of his fingers to Dell's scalp. "I can do whatever you want."

Dell *really* didn't know what the hell he was doing, then, looking into Luca's hazel eyes. This perfect specimen whose bed he was somehow lucky enough to share every now and then. Who he wasn't beholden to, because Dell had made sure that was the case. Because Dell, when he first moved to Greyfin Bay, hadn't trusted himself to be close to anyone.

And now, after years of being goddamn careful, Dell might have accidentally gotten himself just...absurdly fucked up.

"Will you still make me coffee in the morning?"

"Yeah, Dell. I'll still make you coffee."

Luca ran his other hand along Dell's stomach, and like that, Dell was back again. Luca noticed, running his hand lower, giving Dell a slow stroke.

"I just have one request," he said, eyes focused somewhere on Dell's chest. A rueful look pulled on his lips before he lifted his gaze to Dell's eyes.

"Anything," Dell gusted out, already breathless from the combination of what both of Luca's hands were doing.

"When we're doing this," Luca said, eyes suddenly serious, "if you start picturing Mae? When I'm touching you? I'm out."

"Luca," Dell managed. Except Luca was increasing his speed down there, spitting into his hand, digging his nails harder into Dell's scalp, and Dell groaned, eyes closing as his back arched.

"Dell. I'm fucking serious."

"Know you are," Dell breathed. "Fuck." He couldn't believe this was still feeling so good, so electric, after how vigorously they'd both gone in the first round. After the conversation they'd just had. "Luca." He fluttered his eyes back open, made himself use every inch of focus to meet Luca's stare, even as Luca continued his punishing pace on Dell's dick. "If you think *anyone* could focus on anything other than *you* when you're touching them—" Dell sucked in one more breath. "You're out of your fucking mind."

Almost too fast for Dell to prepare for it, Luca kissed him.

And kissed him, and kissed him, until, blessedly, Dell's brain shut off, and Dell and Luca returned to the spaces they knew best.

It would have taken Mae longer to notice if it hadn't been for the breeze.

"Cold as tits in here," she mumbled to herself as she booted up the computer. She took a sip of her tea; she'd installed a kettle on the small table next to the fridge in the office. Speaking of tea—Mae needed more. Which, as a life-long hoarder of overflowing tea drawers, was hard to believe, but if she was going to maintain a reasonable stash at both 12 Main and Dell's ADU, she needed more of the good stuff. Meaning, the good stuff from her favorite tea shops in Portland, varieties not stocked at the IGA.

Although maybe there was someone, some small farmer somewhere, who made good stuff here, too. Maybe she could sell it in the shop. She rubbed her hands together, trying to get warmth into her fingertips, before noting *tea research* on her to-do list.

Secret good coastal tea or not, she knew she'd have to return to Portland sometime soon, regardless. She'd been putting it off, didn't want to seem too weak, too needy, returning to the city too soon. Wanting to prove to herself, to Dell, to Liv, to Greyfin Bay, that she was *here.* All in.

But the air was getting colder as the days grew deeper into October, the winds from the sea stormier, and she hadn't packed the bulk of her winter clothes. She needed to visit the storage unit to retrieve her good boots, her winter coat, all the hats and scarves Vik and Steve had knitted her over the years. There were other things she missed from the storage unit, too, that weren't as necessary but that she longed for, the more the ADU felt like home: framed photos, more books, kitchenware.

She could probably make it another month, though.

She took another sip, shivered. She'd turned on the heat as soon as she'd walked in the back door, like always; it didn't normally take this long to warm up.

And then her trans flag fluttered.

Mae looked toward the front window.

And saw the brick, sitting a few feet from the fluttering flag, surrounded by broken glass.

She brought her tea with her when she walked around the counter. Took another sip as she stood by the broken window. Stared down at the shards lying on her beautiful new rug.

"Well," she said to herself. "Shit."

She pulled her phone out of her hoodie's pocket and called Vik.

"Hey," she said when Vik picked up. "I think I've been hate crimed."

"Excuse me?"

An irrational laugh threatened to escape before she could get the words out.

"I think someone threw a brick? Through the front window of the shop?"

"*Shit.* Mae, oh my god. Are you all right? Did it just happen? Were you there?"

"No, no, they must have done it overnight. I just got here. I'm fine."

"Do you have security cameras?"

An actual laugh rumbled through Mae's throat. "No. No, in all my meticulous planning, somehow I never thought about security. But—" She laughed harder. "It's a small town, right? I thought shit was supposed to be safe here."

"Mae," Vik said. "Are you all right?"

Mae knew, in her rational brain, that she should be more upset. But it felt like such a cliché that it was almost hard to take it seriously. She stared at the rust-colored brick at her feet and her first thought was if she could make it into some kind of cute display piece for the shop, or to help fortify her raised beds out back.

"It's possible I'm not processing this correctly," she assessed.

"I have to say," Vik said on a sigh, "I particularly hate whenever people throw shit through windows. Feels a little too Kristallnachty for me. Even when the protestors I agree with do it."

"Oh." Mae immediately sobered. "Yeah."

"Here with the Jewish trauma to bring down the party any time. So should I come?"

Mae blinked, still staring at the brick. It, unfortunately, seemed less funny by the second.

"What?"

"I want to come. I'm sure you'll have it cleaned up by the time I'm able to get there, but I want to be there anyway. Feels like being there when one of us is hate crimed is sort of a friendship requirement."

"Oh." Mae finally tore her eyes away from the floor. "No, Vik, it's okay. I promise. You don't have to do that."

"I can tell Heben there's an emergency. Because there is."

"No, no." Mae scratched her head. "Isn't it high holy days time for you anyway? It's—"

A knock on the door. Mae jumped, heart suddenly thudding in her chest. Vik was talking, but Mae couldn't hear them. Cautiously, from somewhere outside herself, she took the five steps to the door.

On the other side stood Liv and Olive.

"Hey, hon," Olive said. "Where's your broom?"

They were inside before Mae could say anything.

"Mae? Mae, you there?"

Distantly, Mae knew she needed to respond. To anyone.

But she found herself unable to do anything but stare at her beautiful turquoise front door, marred by black spray paint. Two simple words, dripping and ugly:

*Go Home*

Dusty from the hardware store was boarding up Mae's front window when Dell arrived.

Olive and Liv had made quick work of cleaning the glass, which was good, as Mae's limbs, like her brain, were having trouble working correctly. Her feeling of uselessness as they shuffled around her, as Liv made calls, only increased the panic in her chest. She needed to do something. This was her store. *Her* store.

"Thank you," she said again, flushed and frustrated, as Liv handed her the piece of paper with the contact info for the glass guy, who wouldn't be able to come up from Newport until next week.

"Gotta stop thanking me, love," Liv said. "Like we've said about ninety times now, you need to go take a rest."

When the heavy clomp of feet sounded behind her, Mae closed her eyes. How could she take a rest when people kept showing up? She'd already talked to the police, which had made her skin crawl; Marty from the Small Business Association had shown up, too, full of frowns and platitudes like, "This isn't who we are," and "We'll make this right." Except this *was* who we were, not just Greyfin Bay but everywhere, and you couldn't quite make it right.

Even Freddy Hampton had stopped by. Kind of. He mostly just looked at the damage and rubbed his jaw, a tense look on his face, before muttering a quick, "Let me know if you need anything," before leaving.

Mae knew, in the last corners of her brain, that Olive and Liv were probably holding back even more people from showing up, but each new pair of eyes only made Mae more embarrassed. Olive had asked, once everything was cleaned up, if they should start a GoFundMe for the cost of the glass replacement; Mae had only shaken her head. She found, with each passing second, that she didn't want to post about this, on GoFundMe or Bay Books's socials or anywhere else. She didn't want anyone else's money but

Jesús and Steve's. She just wanted her window and her door back, and for no one else to know this had ever happened.

"Mae." Dell's voice was low and quiet. "What's going on?"

For the first time in hours, Mae's chest loosened. But only by a degree.

She turned to see his furrowed brow, his downturned lips, almost hidden underneath his beard.

She wanted another hug.

Simultaneously, unbidden, the image of the Dell she first met flashed behind her eyes: scowling at her on the front porch, rolling his eyes at her across an empty room. This room.

*Told you so,* that Dell whispered in her ear. Next to every sidelong glance she'd received from every stranger since she'd hung up her flags. *What did you expect?*

"Everything's okay," she pushed out. "Liv fixed everything for me."

"Not true, actually," Liv said from her side. "If I could fix everything in this town..." She trailed off, staring toward the front door. "Well. Life would be different."

"What happened?" Dell asked, more forcefully.

"Just a tiny case of a brick thrown through a window overnight." Mae shrugged, avoiding Dell's gaze. She felt jumpy, anxious. She acutely wanted to be alone.

"And a little spray paint," Liv added. She shot Mae a look. "We can take care of that too, you know."

"No." Mae rubbed her forehead. "I can do that. I would like to. By myself," she added, looking first at Liv, and then Dell.

Liv acquiesced first. "Got it. We'll get out of your hair, then." She squeezed Mae's shoulder, gave Dell a nod. Mae sensed more than saw her gather Olive and finally, a minute later, quietly leave the shop. *I need to get them a present,* Mae thought. She'd get them each something nice. Like flowers, or candy not purchased from bigots. Something the opposite of broken glass.

Dell remained unmoved.

Until the door clicked shut, and he took a step forward, arm outstretched.

"Mae—"

She stepped back, away from his embrace.

"I just have to get the paint from the office," she said, leaving a wide berth as she walked around him.

He was still standing there, still frowning, when Mae returned with the can of turquoise paint she'd purchased a month earlier, a fresh roller and tray. And after only a second of awkward silence between them, Mae's shoulders sank. She wanted to be alone. But maybe she didn't want Dell to go. Not really.

"Is it okay if I work on the shelves?"

She breathed out. "Yeah. Yeah, that'd be okay."

And only then did the memory flash through her mind. Her and Dell, asleep right here on the rug, a mere few days ago. Only then did she wonder what would have happened if the brick-thrower had acted that night. If it would have hit the back of her head. Dell's face.

She swallowed down a swell of nausea.

Dell gave her one last look, like he was mentally calculating the pros and cons of saying anything else. Of reaching for her again. But eventually, he only gave her a nod before heading to the back door. Mae took a deep breath and put on her headphones. Started Jesús's playlist.

And then she stood on the front walkway, in full view of Main Street, and poured out her cheerful paint once more.

Hours later, Mae rubbed her eyes as the computer screen started to go blurry.

Dell had left an hour ago to feed the dogs. He had installed two of the floating shelves before he left, just offset from each other in the brief wallspace between the counter and the window on the left side of the building. Mae's eyes kept drifting toward them, the shine of the varnish Dell had lacquered over the reclaimed wood they'd purchased together. A relief, a gift, to keep her eyes distracted from the cheap plywood that now constituted her beautiful picture window.

Mae gave herself a shake before focusing again on the order form in front of her.

She knew she should head home, too, or at least, back to the ADU—*go home*—but somehow she couldn't make herself leave the shop. As if her mere presence could stop anything else from happening. She didn't think anything else would, really; cowards were typically not super persistent. They had done their job. And it had been effective.

Still, Mae lingered.

Maybe something in her body knew. Maybe she knew she was waiting.

The knock on the door made her jump, but for the first time all day, she didn't feel scared.

"Everyone else wanted to come," Vik said, bag dropping off their shoulder onto the floor. They didn't look at the window, didn't glance at the rest of the shop. They only had eyes for Mae. "But I told them no. Since you said you didn't even want me to come, I thought it'd be too much. Is that okay?"

Mae let herself be wrapped in Vik's arms.

"Yes," she said. "Yes, this is okay. This is perfect."

"Well," Vik added, into Mae's hair, "I would've let Jackson come. But he has to watch his sourdough."

And Mae laughed, before she finally started to cry.

# *fifteen*

"IT'S BEEN a while since I've slept this close to someone," Mae said to the back of Vik's head three hours later, as they spooned under the Pendleton blanket in the ADU. "I apologize in advance if I end up humping you."

After Mae had gotten ahold of herself and shown Vik everything that existed of Bae Books thus far, she'd given them a tour of the town. Which took about ten minutes—and Liv hadn't even been at the IGA, making the whole venture a bit of a bust—so then they'd gone to the beach. Where Mae got weepy again, over Jesús, over the fact that she didn't visit the beach as much as she'd thought she would, over the fact that such a beautiful place that spoke to her so deeply could also be so cruel and complicated.

Finally, she'd brought Vik here. Vik had fallen in love immediately, video calling Jackson to show him the tiny space. Jackson, in turn, showed Mae his breadmaking station, and Mae's chest hurt, seeing his and Vik's home again, even if it was through the jerky, pixelated view of Greyfin Bay Wi-Fi.

Vik let out a half asleep snort.

"No one since Eden, huh?"

"Nope." Mae popped the *p* into Vik's curls. Her mind was barely functioning, but still, she tried to do some mental calculation. It must have been at least a year now, since it all blew up with Eden. Felt longer, though.

Some years felt short. The ones where you lost someone, though. Those felt like forever.

After a moment, she added, deep in the reflective haze a surprising, exhausting day thrusts upon a person, "You know, I think Jesús partly gave me all this money because he was so horrified by what she did. Like he worried I was so heartbroken by it. But..."

Vik shifted, blinking open their eyes to look at her.

That day in the hospital with Jesús had receded in Mae's mind, faded in the loud hum of her new life. But it was always there, every word he'd said, whenever Mae was strong enough to retrieve them. *I know that woman hurt you.*

*I want you to trust the world again.*

"The honest truth is...I've hardly thought about her. I know what she did was fucked up."

And maybe it was weird, that Mae had been able to get over it so easily. Finding out that Eden had actually been married the whole five months they'd dated. With a kid, no less. It had hurt like hell at the time, of course. One of the most appalling things that had ever happened to her. But when Mae thought of Eden now, she simply felt...nothing.

"The only people I actually keep thinking about, since I've been out here? Are Jesús and Becks. The first girl I fell in love with, like, ages ago." Mae huffed out a small laugh at herself. "Like all the shit that happened in my life in between Becks and Jesús's death..."

Mae trailed off, wondering what she was actually trying to say.

"Your body remembers," Vik filled in. "The shit that's important."

"Yeah." Mae nodded, looking into Vik's eyes in gratitude. "That...feels exactly what it's like." She turned onto her back, staring at the slanted ceiling.

*Your body remembers the shit that's important.*

And in the end, someone who betrayed so many people in their life for that many months simply wasn't that important.

Maybe Becks felt nothing when she thought about Mae now, too, even though Mae told herself it was different. That Eden had betrayed her family and Mae for months as a grown woman, while Mae only harbored one misguided night after a show when she was young.

But maybe it was still okay if Mae wasn't the important shit to Becks anymore.

She wished she could go back to the hospital that day. The acute need to assure him that he was wrong filled her bones, the injustice that he died worrying about the wrong things. *Eden hurt me but I'm okay*, she wanted to shout. *I wish you could see our store, Jesús.*

"You know what's funny, though," she added, the words seeming to come out of nowhere, "Dell acted like it wasn't even a big deal, what I did to Becks."

Vik had turned to stare at the ceiling too; their shoulders smooshed tightly together in the small bed. Mae felt Vik turn their head.

"You told Dell about Becks?"

"Yeah." Mae's cheeks heated. "In my defense, there was champagne involved."

Viks snorted again before returning their gaze to the ceiling. "Huh."

"Get out of here with your *huhs*." Mae attempted to shove Vik's shoulder with her own.

"I'm just saying!" Vik laughed. "I knew you had a crush on the guy; I didn't know you were in *love* with him."

"Excuse you!" Mae exclaimed. "I will kick you out of this bed this instant!"

"Dell's bed, you mean?"

Mae sighed. "Fuck." And then, "When did you know I had a crush on him?"

"Oh, pretty much the moment you came back to Portland after we spread Jesús's ashes. You got all flushed and flustered anytime you talked about him."

"I—" Mae crossed her arms over herself under the covers, accidentally elbowing Vik in the gut in the process. *I hated him, actually*, almost slipped out of her mouth, but Vik was too smart for that. "Okay, but I am not in love with him. I can't be."

"What do you mean, you can't be?"

"Because I think he's seeing someone else."

"Oh." The laughter died from Vik's voice right quick.

"Yeah. They might just be fuck buddies, but either way—"

"Complicated."

"Yeah." And then, "Do you think I attract *complicated* or something? Am I involving myself in toxic cycles without fully understanding myself?"

"Oh, Mae." Vik flopped dramatically back to their side, throwing an arm over Mae's stomach. "You know it's sexy when you talk psychology to me."

"I'm serious. Maybe I'm more fucked up than I think I am."

"Mae, I think you might be the most well adjusted of all of us."

Mae released an affronted guffaw. "That cannot possibly be true."

"Have you seen that gorgeous bookstore you've created in like, a month?"

"The bookstore's not done. And functional doesn't mean well adjusted."

"I really think you're both."

"Why do I feel weirdly offended right now?"

Vik smiled into Mae's shoulder. "And I know you're in love with Dell," they said, "because you're drinking champagne with him and telling him about Becks. Am I wrong that the only other people you've told about your one youthful foray into cheating are me and Jesús?"

Mae opened and closed her mouth as she contemplated the question.

"No," she finally admitted. "Not wrong."

"Anyway," Vik added, "I'd fall in love with the person who built this ADU, too."

"*God*, Vik." Mae groaned. "He is so fucking sexy I can barely stand it."

"And we're sure he's attached to this fuck buddy?"

Mae bit her lip, thinking about that blush on Dell's cheeks yesterday. God. That had only been *yesterday*.

"Yeah," she whispered. "I think so."

"Well," Vik said on a wistful sigh, "either way, I can't wait to meet this Dell McCleary."

"Yeah." Mae smiled sadly at the ceiling. "You should give him as much shit as humanly possible." And then, after a minute, the words tumbled out of her, spoken in barely a whisper but feeling like they were screaming out of her chest: "Vik, do you think I'll ever actually belong here?"

Vik raised their head.

"I need your brutal honesty here."

Vik took their time before answering.

"I think you've moved around a fair amount, Mae, like most of us have. So I think you know that it takes a while to belong anywhere."

"Yeah." There were a few native Oregonians among them: Jackson, Ozzy. Steve had been, too. But most of them, like Mae, came from other places. Sometimes, many other places.

"This place might just feel a little scarier than the others. For lots of reasons. But if you *want* to belong here, Mae? You will." A pause. "You can belong anywhere."

Another pause, just long enough for a lump to form in Mae's throat.

But still.

Still.

Even with Vik's kind words.

Mae was scared.

"Someone threw a brick through my window," she whispered. "What if I never get over that?"

Vik's hand came to Mae's face. Caressed her cheek.

"The human brain is incredible," they whispered back. "It has gotten over so many worse things than one brick."

Mae knew the words were true. She still felt pretty scared, just then, but she tried to tell herself to remember. That she still had books. That Vik's words were true.

And then a totally different question formed out of the ether, one she was shocked, upon its arrival, she hadn't already contemplated.

She supposed she had been too busy being selfish.

"Vik?"

"Hm?"

"Is anyone mad at me? About the money?"

Vik shrugged; their shoulder dragged against Mae's.

"I doubt anyone's *mad* at you. We all knew how close you and Jesús were; it wasn't like it was a surprise. Jackson and I are in a good spot these days, so jealousy didn't occur to me. Honestly, if anyone is salty about it, I feel like there's probably grief mixed up in those feelings, which...isn't on you."

"Yeah."

"And even the salty among us probably knows, deep down, that you were the best person to receive Jesús and Steve's money anyway. Like, I hate that it took you away from Portland, but it also didn't surprise any of us that it took you literally less than twenty-four hours after spreading the man's ashes to create a whole new life plan with his inheritance."

Mae's mouth curved.

"You know what I would've done?" Vik continued. "Put it into savings and guilt-stressed about it for years."

"I mean, that sounds like the much smarter option, by far."

"Nah." Vik shook their curls back and forth. "Jesús would've hated that. He would've loved this, though."

"I hope so," Mae whispered.

"Nah. You know so."

Mae kept staring at the ceiling. The atoms inside her, around them, settled, deep and peaceful.

"Thanks for coming, Vik. Even when I told you not to."

Vik kissed her cheek.

"Any time."

When Dell entered the bookstore the following day, the first thing he heard was giggles.

Which was a bit confounding, as the last time he'd seen Mae, she had seemed barely functional. He'd stayed away this morning for as long as he could stand it, giving her space.

He frowned when he walked further into the shop and deduced that the giggles were coming from the bathroom. And that they were coming from more than just Mae.

When he turned into the alcove that was to be Mae's planned reading area, where the restroom was tucked into the corner, he saw first the head of dark curls next to Mae's pink bun. And then he noticed the walls.

"Mae?"

The dark-haired one jumped, turning with a smile.

"Dell McCleary," they said, in such a way that Dell temporarily wondered if he should twirl on his heel and get out of dodge now.

"One and the same," he eventually mustered.

"Dell!" Mae emerged behind her friend, eyes bright with laughter. Somehow, in the last twelve hours, Mae had apparently gone through a 180. Dell was glad to see it, and simultaneously, pettily disappointed that he hadn't had a damn thing to do with it.

"Dell, this is Vik, Bay Books's graphic designer and my friend from Portland. They use they/them pronouns. Vik, this is Dell."

Vik had a sturdy handshake. "It's a pleasure," they smiled.

"Likewise." Dell's eyes slid to Mae. "And Vik is helping you decorate the bathroom?"

"Oh, yes. It's been one of the last big jobs on my list for forever. I think I was waiting for Vik to come help me." Mae stepped back inside the small room, gesturing for Dell to follow. He'd almost laughed at *for forever*, almost reminded her that she'd been in Greyfin Bay for barely over thirty days. Most folks took months to accomplish what she had somehow done in one. There was something so cute about her berating herself for not getting to bathroom decoration yet, when he still had at least seven bookshelves to complete, that he struggled to keep the grin from his mouth.

When he fully blinked inside the surprisingly bright room, though, the grin came to an abrupt halt.

"What do you think?"

Dell attempted to gather his thoughts.

"More wallpaper, huh?"

"Yeah, and let me tell you, having someone help you wallpaper makes the job go by *way* faster. And I've been *dying* to put these prints up."

Mae held an illustration of Bea Arthur against a turquoise background, encased in a gaudy gold frame, up to her chest.

Dell glanced, again, between the huge palm fronds of the wallpaper, the pastel-painted Golden Girls in their Rococo frames, and the much more sophisticated palette Mae had cultivated in the store.

"This design style is...different." He had never felt so fully South Florida in the middle of the Oregon Coast.

"It's for Jesús!" Mae shouted, eyes glittering even brighter.

Vik circled a hand in the air, speaking in capital letters and an indiscernible accent: "Une Toilette pour le Gay Men of a Certain Age."

Dell stared at both of them.

"You're dedicating...the bathroom? To your best friend?"

"Oh, I think he'd be honored," Vik said easily, and Mae nodded forcefully in reply.

"It's an important room."

And...Dell found he could not disagree with Mae there, at least.

"What do you think?" Vik held up another framed painting. "Is Dell more a Blanche or a Rose?"

"Sophia," Mae answered immediately, and Dell frowned. He was obviously, clearly, a Dorothy.

"I'll leave you to it," he said, finally turning to leave as he should have done ten minutes ago.

"Dell, wait! I have an important question for you."

Mae scampered into the shop after him. Dell absolutely did not turn in time to note how Mae's scampering made her chest bounce.

"I'm actually going to head back to Portland with Vik tomorrow, to get some more of my things from storage. I left a lot of winter coats and things and there's some furniture I want and—well, I know it's a big ask, but I was wondering if I could borrow your truck. I won't be able to bring back as much in my little Kia. And I *have* had experience driving trucks before, just as an FYI, so I'd take good care of it."

Dell stared at her. His brain had stopped fully comprehending things the moment she'd said *head back to Portland*, but slowly, delayed, it filled in the rest.

"Your little Kia won't make it over the pass in winter," he heard himself say.

Mae frowned.

"It does just fine. But also, it's not winter yet. And also, I'm asking to use your truck."

Dell looked away, scratching at his beard. "Just something I've been thinking about."

And now Mae stared at him.

"Anyway," she said after a long beat, "so can I use it?"

Eventually, Dell returned his gaze to her face. She looked so happy, like Vik's visit had restored her, and it made some jealous, irrational part of him frightened, in a real way this time. Not in the bullshit way he'd reasoned it away to Luca.

Mae needed friends like Vik.

She wasn't admitting it to herself. But she probably needed Portland, too.

"I'll take you," he said.

Mae blinked. Something in her face softened, her shoulders sinking.

"You'll...go to Portland with me?"

"Yeah." Dell scratched his beard again. "You can use my truck, but only if I'm driving it."

Mae looked at him, eyes inscrutable.

"You don't have to do that, Dell." Her voice had turned too gentle, in a way that itched underneath his skin. "I know you don't like going to Portland. It's okay; I can just take my car. I certainly crammed an impressive amount of stuff in there the first time. I understand if you don't trust me with the truck."

Dell did trust her with the truck. Mae was an incredibly competent person.

But...dammit, she hadn't let him help her yesterday. It was still hard to swallow, that while he'd been sipping coffee with Luca twenty miles north, Liv and Olive had been cleaning up the mess some asshole had made for Mae. On any other day, Dell would've already been here. Maybe he would have been able to fix it before Mae had even seen it. He could not believe he didn't already have security cameras installed on the building.

He could at least help her with this.

"It's fine," he said. "I can handle Portland for a day. I'd like to help. Unless..." He swallowed, unease finally sliding through his bluster, shame hiding behind that unease. "Unless you were planning a longer trip."

Mae broke her stare, stealing a glance at the front window.

"Honestly, part of me was hoping I could hide away until the glass is replaced, so I don't have to keep staring at that plywood, but...realistically, I was planning on staying just a couple days, to get my stuff and see my friends. Thought I'd head back here Saturday morning. If...that would be okay with you?"

Her eyes flitted back to Dell's. And even if the idea of spending two days in Portland made his stomach tight, he saw it then, in the gleam of her eyes, the twitch in the corner of her mouth. She looked...hopeful. Like she *wanted* him to come.

And goddammit. Hell and tarnation. Dell was lost with that.

"Yeah," he said. "That'd be okay with me."

# sixteen

MAE HAD BEEN PLANNING on driving back to Portland with Vik, but they turned the tables on her the next morning. Like a tricky bitch.

"You two should drive together," Vik said, just as Dell returned to the gravel drive with some tarps in hand for the truck bed, the dogs in tow. Vik crouched down to throw their arms around Nash's neck, smiling as he licked their chin. Mae wasn't surprised that Vik had fallen in love with the dogs, especially Nash, when they finally returned to Dell's house late yesterday afternoon. Dell had been on his deck with his guitar; the whole pack had bounded over the moment Mae and Vik stepped out of the car. The light had been just perfect, the sun low in the sky, the air cool but with enough warmth lingering inside of it to make you want to slow down, look up, hold on. A perfect October day on the mid-Oregon Coast. And as Vik had tussled with the dogs in the grass while Dell looked on, guitar resting on his casually bent knee, Mae had wanted to hold on forever.

"I'm going to stop on the way back to get a hike in," Vik said now, squinting up at Mae in the morning sunshine as

Young pranced around them. "And I know how you feel about hiking."

Mae pouted. "Yeah. It's hard." She thought she heard Dell snort behind her. "Makes sense, though," she said, still pouting. "It's a beautiful day."

"Yeah, and even if it wasn't, Ben and Alexei are apparently planning to hike part of the Continental Divide next summer and they have been *super* irritating about it." Vik stood with a huff. "Constantly going on hikes to 'prepare' and it's like, we get it! You're fit and outdoorsy and have adventures all the time!" They crossed their arms and scowled into the distance. "I want to be fit and outdoorsy and have adventures all the time," they said in a smaller voice, and Mae patted their shoulder.

"I know, babe. I know."

"Anyway." Vik brightened, leaning down to give Nash's head one last pat. Vik and Jackson had adopted a sweet old pittie a few years back, but she'd passed away last year. While they hadn't been able to bring themselves to get another yet, Mae could see in Vik's eyes that Nash might have nudged that healing along. "I'm gonna miss these fuckers."

"They'll be here," Dell said. "Anytime you want to visit."

Mae flashed Dell a grateful smile.

"CSNY." Vik shook their head with a small laugh. "I reserve the right to change my mind at any time, but I think I might like you, Dell. Still." They lifted their chin in his direction. "You take care of this one while you're driving or we'll all kill you."

Dell nodded. "Will do."

"Okay then." Vik's face broke into a smile again. They'd been especially smiley, this trip. It healed something in Mae she hadn't known she'd needed. "See you two back in PDX."

And with a wave, they jumped into their car and roared away.

"These all your bags?" Dell asked, already tossing Mae's canvas tote and overnight bag into the cab of his truck. As if the matter had somehow been decided.

Mae turned from watching the dust Vik's tires had spurred down the lane. She leaned down to pet Young, who was jumping for attention, soft collie paws on Mae's knees.

She could drive herself in the Kia. Pack more for the drive back that way.

But...she also couldn't stomach the waste of unnecessary carbon dioxide.

"Yeah," she said. "I'll go lock up the ADU."

When she returned a minute later, Dell had corralled the dogs back into the house, where they would wait for Liv's arrival later in the day.

And without anything else to stall them, Mae somehow found herself on another road trip with Dell McCleary.

And even though it should have been easier this time—she'd been in this truck with him before, knew its dimensions, its smell, the feel of the seats, the proximity of Dell's thighs to her own—she clenched her hands in her lap and stared out the window, any conversation starters that might have previously existed in her brain dead on arrival. Nerves jingled in her joints along with the potholes on the road as Dell navigated down to 101 and turned north.

They were quiet all the way until Lincoln City, where wordlessly, Dell turned into Starbucks. And for the first time in a half hour, Mae smiled.

"So," Dell said as he turned back onto the highway, drinks in cup holders, "You should probably tell me about these friends of yours I'm about to meet. I'm assuming there's more than Vik."

Thank Christ this was apparently the right thing to say. After feeling the tension vibrating off her all morning, Dell knew he'd already started wearing her down with matcha. But only now did her shoulders finally fully relax.

"Well, Vik is married to Jackson, and since we'll be staying with them, I guess I should start there. They're both graphic designers, so, you know. Obviously they're the hottest power couple of the crew."

"Sure."

"And then there's Theo and Ozzy"—Mae's voice started to lift in excitement, her knees turning toward Dell as she shifted in her seat—"who were the, like, ultimate slow burn friends to lovers. We always knew they were in love with each other but they were always dating the wrong people, which was excruciating to watch for *years* until they finally got a clue and got together. And as soon as they did they were like, boom, old married couple making soups and casseroles together. They adopted two cats after living together for a month."

Dell could see Mae's smile from the corner of his eye, bright and wide until it faded, her head tilting as she looked out the windshield.

"Theo and I butt heads sometimes, but I think it's because we're a lot alike, if in different ways. There used to be Dorsa and Camille, too, but they...kind of disappeared, last year, after they had a kid. Which it's possible I'm still slightly bitter about, but! You'll definitely meet Ben and Alexei."

Mae's voice perked back up.

"And I think you might like them the most. They're the newest members of the group; we've only known them for a year or so. Which is wild to think about, because as soon as you meet them, they're the kind of people where it's like...*I'm pretty sure I've loved you forever,* you know?"

Dell did not know.

He made a noncommittal hum. Mae seemed to accept it.

"Jesús actually met Alexei at his church. Maybe I've mentioned that before? Anyway, Jesús and his husband, Steve, normally kept their church friends separate from our crowd, but Alexei sort of naturally bled over, and his boyfriend Ben came along with him."

Mae paused, but in that pregnant way, like she had more to say burning inside her. Dell held his breath, eyes steady on the road. Maybe this was the day Mae finally talked more about Jesús. The best friend who had given her all the money that led her to 12 Main Street. The one who made his own death party playlist.

The bizarreness of the playlist, honestly, already explained to Dell why Mae and Jesús had been friends, but still. He wanted to hear her talk about him.

"Steve actually died, too, a few months before Jesús."

"I'm sorry to hear that."

"Yeah. It was a heart attack, out of nowhere." Another pause before she allowed herself to continue. "Steve was rich. Worked in something-whatever-finance. He always showed up to our trivia nights and movie nights and board game nights or one-of-us-needs-to-process-something nights, at least on the days he was able to leave the office in time, in these bespoke suits that made Jesús purr and pet him like a cat."

Dell kept his eyes on the road, but he heard the smile in her voice.

"Jesús was the one who actually made him *use* his money. Like until he met Jesús, Steve had been good at accumulating wealth, but Jesús made him actually enjoy it. Jesús worked hard, too; he was the whole heart of the community center where we worked, but...he made sure their lives were broken up occasionally, you know? By Disney cruises and trips around the world. At least, trips around the world to the places that are safe for gay men."

Dell's mind flashed to Luca. He continued to keep his eyes on the damn road.

"Anyway, I'm talking a whole lot."

"It's okay," Dell said. "I want to know." But Mae closed herself into another silence. Until Dell encouraged, "So Jesús passed away only a few months after him? Was that a surprise, too?"

Mae sighed.

"Yeah, definitely a surprise, but slower. He suddenly had pneumonia, and then he was in the hospital, and then..." She shook her head, trailed off.

"I can never decide if it's romantic or just sad," Dell said eventually. "When a couple goes like that."

"Jesús definitely thought it was romantic. Sometimes, in those last days, it almost felt like he—"

Mae's voice cut off, suddenly choked with emotion. She took a second to gather herself, and Dell wondered if he had pushed too hard. His fingers twitched on the wheel, yearning to touch her.

Her voice was smaller when she continued.

"It felt like he wanted to go. Like he'd willed his body to get sick on purpose. And it pissed me off. Even though I know it's not logical, that he didn't actually have control over his organ failure, but anyway. I might, *might* be inclined to agree with the romance part if they weren't both way too young."

"How old were they?"

"Mid-sixties."

Dell winced so hard he almost swerved off the road.

"Yeah. Sixties feels ancient when you're young, but from the view of your forties, it feels like fucking tomorrow."

Dell let out a gust of air. "Yeah."

"But Jesús was so into his faith that he was so...at peace with it. Alexei, too, even though Alexei was probably as close to Jesús and Steve as anyone. He has this whole fucked up family that disowned him for being gay, so Jesús and Steve became like...parental figures to him. I know they always spent every Sunday together, after church. But even though them both dying within four fucking months of each other was like losing his parents *again,* Ben said that Alexei felt at peace because...he got to say goodbye, on his own terms, and I am telling you a lot of personal shit about Alexei that's probably violating some boundaries but he won't tell you anything about himself on his own because he's a super quiet dreamboat and I am now realizing that I am *super* jealous of his processing abilities."

Mae took a deep breath before crossing her arms over her chest. She turned her head, staring out the window, and Dell felt a perhaps inappropriate level of affectionate amusement. Being that they were discussing the death of two men. But yet—

"Makes a bitch want to believe in God," Mae said, and Dell let out a short guffaw of laughter before attempting to smother it with his palm.

"Liv goes to church, you know," he said after a moment.

Mae looked at him in surprise. "Every Sunday. Sings in the choir."

Mae's jaw gaped open at that.

"No fucking way."

Dell grinned. "Yup." He shrugged. "According to her, she's not truly that religious, but it's the church her family's always gone to, and she likes the community."

"Huh." Mae faced forward again. After a moment, she said, "Damn, Liv is *good* at being a small town queer."

Dell's grin dropped, his brow furrowing.

"You make it sound like it's a vocation or something."

"I don't know." Mae returned to staring out the passenger side window. "It feels like it is, sometimes. To me."

Dell didn't agree in the slightest—a person was just a person, no matter who they were or where they chose to live—but he wasn't in the mood to argue, to break whatever fragile thing had draped across their laps and made Mae open up. He knew Mae might not believe him about this philosophy, anyway, what with his view of outsiders. Or what she perceived that view to be, anyway. But it wasn't really about where a person was from. It was about trust. Dell had simply learned to not have much of it.

"Jesús had this line," Mae said some minutes later, "that he'd use with new clients at the center. He called himself *a bit more fabulous than the original, but don't tell Him I said that.*"

Dell smiled. "He sounds like a fun guy."

Mae was quiet for too long before she simply said, "Yeah."

It felt like a bookend, that *yeah,* confirmed by the silence that stretched behind it, and Dell decided to let it lie. His own mind wandered in the quiet, as the road approached

McMinnville, as the traffic piled up. He fucking hated this part of the drive, an endless stretch through suburbs, the peace of the Coastal Range gone too fast. He focused on letting his mind wander, to anywhere that wasn't here. Anywhere that avoided the reality of Dell soon being in Portland, of his own volition.

He traveled to Michigan instead.

Dell had already forgotten half the names Mae had just filled the last hour talking about, but it made him wonder. What names Dell would list, if Mae turned the question around. Asked him about his own friends.

Mae already knew Liv.

She didn't know about Luca, not really, even though he knew he should tell her more about him soon, if hopefully in a better manner than he'd told Luca about her. But was Luca truly a friend, anyway?

His chest hurt with the answer.

He'd had friends, back in his Portland days, but looking back, any of the decent ones were really Lauren's friends. He wondered if they'd even mourned his absence much, after he left in the abrupt way he did, but he stopped that line of wondering real quick. There wasn't a point, especially this long after the fact, to wonder shit like that. The co-workers he'd gotten to know, the wide community of real estate agents in the city had been friendly but largely superficial. There was a small portion of folks he'd have a beer with again.

But when it came to *friendship*, the kind of bond Mae clearly felt with all these people he was about to meet—Dell wasn't sure if he'd had any of those since the UP.

It had felt logical to him for most of his adult life. That there simply wasn't anything else exactly like childhood to connect you to another human being. That there was a rawness, a realness that you lost once you became an adult. And Dell was a person who'd felt like an adult since he was about fourteen.

Still, for the first time in a long time, he let himself think about Ryan, about Chris and Waylon. The rest of the guys from the baseball team. Wondered what they were up to, these days. If Chris and Waylon were still in the UP. If Ryan was still in Chicago.

"Hey," Mae said, and Dell blinked back to the present. They were already cruising through Tigard, on the outskirts of the city. His skin prickled. "Did Bay Books ever make the cut? For who you follow on Instagram?"

For a half second, Dell didn't respond, still mentally navigating back to here, to the fact that he was about to be in Portland. A fact he'd somehow been real good at ignoring, even as the miles passed by.

And after that half second, once Mae's question actually sank in, he still didn't respond, feeling caught out. He'd waited a day or two, so as not to be obvious. But he figured she already knew. That he'd followed her that very first week, when she'd told him the username.

"Yeah," he said. "You did."

She turned her head toward her window, but he still caught her smile.

# seventeen

"HEY NOW." Jackson took one of Dell's hands in his, lifting it toward his face, turning Dell's palm to better examine his nails. "These are real nice."

"Jackson." Vik hit their husband on the shoulder. "My man. This one is not for us."

Jackson frowned, still inspecting Dell's fingers. A fierce blush was sweeping rapidly up Dell's neck, and Mae bit her lip, unable to keep her eyes from it.

"I can still look." Jackson's eyes flicked to Dell's. "As long as it's okay with him."

"Um," Dell said.

"Let's start the tour!" Vik clapped their hands, and Jackson finally let Dell's hand drop. "This, as you can see, is the kitchen. And moving through here—"

"That's a beautiful dog." Dell stopped five seconds into the tour to point to a picture on the wall of Daisy, Jackson and Vik's old pitbull. And, well, if Dell *didn't* want Jackson's adoration, complimenting Daisy wasn't the way to go about it.

Jackson stopped alongside him in the hall. "She was the best dog."

"I'm gonna show Mae where they'll be sleeping," Vik called, dragging Mae away. "Catch up with y'all in a sec."

"Vik," Mae said as she was hauled into Vik's office, where the loveseat folded out to a bed. "You know I know where I'm sleeping. I've slept here like, a bunch of times, even if it's always an awful decision for my back."

"I know." Vik let go of Mae's arm with a shrug. "But I wanted to give those two a moment. And ask you how the drive was."

"It was..." Mae stared at Vik's desk. "Good."

"That's seriously all you're going to give me."

"Listen, it was! I...talked about Jesús, a little." Mae shifted on her feet. "I got sad."

Vik looked down, shifting on their feet right alongside her. "Yeah?"

"Yeah. But I felt...okay. Being sad with him."

Vik glanced up at her.

"You really have to find out more about this fuck buddy."

Mae sighed. "I know. Anyway, your hike was good?"

"Yeah. It was great."

Mae and Dell had already been to Mae's storage unit, filling up half of Dell's truckbed before she got overwhelmed. She had forgotten, somehow, about half of the things she owned. How much she had missed those things.

And how she had no idea, aside from the things she wanted to use for the shop, where she was going to put them.

She should have thought through this trip so much more. About how it would make her face the fact that she couldn't live in Dell's mother's ADU forever. About how being in Portland again would make her feel, a Portland where she no longer had her own home: a confusing, overwhelming combination of comforted and hollow.

It had simply seemed like a good idea, back in the warmth of Vik's surprise visit to Greyfin Bay. A way to not have to say goodbye to Vik. To not have to deal with the plywood in Bae Books's window.

Dell had taken it in stride when Mae had to stop only a third of the way through the storage unit without being able to fully explain why. "We'll have plenty of time to come back tomorrow, right?" he'd said with a smile that made her want to kiss him, and they'd gotten a late lunch at one of Mae's old favorite sandwich shops, where Mae consumed a sandwich that tasted so good she'd almost cried.

"We're not both supposed to sleep on that, are we?"

Mae turned at Dell's voice. He stood in the doorway, casting a skeptical glance at the foldaway.

"Oh, no," Vik said. "I figured you'd take the couch in the living room."

"The couch is good," Dell said, a second before Jackson appeared behind his shoulder.

"Or," Jackson said with a smile, eyes sparking at Vik, "You could join us in our—"

"Let's show you that couch next." Vik plowed through both Dell and Jackson at the doorway, giving Jackson a smack on the hip as they passed.

Dell stopped short as they entered Jackson and Vik's light-filled living room.

"There are...a lot of plants in here," Dell observed. Mae held a hand to her heart. She had *missed* this house.

Jackson laughed.

"It's these two." He tilted his head toward Mae and Vik. "They're like a they/them gardening platoon."

"A *platoon*?" Vik asked incredulously as they walked toward their army of monsteras. "That's the best word you could come up with?"

"I like it," Mae said. "It sounds like...a cute fat duck or something."

Vik shook their head. "Never tell that to the armed forces."

"Oh, these are looking *great*." Mae leaned closer to take a look at the African violets, the Christmas cactus, the numerous jades.

"Yeah. The sun's been kind to us this fall."

A vision hit Mae of Dell in his safety goggles, leaning over his work bench on the back porch of the shop, a ray of light slashed across his hair.

"Yeah," she agreed.

And then she turned to look back at Jackson and Dell, standing a few feet away, together in a pool of light from the wide window. And—

Mae stared at them a moment more, suddenly agog.

Vik snorted. Mae's phone vibrated in the pocket of her hoodie.

**Vik**: are you really just seeing it?
**Mae**: they look EXACTLY ALIKE
**Mae**: okay not exactly
**Mae**: but close enough

Jackson was thinner, and didn't have The Voice—and Mae felt grateful for that, because their friendship would have been perhaps a touch different, if he did—but still.

Vik was full on laughing now.

**Vik**: told you I understood falling in love with Dell
**Mae**: there is something too queer about this
**Mae**: I just can't put my finger exactly on it

"Hey. Earth to Vik and Mae."

Mae glanced up at the sound of Jackson's voice. And noted his single raise of an eyebrow. Which was...almost exactly mirrored on Dell's face.

She dissolved into giggles.

"You do realize," Jackson continued, "that the two of you are just standing there, right next to each other, texting each other?"

"Yeah," Vik shot back, "as is our right, as friends."

"Well, sorry to break up this weird moment," Jackson said, "but we should get going to dinner soon."

"Dinner?" Dell put a hand on his belly, glanced at Mae. "We sort of just ate..."

"Sorry." Mae stuffed her phone back in her pocket, ran the backs of her thumbs over her eyes to calm herself. "We're meeting everyone for dinner soon. You can stay here and relax"—she returned Dell's glance—"if you want."

But Dell only held her gaze for another beat before he shrugged and said, "Nah, that sounds good. I'd like to meet everyone."

Jackson led Dell back to the kitchen then, chattering on about his sourdough starters. Mae watched Dell's retreating form. She never quite stopped watching Dell, really: as they met the whole gang at their favorite pizza place—minus Dorsa and Camille, as expected, and of course, Steve and Jesús. As he dozed in an armchair back at Jackson and Vik's afterward, his beard nuzzling into his chest. She watched his shoulders move under his T-shirt as he prepared to sleep on the couch. "I'm all right out here,

Mae," he finally said to her as she lingered. "I've slept on couches before."

And yet Mae hovered a minute more. Struggling to see, as she had all day, any signs of tension in those shoulders, hiding in the corners of his eyes. Any indications that he was regretting this, being here, in Portland. But he only looked back at her, eyes tired but calm.

"Go to sleep, Mae."

She bit her lip.

"Thank you," she said softly. Vik and Jackson were already in bed. "For coming with me."

Dell's gaze was steady.

"I'm having a good time."

And maybe he was telling the truth. He'd smiled with everyone, laughed a few times at dinner while he nursed a soda. Maybe he only wanted her to go to bed.

"See you in the morning," she finally said.

"See you in the morning."

And as she tucked herself into the foldaway in Vik's office, only a wall away, she thought about how nice it had felt, saying goodnight to Dell.

# eighteen

"WHAT DO you think about the place?" Mae glanced at Dell, who was looking over the landscape of Moonie's while their favorite butch bartender grabbed their drinks. One of Dell's hands rested on the edge of the bar, his body just behind hers. She liked it a little too much, the brush of his chest against her shoulder. It felt like a distinctly couple-ish pose, like she was meant to lean back into him. "I can tell you're thinking something."

Dell looked down at her, quirking a brow as the bartender brought them their drinks.

"I was just thinking," he said after giving the bartender a nod and retrieving his IPA, "that this place looks like any other dive bar on the coast I've ever been to."

Mae smiled around the tiny straw of her vodka cranberry as they pushed away from the bar.

That *was* what made The Moonlight Café so great. In a city chock full of hipness, it was decidedly a dive, on a lonely stretch of industrial wasteland in the north of the city. A place meant for truckers, taken over by queers.

"It's different, though." Mae stepped to the side, paused

along the wall underneath a mirror that advertised Miller High Life. She wanted to talk about this with Dell before they made their way back to the group. "Because we're safe here. You know?"

Mae hadn't been surprised that Dell had never been to Moonie's, that he seemed to have never even heard of it. Every queer Mae knew had been here at least once, but Dell was clearly a person who wasn't super obvious about his queerness, and she had no idea what his life in Portland had been like. She'd been dying to ask him more about it, this last day and a half, today especially, as they explored the city more well-rested. They'd spent a healthy chunk of the day at the storage unit, but she'd also shared her favorite breakfast sandwich, her favorite matcha, her favorite scoop of gelato. She'd made him drive past her most recent apartment, partly to see how it made her feel—sentimental but not regretful, the optimal result—but mostly just because she wanted to show him.

He had been calm and good-natured the whole time, even as she'd continued watching him for signs of stress. But he had never once broken his easy I'm Just Visiting facade, never given any indication that he knew the place. No *I used to go here, too*, no *this was my old neighborhood.* She wanted to know his old neighborhood, the places he used to go, as badly as she wanted to show him hers. But she'd kept her mouth shut, because she knew it was likely a miracle he was here with her at all. She'd kept her mouth shut because she didn't want to hurt him.

But for her sanity, she had to know that he understood Moonie's.

"I *want* to feel comfortable at any old dive bar on the coast," she continued. "I *want* to feel safe at Freddy Hampton's. But I don't. And I *know* I am here, from the moment I walk in the door. You have to get that, right? That that's important."

She looked into Dell's brown eyes, imploring.

"Yeah, Mae," he said, those eyes suddenly as gentle as his voice. "I get it."

She wanted to keep looking at him. She wanted to lean into him, hidden here against the wall. She wanted to taste the hops on his lips.

She turned and walked to their table instead, in the middle of the main room on the other side of the bar, to the right of the dance floor. She slipped into her seat next to Vik, Dell sliding in next to her. The karaoke was already in swing, a singer Mae didn't know doing their best Avril Lavigne.

"Hey, Dell, good to see you again." Ben leaned across the table. "I forgot to ask you yesterday—do you happen to know Emerson King? He owns a farm out on the coast, just a bit north of Greyfin Bay."

Dell shook his head, taking a sip of his beer. "Can't say I do."

Ben slumped back against his seat.

"That's too bad. He comes up to farmers' markets here sometimes; we somehow befriended him last year."

Alexei shook his head. "*Somehow*," he said with a small smile at Ben. And to Dell: "Ben befriends everyone."

"Couldn't relate," Dell said. Alexei's smile grew.

"Anyway, he sells some delicious stuff, and takes care of our dog whenever we fly back East. He just went through a divorce recently, and I think he could use some friends. He's a good guy."

"Ben." Alexei shook his head again. "Stop trying to set Emerson up. I think he's doing just fine."

"What's his name again? Maybe I can sell some of his

stuff at the store." Mae got out her phone and opened up the notes app, her newest best friend.

"Emerson King. Owner of Short King Farms."

Mae threw her head back and laughed. Even Dell chuckled beside her. It was hard to hear anything at Moonie's, once the karaoke got going, but Mae could still feel the vibrations of Dell's chuckle, like they rumbled through her own chest.

"Okay, *yes*," she gathered herself enough to say. "I remember you mentioning this now. This is excellent."

Dell said, "You guys have a dog?"

Mae turned then, as Alexei and Dell exchanged slide shows, to listen in as Theo complained about a new coworker to Vik. As Ozzy lamented one of their old favorite restaurants shutting down. As Jackson talked more, somehow, about bread.

Until one of their favorite Moonie's regulars, an attractive, athletic-looking guy, approached the mic.

And he opened his mouth to sing Taylor Swift's "Cruel Summer."

Jackson's story slowly died from his lips. As one, they all turned to watch the singer move his hips, rotate his shoulders, shuffle his feet just perfectly. Vik's hand found Mae's under the table and held on tight.

This had been Jesús's favorite Taylor song.

It was a difficult song to sing, and the dreamboat on the dance floor wasn't doing it particularly well, but that technicality was canceled out by his enthusiasm. Along with the enthusiasm of half of the gays in the bar.

"At least Jesús lived through the Eras Tour," Vik murmured halfway through.

"He actually said that," Mae said with a tremulous laugh, "at the hospital."

"Of course he did," Ozzy said with a sad smile.

Mae had been uncertain about whether she'd sing tonight. She always had, before. But it was a vulnerable thing, if silly, singing karaoke, and she hadn't been sure if she was up for it with Dell in the room. Even if he had already witnessed her solo dancing to Judy Garland.

But when the singer returned to his seat, giving his boyfriend a kiss on the forehead, Mae rose from hers. Walked over to Kiki, the karaoke jockey, and wrote her standard selection on a slip of paper. Like she had at least ten times before. Except this time, the slip of paper only read *Mae.*

By the time she returned to the table full of people she loved, the moment that had settled over them during "Cruel Summer" had been mercifully broken by the next song, by the next exchange of stories, shouted over the sticky table.

Mae grew true Moonie's-loose after one of their own approached the mic, Ozzy with a rendition of The Fugees' "Killing Me Softly with His Song." After she'd spent time on the dance floor, bumping hips with Theo, lip syncing and dipping low with Vik.

Once Kiki called Lily to the mic.

"What's she gonna do, what's she gonna do," Ben chanted, drumming his hands on the table.

Mae, face flushed from the previous song, leaned over to speak into Dell's ear.

"This one has the best set of pipes of anyone in here." She wondered if Dell could feel her breath on his neck. If he had goosebumps, too. She knew she was leaning in too close, that she could've shouted it at a normal distance instead.

But there was something about Moonie's that made you want to play with fire.

"We *live* for her performances," she finished.

Even now, more than twenty-four hours since they'd departed from Greyfin Bay and his workshop, Dell still smelled like sawdust. So strong Mae almost sneezed with it.

As the music started to play, the big blonde woman stood with her hands behind her back, head down as the recognizable guitar intro echoed through the room. Goosebumps returned to Mae's skin. Vik released a small groan.

"Oh, *fuck me*," they muttered. "I am cooked already."

By the time Lily stepped to the mic, singing the first lines of "Dream On," the whole room had settled into a hush. Moonie's knew to shut up when Lily was singing.

By the time she reached those high-pitched *dream on*s of Steven Tyler's youth, the whole crowd was on their feet.

Even Dell.

Tears stung the corner of Mae's eyes; she blinked them away as the bar cheered Lily off the stage. Even the butch bartender gave a hearty clap, the highest sign of Moonie's approval. Lily curtsied with a shy smile before retreating into the waiting arms of her partner at the bar.

"Now that," Kiki said into the mic, "was one for the ages. And now let's welcome up...Mae!"

"What!" Mae shouted. "Oh, this is some bullshit."

But the rest of her table only laughed. Vik shoved her shoulder. "*Go.*"

Kiki handed over the mic with a kind smile. "You got this, babe," she said.

Mae squinted into the lights. Attempted to take a breath.

Traditions could still live on. Maybe the shape of things

changed, the walls painted new colors, but the foundation could still be there.

Her face grew hot with a pulse of embarrassment as she stood in front of the mic, as the iconic tinkling piano of Vanessa Carlton's "A Thousand Miles" splashed through Moonie's. She didn't have a good voice like Lily or Ozzy, but Jesús hadn't, either. They had always completely trashed this song, together.

And the point of Moonie's wasn't very fine singing. It was about laughing with your friends and feeling nostalgic about the stages of life that had passed you by, painted through old pop songs. And Jesús had always done that, alongside her on this stage, so very well.

And for the first half of the song, she felt him there next to her, still doing it. Still making her laugh. Vik and Ben hollered and clapped; the familiarity of how many times she'd sung this song, right here, made the words come easy. She tried to make her off-key voice as pouty as Vanessa's; she bounced her shoulders up and down along with the strings.

But then Mae caught Theo's eye. He was turned in his chair, staring straight at her. His eyes were glassy.

And the facade crumbled.

All at once, the words she was actually singing crashed through her in the most horrible, discordant way. Because she did still need him. She did still miss him. She would walk a thousand miles to see him again.

She had no idea how she had thought this was a good idea, singing this song that she had only ever sung with Jesús Herrera-Baptiste. It was too much, that he didn't get to hear Lily slay 1970s Aerosmith. It was too much, that he would never get to meet Dell.

Her voice caught in her throat at the last line, her

mouth open without any sound, the words bouncing uselessly off the screen in front of her.

She needed to get off this dance floor.

And so she did. Returning the mic to Kiki before the song was even fully over, she turned on her heel and marched swiftly away from the bar, through the narrow hallway that held the bathrooms, straight out the back door to the crumbling patio.

She pushed her palms into her eyes, taking deep breaths of the cool night air before she heard the door swing open behind her.

"Hey, Mae." Vik's arms were around her first. When Mae finally dropped her hands and turned, she saw everyone, save Dell: Vik and Jackson, Theo and Ozzy, Ben and Lex.

"Sorry," she said, before bursting into tears for real.

And then they were all hugging, and it was too dark out here to tell, but Mae thought half of them were crying, too, even as almost all of them laughed.

"Do you think," she eventually recovered enough to say, "this is the first time anyone's had an emotional meltdown to Vanessa Carlton?"

"Oh honey," Theo said. "You're not the first and you won't be the last."

Mae smiled.

Vik squeezed her arm. "Jesús would be proud of you, Mae."

"Well, that's too much," Mae laughed. "Fuck you."

Vik smiled back. "Fuck you, too."

They separated to give each other some room.

"I don't think I really thought about it," Theo said. "How hard it'd be to come here without them."

"I keep thinking I'm doing okay," Jackson said, wiping a

hand underneath an eye. "And then karaoke night shows up and punches me in the face."

"Yeah," Vik said. "Grief's like that, sometimes."

"Okay." Mae took a deep breath. "Steve and Jesús wouldn't want us crying out here all night, though. We okay now?"

Both Theo and Vik kissed her cheeks.

"Yeah, girl," Theo said. "We're good."

And when Mae finally did feel ready to re-enter Moonie's, she was stopped short by Dell. Leaning against the wall in the narrow hallway by the bathrooms, arms crossed. Waiting for her.

The rest of her friends squeezed around them. She avoided their eyes, focused on Dell's face. Curling photographs were tacked onto the wall next to them, flash-heavy shots of Moonie's patrons from years gone by.

"Hey," he eventually said once they were alone. Well, with the exception of the occasional bargoer coming in and out of the bathrooms. Nothing about Moonie's was exactly sanitary, but this corner of it in particular was rather dire. Mae couldn't believe Dell was willingly standing here. "You okay?"

"Yeah." Mae swallowed, caught between wanting to make a joke about what he had just witnessed—it was, objectively, pretty funny that she had broken down, publicly, while singing "A Thousand Miles"—and wanting to step even closer to him. To do something in this dark hallway that wouldn't involve laughing at all.

"Just needed a little moment of catharsis," she eventually said. He wouldn't stop looking at her. It had been cold outside, a second ago, but her skin felt at once overly warm under his attention.

*Dell*, she almost opened her mouth to say. *What the hell are we doing?*

But he pushed off the wall before she could.

"We can leave early if you need to," he said.

"No." She shook her head. "I'm all right."

But she had liked the way he said it. *We.*

With a grave nod, he turned. She followed him back to the table, still avoiding the eyes of her friends.

But before Dell could retake his seat, Kiki read out his name.

Mae jerked her head in his direction, mouth parting in surprise.

Dell tilted his head, scratched behind his ear, as if he was going to explain. But then he simply left, walking toward Kiki.

"Hell yeah," Vik said, voice low. "I am ready for *this*."

"Do you know what he's singing?" Ben asked.

"No. I—"

And then she was truly struck speechless as an easy, gentle acoustic guitar swept through the room.

Mae never would have expected Dell McCleary to actually sing at karaoke. And she certainly never would have predicted he'd sing *this*.

In general, Mae held high standards for anyone who dared to sing Tracy Chapman. But the moment Dell opened his mouth to begin "Baby Can I Hold You," it became clear to everyone in the room that of the small percentage of people in the world who could do her justice, Dell McCleary was one of them.

By the time he got to the first chorus, Theo swooned into Ozzy's lap, hand over his heart.

Alexei, who had started putting on his coat, froze.

Mae dared Dell to look at her, at the same time that she

was terrified of what would happen to her already alarming internal temperature if he did. But he only stared straight ahead at the screen, even if it was clear he didn't need the prompted lyrics. As whenever he wasn't looking at the screen, he had his eyes closed.

Which he *had* to know was the sexiest move he possibly could've pulled.

With each passing second, the sensation that had been haunting her for the past two days grew heavier, deeper, a weighted blanket sinking over her chest. Because dammit, everything about this trip *had* felt couple-ish, and not just because of his skill at holding his body behind hers at the bar, although that was part of it. It was Dell asking teasing questions about her belongings inside her storage unit; it was wanting to share her favorite memories with him. It was Dell waiting for her to click in her seatbelt before he started the ignition; it was Dell sharing his radio. It was Dell, sitting with her friends last night over pizza, sitting at the table with her friends here at Moonie's: simultaneously in-line and on the outside of their group, connected to this world only through her.

Even if it wasn't rational, even if she shouldn't have thought it, every time her eyes snagged on him at those tables, she thought: *Mine*.

When he finished, the screams of applause were so loud as to almost be painful, a ringing in Mae's ears. She still couldn't look directly at anyone else at the table. She couldn't move. She focused on her breathing very, very carefully, her hands trapped between her thighs under the table.

Dell had barely returned to his seat when a hand slid down his shoulder. Mae broke her statue-esque meditation to look at the man currently caressing Dell's flannel.

"Hi there, honey," he cooed. "My entire table was just wondering if you're single."

Distantly, Mae heard the rest of the table barely conceal their laughter. But she could only focus on Dell's face. He glanced at her for a fraction of a second.

"I'm not looking, at the moment," he said to the man, not unkindly, though his face remained passive. The man retracted his hand with a small pout.

"Well, you can't blame a girl for trying," he said before returning to his friends.

Mae watched Dell take another sip of beer.

And then, unable to stop herself, she leaned in too close, again—entirely too close, this time—to say it directly into his ear.

"You know everyone in this room wants to fuck you now, right?"

When he didn't respond, when he didn't move a muscle, she pulled back. He turned to stare straight at her, eyes dark in the dim light of the bar.

"Do you?"

*Of course I do*, she thought. No one asked that question, in that way, if they didn't already know the answer.

"It's not fair," she murmured instead. "It hasn't been fair since the beginning."

"What isn't?"

"Um. Mae?"

With a blink, Mae turned at Alexei's voice. He stood behind Ben's chair across from them, coat zipped, pale cheeks pink. He gave them a small wave.

"I was just, uh. Saying goodbye."

"Of course," Mae said smoothly, picking up her glass to take a healthy gulp before realizing it was already empty. Alexei could only handle about an hour of Moonie's karaoke, or any activity, really, that involved potential sensory overload. She always loved him a little bit more, each time he decided to leave an event. She loved a person with boundaries. Perhaps there were limitless ways Mae should strive to be more like Alexei. "It was great to see you."

"See you at home." Ben lifted Alexei's hand for a kiss of Alexei's knuckles before Alexei waved to the rest of the table on his way out.

"I'm going to get another drink," Mae announced. "Anyone need anything?"

The five minutes alone, away from the heat of Dell's body, helped. A little, anyway. When she returned to the table, she vowed to keep her mouth away from Dell's ear, her eyes on her friends. Exhaustion started to set in: a long drive followed by sleeping in a house that wasn't your own, the physical labor of moving things around the storage unit, the emotional whiplash of this whole night.

But then...another stranger sang another song Mae used to love.

And like always, a night at Moonie's began to take on an insular, outside-of-time-and-space quality, where nothing else quite mattered other than singing until your throat was raw. Dell never joined the dance floor, during the songs when the rest of the table was inspired to dance, but even he visibly, slowly loosened as the night progressed, opening his mouth to sing along on almost every song. Mae tried to not be impressed with it, how many songs he apparently knew by heart, but it was hopeless. And when she thought about him sitting on his porch with his guitar, she wasn't truly surprised. The depth of ways Dell could make her attracted to him knew no bounds.

And she tried to be good, keep the leaning of her body

toward his to a minimum, but he started changing the rules. Started being the one to lean into her, listing his random observations of the night into her ear, the bristle of his beard brushing her neck. He laughed more than she'd perhaps ever seen him laugh. When he leaned in again just after midnight to say, his naturally scratchy voice scratchier than she'd ever heard it, "I think I have to turn in soon, Mae," she just about fainted with relief.

"Yeah," she said, even though the rest of the table was currently fully engaged on the dance floor with no signs of slowing down. "We can go."

They had both stood, started to pull on their jackets, when Kiki said Dell's name again.

Mae looked up at him in surprise.

"Oh shit," he said, eyes just as surprised, before he let out a startled laugh. "I forgot I put another song in."

The portion of the crowd that was lucid enough to remember Dell's first performance was already chanting his name. Cheeks turning crimson, he draped his coat back across his chair.

Mae sank back into her own, defeated. She had barely survived his first song, and her defenses by now were practically nonexistent. This...was not good.

But yet, when Dell took the mic with a half-nervous smile and the words "Teenage Dirtbag" displayed on the screen behind him, a laugh managed to burst out of Mae's lungs.

"I mean," Vik rushed back to her side to say, breathless, "the *range*."

"I know," Mae agreed, still laughing. "I know."

The vibe could not have been any different from "Baby Can I Hold You," yet Dell attacked "Teenage Dirtbag" with the same intensity and absolute capability that he had shown hours earlier. Except...goofier, as fitting the song and the hour of night, and Mae could barely process this version of the song. The high, nasally vocals of the original were replaced with the deep raggedness of Dell's, and particularly when he certifiably yelled out the chorus, it was as if pop-punk had been smashed together with metal. It was utterly perplexing and hypnotizing and Moonie's could not get enough of it.

He looked at her this time.

He looked at her a lot.

A sensation creeped over her skin, one she typically only found at live shows: when she could feel every single breathing atom of a song, each chord progression a miracle.

Mae thought she was possibly vibrating.

"When I tell you I thought I was obsessed with this man before," Ben said across the table.

Mae didn't know what to say, either during the performance or when Dell returned to the table, promptly putting on his coat and gesturing toward the door, eyes on hers.

Dear god.

She had truly just gotten wet from watching a person sing Wheatus. She was never going to forgive him.

"We're going to go now," she heard herself say, distantly, to Vik, whose lips were quivering with holding in their laughter.

"Yeah, you are," they said.

And then she was up, and out, and the harsh night air revived her brain for a few precious seconds. Until Dell twined a hand through hers as they walked toward his truck, and she lost it again.

A second before they got there, before they separated for their respective doors, Dell pulled off some kind of clever maneuver that resulted in both of their hands grasped together, face to face. And with a tug and a push, Mae found her back against the metal of the driver side door, Dell's stomach against her own, hands pinned just above her head. Mae couldn't stifle the sound that escaped her at the relief of their bodies pressing together, everything she'd been aching to feel for so long, boiling up through her.

"Dell," she said, needing to be honest, to finally get it out in the open. "Dell, I want you so badly."

His face was in shadow; she couldn't make out his expression. But the minute step he took, pressing their bodies even further together, said enough. She wanted to drag her hands away from his to slip underneath his clothes, to scratch his back, to squeeze his ass, to pull him, somehow, even closer than they already were, until she couldn't tell where her body ended and his began.

"Mae," he said, voice low, almost broken, breath hot against her cheek. Mae liked to imagine she could feel the rumble of that single syllable, vibrated from his chest to hers.

Her eyes drifted closed; she arched her neck. Dell groaned, and it wasn't only her imagination this time. She felt it, his noises absorbed into her own skin, like they belonged there.

She was molten lava.

"Mae," Dell said, voice strained. "I have a fisherman."

It took a few long seconds for the words to process.

When they did, the lava plummeted, hot and icy all at once, through the cavern of her chest.

She had forgotten. She had somehow *forgotten*, in the heat of the moment, the blur of Moonie's, that Dell already had someone.

She licked her lips.

"Your—your novelist is also a fisherman?"

A breath that might have been a laugh or a whimper, against her chin as Dell dipped his head.

"Yeah." And it was hard to think against the force of her lust, but confusion began to pierce through. Because it was Dell's hands, Dell's body capturing hers against this truck. It had been Dell, singing to her inside, whispering in her ear. Dell who offered to come to Portland with Mae in the first place.

Mae had *told* Dell about Becks, about how shitty her history with cheating made her feel. What was he—what was—

"But Mae, it's—"

A shot rang out.

Then two.

Mae recognized the sound, an instinctual alert felt deep in her mind. She'd been close enough to a shooting before—and one time was too many—to know the difference between the loud blast of a firework, the surprising boom of a backfiring truck, and this—the pop, so quick your mind might think you'd imagined it, if your body didn't know.

And Dell's body reacted immediately.

"In the truck." His voice was quiet, deadly serious; his hands had disappeared from Mae's in the blink of an eye. He already clutched his keys in his fingers. "Mae. Now."

And even though somewhere in her brain, she knew the pops had been far enough away that they likely weren't in immediate danger, Mae was scrambling around the hood, fumbling with the handle of the passenger side door. It was only when she was clicking in her seatbelt that her brain caught up.

"Dell, should you—"

"I'm fine." The truck was already moving, tires

crunching toward the parking lot exit. Mae stared at him in panic, remembering the blank anger on his face when he'd thrown that mug. That was not a face that should be driving. In a shitty neighborhood. Of a city he hated. In the middle of the night.

That—fuck—*she* had brought him to.

But he glanced at her then, pausing just before he pulled out of the lot to reach over and take her hand. It was only a small squeeze, before his hands returned to the wheel and his foot to the gas, but it was something.

"It's okay, Mae," he said as he pulled onto Columbia. "I'm okay. I just need to get home."

Mae stared straight out the windshield, heart still hammering as the dark night passed them by. She knew Dell didn't mean Vik and Jackson's. She knew, as Dell navigated down the road toward the I-5 ramp, that they were going back to Greyfin Bay.

And maybe the fretting, rational part of Mae's brain worried about Dell, driving almost three hours in the middle of the night in the midst of a trigger, and her own safety next to him.

But the more she watched him from the corner of her eye, his hands never leaving 10 and 2 on the wheel, his profile hard but calm, something in her gut settled. She sent Vik a quick text: *Something happened, and we're okay, but we're heading back to Greyfin Bay right now. I'm sorry promise I'll explain later.* She understood, somehow, that this was what Dell needed. She trusted him.

And she found, as the quiet miles went by, that she didn't really care about whatever belongings she'd left back at Vik's place. The things on her Portland to-do list she hadn't yet gotten done. She just wanted Dell to be able to get back to Greyfin Bay. To be with his dogs. To be in his workshop.

Every time her eyelids started to droop on the long drive, she pinched the skin on her wrist. Dell always seemed alert, every single time she glanced at him, but she had to stay awake to make sure. That he was okay. That they were almost there.

Almost home.

# nineteen

AS SOON AS the ignition turned off, the adrenaline hit.

Dell supposed it had been there all along, these last two and a half hours—traffic had been light in the middle of the night; they'd made good time—that it was what had allowed his mind to go quiet, hyper focused, intent on only the road in front of him, the wheel in his hands. He had expected Mae to protest more, to be worried about the state he was in, but he was grateful she'd barely complained at all. That he hadn't had to explain—not that he would have been able to—that he'd never felt like such a competent driver in his life.

But now that they sat in his drive, the engine cooling, all that tension maintained by his adrenal gland seemed to heave an enormous sigh. He attempted to pull his keys out of the ignition, but found his hands were shaking too badly to do it.

"Fuck," he muttered.

"It's okay." Mae's voice was soft, but her fingers over his were steady. "I got it."

"Sorry." His voice sounded slurred; he couldn't tell if it actually was or if his mind had just started to go sideways. "Swear I was a safe driver."

"I know you were," Mae said. "Come on. Time to rest." She opened her door, and somehow, he was able to follow suit. Until his eyes spotted the extra car sitting in his driveway, and his feet stopped. Mae paused at his side.

"Liv," she explained, voice still soft, and Dell's stomach lurched.

"Fuck," he said again.

"It's okay. I'll take care of it." She already had out her phone, was typing rapidly. The bright screen in the dark hurt Dell's eyes; he squinted away. "Okay. I'll help you get inside, okay?"

"I can get inside my own house," he mumbled automatically, but he didn't mean it. He was pretty sure her hand was on his lower back, pushing him gently along. He never wanted that hand to leave.

"Blue one," he said when they arrived at the back door, the one that led to his workshop. Mae fumbled through his keys before she found it. She turned the lock quietly, but as soon as they stepped inside, there was still a sudden cacophony of barks.

Dell wasn't sure if he should be embarrassed that he started crying as soon as he heard it.

He also wasn't sure how long he kneeled in the middle of his workshop, hugging CSNY once they all arrived, licking his face and wiggling their butts against his side. Liv never followed them in, and in the rational part of his brain he was able to access, he was grateful: that she must still be in the guest room, that whatever Mae had said to her resulted in Liv not seeing him like this. Mae was still there, her hands brushing through his hair, but that he didn't mind.

"Hey," she whispered eventually, once the dogs had begun to calm. "Let's get you all to bed."

Getting back to his feet felt like the hardest thing he'd done all night, but somehow he accomplished it, leading Mae and the dogs into the hallway, through the living room, past the kitchen, into his room.

As soon as they walked through the door, Dell kicked off his shoes.

"Okay," Mae said again. "I'll let you—"

His hand shot out to wrap around her wrist.

"No." He swallowed. "I need—can you—"

A beat of silence. He felt her pulse underneath his fingers, and something about that sharpened his mind, brought him back to himself for the first time since he'd turned off the truck.

"You want me to stay?"

"If you're not uncomfortable."

"Yeah, Dell. I can stay."

The second he heard the confirmation, he dropped her hand and began undressing. He was sure he'd had better fantasies about getting naked in front of Mae Kellerman, but at the moment, he didn't really give a shit. He just needed these jeans off his body, and this shirt, and—

At the last second, he had enough sense of mind to keep his underwear on, even though he didn't truly want to. He exhaled as he collapsed into bed, *finally*, back in his fucking bed, where he was never going to leave again.

"Mae?" he said after a second. They'd never actually turned on the lights; it was dark, and felt suddenly too quiet. He didn't know where she was, what she was doing, and a fraction of panic started to rise in his chest.

"I'm here," she said. "Just..." A hint of laughter. "Trying to get Crosby out of the way."

"Sorry," he mumbled, patting the comforter lower on his thigh in an attempt to encourage the old man to move. "Just push him. 'snot used to anyone else being in his spot."

"I get it," she said. "Sorry, Cros."

Dell smiled, any bad feelings left in his brain somehow wiped away with his own nickname for the retriever leaving Mae's mouth.

The bed shifted under her weight as she settled in. Dell was just about to instruct her to move closer when she said, "Dell, can I—"

And then her voice broke apart into quiet laughter.

"What?" Dell's mouth curved helplessly into a smile against his pillow at the sound. "What's so funny?"

"Baby," she said, and even if she was still laughing, the word caused another lurch of Dell's stomach, "can I hold you?"

"Yeah," he answered, a confused frown replacing his smile. "I want you to. But I still don't get what's funny."

Mae's arm wrapped around his stomach then, the skin of her forearm warm against his own, and he realized he didn't give a shit about this, either. Understanding the joke. Mae inched closer, her stomach against his back, and even though it wasn't fully the skin on skin he wanted, as Mae was still wearing a T-shirt, the warmth and pressure of it was enough. It was just fucking right.

"Your song," she said into his hair.

"Mm," he said, noncommittal, still confused. His eyes fluttered closed as her knees curled up behind his.

"Tracy Chapman," she whispered after another second, and memories of the night finally started to peer through the haze. Even if he didn't want them to.

*You're safe,* his mind reminded itself. *You're safe here.*

"S'a good song," he mumbled, as he let the haze take over again.

"You sang it so beautifully, Dell," Mae said, still whispering, her voice still right there behind his ear, the warmth of her breath tickling the back of his skull, and it was the last thing he remembered before his body finally dropped into sleep.

A creak of the floorboards woke Dell the next morning.

"Shit," Mae said, voice low, before she slipped back under the covers. She shivered, yanking the comforter up to her chin. "Didn't mean to wake you. Had to pee."

Dell stared at her.

Mae was in his bed.

And in the blur of his just-woken-up memories of five seconds ago, he was pretty sure she was only wearing a T-shirt and underwear.

None of which he, or his dick apparently, was opposed to, but why, and how—

Oh.

Right.

Mae turned on her side to face him, still snuggling aggressively into the comforter. She kept her body on her side of the bed, but he remembered it, then. How it felt to have her legs curled against his. The weight of her breasts against his back.

Gauzy light shone through the curtains of the wide window above his bed; he could tell from the strength of it that it must be at least late morning. His body tightened in anxiety at the wrongness of it, even as he knew that whatever rest they'd gotten wasn't enough. He couldn't bring himself to move, but he hated that the day already felt wasted. He was most calm when he rose with the sun. And—

"Liv let the dogs out," Mae said, "before she left a few hours ago to open the store."

Dell tried to exhale slowly.

"Okay," he rasped, the first word he'd spoken. He attempted to clear his throat. His eyes roamed past Mae's shoulder, saw her leggings, skirt, bra folded on top of his dresser.

"They're okay," she reiterated. "Everything's okay."

His eyes narrowed, flashed back to hers at the way her voice had turned soft. He didn't want her pity. But then...

God, even if they weren't technically touching anymore, staring at each other face to face like this, in the light of day, felt a hundred times more intimate.

He shifted onto his back, escaping her gaze.

She had come back with him last night. Had stayed with him. Without question or protest.

Mae deserved answers.

He sighed. "I suppose we should talk about some things."

"Only if you feel ready to talk."

Dell contemplated this as he studied the ceiling. And concluded, once his brain grew more awake—somewhat to his own surprise—that maybe he did feel ready. As ready as he'd likely ever feel, at least.

"Yeah. I can talk."

"In that case..." He heard Mae's intake of breath, felt her slow exhale make its fluttery way to the side of his neck. "Do you want to tell me about your fisherman first? Or why the gun shots triggered you?"

Dell closed his eyes.

"Mm," he mumbled. "So many great choices." But then he opened his eyes, turning his head toward her. "Wait. They were definitely gunshots? And you heard them, too?"

She nodded against the pillow, holding his gaze. Damn, her eyes were pretty.

"Yeah. They were, and I did."

Dell returned his gaze to the ceiling.

"Thanks. It makes me feel...less crazy. To know that. Even if I know I'm not crazy. And that I shouldn't use that term." He sighed again. "Fuck."

"Dell." Her voice was serious, almost reprimanding. "You can explain your story to me using any language you want. It's your story. I'm not going to judge."

Dell wiped a hand over his face, gusting a breath onto his palm.

And then, almost without his conscious decision, the words just...came out.

"There was a break-in. A home invasion." His hand flopped to the comforter. "My old house, in Portland, someone broke in. In the middle of the night. I was sleeping." A pause. "I lived alone."

A longer pause. Dell swallowed.

"I had an alarm, for the house I mean, and I guess it went off, but I'm a heavy sleeper, or, well, I used to be. I only really remember waking up when I heard something, someone, right outside my door, and then—the pops."

For the first time in the story—well, if one could count Dell's awkward sentence fragments as a story—Mae gasped, a short, quiet intake of air.

"They had a gun?"

"Yeah. I was shot here"—Dell pushed down the comforter an inch or two, pointed to the scar on his shoulder—"and in my thigh. Both shots were lucky, according to the doctors. Both that they missed more essential parts of my innards, and in the kind of gun they had, that it was just a handgun. That the bullets didn't rip me to shreds like the rapid-fire assault shit people have now." Dell's face twisted in disgust, another angry huff leaving his lips. "Feels weird to be grateful for the simplicity of being shot with a handgun, but here we are."

"Jesus," Mae whispered. "Dell, I'm so sorry."

"Yeah. Anyway, because of the alarm, I guess first responders got there pretty fast, and like I said, the doctors said I was lucky, and did a good job in helping me heal, so."

And now that the story was out there, Dell didn't quite know what else to say.

"The wounds get sore sometimes when the weather changes, when it's cold, but mostly they don't bother me too much anymore."

A short silence stretched until Mae said, "But...but what happened then?"

Dell turned to her. "What do you mean? Me moving to Greyfin Bay after? I don't know; it just felt—"

"No." Mae shook her head. "I mean, yes; I want to hear about that, too, but...what happened after you were shot? Was the intruder caught? Did you know them?"

"Oh."

Dell turned back to the ceiling.

"I don't remember anything, after I was shot." Dell had worked on the shame about that in therapy, but part of him still felt like an idiot saying it out loud. That his body held on to this trauma over an event he couldn't even fucking remember.

Then again, Mae was the first person he'd said any of

this out loud to in years, so he supposed his therapist would've told him to give himself a break.

"And...no, they were never caught. The police guessed, due to the erratic nature of the break-in and the shooting—they barely even stole anything good—that it was likely someone, or multiple someones, on drugs. Like half of the shit that happens in our country is because of people on drugs."

"Dell," Mae said. She sounded almost breathless, pained, and it made Dell wince. "No wonder you don't like going back to Portland, when this person that hurt you could just be...out there. I can't—"

"It's okay." Dell lifted his hands just slightly, flattening his palms against the air. "I'm not..." He sighed, unsure how to explain it. He'd almost said *angry*, but that wasn't exactly right. He was still angry, at a lot of shit. He'd just learned to not invest too much energy in that anger. "It doesn't matter so much to me who the person actually was, if they're still in the state, whatever. Honestly, even if they did find them, the idea of taking someone to court, having to live through everything again, knowing they'd probably be thrown in jail when I would just want them to get treatment—" Dell rubbed a hand over his face again. "A fucking nightmare. But yeah, I couldn't sleep in that house again. Moving here, after, felt like the right thing to do."

"I get that," Mae said. "God, Dell. I do. I just—fuck."

"I've been to therapy," Dell said, unable to repress the defensive note of his voice. He knew Mae had been a social worker, knew she probably had a ton of stuff to say about trauma, but he just...didn't *want* that from her, at least not right here, right now. He just wanted her bare legs against his again. "So you don't need to therapize me yourself, or say anything else. I'm okay. My triggers lessen by the year.

I'm *good* in Greyfin Bay. I hate that you've had to see me lose it fucking twice now, but this week was the first time I'd been in Portland in a long time, and the other week when I mistook your knocking for gunshots, it was right around the anniversary of the break-in, which isn't an excuse for me almost hurting you, but just so you know that this isn't a super normal occurrence anymore."

"Okay," Mae said, voice placating. "I get it. I won't therapize you, promise. I feel honored that you told me, but if you never want to mention it again, that's good, too. It's good, Dell."

Dell closed his eyes, worked to calm his heartbeat.

"I'm glad I was with you, though," she added, voice soft again. "Last night."

Dell swallowed, eyes still closed. "Yeah," he managed. "Me too."

A torturous moment passed before Dell felt her shift toward him. Just enough for her body to brush against his side. *Thank god,* he almost said out loud.

"That was a lot," Mae said after another beat, "so if you don't want to talk about the other thing, we can wait." Another pause. "We do have to talk about it, though."

Dell's mouth twitched into an almost-smile. It was that moment—Mae, still standing her ground, not actually letting him off the hook—that confirmed telling her had been okay. That maybe everything was as okay as it could be.

"The other thing...meaning my fisherman," he said, after a long stretch of silence.

"That's the one." Mae's voice had gone soft again. She danced her fingers up Dell's shoulder, and he repressed a shiver.

Eyes still closed, he started.

"His name is Luca."

And...guess he should have thought through what he would say to Mae Kellerman about Luca Yaeger. Maybe he'd thought the words would just tumble out of his mouth, like they had a second ago, about the break-in.

But the seconds ticked by, and the words had yet to arrive.

Maybe because he'd had more time for words about the break-in to marinate. Maybe because he'd already used those words, a bunch of times, in therapy, in conversations with his mom. But he'd never actually talked about Luca out loud. And maybe he didn't know what the fuck he was doing, here.

And that probably meant he didn't deserve either of them.

"Fuck." He ran a hand down his face again, blinking his eyes open. He should at least have the courage to look at the world while he talked about this. "Sorry."

"Dell," Mae said, voice even. "I'm not...interrogating you about this. I'm not upset. I just want to know."

Another beat passed before Dell blurted, "Fuck, he'd probably hate that I described him as a fisherman to you in the first place. He doesn't actually want to be one."

"Because he wants to be a novelist instead."

Dell swallowed. "Yeah. But fishing's all his family's ever done. Anyway, we have a sexual relationship. We meet once a month. That's it."

"Yet...you know his hopes and dreams."

Dell let out a rough laugh, about to reply with an incredulous denial. If only Luca had shared his hopes and dreams with Dell, their road might have turned out differently.

But he stopped himself at the last second. Because

maybe Luca *didn't* talk about his book with anyone else. But...god, Dell really had no idea.

"We talk, sometimes," he said. "After. But mostly...we were clear about it, when we started. It's not...a romantic relationship."

Mae's fingers were still dancing around Dell's arm. It was both distracting and oddly focusing all at once.

"How long have you and Luca had this arrangement?"

"About two years."

Mae's fingers paused.

"That's a long time to have..." She hesitated, as if she knew Dell would hate the term *fuck buddy*. "A friend."

Dell rumbled an assent.

"Do you care about him?"

"I do." He didn't hesitate in his answer; Mae deserved his honesty. But his voice was shakier, a fraction less assured than he'd planned. "But it's also different. It's different, Mae, from..." He turned on his side, finally, to face her, even if it made his stomach lurch the most of all. "This. From you."

He wanted better words to explain it. There were compartments in his heart for both of them, but Mae knew Dell in ways Luca had never even touched. She lived on his property, knew his dogs. And maybe those were superficial things, but they were things he had never let anyone else do. She made him feel a little more alive each time he saw her, whereas something inside him only grew tighter, more frustrated, each time he left Luca's cabin. She made him *laugh*.

He tried to imagine if he'd have let Luca see him last night, triggered and raw, like he had Mae.

The honest truth was, he really didn't know.

But he had let Mae in without question.

"But it still matters," Mae said, hands retreated, tucked back under her head. "Even if it's different."

"Yeah." Dell breathed in and then out, deep and slow. "Mae, listen. I got too close last night, outside the bar, before those shots rang out. I'm sorry. I shouldn't have... shouldn't have touched you, without working out my shit with Luca."

"You had started to tell me, though," she whispered. "You were going to tell me, before we almost kissed."

Dell's heart galloped in his chest at the memory. At how badly he wanted to kiss her, still, right fucking now.

"Yeah," he said, voice rough. "I've wanted to tell you for a while."

"I've wanted you to tell me for a while, too." She smiled, just an inch, but it was a little sad, her eyes a little glassy.

Dell almost opened his mouth to ask her what she wanted, to ask for confirmation that they were traveling down the same wavelengths here. But then her words from last night came back to him, blessedly clear, even with the hazy memory of the trigger soon after.

*Dell, I want you so badly.*

"Mae." He tried to clear his throat again; it'd gone thick and tight. "Mae, I want you so badly, too. But...it might take me some time. To end things with Luca, to...take some time with that." Because hell if Luca didn't deserve to be mourned. Because two years of letting each other's bodies in *was* a long time, and it *was* something, even if it wasn't as soft and open as this, Mae's ocean eyes staring earnestly back at his.

Dell's stomach was really hurting now with the brutal truth of it. He'd never get to touch Luca again. Never again get to fall asleep in that cabin.

If Mae still wanted to try this, anyway.

Fucking A, Dell was a selfish bastard.

Mae only stared at him. She blinked faster, eyes more glazed by the second.

"That is..." he started, more uncertain than ever. "If you still want to try something here, Mae. I understand it's messy, and..." Giving in to cowardice, he closed his eyes again. "I'm sorry," he said again, voice now as soft as hers.

A few seconds went by, and Dell's stomach sank in a different way, a kind of predictable resignation. He almost felt calm about it. Lord knew life would be quieter, *easier*, more familiar if he just continued as he'd been, Mae-less.

He would have to kick her out of the ADU, though. And probably finally sell 12 Main to her outright. He should probably do that either way. It'd be too messy otherwise, and this moment right now was enough evidence that Dell was not equipped for mess. It'd feel like a huge chunk was cut out of him for a while, he was sure, the ADU sitting empty again, his driveway only ever holding his own truck, not being able to help with the store. But it would heal, eventually.

"This feels different," Mae said.

Dell blinked open his eyes.

Mae was still staring at him, but a look of almost...awe had taken over her face.

"It *is* different, Mae," he said, voice full of feeling. "Luca and I never really let each other in, but you're like...a bulldozer; it's impossible to *not* want to let you in, and—"

"No, no." Mae smiled, eyes seeming to come into focus again. "I believe you, and I get it. *Every* relationship in our lives is different from all the others, but they all matter. I understand you have lots going on inside you right now. I'm not angry about it."

Dell faltered.

"You're not?"

"No. I was last night, though, for a *real* hot second, before everything happened." She kept smiling at him. "Because I'd already told you about my big guilty feelings about cheating on Becks, and..." Another look washed over her face as she shook her head. Dell couldn't quite discern anything that was happening here, but he focused on the fact that her mouth was still tilted upward. "God, I didn't even tell you about *Eden.*"

"Eden?" Dell frowned.

"Yeah, the last person I dated." And she was almost laughing when she said, "We dated for five months, and she was *married*, with a *kid*, the whole fucking time!"

Dell felt the blood drain out of his face.

"Mae. I'm so sorry."

"It's okay!" Still laughing, Mae wiped at an eye. "Sorry, I'm only laughing because it's such a fucking cliché, that she lived out her queer fantasy with me while I was oblivious, and she went through such *depth* in her deception, like rented a whole fucking apartment for our affair so I wouldn't know she actually lived with her husband and kid and..." Mae took a big breath. "I just...don't even feel bad, that I never even think about her anymore."

"Good." Dell was suddenly lost, drowning in a swamp of how people treated each other. Worried—no, knew—that he was part of its murky depths. "You shouldn't."

"But anyway, so I was real fucking angry for a second last night that I was about to somehow be caught in some kind of mess *again*, but this right here, right now, *you*, lying here telling me everything..."

The laughter faded from her lips. And she looked at him in a way...fuck, she was looking at him in a way that felt like the ocean, deep and fluid and vast. The most simultaneously frightening and grounding thing he'd ever known.

"Am I jealous this guy's been getting to fuck you for two years? Sure. But mostly I just feel...so glad, Dell." Her eyes somehow turned even softer. "That you've had him."

"But—" Dell couldn't help his frown. "Do you not—are we not—" He sighed. "Fuck, Mae, help me out here."

Mae only smiled again.

"Tell me something," she whispered. "Dell, in an ideal world, would you want to keep seeing him? While we start..." She let a hand escape the weight of her body, pressed a palm against Dell's chest. "This?"

Dell's body tensed beneath her fingers.

"In an ideal world," he eventually repeated, dumbstruck.

"Yeah." Her eyes sparkled at him. "I think I'm finally realizing that what made all those other relationships feel so bad was the *lying*. I lied to Becks, should have told her I was developing an attraction for that asshole far before I kissed him. Eden lied to me and to her family for five whole months. It's the lying that's the betrayal, right?" She shook her head again. "Maybe having feelings for multiple people at the same time is just the way the world works sometimes, because love is fucking messy. Maybe we don't have to feel shame about it if we're honest about how we're feeling."

Dell felt like he was losing his mind. He pushed himself up on an elbow, needing to...break the intimacy of the moment even an inch, needing to pierce a needle into the riot of things he was feeling.

"You're telling me you'd seriously be okay with it. Us dating, while I'm still sleeping with Luca once a month."

Mae shrugged. "Honestly? I don't know. I've never tried it. Do you think he'd be okay with it?"

Fuck. He couldn't believe they were talking about this. Maybe Mae had lots of friends who were into open relationships—shit, Jackson *had* been super flirty with him, and Vik had seemed fine with it—but Dell had never truly contemplated anything like this before. Up until a couple months ago, he'd considered himself a simple being, the holder of a life structured around the boundaries he needed.

"I...don't know."

Mae sat up too then, brushing stray hairs behind her ears as she rearranged her body, pretzeling her legs to sit across from him. At the last second, she seemed to remember she wasn't wearing any pants; she hurried to shuffle the sheet over her thighs. It was a second too late. Dell had already seen her silky purple underwear. It made Dell's stomach swoop, being below her like this. He went ahead and gave in, giving his elbow a rest and flopping all the way onto his back again.

Dell's stomach was a real fucking mess.

"Sorry, Dell. I don't mean to, like...pressure you into polyamory here." Mae gave a nervous laugh, a flush entering her cheeks. "We could not start anything at all. I could..." She swallowed, visibly uncomfortable. "Move out, get out of your hair, and—"

"No," Dell said shortly. Mae tucked more hair behind her ear, the flush on her face deepening.

"Okay. So then if you want to break it off with Luca, and give it some time, before...starting something with me, I'll still be here, living in your backyard, working in your town. If that's what feels right to you, I totally understand. But it just..." She shook her head, averting her eyes as she messed with the sheet in her lap. "I don't know. It feels wrong.

Making you give up someone you care about so that you can be with me."

"To me," Dell said slowly, "It feels selfish to not do so. If I got to keep you *and* Luca..." He looked over at her. "It feels imbalanced, for you."

"What?" Mae tilted her head and threw him a grin. "You wouldn't invite me to take part?"

Dell's face immediately flushed hot.

"I—I don't—I'm not sure he—"

"Sorry!" Mae practically screamed, throwing her hands over her face. "Sorry, I got excited and ahead of myself. I don't know what I'm doing here."

After he'd had a second to get over his shock, Dell's skin was still overly warm, yet...somehow, he found himself grinning.

"But you'd be into that, huh?"

Mae dropped her hands, face still red, an impish smile on her lips.

"I mean, all I truly know of threesomes is what I've seen in porn, but...I don't know, just something about the name Luca already kind of turns me on. Lots of things turn me on, though. Is he hot? I bet he's hot."

A small, unexpected laugh rumbled through Dell's chest. Fucking Mae Kellerman.

"He is...extremely good looking."

Mae swatted at his shoulder. "Of course he is! Do you have a picture?"

"Only the profile picture from the app."

Mae's jaw dropped. "You, Dell McCleary, use an *app*? This alters my whole perception of you somehow."

Dell shrugged.

"Haven't opened it since I connected with Luca. But when you live in Greyfin Bay and are searching for queer friendly options? Yeah, apps can be pretty helpful, Mae. Although even the apps..." Dell trailed off, staring at the door frame across the room. "You have to be careful."

Mae sobered. "Yeah."

But she was back a second later. "Okay, so show me the profile picture, then." And she flopped back onto the bed, snuggling her head into the crook of his shoulder.

Dell only really processed it then. That Mae's grapefruit scent was going to be embedded into his sheets.

With a half-hearted grumble, he leaned over the side of the bed to retrieve his phone from his discarded jeans.

Mae snuggled her chin right back into position when he returned.

Swiping open the app for the first time in two years, he found Luca's profile in his history and handed over the phone.

Mae lifted her chin with a gasp.

"Ohmy*lanta*. Dell!" She smacked him on the arm again before settling back against the pillows with his phone. "Good for *you*."

Dell plucked his phone away, chucking it onto the side table.

Mae turned back on her side, facing him.

A second ticked by before she asked, "Does anyone know about Luca? Other than Liv?"

He shook his head.

"Does anyone know anything about you? Other than Liv?"

He took a second before he turned his head. "Only you," he said.

Mae met his gaze, eyes soft again, before turning half her face into the pillow.

"The way I want to wreck you right now," she muttered. Dell tore his eyes away, taking a long, deep breath.

"I'm not going to touch you again," he said slowly, "until I talk to Luca."

"I know," she whispered. "I won't touch you. I mean—" She blew a breath into the pillow. "I've probably already touched you too much this morning; it's just...we're in your bed and you're over there looking all cuddleable and shirtless—" She briefly smothered her entire face into the pillow to release a scream. "But I'll be good! From here on out. I promise."

"I get it." Dell smiled back toward the ceiling. "Believe me, I get it. I...have made some unfortunate life choices." And then, his smile sliding away: "I hope it wasn't too inappropriate, last night when we got here, to ask you to stay. I'm sorry if—"

"No." Mae cut him off. "No, I know there was nothing sexual about last night. And I wasn't uncomfortable being here. I'm glad you asked."

Dell exhaled. "Mae. How are you so...understanding."

He felt her stare, burning on the side of his face.

"Maybe I'm just old enough now," she said, "to trust my instincts. Or maybe...I just trust you." A pause. "Even if you still need to sell me my fucking store."

Dell's mouth twitched.

"In seriousness, though, Dell," Mae continued before he could reply, before he could tell her she was right, "think about what you want. Take your time with it. Talk to Luca. Realistically, I imagine it would just be a hinge type situation."

"Hinge?"

Mae shifted onto her back and held her hands in front of her in a V.

"Me." She wiggled one set of fingers. "Luca." And the other. Then she tapped her palms together. "You. You're the hinge."

Dell, again, couldn't help the grin that stretched the corner of his mouth. It was a hell of a diagram. Preposterous, probably, but still a hell of a diagram. "Huh."

"*Huh*," Mae mocked him with a smirk as her hands fell back to the bed. "You can admit to wanting to be a hinge, Dell."

"I..." Dell huffed another half-laugh. "Mae, I just learned the term two seconds ago."

"I know." Mae's voice turned serious again. "Which is why you have to think about it." She shifted suddenly, swinging her legs off the bed. "I'm going to get dressed now, if you want to cover your precious eyes."

Dell did close his eyes, but he listened to every bit of rustling fabric. Imagined every piece of it sliding over her skin. Mourned the loss of her body weight and heat next to his.

His mind was still processing the rollercoaster of a conversation they'd just had, but his tongue tingled with the possibility of it. That he could have her back here, in his bed. That he could finally taste that skin, one day soon.

The floor creaked as she walked across the room. He blinked his eyes back open.

She stood at his open door, glancing into the hall.

"I'm going to get some of the stuff from the truck," she said. "Do you think you could help me unload the things I want at the store later?"

Dell hoisted himself onto his elbows.

"Maybe not today," he said honestly. That hazy post-trigger exhaustion was hitting him now. "I think I need to rest more, from last night. But tomorrow. I promise."

Mae nodded, readjusting the strap of her bag on her shoulder. “Of course.”

“Mae,” Dell said, the last twelve hours fully sinking into his consciousness. “I’m so sorry. About the way we left. I know you still had stuff you wanted to do, and we left things at Vik and Jackson’s—”

“It’s okay.” Mae shook her head. “I can get it all later. Truly, it’s okay. I’m just...glad to be home.”

Home.

Dell willed his heart to believe her.

But part of him—the part who had gotten to see Mae come alive, surrounded by the friends she loved, the city she clearly still loved—was, even now, more doubtful than ever.

Maybe he’d be able to have her for a little while.

But he couldn’t completely trust he’d have her forever.

“Take your time,” she said. “Talk to your fisherman. I’m here for whatever you need, Dell McCleary. Until then...” Another small smile, thrown his way. “You know where to find me.”

# twenty

MAE DECIDED to approach Bae Books from the street.

She normally parked in the back alley, checked on the plants in her raised beds, entered via the office door. But maybe she should start facing her dream the way the rest of Greyfin Bay saw it: from the outside. A boarded up window, a bright turquoise door. Planters holding wilting flowers. A small storefront next to a small pub, at the end of a small street.

Mae inspected the drooping fall daisies with a frown. She needed to tend to them more, cut them back for winter. Decide what she could plant for the dreary months.

She stepped back to survey the storefront once more.

Flora aside—

It was perfect.

Even with the boarded up window. That would be fixed soon. Most things could be fixed, with time.

Mae unlocked the door, and her first thoughts were somehow simultaneous:

*Oh god, I still have so much to do.*

*Look at what I've done.*

The bookshelves, the rug, the mural behind the counter. The *pilea peperomioides* on the counter.

She'd remembered last night, even in the dark, even in the exhaustion. She knew it again now. What the most important part of moving somewhere new was.

Leaving, and then coming back again.

Even a short time away made you appreciate all the details you had forgotten to appreciate. It didn't take long at all, Mae had learned, to stop seeing the details in a place.

You also didn't have to be in a place very long to know it was where you wanted to return to. At least for that exact moment in time. The place that life had led you to, for whatever reason, right here, right now.

It wasn't quite a bookstore, not yet.

But it was hers.

She put her keys and IGA coffee behind the counter, and she propped open the front door. Began bringing in what she'd been able to transport in her car. The bigger things she'd need to wait for Dell for, and a lot of what she'd dug out of the storage unit were creature comforts she simply wanted for the ADU, even if the ADU didn't exactly have the space for any of it. But there were knickknacks, framed photos, artwork, pottery, small furniture pieces she wanted for the shop, either for the front desk or the office, to make 12 Main even more her own. It was Saturday morning. She kept the door propped, started taking her time with the trips the more folks she started talking to.

*Say hi, sometimes.*

It was the height of whale-watching season; weekends in Greyfin Bay in October and November were often as bustling as they were in July. She stuffed a stack of Vik-designed, newly printed business cards in her coat pocket, handed them out to any passerby who paused even a moment. Encouraged them to peek their head inside. Asked them about their favorite books. When she explained that the glass of the front window was being replaced soon, nobody even blinked.

By the time she kicked away the doorstop, several hours had passed, and Mae was almost high on the enthusiasm of strangers. What a kind thing, to earnestly wish someone luck.

What a blessing, to have several hours' reprieve from remembering the feeling of Dell McCleary's body, tucked alongside hers.

Taking a big swig of now-lukewarm coffee—Mae's nose wrinkled as the bitter taste slid down her throat—she flipped on the lights in the office, opened the back door to make sure homophobes hadn't fucked with her raised beds while she'd been gone.

And then she almost fumbled her coffee entirely into her mums and black-eyed Susans when she saw what Antonio from UPS had left for her.

She rushed back into the office to put the coffee down and retrieve her phone to document them, and maybe call Vik to squeal.

Whereupon she discovered her phone was...completely and utterly dead.

"Dammit," she muttered, reaching for the charger on her desk. She stared at the dark screen, biting her lip and tapping her feet, before twirling on her heel to grab the boxes. This would have to be a *let's just remember in our hearts* situation.

She carried them to the front counter, found her favorite pair of scissors with the glittery pink handles, and carefully, preciously opened her first box of books as a bookseller.

She smiled when she saw the first books, sitting on top, glossy little mass markets: Tessa Dare's Spindle Cove. She plucked them out, inspected the spines and corners for damage. Her heart swelled with the appropriateness of it all. Maybe everyone had to get swept away, at some point, by a whimsical coastal fantasy.

And then she unpacked more, romance novel after romance novel, and the smile began to slip from her mouth.

She stared at their colorful covers, every depiction of embraces and longing glances scattered across the dark wood of the counter, and felt suddenly dizzy. She realized, dimly, that she had missed lunch.

In all of these stories she'd read, all the comfort she'd escaped into over the years, the characters met the loves of their lives at the exact right time. Maybe it didn't seem that way in the first chapters, of course; there had to be some hurdles for them to jump over to be together, but...they could always be together by the end. Because they were both unencumbered, ready to let their love interest in.

They weren't already fucking other people.

Mae sank into her chair, dropped her forehead to the counter.

After a deep breath, she walked into the office to retrieve her phone.

Where several panicked messages from Vik yelled at her from the screen.

*Are you okay?? Are you back in Greyfin Bay?*

*ARE YOU ALIVE PLEASE TEXT ME*

*I am imagining you just had so much wild sex into the early morning that you are now sleeping it off and that's why you're ignoring me and you're not actually in a ditch somewhere in the coastal range*

*Just kidding i'm absolutely picturing the last thing CALL ME*

"Shit." Mae pressed Call so hard it hurt her finger. "I'm sorry! I'm safe! Everything's fine!"

Vik's sigh was loud in Mae's ear; Mae couldn't quite tell yet the balance of angry and relieved.

"*Good,*" they said, and Mae'd say it was 50/50. Which was probably kinder than she deserved. "Thank fuck. But Jesus, Mae, never leave Moonie's again like *that* and then send me a text message like *that* and then go radio silent."

"I know, I know. You're right." She was about to jump into the story when she paused. "Wait, how did we leave Moonie's?"

"Like you were about two seconds from jumping each other's bones. Jackson was extremely jealous. What am I saying, we all were."

"Right. That didn't...*quite* happen."

And then Mae did jump into the story.

Vik, as always, was a patient, attentive listener.

"Wow, Mae," they finally said.

"I know."

"And you're..." Vik sighed. This gust of air was clear: 100% worry. "You're sure you're okay with this, if it moves forward? You know we've seen it...go wrong."

Mae winced. *Fuck.* It had gone wrong, specifically, with Vik and Jackson. It had been a long time ago, before Mae knew them; she didn't even know the third's name. But Vik had told her about it, after Mae had told them about Becks. It hadn't been the same thing, but it had been soothing for both of them, Mae thought, sharing their mess. Knowing that people you loved had mess, too.

They still cautiously practiced openness, sometimes, but they had clear boundaries now. Sex only. No deeper feelings.

And it was clear, even if Dell tried to argue that it was *different*, that Dell had feelings.

"Fuck, Vik. I should've thought more before I presented this to you. Sorry if I said anything that brought up old hurts."

"No, no." Mae could hear Vik's bittersweet smile through the line. "You're fine. And it's good, sometimes, to bring up old hurts. Make yourself remember the things you've learned. And it wasn't all bad, our thing."

"Yeah." Mae bit her lip.

"Just...you have to be really, really honest with yourself, and each other. All of you."

"Yeah," Mae said again.

"I'm not...trying to reprimand you, or be condescending or—"

"No," Mae interrupted. "This is good. Thank you, for talking to me seriously about it."

"Of course. It could work out just fine. I just...please, Mae, don't let your heart get broken, okay? I know you say you're fine after what happened with Eden, but...you deserve something really, really good, Mae, and...I saw you and Dell together. Not just at Moonie's, as hot as that sexual tension was, but...from the moment I saw you two in Greyfin Bay. I know your heart's already involved here."

"Yeah." A whisper this time, before she cleared her throat. "I'm going to be careful, Vik. I have so much to do with the store to distract me, and...it'll be okay. Either way."

And she realized, as she said it, that it would be.

It would hurt. In the case that...no, no matter what

happened, someone would likely hurt, somehow, at some point.

But maybe that was always the risk with love.

And even if she never got to touch Dell McCleary again for the rest of her days, Mae had already experienced an abundance of love in her life. Jodi and Felix. Becks. Jesús. Vik. Others, too: the people who flitted in and out, the intense bursts of friendship, the mentors and the teachers, the relationships and nights that were brief but warm. Maybe you experienced a multitude of loves in your life, and Mae had already experienced her fair share. Maybe anything from here on out was a bonus. This store, Jesús's inheritance, the little house in the woods she'd been able to fall asleep in every night for the last month and a half, the ocean, pounding steadily behind her: all of this, clearly, was a bonus.

She'd cherish every drop she could.

"I should go." She wiped at her suddenly damp face. "I have a lot to do. Thank you so much for listening, Vik. It was...so good to see you this week."

"I miss you already, Mae."

"I know." Mae sniffled, straightened. Walked as she talked, back out to the counter. Straightened her stacks of books. "But we'll do it again. Soon. You saved me this week. Can you...keep making sure I don't lock myself away over here?"

"You can count on me, Captain."

"Thanks, babe."

"Keep me updated on that sitch of yours."

"I will. Mwah."

"Mwah."

When she hung up, she turned on Jesús's death party playlist before she placed the phone back on the counter.

And then she woke up the computer, and got to work adding these fresh and shiny books into her inventory. As she typed and scanned away, a memory surfaced: standing in the IGA her first day in town, talking to Taylor Nguyen about buying Pokémon books for Lanh.

She opened a new browser right then, searching for all the Pokémon she could find.

Like that, it hit her.

Why didn't she know *all* of Greyfin Bay's favorite books? She'd asked some tourists this morning for theirs, but—

Maybe she hadn't actually been doing the work at all.

She picked the phone back up and sent a text to Liv. *Hey —mind if I come bug your patrons for a while?*

Then she grabbed another stack of business cards, and locked the door behind her.

Dell showed up mid-morning the next day.

Mae smiled, cautious but true, at the sight of him.

His skin was wan, the space under his eyes almost purple, shoulders tense. Just like he'd appeared the last time she'd seen him post-trigger. Her smile faltered as she took him in, as she held back the urge to go to him, wrap her arms around his back and rest her head on his chest.

But Dell had been living with this for years now; he likely had his own routines. Likely didn't want to keep talking about it. She'd promised she wouldn't touch him.

"Hi," she said, turning back toward the bookshelf where she was arranging the books that had arrived yesterday. This wouldn't be their final resting spot, but books still deserved to be on bookshelves.

"Hi. I brought the rest of the stuff from the truck, if you want to help me unload it. And then I'm going to get to work on the rest of the shelves."

She put down the paperback in her hand. She'd almost forgotten about the rest of the stuff.

"Of course. Thanks, Dell."

He dipped his head in acknowledgement before heading outside, Mae at his heels. She couldn't quite tell if carrying furniture together helped with the awkwardness between them or only enhanced it, but either way, she was grateful for the bits of familiarity they brought to the shop: a favorite old table, placed under the window by the front counter. A dresser she planned on using for storage in the office. Her favorite comfy armchair, placed in the reading area. And then a few random pieces she wasn't quite sure where to put, so they were put upstairs for now, one creaky step at a time.

Mae wiped at her sweaty brow when they'd placed the last one against the wall in the otherwise empty second floor.

"Thanks," she said. But Dell was already walking away, toward the two windows at the front of the room. Mae followed. And then they stood a while, watching. The view of the ocean, of Main Street, of the entirety of Greyfin Beach and the cliffs that enclosed it was so much clearer from up here. Something special.

"I know it seemed like my move to Greyfin Bay was impulsive," she said after a spell. "I know there's still a lot I have to learn about the town. But in a way...it feels like my body's always been waiting to get back to the ocean, you know? I've always loved it so much."

Dell was quiet, his eyes still focused on the view. But she knew he was listening. Dell was also good at listening.

"And my parents are here now, too. It feels like...I don't know. I've never believed in fate, or anything like that, but it does feel primal, somehow. Ending up here."

After a long moment, Dell asked, "How come I've never met your parents, if they're so close?"

"For one thing," she said with a smile, "my dad's eyesight has gone to shit, and my mom's always been a nervous driver. That's one of the reasons they're at this senior living place; the staff can take them where they need to go in town or get stuff delivered for them. But...I've also told them I don't want them to see it until it's all done."

Dell turned to look at her then. Her smile deepened at his stare. She shrugged.

"I love the idea of a grand reveal. I want to see the look on their faces, you know?"

Dell turned back to the window.

"I feel the opposite," he said after a beat. "If my mom was here, I'd want her to see everything. To always be in my workshop, watching every piece I made. Telling me how to make it better." Mae turned her body toward him, resting her hip against the window frame. "I think most of the time, that's what I imagine is happening, in my head."

Mae let herself stare at him, the tired lines of his face, the rough stubble on his neck.

"Tell me about her," she said softly. "Georgia."

Dell glanced at her, once and then away, back to the ocean.

"She's just..." He raised his shoulders, let them drop. "Always been a good mom. My bio dad left when I was little, so she raised me by herself through most of my childhood. Ours was the house my friends always wanted to hang out at, because she made everyone feel so welcome. Like she was everyone's mom, you know?"

Mae nodded.

"She met Henry, my stepdad, when I was in high school. He was a good guy; I was happy for both of them when they got married. Made it easier to move out here, knowing she wasn't alone. But he died a few years ago, and...now she is alone. And I'm stuck here, because it's where I feel safe now." He shrugged again, in a somehow particularly self-deprecating way. "I don't know," he said, voice quieter. "She's always been my favorite person. I just want her here." A second later, frustration lacing into the words: "I know she'd like it here."

Mae could only smile sadly at him. She'd promised not to touch him.

"I'm glad you had a mom like that." And then, before she thought the words through, "I hope I get to meet her someday."

Dell's eyes flashed toward hers.

"She would..." And then he shook his head, a grin cracking onto his lips. "She would fucking love you."

And before Mae could even absorb that, he stuck his hand in his pocket, checked his phone with a slight frown, and twisted away from the window.

Mae watched his long strides in silence, the swiftness with which his large body swept across the floor, disappeared down the stairs.

And with a deep, slow breath, she turned back toward the dusty glass, and watched the waves a bit more.

# twenty-one

DELL WAS FINISHING his second bookshelf of the week when Luca finally texted him back.

His stomach sank when he saw the reply to Dell's request to talk, sent only a few hours after Mae had left his bed, four days earlier.

*Okay*

Luca had never been the most garrulous guy, but even for him, a single *okay* didn't portend enthusiasm. Dell supposed he should be grateful that he at least included the *ay*. Dell supposed he should be grateful Luca responded at all.

*Is it okay if I come over later?* he typed back immediately, not even concerned about how thirsty it appeared, texting back within thirty seconds. He wished he could express it somehow over text, that he wasn't coming over to say goodbye. But he didn't know how to say any of this, really.

At least Luca didn't leave him hanging now.

*sure*

Which was how, three hours later, Dell once again found himself in front of Luca Yaeger's door.

He sucked in a small breath when Luca opened it. Luca's hair was starting to get curly again, and it looked like he hadn't shaved in a few days, making him appear rather scruffy, all over.

Dell was into it.

Dell had always been into all of it.

"Hey." Luca stepped back. "Want a beer?"

"Yeah." Dell closed the door behind him. "A beer sounds great."

Luca cracked open a can, a bit of foam running over his thumb. He sucked it off after he handed it over, before he opened his own. Dell felt hyper aware of every move Luca made. Hyper aware of every hop running down his throat. Hyper aware that Luca hadn't made eye contact since he'd opened the door.

"So." Luca leaned his forearms on the counter, looked over at the view of the surf from the kitchen window. "I feel like you should just get to it. Whatever you wanted to come here to say."

He was right. There wasn't need for small talk. Dell had to use his words; Luca deserved that.

Dell stuck his hands in his back pockets after taking another sip for bravery.

"The person who's opening the bookshop. Mae. Who I told you about last time. We've gotten a little...closer. I told them more about you."

Luca remained still, eyes still focused on the outside world.

"And they..." Dell swallowed. "They suggested...if we wanted to...that you and I could keep up our deal. While I start seeing Mae, too. Sort of an..." He waved a hand. "Open relationship deal. So we wouldn't have to stop this. If you didn't want to. Because I don't want to stop, Luca."

The truth was, while Dell had been skeptical when Mae first suggested it, he'd been doing a shit ton of reading over the last few days. And a shit ton of wondering if his initial discomfort had only been due to the societal pressures that prioritized monogamy, a culture he'd been immersed in his whole life. Maybe he *didn't* have to feel shame about harboring feelings for two people at once. Maybe it was okay to want to hold onto all of this.

Finally, Luca looked up at him, an eyebrow arched.

"So you came here to ask me if you can keep fucking me, while you start fucking them?"

Dell blushed, looking down at the counter.

"I, uh...yes." It sounded cruder, the way Luca had just put it, than everything Dell had been reading about openness and communication and boundaries and trust. But— "That's about it."

Luca made a noise Dell couldn't interpret before grabbing his beer and walking to a chair in the living room. After a moment, Dell sat in the opposite chair, joining him in his stare out a different window.

"So you're into open relationships," Luca summarized after a silence, tapping his fingers against the side of his can. "This wasn't exactly what I was expecting."

"I know," Dell rushed to say. "It wasn't what I was expecting either. But I've thought about it a lot, been reading about non-monogamy. I've never actually tried it before, but caring for Mae doesn't mean I suddenly don't care about you. I think...we work well together, you know? Or else we wouldn't have kept this up so long."

Luca nodded slowly. "You don't want things to change."

"Not really, no." And then, unable to help himself, he blurted, "Do you?"

Luca only stared straight ahead before he said, "I have a

feeling that what I want isn't the most important factor here."

"No, it is." Dell pushed to the edge of his seat, turned his knees toward Luca's. "That's why I'm here, talking this out with you. I want to know what you're thinking. What you want. It should be about what all of us are comfortable with."

Luca closed his eyes.

Dell had known this might be an awkward conversation to have, but his gut told him, even by his low expectation standards, it wasn't going well.

"I haven't kissed them or...anything," Dell stuttered out, face flushing as Luca's silence stretched, as the shame he'd been training himself not to feel came creeping back. Wondering, after the words came out of his mouth, if that statement was even true. If the looks, the nearness he and Mae had shared in that karaoke bar, if spending a night in the other's bed counted as *anything*. "We promised we wouldn't, until I talked to you."

Luca continued to be quiet for a long time. At least, it seemed like a long time. It might have only been an awkwardly prolonged pause before he spoke again, but maybe it was also an eternity.

"You could've kissed them if you wanted to," he said, rubbing a hand over his face, like the conversation was making him tired. "You're not...obligated to me, Dell. I thought we were clear about that."

"Yeah." Dell cleared his throat. "I guess I just...want to be obligated, a little. To you."

Luca leaned forward in his seat, resting his elbows on his knees, his face in his hands.

"Did you really think I was seeing other people, while

we've been...doing this?" Dell asked after a moment, genuinely curious.

Luca sighed, dropping his hands.

"I guess not. I mean, it's a small town. I figured if I heard about you being with anyone else, and you were still coming around, I'd ask you about it. Or..." He raised a shoulder, a small smirk on his lips. Dell breathed in relief at the hint of amusement on those lips, no matter how faint. "Shit, maybe I wouldn't have asked you, and just kept having you while I could. I don't know."

Dell's brow furrowed.

"But isn't that...what I'm proposing?"

Luca was quiet again. Before he leaned back and looked directly at Dell, fist propped just below his mouth.

"Mae would be your primary. Right?"

Dell's mouth gaped open and closed at the terminology coming out of Luca's mouth so casually. But eventually, he nodded.

"So it feels, to me, like what you're proposing is that you and Mae get to fall in love, while I get to be your open relationship side hustle experiment."

Dell couldn't hold his gaze. He blinked away, eyes suddenly stinging.

"I'm sorry, Luca. I didn't mean..."

The rest of the words caught in his throat, but they felt obvious. *To hurt you.* Luca's tone was even, almost clinical. But it was impossible to not hear anger in the actual words.

Except...wait. What was happening here? Why was Luca getting to act offended? They had met once a month for exactly one thing for a long time now. Luca had never offered anything more than that. Had never even seemed to *want* to. He had iced Dell out just as much as Dell had iced him out. So yeah, maybe Dell didn't actually understand how he was the bad guy here.

"If you *want* more than this, Luca...listen, I'm not opposed. I..." Dell stopped himself to gather the right words. *Honesty*, that was what he'd read over and over this week. This kind of shit only worked when everyone was honest. "I haven't been opposed to that for a while."

Luca took a long, audible breath. His knee bounced, until Dell could see him make himself stop.

"I think...that might be what freaks me out," he eventually said. Dell turned to him, a lick of...something stirring in his chest. "If we were all just fucking each other—fucking you, I guess—it'd be one thing. But something about... approaching it this way, all open and honest..." Luca laughed a little. "Maybe I'm just not equipped for that level of maturity, or something, but it's hard to not see it all leading to deeper feelings, and..."

Luca's mouth opened and closed a few times, before he finally met Dell's gaze.

"You already have those deeper feelings with Mae, right?"

Dell swallowed. "I think so."

Luca looked away again.

"I think it'd be best for everyone if you just let yourself have those feelings, Dell. I fear I would just...muck everything up. You deserve a good thing."

"You deserve a good thing, too, Luca," Dell said, voice quiet.

Luca raised a noncommittal shoulder, let it fall.

"I'm sorry I can't let it be this."

"Yeah." Dell cleared his throat, interlocked his fingers over his stomach. Finally accepting Luca's answer. "I get it. Sorry. I just...got excited about the possibility, I guess."

"I mean." Luca adopted a similar position, crossing his arms over his chest. He settled deeper into the chair, a smile lifting his mouth. "I get it, too, Dell. Getting to fuck two people you like? I'm just sorry I can't give that to you."

"Oh god." Dell covered his face with his hands, chest suddenly full of laughter. "Do you hate me right now? Have I just...made this the worst breakup of all time, or something?"

"Nah." Luca's grin turned bittersweet. "I didn't give you much to break up with, Dell. I know that, too."

For the first time in what felt like a while, Dell picked up his beer again.

"I didn't, either," he said.

Except...part of him wanted to keep pushing. This conversation was never going to be easy, but this conclusion they'd somehow come to didn't feel exactly right. Mae: feelings. Luca: sex. Like Luca was trying to fit them into little boxes so this split would make more sense.

But no relationship ever fit into little boxes. The truth was, Luca and Dell had shared something. Even if it was mostly physical, it had come with a sense of trust, of safety, that wasn't exactly easy for a person like Dell to find. It had lasted almost as long as Dell's longest relationship.

Maybe they had iced each other out at times; maybe they didn't share all the details of their lives. But they had spent a lot of hours in this place, even when they weren't actively fucking, in quiet acceptance, skin to skin. It meant something to sleep next to another person, close enough to feel their heat, to wake up next to them. To learn the shape of another person's body, the secret spots that made them shiver. It was fucking vulnerable. They *did* know each other, Dell thought, in a way that had been singular, unique to them. Dell imagined Luca would find a man, eventually, that he'd be able to open his whole self up to. Who he'd share all the secrets hiding behind those mysterious, brooding eyes with, in addition to all the private pleasures of his body. Dell's chest ached with jealousy at the thought.

But still, that man wouldn't know Luca in the exact same way Dell had known him, these last two years. Just like Mae wouldn't know the Dell who had existed in this cabin exactly like Luca did. None of it lessened anything else; no amount of care minimized other care. It was still all care. It all carried weight.

But Dell knew he'd likely already pushed Luca too far. He'd already put enough of his thoughts out there, and they weren't Luca's burden to bear if he wasn't interested in hearing them.

So he kept his mouth shut, and Luca took another long sip of beer before he said, "It was what we agreed to. Sorry if I reacted badly to this. I had just thought that we'd already said goodbye, so...I don't know. This caught me off guard."

"Wait. You thought we'd said goodbye?"

Luca cut his eyes toward Dell's.

"Yeah, Dell," he said, quiet but not unkind. "We did."

Dell looked away, back toward the Pacific, feeling suddenly childish.

Another long silence passed, but this one felt off-balance. Like Luca had finally relaxed, and Dell was glad for that, but Dell was, himself, increasingly lost.

"So we can't..." And Jesus, maybe Dell really was a crude ass, but apparently he was going to ask anyway. "Go one more time?"

Luca slowly shook his head.

"I mean." He gestured vaguely toward Dell with his beer, even as his eyes remained focused on the window.

"My body has a Pavlovian response to you at this point; I'm pretty much crawling out of my skin to touch you." Luca cleared his throat. "But if we went one more time, I think it'd just make me sad. And sad sex isn't up my alley."

Dell's throat went tight.

Luca had described it perfectly. *Crawling out of my skin to touch you.* He knew Luca was right; following every instinct in his body right now likely wouldn't be a good idea.

Part of him was bitter, though, that Luca had known the last time had been the last, and he hadn't.

But maybe...a tiny part of him had.

Either way, the fact that he and Luca would never have another time, that he would never have *this* again, a moment alone in Luca's cabin, made the hyper awareness of Dell's skin shift from arousal to something painful. Like it wanted to rip right off of his bones.

Even if he was the one doing the ripping.

"Well." Dell stood abruptly, placing his can on the table. "Probably shouldn't drink too much more of that."

Because maybe he could have stayed to shoot the shit with Luca until the beer ran dry, but something about that felt even more painful than sad sex. Even more of a misdirection than whatever Dell had already done here today.

"Yeah." Luca joined him, placing his own can next to Dell's. "Sorry. Probably shouldn't have given you one at all; it was just..."

"Routine." Dell smiled sadly. "Yeah, I know. But I should go."

"Yeah." Luca attempted to give him a smile back. "You probably should."

Dell paused at the door, glancing behind his shoulder.

"It won't be weird between us, if we run into each other

at the IGA or something? I don't want it to be weird between us."

Luca's smile didn't fade, but he said, "I can't guarantee that, Dell. At least not for a while."

Dell looked back at the door.

"I'm sorry, Luca."

A moment passed. He felt, more than saw, Luca's shrug.

"I'm not. I mean, I'm sorry as hell right now, but...it had to end at some point. Right? And you deserve to be happy." And then, a true kindness: "It's okay, Dell." Another shrug, small this time. "We're okay."

And even if Dell had had any more words, he wouldn't have been able to say them.

With a nod and one last glance, he shut the door behind him.

# twenty-two

DELL'S MIND went fuzzy when he returned to his truck. When he backed out of Luca's driveway. When he turned south.

And somehow, a seeming blink of an eye later, he found himself standing inside of Bay Books, in front of Mae, who was arranging books on Dell's bookshelves. Mae had been arranging books on Dell's bookshelves all week. She had this look on her face, every single time he walked in and saw her like this, that made him want to take her lower lip between his teeth.

"He said no."

Mae turned, eyes blinking up at him in surprise.

"What?"

"Luca."

Recognition dawned, and her eyes turned to pools of pity.

"Oh. He's not into it?"

Why had Dell come here? He didn't want to be here. He wanted to be...somewhere, anywhere, outside of his own skin. He'd needed to tell Mae, straight away, some bone deep, instinctual feeling that had swept over him as soon as he'd left Luca's cabin, like when he needed to talk to his mom after a trigger. But he could have just sent a fucking text. Why was he here?

"No," he managed.

"Dell." Mae's eyes were entirely too soft, and she smelled entirely too good. "Oh, Dell, I'm so sorry."

All that honesty shit piled up in his brain, and he almost blurted, *I'm sad,* but stopped himself just in time. He'd felt like enough of an amateur at Luca's.

"I need some time."

"Of course." Mae nodded, taking a step back, as if they needed an extra barrier between themselves for Dell's processing. Which, well, they probably fucking did. Dell had no idea what he was likely to do, just then. "Take all the time you need. Seriously, Dell."

"Okay." Dell scratched his beard. "Okay."

And he turned and left.

He found himself at the house next, grabbing the dogs. He gathered every single one, even Young, and opened the door of the truck, watched them all hop in, even though he'd never had them all in the truck because Young was still too much of a loose cannon. But he closed the door behind them all with a bang and hoped for the best.

And then they drove.

When Dell got back to his house that night, an email from The Nature Conservancy sat in his inbox, finally signaling movement about the wetlands at the edge of the old Edwards' farm.

Dell thanked whoever was out there for saving graces.

They'd been in protracted communication about the Edwards tract for months. While Dell always tried to reach out to local land trusts first with spaces like these, all the non-profits in Lincoln County had been strapped for cash lately. But he knew The Nature Conservancy could do something with it, if only the guy in Eugene would come out and walk it with him. Which it sounded, finally, like he would.

Dell was behind on orders for his online shop, too. Had been for weeks.

And so he hunkered down in his workshop, and walked through a marsh with someone who would help save it, and hammered out paperwork, and continued working on Mae's bookshelves, when he could.

Even if he barely talked to her, barely stepped inside the shop, when he did.

The truth was, he wasn't entirely sure how to make this transition. He still felt more raw over Luca than he wanted to be, even if he knew he was being dramatic about it. Sadder about the loss of their potential, perhaps, than what they truly were. Either way, it had been his favorite routine in his new life, and now it was gone.

And approaching Mae—god, he'd really fucked things up with her from the start. Didn't want her to feel like she was just his second choice, now. She was always reading romance novels. She deserved a better start to a relationship than...whatever the mess of the last week had been. Whatever the mess of the last two months had been, maybe.

Did he ask her on a date?

He hadn't been on a date in what felt like a decade. Had never been very good at them, even when he was younger.

God.

A mess.

And then Friday afternoon hit him in the gut.

Maybe it was something about the turn in the road, on his drive home from the post office. The slant of October light through his windshield, the glint of it off the ocean in the corner of his eye. Or perhaps his slow brain had simply finally had enough time for things to sink in.

A few years ago, he'd looked death in the face.

And here he was, next to the Pacific Ocean, safe and fucking alive, feeling bummed because he'd only been able to sleep with a gorgeous man for two fucking years. Feeling conflicted, or guilty, or *something*, because a beautiful person who made him laugh somehow wanted his sorry ass, too.

If you had told the Dell McCleary of three years ago, newly moved to Greyfin Bay, still recovering from multiple surgeries, nothing but hollow and a little stunned inside, that in a few years he'd be surrounded by the ocean breeze and the dogs that made up his heart, feeling a little sad that his attempt at polyamory didn't quite work out, he would have simply dissociated the entire thought.

Luca had let him go.

Luca had maybe let him go weeks ago.

And Mae was there, waiting. Like she'd always been there, waiting, in his ADU, in his damn Main Street property, inside his skin since she'd first shown up at his doorstep over two months ago.

Life was short. *God*, life was short. If he hadn't learned that, what was even the point of anything?

What the hell was he waiting for?

Except one tiny detail snagged in his brain. Luca in his cabin, saying *you're not obligated to me.* Dell was pretty sure they were safe, but *pretty sure* wasn't good enough for Dell.

Wasn't good enough for Mae. He glanced at the time on the dash.

With a squeal of his brakes, he turned around in the parking lot of the Fin Inn and turned north again, toward the clinic in Lincoln City.

Mae sat on the kitchen counter, eating out of a carton of Ben & Jerry's (prohibitively expensive out here on the coast, but every time Mae waffled in the frozen aisle of the IGA, Jesús nudged her shoulder and said, *"I am TELLING you—"*). It was a bit of a precarious thing, sitting on the counter; she had to help herself up with a footstool, and her big ass just barely fit before the cabinetry bit into her back.

But she'd discovered recently that it was worth it to sit on this corner. From this corner, she could see around the edge of Dell's house, where the sun peeked through the trees on its way down the horizon. Shining on Dell's overgrown patch of lawn, over the landscaping between his space and hers. She could best picture the ocean here, past that grove of trees, down, down past a few more, until you reached the highway, and then sand: as close to the sun as one could come.

And so Mae sat and ate her ice cream and watched the sky turn peach, and told herself she was just fine.

It was just fine that Dell had barely said two words to her since last Tuesday, over a week ago now, the day he must have spoken to Luca. She had meant it when she'd told him he could take his time, but she hadn't thought she'd be so thoroughly shut out while he processed. She had thought, perhaps naively, after their conversation in his bed, that perhaps they could process whatever had happened together.

But of course, Dell was still Dell. She'd witnessed how he processed things. And so it shouldn't have bothered her that he'd only shown up at the shop intermittently, this past week. That he'd barely even looked at her when he had.

She...well, she missed him. The shop was quieter without the sound of his saws and drills and sanders in the background. He felt almost more remote to her than when she'd first moved in. Remote enough that her doubts began to get the best of her. Maybe, instead of bringing them closer, going to Portland and the night she'd spent in his bed had only spooked him. Maybe something had changed between them, something that couldn't be recaptured now.

Maybe she'd have to drink all of her future matcha lattes alone.

Which, she reminded herself with another shovel of ice cream, was okay.

It had been a bonus. Seeing Dell sing at Moonie's. Getting to hold him that night.

It was okay if all of this had only been a bonus.

His silence would hurt less soon. She was sure of it.

The sound of Dell's truck swept up from the road like an incoming wave, ending with the close crunch of gravel, the abrupt quiet in the cutting of the engine. A moment of stillness, like the holding of a breath before the air was punctuated by the slam of his door. The dogs barked. Mae bit her lip, wondering where he was coming from. What he was wearing today.

And then—

Three loud raps, right on Mae's door, and she almost fell off the counter.

She couldn't remember a time Dell had knocked on her —his—door, a time he'd even set foot inside the ADU since that first day he'd let her in and handed over the key. Yet before she could even gather herself to get off the counter with grace, another key turned in the lock.

And Dell McCleary strode inside, door slamming behind him. In three long strides, he was there, in front of her, standing at her knees.

Mae blinked.

He appeared almost out of breath, eyes dark and serious. And even if the week of silence between them had, perhaps, hurt her feelings, she was so damn happy to see him that she couldn't help but smile.

"Well, hello," she said.

"Sorry," he answered, running a hand through his hair. "Sorry I didn't wait for you to get the door, sorry I haven't—"

He grabbed the ice cream from her hand, followed by the spoon. Placed them on the counter a safe distance away.

And when he was done, he rested his hands on her thighs, which had, unbeknownst to her, parted to make room for his.

"I'm sorry," he said again. "I wanted to do this right, and I'm sure everything was probably fine anyway, but I wasn't completely sure, that Luca hadn't slept with anyone else, and so I went to get tested, and I've been waiting, but I just heard, and—are you good, too? Health wise?"

Mae was overwhelmed at the sudden closeness of him, so very close and surprising and wonderful, his hands moving up her thighs to grip her hips.

"What?"

Dell's mouth twitched. "Have you been tested since your last partner?"

"I—" Oh god, he smelled like *Dell.* He was so close. She swallowed. "Yeah. I have."

His hands moved again. They wrapped around the back of her neck, fingers gripping into her hairline, thumbs pushing upward against her jaw. She inhaled a breath she couldn't quite release.

The amusement faded from his eyes, replaced by that dark seriousness once more.

"These lips," he said, right hand crawling over her jaw, until his thumb pressed down on her bottom lip. "You are always biting this lip. Drives me fucking wild."

And Mae had meant every word she'd said to Dell that night in his bed. She had been patient and understanding and she knew he'd stood behind her at the bar like he owned her, had pressed her against his truck; she knew he'd said the words the next morning—*I want you so badly, too*—but it was possible she hadn't fully believed them until this moment. It was possible she'd forced herself to not believe them, this week. Until now. Until she saw the desire in his eyes. For her. Until his thumb pressed down into her bottom lip.

"Mae," he said, voice quiet as sin, "do you still want this?"

Wordlessly, as much as she could under the command of his palms, she nodded.

The moment he clocked the movement, before her chin had barely dipped, he closed the gap and kissed her.

# *twenty-three*

DELL KISSED like he had his safety goggles on: with focus and a quiet intensity. A powerful but controlled force, art left in its wake. And as with the first time Mae had seen Dell's brow furrow as he contemplated a stretch of wood, she was gone for it from the start.

She hadn't kissed someone with a beard in a long time. It tickled her chin, her cheeks. Her hands scrambled for purchase, grabbing at his shirt, wrapping around the prickle of his neck until they mirrored his. When his mouth opened to hers, a small, uninhibited sound emptied from her throat, landing on his tongue: surprise and relief and *finally*. They were so close, but she needed to be closer; she scooted an inch forward. A darker sound, almost a growl, rumbled through Dell's chest, because *yes*. It was just right, here on the counter: the apex of her thighs fit *just there*, against the bulge in Dell's jeans.

Mae pushed against him, wrapped her legs around his hips, kissed him with a sudden, bone-deep clarity: Dell McCleary was the one thing, other than her books and the ocean, that made her feel at home here. That made her feel safe. Like she belonged. And maybe even her books, maybe even the ocean couldn't compare to this. Maybe Dell wasn't just a bonus. Maybe he had been entwined with this dream from the start. Maybe he was everything. He kissed her back like he was letting her see the whole of him for the first time, someone a little angry but mostly soft—a quietly desperate person—and she was *here* with him, fully here, like seeking like, kissing him fast and sloppy now—*slow down*, a tiny part of her brain whispered, but she couldn't stop rocking against him, until everything hit her at once. That she'd wanted this for so long. That it felt so good. She needed to breathe or she was going to explode. She needed —she needed a breath.

She broke away with an unsteady gasp, turning to rest her cheek on his shoulder.

"You okay?" His voice was soft, ragged.

"Yeah, I just—" She tried to wipe surreptitiously at her face. Tried to swallow down her heartbeat, thudding in her throat. Tried to think of something to distract, to help her calm down. "I can't believe you're doing this now."

"I'm—I'm sorry. I came as soon as I got the results, didn't really think—"

"No, now is good," she assured him. She turned to kiss his neck. "Now is great. It's just—" She attempted to gesture at herself, but found her control of her limbs had gone a bit loosey-goosey. "I'm wearing sweatpants and a Wisconsin Badgers T-shirt. Objectively the least sexy outfit I own."

"I don't give a shit what you're wearing," Dell said, before he pulled back an inch. Assessed her with a frown. "Actually, I change my mind. The shirt has to go." And he was pulling back even further, hauling the shirt over her head.

"Ow!" She laughed as the collar got stuck on the earrings she'd forgotten she was still wearing, and it shook her back inside her body just enough. Just enough to catch her breath. "Hold on a second."

She was still disentangling herself from the fabric when she heard Dell say, "Let's go blue."

Mae slapped the T-shirt to the floor, mouth gaping in disbelief.

"Dell," she said, "did you really just say *let's go blue* while attempting to have access to my vagina?"

"Accept me as I am or don't have me at all," Dell answered, a clearly disingenuous statement as his lips were already back on hers by the time he'd finished it. She laughed into his mouth, heart swelling at the look in his eyes she'd just glanced—light, sparkling, playful—before her pelvis found a rhythm again and her laugh turned into a gasp once more. But this was the Dell she wanted. The Dell that challenged her. That laughed, sometimes, just for her.

Dell's hands found her breasts, bare now to the air, nipples smarting against the soft-roughness of his flannel shirt until he covered them with his palms instead, kneading, gripping, the calluses of his fingertips rasping against the smoothness of her stretch marks, and Mae was so very, very gone.

"Dell," she rasped. "Dell, let me touch you, too."

She broke away from his mouth, concentrated on the buttons of his shirt; he moved the attentions of his tongue to the side of her neck. Her fingers faltered, head lolling to the side, eyes fluttering closed. Thighs cinching around Dell's body even tighter, clenching him even closer as she found a rhythm again, until Dell had to pause to curse against her clavicle.

"Mae. If we don't slow down—"

"I know, I know," she breathed, opening her eyes to focus on his buttons again. "Fuck, it just feels so good."

She managed to shuck the flannel off his shoulders, but he was still wearing a thin T-shirt underneath. She paused as long as she could manage to admire the way it hugged his stomach, how it molded around his thick, strong arms, until she shoved the hem up to find skin.

Dell sucked in a breath when her fingers found his belly.

"Sorry," she murmured. "If you remember, I'd been holding ice cream."

He chuckled against her skin, mouth still attached to her neck, and she needed it, that little rumble of laughter, to rein herself in again, before she rubbed herself to completion in the next five seconds. It was possible she'd already come a few minutes ago. It was possible her body was simply in a rolling cycle of freefall. She decided to smooth the fabric back over his stomach. She liked Dell in a thin T-shirt. She wanted the friction of it against her tits.

Her hands moved to the front of his jeans instead.

He mumbled something incoherent against her shoulder as she worked at the top button.

"Okay," he breathed once she reached the zipper, pushing his palms against the edge of the counter. "Okay, give me a second." He reached a hand into his back pocket, passed her a condom. "Hold onto this for me." And then he was bending down as the packet crinkled between her fingers, kissing the tops of her breasts, the sides, taking her nipples into his mouth as those calloused fingers inched beneath her underwear, spread over her ass, pushed her sweatpants over her hips. She wriggled on the counter, undignified and shivery, attempting to help the process, until, with a last kiss of Mae's hip, Dell straightened again, and Mae pulled him close by the belt loop of his loosened jeans.

Distantly, she knew the counter was cold against her ass, that neither of them were the most limber people for this kind of situation, that there had to be a more comfortable way to do this for the first time together, that there was so much more she wanted to examine about this person between her legs when she could take her time. But mostly, as she shoved down Dell's jeans, his navy briefs—and oh, those were *good* briefs on those thighs—and oh *shit*, oh god, there was that tree tattoo on his thigh that she had never once forgotten about, and it was *glorious*; she was going to have to examine it in so much more detail later—as she wrapped the condom over him, all she felt was hot and urgent.

Dell moved a hand between her legs but she slapped him away. If he touched her clit now she'd come on the spot. "Later," she said, grabbing his ass, lifting her stomach, helping position him. And then: "This is extremely unsanitary, you know."

"Don't care."

"Oh, me neither," Mae said breezily. Or, as breezily as she could. Which, at the moment, was likely not very breezy at all. "I was just making conversation."

Dell paused to drop his forehead onto her shoulder, another small laugh tumbling onto her skin. "Jesus."

"What?" she asked, but she was laughing, too. Until, suddenly, Dell pushed into her and the air was plum stolen from her throat, laughter cut short. Other words flitted through her mind: *fuck, oh shit, FUCK*, but out loud, all she could manage was a feathery whimper.

Dell's face had that focused look again, brow furrowed, hands gripping her hips as he pushed in, and in, and Mae dipped her back, one hand clutching the counter to hold herself there, the other holding onto his forearm, because she could, and she wanted to. She wondered if she could ask him to put those safety goggles on for her, next time.

He took one pause, one second to close his eyes, and then he was moving, and Mae simply went blank for a while, no thoughts just Dell, no thoughts just skin and muscle, no thoughts just heat and breath, until her head started to smack against the cabinet behind her.

Without breaking rhythm—*god*, Dell was an impressive fuck—his hand was there, calluses scratching into her scalp, cushioning her skull, his knuckles taking the blows instead.

"No head injuries," he gusted out, "on my account."

Mae could only manage another whimper in reply.

And soon, very soon, she was grabbing his other hand, guiding it under her belly and between her thighs.

"Now," she gasped, pushing his fingers against her clit, *now*, nownownow, and she seized around him in waves, no thoughts and all the thoughts at once, until she could breathe again.

Dell gave a last thrust, a groan, dropping his face into her shoulder. His fingernails dug into her as he came, biting at her scalp, her thigh where he'd been holding one of her legs against him, and this last, surprising jolt of pain breaking through her post-orgasm haze almost made her come all over again.

But she only wrapped her arms around him instead, scratching her own nails underneath his T-shirt, up over his shoulder blades.

"Shit," he said into her collarbone a minute later, voice threaded with tired laughter.

"Yeah," she agreed. "Same."

And then, like some kind of sneaky snake, his arm stretched to the right. When she realized what he was going for, she slapped his hand with a gasp.

"Dell McCleary. Get your dick out of me before you touch my ice cream."

"It's gonna be like that, is it?"

"You always knew it would be."

And when he leaned back, sneaky hand grabbing the ice cream anyway, his grin crinkled the corner of his eyes.

Letting his other hand fall from the strands of her hair, he picked up the spoon. And slowly, fucking *sensually*, he dipped it in and out of the carton before bringing it to Mae's lips.

They'd fucked so quickly that the ice cream hadn't even had time to fully turn to soup. It was only perfectly soft at the edges, and when Mae opened her mouth to accept the spoon, when the creamy sweetness melted on her tongue, her eyes never leaving Dell's, she thought, again: FUCK.

And then, with a hiss and a half laugh, Dell withdrew the spoon, hitting her front teeth on the way out, dropping both spoon and ice cream onto the counter as he focused on withdrawing himself instead.

"You like—*squeezed* me," he said, with a look that might have attempted to be accusatory if he wasn't laughing. "I wasn't ready."

"Your fault for lingering and doing *that*," she countered, picking the ice cream back up herself. "Wait." She straightened, leaned forward as he began to pull away.

"I have to—" He motioned toward the condom, but Mae grabbed his forearm.

"*Wait.*"

And she spoon fed him his own mouthful of Ben & Jerry's.

"Okay," she whispered, eyes on his lips as his tongue dipped out to grab a last drip. And helpless not to, she leaned forward to kiss him, lips sweet, beard rough, until he pulled away, eyes soft.

"I'm going to take care of this," he said, "and then I'm going to go let the dogs out. You can follow me, if you want, if you want to sleep in my bed without any clothes this time. Or you can stay here, if that's what you want." He kissed her once more, a barely-there brush of lips, before he opened his eyes again to smile at her. "Hi," he said.

And then he turned and left the kitchen.

"I only have one question," Mae said to Dell's back fifteen minutes later. He'd left the workshop door unlocked for her, but she'd still tried to make her entrance as conspicuous as possible, shuffling her feet along the hardwood floors so she wouldn't spook him. "Does your bed also have a Pendleton blanket hiding somewhere?"

She couldn't quite remember, from last time. A lot of that night still felt like a dream.

Dell turned from the kitchen counter, that small smile lifting the corner of his mouth.

"No. Felt Georgia deserved one, though."

"Hm." Mae crossed her arms over chest. "Guess I'm going to need a thorough tour of the whole house then, to make my final decisions."

Dell's smile grew before he attempted to flatten it, a superficially serious look creasing his brow.

"Fair." He cleared his throat, motioning to his left. "Well, what drew me to the house, along with the location, was all the natural light, especially here in the kitchen—"

"Oh my god, Dell," Mae burst out. "We totally fucked on your mom's future kitchen counter."

Dell looked at her, mouth open for a solid ten seconds before he snapped it shut.

"I am choosing to maintain a solid cognitive dissonance about that for the rest of my days."

Mae nodded. "Good call."

"Anyway." Dell cleared his throat, picking up a mug from the counter and stepping out from behind the kitchen island. "Then we have the living room..."

Mae followed him into the high ceilinged, straight-out-of-a-magazine living room and gasped, interrupting whatever he'd been saying.

"Hey!" She smacked him in the arm. "I have that same exact poster in my office! The Joshua Tree National Park one."

"I know." He cleared his throat. "You also have..." And he walked a few steps further into the hallway, switched on a light. "This one."

She gasped and smacked his arm again. "Hot diggity dog!"

Dell's lip twitched; he covered his mouth with a hand as if to hide it.

"I also..." He dropped the hand and cleared his throat again. "I'm also pretty sure I went to that same Decemberists show, at Edgefield. The one you have a poster of."

Mae turned her gaze from the Olympic National Park poster to Dell's face.

"No shit," she said.

"Yeah." Dell laughed a little, looking away. "Anyway. I

usually work on the computer in here..." He walked through the hall, back toward the kitchen, and Mae followed, a sense of awe infused in every single thing that was happening just then.

The matching posters.

The way Dell seemed almost nervous, showing her around the details of his clearly beloved house, scratching his beard every ten seconds, clearing his throat every thirty.

Mae could only watch him until the awe filled her lungs, her throat, the corners of her eyes. She wanted to grab his hands every time he gestured to something, every time he ran them over a piece of furniture, and kiss every fingertip.

They were in Dell's laundry room when she thought, *here I am again.*

Each time her heart had been broken, whether through someone else's actions or her own—from Decree in the sixth grade, the first crush that had truly consumed her, to Becks, to Eden, and all the aches that had come in between—she always told herself she was done. She was her own best love; she didn't need any more of this mess. She'd never felt it as strongly as after Eden. She was *old*. Who needed it.

And then someone new showed up. Some new surprise. And she found herself here again.

As Dell pointed out random corners of his house, as they stood in each other's way in the bathroom and laughed, mostly breathless, like awkward kids, Mae thought maybe this realization should concern her. What had she just asked Vik the other day? Was she simply too susceptible to throwing around her heart? Did she attract heartbreak?

But as she examined every grain of wood in Dell's walls,

as she studied the crinkles of his eyes every time he glanced back at her, she only felt...grateful. To be here again. To feel this glow again.

How many times did one fall in love, over the course of a lifetime?

Maybe there wasn't only one answer.

Maybe there was no limit.

# *twenty-four*

"AND THEN, well, you've seen this one before—"

Dell had barely opened the door to his bedroom before Mae was on him.

He stumbled back at the force of her, a hand reaching for the wall to steady themselves, a laugh tumbling from his mouth into hers.

"Hi," she said, before swallowing his laughter down, commanding his lips with her own, swimming her tongue inside his mouth, her hands underneath his T-shirt.

"Mae," he managed to say after a minute, pulling away. "I want to go slower this time."

"Yeah," Mae breathed, eyes blown out, mouth so very pink. "I want to see you."

But even with the best of intentions, somehow the next ten minutes went by very fast, clothes shed without grace, hands moving with fervor, until he was on his back and her hands were on him, guiding him inside, and she was sinking down, down, eyes fluttering closed, sounds escaping her throat, tiny gasps and long breaths and it was only when she was seated, only when she started a slow, languorous rhythm, leaning over him to kiss his chest, his shoulders, bellies pushed together, that Dell caught his breath.

Not completely. But enough to breathe, to blink his eyes wide open and look.

He had been in such a hurry when he'd entered the ADU, taken over by such a desperate need, that he hadn't been able to fully absorb the details of her. When Dell had taken off Mae's shirt on that counter, revealing she was braless, Dell's main thought had been *TITS.* But now he took the time as Mae moved over him to run his hands over her shoulders, taking special care to investigate her left arm. The one with the tattoos. All the black lines and color.

"Incongruous," he said with a soft smile.

She smiled back.

"Incongruous does it for you, huh?"

"Yeah." He met her heavy-lidded eyes. "It does."

He'd spent enough time with her now, had cast enough glances at her arms to already know most of the tattoos, every flower, every trailing leaf and vine. But he had never had a chance to kiss them before. Had never had a chance to bite her tattooed shoulder, until now.

Her skin was salty underneath his tongue, soft underneath his teeth. She whimpered as he made his way down her arm, past the lavender and poppies and forget-me-nots, the barbs of all the stems and thorns in between. Until she lifted his own arm, removing it from where it caressed her side, to bring his hand to her mouth. His head dropped back onto the pillow as she kissed his fingernails, one by one.

"They're starting to chip," he rasped, wishing it hadn't been weeks since his last manicure, wishing they were fresh for her.

"They're perfect," she said before sucking his pinky into

her mouth. Each of his fingers followed, each digit wrapped inside her tongue until he couldn't help but push up into her, even deeper inside, until she was moaning around his thumb.

"Dell," she whispered, eyes closed as she finally let his hands drop. "Slow."

And Dell tried; he really tried to listen. To do his part.

But then Mae found a spot. A spot where the friction on her clit must have been just right. Where he was hitting her inside just so. Whatever was happening, a sharp gasp escaped her throat as her mouth dropped open, as those ombré eyelashes fluttered against her cheeks. It was a sound Dell heard in a place deep inside himself, deeper than his own pleasure, a sound he would never forget.

"Oh, *fuck*," she whisper-screamed. "Oh fuck oh fuck oh fuck."

Dell tried to lift his hips, to meet her halfway, but she smacked his arm.

"Don't," she breathed, moving against him abruptly, shockingly fast. "Don't you move. This is perfect. Perfect. Oh god."

"What are these?" Dell tried to grasp the pendants of her necklace in his fingers as they bounced against her chest. "These flowers. Do they mean something?"

"Dell. You cannot seriously be asking me this now."

"I want to know. I've always wanted to know."

"Oh god don't move. They're the state flowers of all the places I've lived. *Fuck*."

Dell dropped his hand and didn't move, only held onto her hips as she rode him, as she kept saying *fuck* over and over, barely audible, high pitched, a sloppy pleasure-filled symphony, until she was shouting and then suddenly silent. Her face was cherry red, forehead creased, and Dell could only look at the palette of her as she came, the pink of her hair and red of her cheeks, the pink of her mouth and the red of her tongue, the gold pendants quaking on her chest, the pastels of the tattoos caging his body in, and as he came soon after all he could think about was how she looked like dessert, like a sticky summer treat, like a spring garden showcase.

"Fuck me," Mae shouted as she collapsed on top of him, her breasts smooshed against his, her breath hot on his neck. "Oh god Dell that was so good."

"I'm glad," he murmured, arms wrapped around her back, holding her close, the way he always wanted to hold and be held, after. "I'm so glad."

On Monday, the glass in the picture window of Bay Books was finally replaced. Mae hesitated only an hour or two after the workers had left, and then she put up her flags once more.

On Tuesday, Mae and Dell fucked in the office.

She hadn't planned that particular chain of events, but Dell had taken to sneaking up behind her as she arranged and rearranged books on her shelves—Dell had installed four more of them; there were only three to go; there was so much space, now, for her to play with her books—and kissing her neck, wrapping his arms around her belly. It was a rather rude trick, she thought. She really did have a lot of work to do.

It was his fault that all the neck kissing inevitably led to Mae grabbing him, pushing him back, back, away from prying eyes, until they landed at her desk, until she was somehow in the same position she'd found herself in the first time they'd fucked, sitting on an inappropriate surface, Dell's thick body between her knees.

And as he slowly slid to his own knees, as he stripped her and then kissed her—breasts, stomach, thighs, the center of her—a tiny part of her brain held up a red flag.

*Not in your store,* it said. *Not here, not on this desk.*

Because she had told Liv she would die here. And if something went wrong with this, if something broke between her and Dell—

She wanted this store to be *hers.*

But as Dell broke her apart with his tongue, as he pushed her down and produced another condom from his pocket, as he eased inside her once more, the red flag disintegrated, tore into tiny shreds.

Because ever since Dell had set up his power tools outside the back door, just yards away from where he was currently inside of her, ruthless and almost painful in the middle of the day, Bay Books had become a bit his, too. Maybe it had always been a bit his. Maybe Mae couldn't fully imagine, now, not sharing every estimate and invoice with him. Not talking through every new idea and design with him. Not visiting the lumberyard together. Maybe, whenever she had a new idea, she thought, *we could do this.* And maybe at first, that *we* had meant Jesús. Because it had always been so easy to feel Jesús here, in this town, inside this old building. Maybe the *we* had often meant Vik.

But maybe whenever she thought *we* now, she actually meant Dell. Maybe she had meant Dell for a while.

"Shit," Dell muttered, soft and shaky in her ear, and he gave a final thrust, accompanied by that low, guttural sound he made just before he came.

He stayed there after, forehead pressed against her neck, after she navigated a hand between their bellies and rubbed herself over the edge, his beard prickly against her collarbone, his breath gusting down her chest.

"Which is which," he said while she was still shaking; eventually, she realized his hand was once more holding the pendants on her necklace. She brought her own sticky hand up to clumsily clasp around his.

"Flowering dogwood," she said, eyes drooping closed. "North Carolina."

Dell's fingers twisted underneath hers, holding another tiny flower.

"Blue violet. Wisconsin."

"Rose," Dell murmured, and Mae smiled.

"Yeah, that's the easy one. New York."

"So this weird one must be—"

"Oregon grape."

Finally, Dell let the pendants drop. Focused on Mae's fingers instead. Brought each one to his mouth, licked them clean.

On Thursday, Mae found her perfect centerpiece New Releases table at the flea in Florence with Olive. It was scratched, and a darker wood than her shelves, but it was the perfect size and had the perfect dramatic legs and she thought she might paint it, turquoise or pink or blue, something to match the rug and Gemma's murals and the waves of the ocean.

Olive owned an even bigger truck than Dell, and she wrapped the table in a packing blanket and secured it to the bed. And even though it was dark by the time they got back to Greyfin Bay and they were both sore and tired and the table was heavy as an anvil, Olive helped Mae get it through the front door of 12 Main, until it stood on the rug in front of the window. Until it was home.

"Hey," Mae said on Friday night, almost casually, as if she wasn't currently riding his dick. "If I ever found someone I wanted to fuck on the side, or...have something else with, would you be cool with it?"

Dell's brain, and his pelvis, stuttered to a stop. Mae grunted at the halt in rhythm.

"Sorry," he said automatically.

"Nah, I brought that on myself," Mae said, before readjusting her position over him and restarting her own rhythm. Her nipples tickled against his skin. This was Dell's favorite position with Mae. Fucking her against countertops was hot, but it also hurt his back. He liked her like this: resplendent in her own power.

"Sorry," Dell said again as he tried to bring his brain back online. He knew he should have had a better response to this question ready to go. He knew it was hypocritical if he didn't—if he couldn't—

But the thought of Mae moving this way with someone else made him want to die.

"It's okay, mon cherie," Mae whispered after a minute, and his heart tripped over itself. "You don't have to be okay with it. Or have an answer right now."

"But..." He sucked in a breath as he attempted to find words at the same time Mae was doing...this. "I'm pretty sure I do, Mae."

"No." She leaned down and kissed his neck. "It's not a zero sum game. You don't have to be okay with it." She lifted herself back up. "I don't have anyone or anything specific in mind, for the record; I was just curious. But I asked it poorly."

The flowers against her chest moved, a gentle sway as she slid against him.

"Every circumstance is different. It's probably a question that only really deserves a thoughtful response when there are details, you know? *Oh.*" Mae's eyelashes dropped against her cheeks as she found a good spot. "Oh fuck, please ignore me."

"No," Dell smiled at her, even if she couldn't see. "I find I can't ever ignore you, Mae."

Mae's eyes opened just enough to smile back at him. Until Dell pushed up into her, and her breath hitched, eyelids drooping low once more.

"How are you so..." Dell searched for the words as his brain fought to go offline once again. Rain slashed against the window above their heads. "So good, and open, about all of this."

"Oh, I truly don't know shit," Mae said, voice temporarily breezy again, and Dell laughed. "*Fuck*, that feels good. Fuck. I just..." Her mouth opened as she picked up her pace. Pink. So much pink. "I've just maybe been reading a lot," she finally wheezed, and Dell smiled again.

"Yeah." He leaned up to kiss her neck, this time. "Me too." And then, "Ask me again, if you ever need to, okay?"

"Okay." The pink spread across Mae's chest. "Okay."

"Remind me to work on my core so I can do this better next time," Mae panted on Sunday night. Or perhaps it was technically Monday morning. Time, in general, had started to go fuzzy for Mae. "I'm pretty sure I have one of those, somewhere in there."

Dell wheezed a strained laugh.

"Think"—*wheeze*—"you're doing just fine."

Mae was appreciative of the encouragement. Because while she had been into it from the moment Dell brought out his toy and harness, she hadn't actually done this before. And while it was working for her—there was a grooved lip of the vibrating toy that fit against her *just right*, bless its engineers—she was also sweating in a likely unsexy way, and her thighs were shaking, and she worried she kept fucking up the rhythm.

But her chest glowed each time Dell made another sound. Each second that he was clearly all in on this. That he trusted her with this at all. She dug her nails into his ass cheeks, earning herself another groan.

"Faster, Mae," he growled. And then, a second later, like the fucking angel Dell was on the inside: "If you can." And Mae leaned down to kiss his spine.

"Okay, but if I go much faster," Mae huffed out, re-gripping Dell's hips, "This thing—I'm gonna—"

"Yeah, me fucking too, Mae; that's why I'm asking you to do it," Dell ground out into his pillow, and Mae half wheezed, half laughed before she took a shallow breath and gave it her all. Dell's arm moved underneath himself; his other hand, holding the controller to the toy, clicked it up a notch.

"Oh *fuck*," Mae managed to say before her vision started to go black. It was a wild thing, everything about it completely out of control; so physical and ephemeral all at once, an absolute mess.

Dell had to help her out of everything, after. Mae wasn't sure she would ever move again. Except to move her lips, to say "oh my god" over and over again, until Dell laughed, and she shut her mouth, suddenly embarrassed. Until he kissed her so very gently, until he said "I know" and "thank you" into her ear.

Some minutes later, somehow, Mae found herself cozied under the blanket, cheek resting on Dell's shoulder. Blinking her eyes, she could just see over Dell's chest into his en suite bathroom, the toy and harness cleaned and drying on a towel on his countertop.

"Huh," Mae heard herself murmur. "An excess of dicks really can be fun sometimes. By no means necessary, but fun sometimes."

Dell rumbled a tired noise of assent. He kissed the top of her hair.

"In these particular instances, yeah. Otherwise...I've always been kind of take 'em or leave 'em, myself."

Something inside Mae paused. She made herself stir further awake, pushing back until she could see Dell's face.

Maybe she was reading too much into things. Maybe the hunches she'd always had were misguided. She should probably keep her mouth shut.

"Can I make an observation? One I probably wouldn't make if I wasn't extremely sex drunk?"

Dell shrugged, smiled at her. That barely-there Dell smile. His eyes were half closed.

"Sometimes I wonder," Mae said slowly, "if you aren't completely cis."

Dell's mouth, to Mae's immense relief, only slid deeper into his smile. His eyes closed completely.

"Yeah, well. Maybe I'm not."

Mae held her breath. Waited for him to say more.

"Sometimes I wish I had nice tits," he said suddenly. "God, your tits are incredible."

Mae honked out a possibly inappropriate laugh, immediately smothering it with a hand. But Dell only kept grinning, his eyes remaining closed.

She reined herself in. And slowly, carefully, she moved herself on top, straddling him again. God, she loved being on top of Dell.

She moved her hands toward his breasts. Caressed their sides, molded them in her palms until they lifted, curved and soft next to each other.

"Funny," she said. "I've always thought you already did."

Dell had opened his eyes, just the tiniest bit, to look up at her. After a moment, he lifted a hand, threaded his fingers into her hair, pulled until she acquiesced, dropping her head down for a kiss. And even as every muscle in her body ached, something deep in her belly still stirred as Dell stretched the kiss, as his tongue swirled with hers, both lazy and with intent, soft, soft, soft.

Until her limbs truly did threaten to give out, and she worried she might suffocate him, and she collapsed back to his side, molded herself there, forehead against his neck, arm across his stomach.

"Would you want...to explore different pronouns or anything, ever?"

Dell waved a tired hand. "Nah. I don't...I don't want to deal with all that."

"That's okay." Mae kissed his collarbone, unsurprised.

But a minute later, Dell spoke again.

"Maybe..." The words came as slowly as Mae's just had. "Maybe if you're ever around the house, talking to the dogs about me..."

Mae smiled against his skin.

"Yeah?" she whispered.

"Yeah. Maybe you could use *they* then."

Mae pulled back to see his face once more.

"So you're *they* to the dogs."

Dell smiled back, more relaxed than Mae had ever seen him.

"Yeah," he said. "I like that."

And then he added, "And you."

"Yeah," Mae whispered. "The dogs and me."

By the following Tuesday, Mae was spending every night in Dell's bed.

She hadn't fully meant for that to happen, either. But somehow, she had learned where the dogs' food was, how much they each took, which bowl belonged to Crosby, and Stills, and Nash, and Young. She learned how Dell took his coffee. Had memorized the shapes of his scars. Some mornings, before they headed into the shop, before either of them said a word, she curled herself inside a blanket on his leather armchair, drinking a mug of tea, looking through the sliding glass door at the mist through the trees, and listened to Dell play her favorite songs on his guitar.

On Wednesday, Dell installed the last bookshelf.

# twenty-five

ON THE LAST Thursday of October, Mae sat alone in the ADU and opened her planner. The rainy claws of November and all the gloomy months to follow inched closer, day by day. Even the weekend whale-watching visitors to Greyfin Bay had started to lessen; the weekdays were even quieter. Folks in the IGA were starting to share holiday plans.

And Bae Books was ahead of schedule.

There was nothing truly holding Mae back. She still had orders she was waiting on—she'd learned each vendor and publisher had its own quirks, requirements, and wait times. She still needed to work on signage, still had gaps where she wanted to fit more local merchandise.

But the bookshelves were done. The repairs and major remodeling were done. Dell had a security system installed last week. She had a business license and an inventory system. She had a lawyer and an accountant. She had a business bank account and a credit card reader.

She knew she'd have to hire at least one or two employees, but there were still a lot of unknowns to fill there. She'd chatted this week with Liv about Karizma, a local high schooler who currently worked weekends housekeeping at the Fin Inn, who also found herself pregnant at seventeen. From what Liv knew, Karizma loved to read.

Mae thought working weekends and a few days after school at a bookstore would likely be less physically demanding than housekeeping for a pregnant person, so she hoped to meet with Karizma soon. Send out a wider call when she knew how much help she might actually need. But for now, as the off season loomed on the horizon, Mae thought she could handle a quiet opening on her own. She already spent all of her days at 12 Main Street anyway.

Mae examined her planner. Sipped from a mug of tea.

And eventually, finally, she clicked open her pink pen and circled a date just under a month away, right before Thanksgiving, before holiday shopping truly began.

"November 21st, Jesús," she whispered. "See you then."

On Halloween, Dell was carrying in Bay Books's mail when his phone rang.

Five seconds into the phone call, Mae thought perhaps they had both been transported to a movie set. An alternate dimension where everything happened in slow motion, a scene she must have seen somewhere else before: the way Dell's eyes went blank, his knuckles turning white as he gripped the phone. The way the flyers and envelopes fell out of his other hand, fluttering to the floor like a slow dance.

Mae was afraid to speak when he hung up.

"Georgia had a stroke," he said. And, before Mae could respond, blinking down at the phone in his hand: "She's alive. She's okay. For now." His eyes were no longer blank when he finally looked up at Mae, where she was barely breathing, frozen behind the counter. "My mom had a stroke."

On a Friday afternoon, three weeks before Bay Books's opening day, Dell bought a one-way ticket to Michigan.

# twenty-six

DELL HAD FORGOTTEN the colors of Michigan in the fall.

There were colors in Oregon, yellows and oranges and an occasional red, but not like this. Even at the tail end of the season, the trees of his home state knocked him out.

There wasn't a direct way to fly into the UP, at least not if you didn't have your own prop plane. And Dell might have been milking the fruits of his previous real estate boom life for the last several years, but even he wasn't Luce County Airport rich.

Still, Dell tried to savor the long drive north from Detroit: the lakes and the colors, the peaceful flatness and occasional rolling hill. Told himself he was comforted by the trees, even as he drew farther north, as the branches became more bare. He wondered, distantly, if the UP would have snow. He hadn't thought to look at the weather. He hadn't been able to think about much from the second he'd gotten the phone call. He remembered Mae's eyes, the way she'd cautiously held out a hand in the store after he'd hung up; the way she'd held him in bed before he had to get up at 3 a.m. to drive to PDX. He remembered the drive to Portland, long and alone and dark.

But all of it, the last twenty-four hours, were a bit hazy. The memories blurry at the edges, like he had only been half there.

The only thing he truly knew was that Georgia was in the hospital.

He stopped once at a Culver's for some food—lunch or dinner or something else, he couldn't say; a rest stop or two when he needed it. But mostly he pushed on until he reached the Mackinac Bridge, and then a bit further than that. Until he was actually home. Until he was at that hospital.

And only when he locked the rental car with a beep, only when he walked through the whooshing automatic doors, only when he cleared his throat to actually speak to another human for the first time in hours did the haze go away. When he was being led to his mother's room, he was strikingly, solidly awake.

Dell knew most folks hated hospitals, but there was something about them that soothed him now. Hospitals had taken care of him after he'd been shot. The doctors and nurses and assistants had been kind as his brain and body attempted to adjust to a new life. This hospital was keeping his mother alive. This hospital was holding his mother safe.

Someone else was in charge.

Someone else was going to help.

Maybe he only felt this strange comfort inside these sterile spaces because he and Georgia had been on the lucky side of things. And from the scraps of information he remembered from the phone, Georgia had been extremely lucky. She'd been at the grocery store when she collapsed.

Amelia Hawkins had called 9-1-1 from the bakery department straightaway.

Except then the nurse opened the door, and Georgia was asleep.

"The doctor will be in when she can to give you an update, but her vitals are good," they'd said, and then they were gone, and it was just Dell and Georgia. And she looked so fine, other than the oxygen hooked up to her nose, the IV in her arm. She looked so peaceful. Maybe she was okay. Dell wanted to take her home.

And he had missed her so much, he *always* missed her so much, that seeing her at all, hospital bed or not, made him collapse into the bedside chair like a crumpled up Culver's wrapper.

He didn't cry. But he scooted the chair as close as he could. Rested his head next to hers, the only place there was space, chin on her shoulder.

And within a few minutes, he was asleep.

"Lots of good news here," Dr. Collins said, an uncertain number of hours later. Georgia was still asleep. "Because of how quickly she got to us, we were able to restore blood flow to the brain using the least invasive treatment possible. We'll do another CT scan soon to make sure things are still stabilized and there isn't any excess intracerebral bleeding. In terms of her recovery, we'll be doing plenty of tests in the coming days and weeks, but our initial monitoring over the last few hours has been very positive. Her motor and sensory skills seem minorly impaired, and she was able to swallow some water, which is great. She is suffering from aphasia, which might make it difficult for her to speak with you when she wakes up. It's common after a stroke, but hopefully the effects of that will also lessen over time. Neuroplasticity is an amazing thing. What we'll be focusing on for now..."

Dell prided himself on being pretty good at retention of information, but something in his own brain failed him here. Because about the time Dr. Collins said *she was able to swallow some water* like it was a minor miracle, he had a hard time comprehending anything else.

He had thought, after he'd almost died, that he did a good job at appreciating being alive. At least, he tried his best. Even immediately after a trigger, when he was shaky and weak, he was always grateful to still be alive. To still be surrounded by trees and water and sky, to have his dogs and his house.

But being grateful for the ability to swallow was something that didn't much cross his mind.

He hated that it had to now.

"The most important thing to know, in general, with strokes," Dr. Collins was saying, "is that there's an increased possibility of stroke patients having another one, especially within the first year. I'm hoping your mother's physical recovery from this one will be relatively smooth, but in addition to rehabilitation, we'll work in the coming weeks on a plan for what we call secondary prevention, to make sure Georgia's as healthy as possible in the aftermath. So that hopefully, we'll never have to have this conversation again."

Dr. Collins gave Dell a reassuring smile. Dell attempted to receive it.

*Rehabilitation. A plan. Prevention.* Dr. Collins had a plan. Georgia was safe. Everything was okay.

Dell swallowed.

"Okay," he said. "Thank you."

But after she'd left, all Dell could remember were the other phrases she'd said. *In the coming weeks. Especially within the first year.*

Dell had built her an ADU. He had tried to get her to come to him, but he must not have tried hard enough, and now—

What if she hadn't been at the grocery store? What if she wasn't, the next time? Someone needed to *be* with her.

He needed to convince her.

But for now, Georgia had won. Dell was back in Michigan. And only as he watched the sun slowly break through the darkness outside her hospital window did he fully realize that he had no idea how long he'd be here.

He hoped CSNY would forgive him.

He reached out, again, to squeeze his mom's hand.

He hoped Bay Books would, too.

When Mae was a kid, she always envisioned your forties as being the age you really got old. Jodi and Felix, in her memory, were perpetually in their forties throughout her entire childhood. Even though she knew it wasn't the case, she halfway imagined they were still in their forties now.

But as she stocked her shelves that first week Dell was gone, as she worked on her final project for her small business class, as she made tea and spreadsheets and folded laundry, thinking about Georgia all the while, she understood the truth of your forties. As she had understood when Steve passed away, when Jesús followed.

Your forties weren't really about being old at all.

They were about watching the people you loved most actually grow old.

They were about starting to lose people.

And being utterly unable to stop it.

After almost forty-eight hours of radio silence during which Mae drove to Lincoln City for a matcha latte, and then to Shelly's for French toast, and then to Newport for a walk along the beach with Jodi and Felix, and then to the sea lion caves, to spend some time with other fat and noisy creatures, and pretty much anything else she could do to keep her sanity—Dell did call. As the days stretched, he continued to call, occasionally. To let Mae know he and Georgia were still alive.

Sometimes, when the days stretched just a little too slowly, she broke down and called him. To his credit, he almost always picked up.

But Dell McCleary, as Mae had learned the first time she'd ever spoken with him, simply wasn't that good at the phone.

He answered all of her questions, such as, *How is Georgia doing? Is she talking better? Does she have a release day yet?* And, *How are you holding up? Are you sleeping? What was the last meal you ate?*

But he answered simply—*fine, a little, no, fine, yes, a hamburger*—never offering much more.

And Mae never asked the question she wanted to ask most of all.

*When are you coming home?*

It was selfish. A mother was more important than a bookstore.

Sometimes she also wanted to ask: *can I come?*

But somehow that felt selfish, too. Dell was more than capable of taking care of his mother on his own, a woman

Mae had never even met. It was presumptuous to assume she had that kind of place in Dell's life, after only knowing him for a few months. After a week of vigorous fucking.

She had committed to Bae Books. Had already told Liv and Olive her planned opening day, mere hours before Dell had received the phone call. Meaning that the majority of Greyfin Bay knew her planned opening day, and while it was possible that half of Greyfin Bay didn't want a queer running a bookstore in their town in the first place, she'd be damned if she proved herself to be a flighty queer on top of it all.

And so half of her conversations with Dell were filled with awkward pauses. Stretches of only breathing as Mae clutched her phone. Of wishing she could reach out and touch him, so badly it ached.

While Mae was always grateful to hear his voice, almost every time she hung up, she found herself feeling sadder than she had before.

She tried blasting Jesús's death party playlist around the store to help perk herself up, once she ceased panic-induced sea lion hangs and actually got back to work. But the truth was, she'd listened to these tracks so many times by now that even they started to make her feel sad. Even Judy.

Especially Judy.

Mae didn't want to keep thinking about the death party anyway. About the ocean outside her door that held Jesús's ashes.

She wanted to remember Jesús.

She wanted to remember trivia nights and excursions to try new restaurants; she wanted to remember Moonie's. She wanted to remember that one time they went snow tubing at Mt. Hood Skibowl, how she didn't think she'd ever heard Jesús laugh that hard, cheeks deep crimson with the cold and his glee, and Jesús was a man who lived to laugh. She wanted to remember the year they tried joining a queer bowling league, how Jesús had been the worst among them, his attempts at flinging the ball down the lane so bad they made Steve laugh until he'd cried, and Steve, in contrast to his husband, wasn't a man born to laughter. The nearby team of butch lesbians had been so far superior that it eventually made Theo salty enough that the games weren't really fun anymore, and they'd quit. But Mae wanted to remember how Steve later revealed that Jesús sometimes stopped by the bowling alley on Monday nights anyway, just to say hi to the butches.

She wanted to remember the murmur of his voice, the rumble of his laughter through her office wall. She missed the donuts he always brought to the center on Fridays. She missed hearing his thoughts on the Real Housewives of Atlanta.

She built her inventory, and she posted a countdown on social media, and she cried a little.

And then she went home to the dogs.

Half of her wanted to return to the ADU, to at least temporarily forget the days she'd spent in Dell's bed beside him, but she had to take care of the dogs.

Young adapted to her presence as the apparent new master of the household the best, happily jumping on her thighs each time Mae returned home. Stills was always stoic or sleeping. But Crosby and Nash, the golden retriever and the pittie, whined almost constantly for Dell, in the beginning.

"I know," she said, every night, wrapping herself around Nash, the one most willing to be hugged. "I know. I miss them, too."

# *twenty-seven*

WHILE THE HOSPITAL had let Dell sleep on his mother's shoulder that very first night, they kicked him out the next day. Which Dell had to admit, with guilt, he was okay with. He needed to sleep, and take a shower, and process the fact that when Georgia had finally woken up, shortly after that first visit from Dr. Collins, she hadn't been able to say Dell's name. Only a sleepy, surprised smile, followed by, "I—" and then a frown, and a small confused laugh as she attempted to reach a hand to his face, not fully making it there before her trembling fingers fell back to the bed, and then, "You know."

And then she'd fallen back asleep.

Without much else to do after visiting hours officially ended hours later, Dell returned to his childhood home.

He couldn't remember the last time he'd been here.

Michigan, he only fully understood when he walked into Georgia's kitchen, which still smelled like the lemon dish soap she had used for decades, existed in the Before.

Before the break-in.

He was so used to pushing Portland to the background,

to the Before. He hadn't thought he'd done the same to the UP. He thought about it all the time.

But maybe he only really thought about Georgia.

About getting Georgia out of here. To join him, in his After.

The house was so much the same as it had always been, the photographs and the blankets and the paintings on the wall a brazen declaration of Before, that Dell stood in the living room for a good ten minutes, staring at Georgia's handmade vases on the mantle above the fireplace, unable to move.

Eventually, his skin itched, and he remembered the need to bathe.

He dropped the duffel bag he'd haphazardly packed back in Oregon onto his old bed in his old bedroom upstairs. He'd told Georgia, countless times, that she could make it into something else: another studio for whatever artform she was practicing at the time; an exercise room. She scoffed each time.

"But where would you sleep when you come visit?"

He had to admit, begrudgingly, that he was grateful for her stubbornness at this precise moment. Their old couch would wreck his back, and no way was he sleeping in his mother's bed while she slept at a hospital.

He flicked on the light in the bathroom. And frowned.

And god, he *knew*. He *knew* Georgia had spent months remodeling this bathroom, two years ago now, at least. She'd talked about it throughout the whole process. He shouldn't have been surprised.

But this. This wasn't part of his Before.

This was Georgia's After.

And he didn't like that, either.

He didn't like that at all.

After a week, Dell grew tired of eating out. As in Greyfin Bay, there weren't necessarily a lot of culinary options here to begin with. And so even though he didn't want...to settle in here—and nothing felt more like settling in than grocery shopping—he found himself at the IGA. An IGA that wasn't owned by Liv. An IGA where his mother had had a stroke.

He unloaded the bags in Georgia's kitchen, added his new purchases alongside Georgia's staples; everything was in the same place, every cabinet as he remembered. He was too tired at the end to make anything but spaghetti.

And as he sat alone at his old kitchen table, the spaghetti tasted so good he almost cried.

And then he let himself stop trying so hard.

He wanted Georgia to be better.

He wanted to see her dip her fully functioning toes into the Pacific.

He didn't know how to be here anymore.

He ate and he cried and he fell asleep in a bed that had been too small for him for a long time, wishing for the heat of Mae Kellerman at his back, Crosby at his feet.

By the second week, Georgia still wasn't able to eat solid food or walk without assistance, but her speech was improving.

"Go," she said, irritated, flapping a hand at Dell. "See friends."

Dell stared at her blankly.

"Mom," he eventually mustered. "I—"

"Baseball," Georgia interrupted, even more irritated. And then, light entering her eyes, as it did when she remembered something, when the word traveled correctly from her recovering brain to her lips: "Chris." And shooing her hand again, back to irritated: "Go."

So. Feeling more like a child than he had in years, Dell set out to find Chris, and maybe Waylon, some of his best friends from high school, old baseball teammates, whom he hadn't talked to in well over a decade.

And he had to log on to fucking Facebook to do it.

After an enraging ten minutes of figuring out how to change his password, he sat on Georgia's couch and looked up Ryan first. His actual best friend from Before. But as he had thought, Ryan was in Chicago, with a wife and two kids and a cat.

Part of him still wanted to go see Ryan's folks, though, more than he wanted to see Chris or Waylon. He'd been a child who always felt more comfortable around adults than other kids. Like he was ready to be old.

But maybe Ryan's parents had actually gotten old. Maybe one of them had had a stroke, too.

No, Georgia would have told him.

Georgia had always been so good at telling him things.

Dell rubbed a hand over his face. Released a hard breath. And tried again.

Waylon was still in the UP, but had moved up to Marquette. And good for him.

Chris, though, appeared to still be right here, in the middle of fucking nowhere. The place Dell had romanticized in his head a bit, the longer he'd been away. The place he was struggling to reconcile, now that he was actually here. It was both as lovely as he'd remembered and as rough: a small, hard-working place. He could smell the snow coming in the air.

Dell sent Chris a message, both hoping Chris didn't check his Facebook messages and hoping he did, mostly so he wouldn't let Georgia down.

A couple hours later, they had plans to throw a ball around at the park the next night.

Throwing a ball around in November in the UP was a fucking dumb idea.

"Shit, it's cold." Dell rubbed his hands along his arms, mitt stuck under his armpit. He'd had to root around the garage to find it.

"Yeah, nice to see you too," Chris laughed. He held out a hand, drew Dell into a back-slapping hug when Dell shook it. "We can always head somewhere else if you want."

"Nah, this is good. Just do me a favor?" Dell rubbed his shoulder, already stiff from the wind. "Try not to slug me right here. Got an injury there, few years back."

"I'll do my best." Chris threw a dirty ball up in the air, caught it in his palm. "Been a while since I've actually done this with anyone." He smiled, and Dell found himself surprised at how easy this felt. "Thanks for reaching out, man. It's good to see you."

"Yeah. Good to see you, too."

They walked toward the outfield. The park was almost empty. A woman walked her dog around the perimeter. A bundled-up kid ran around the playground in the opposite corner.

"Sorry to hear about your mom," Chris said. "She recovering okay?"

"Yeah. Just has a lot of occupational therapy to do now. Doctors say she'll hopefully be back home in a few weeks. It was good it happened where someone could call for help."

"Yeah. Shit."

"Your mom doing okay?"

Dell almost said *your parents,* but at the last second remembered that Chris's dad had taken off back in middle school. Funny how many details he'd locked away about the people he used to know. How they were tumbling back open the longer he stayed here.

"Ah, well." Chris rubbed at his jaw. "Been struggling a bit with cancer for a while now."

"Fuck. I'm sorry, Chris."

"Eh, it is what it is. She's in remission now, which is good. But I don't know. You hear enough stories about it coming back harder than before..."

"Yeah." Dell almost left it at that, because what more could you say? But after a second he added, because Chris had answered his message, because he'd met him out here to play catch in the freezing cold: "Hope it doesn't, though."

"Yeah, me too."

And then they threw a ball around for a while. No need to talk. A blessed thing.

Dell had forgotten how much he loved this park, how peaceful it felt, like a secret hiding spot, nestled amongst the trees. Even when half of them were mostly bare now, it felt safe.

Dell missed the ocean.

But this was still nice.

"Shit," Chris said after a while. "My hands are freezing. You still good?"

Dell's hands were freezing, too.

"Yeah. Good for a little while longer, if you are."

"Yeah."

After a minute, Chris moved a touch closer. Easier to hear each other.

"You're still out in Oregon, right?"

"Yeah. Live by the coast now, though."

"Sounds nice."

"It is. How are you holding up here?"

Chris took a couple throws to answer.

"Made some dumb decisions for a while. But"—he threw the ball to Dell—"I'm sober now, so. Been working at the Department of Natural Resources down the road here for a while now."

"Yeah?"

"Yeah. It's a good job." Another throw. "And, uh. You remember Alyssa Welch?"

Dell held the ball in his cold fingers an extra second, frowning as he tried to remember.

"Name sounds familiar. Can't quite picture her face, though. You together now?"

"Yeah." Chris caught Dell's throw. "We didn't hang out much, back in high school. But...you kind of get to know each other. When you're the people who stay. You know?"

He didn't say it like a judgment. Even if he knew Dell *didn't* know.

Georgia knew, though.

Most of the rest of the McClearys had been good at staying.

Mae came to him, as she often did, a gentle pink surprise in his memories. This time, she was lying sleepily on a colorful rug over a hardwood floor.

*Books inspired me to get out of the small town I grew up in. And here I am, over twenty years later. And books have brought me back to another one.*

A feeling pushed in, somewhere in the back of Dell's mind, somewhere behind his ribs. A desire to know more about Mae's own small hometown. Why hadn't he asked more about it?

*Flowering dogwood. North Carolina.*

There were so many things he hadn't asked.

More distant, something his mind resisted, but wrapped up in it all the same: a need to tell Mae more about this place, too. His Before.

"Makes sense," he said, after his next throw. "Happy for you, Chris."

"How 'bout you?" Chris chucked the ball back, blew into his hands to warm them. "You with anyone, out there in Oregon?"

Dell contemplated the ball in his hand. Ran his thumb along the seam.

"Had actually just kind of started something up with someone, right before I got the call about my mom," he admitted. "So...unfortunate timing, I guess. Not that there's probably ever a good time for a parent to have a stroke."

"Or get cancer."

"Yeah. That too."

Another easy pause in conversation. Nothing but the whistle of the ball, the soft thud of it hitting leather.

"Bet she's waiting for you, though," Chris said. "The girl you just started seeing. You're a good guy. Worth waiting for."

And there Dell was, caught between an almost surprisingly earnest compliment and the discomfort of Chris's assumption. Made, Dell knew, without ill intent. Still, he couldn't help but wonder what Chris's reaction would've been if he was with Luca.

Or if he was with Luca *and* Mae.

Which led him to wondering, as he often did—especially during these long, lonely days of being back home—how Luca was doing. If he was back in Alaska. If he was still writing his book.

Dell chucked the ball toward his old friend.

"They're nonbinary, actually," he said. Even though he didn't know if that was the nomenclature Mae preferred. Still, he felt the need to do right by her, as well as he could.

Chris caught the ball. Shrugged.

"All right," he said. Chucked it back. "Point stands."

Dell caught it with a smile.

While Georgia's therapists used ropes and balls and other various implements to retrain Georgia's brain in how to use her body, Dell was issued the responsibility of board games.

She'd been moved to a different wing of the tiny county hospital; flowers and treats Georgia still wasn't quite able to swallow on her own adorned every surface. And in the corner of the room, a stack of old games Dell had unearthed from the closet across from the laundry room back at the house, their cardboard corners held together with curling masking tape.

In the middle of another round of Candyland on a Wednesday afternoon, an incoming text made Dell's phone buzz on Georgia's bedside table, beside the drooping lilies from Rosemary Clark, one of Georgia's best old teacher friends. Georgia motioned for him to check it as she struggled to flip over another of the small paper tiles.

Buffalo Springfield and Jackie Wilson played from a small portable speaker the hospital had brought in. The

Beach Boys and Herman's Hermits. This was supposed to help Georgia's brain, too. She hummed, moved her toes.

"Smiling," she said a few seconds later, and Dell looked up from his phone screen. "You." She reached over and poked him in the belly. Her eyes were bright, the frustration of trying to hold onto tiny objects flown away. "Tell me."

Dell glanced back down at the photo of Young wrestling with a new toy. He wondered if she'd bought it from Cara.

"Mae just sent me a picture of one of the dogs."

He held it out for Georgia to see.

"Young," he reminded her. "Collie mix. She's the newest member of the pack."

Georgia only looked, a faint smile lifting both corners of her mouth.

Dell moved to put the phone back down, but Georgia grabbed hold of his wrist, demanding to look at the photo longer. The strength of her grip—not overwhelming, but an undeniable pressure—made Dell's lungs inflate with hope.

But when she finally released him, turning back to the game, she didn't comment on Dell's dogs at all.

"Mae," she said instead, moving her tiny man to the next green space. Her smile deepened. "That's right."

# twenty-eight

"DO you just feel like vomiting all the time?" Vik asked. "I feel like vomiting and it's not even my store."

Mae smiled, rubbing her tired eyes as she turned away from the computer screen.

"No. But I think that's because I know you'll be here."

"Yeah," Vik replied, voice going softer. "But only for one day."

"Are you seriously feeling bad about offering up only one day of free labor? I can't thank you enough, again, for that one day."

"I know, but...you sure you'll be okay? Sure you shouldn't hire someone else?"

"What if I end up having four customers a day and I'll have made Karizma leave her housekeeping job for nothing?"

"Uh, I have a feeling there are more people in Greyfin Bay looking for part-time work than one teenager."

"I'll look for help if I need help. It'll be okay, Vik. I promise."

Vik was quiet a moment; Mae could envision them

chewing their lip. "Okay," they said. "Either way, I can't wait to see you. So fucking soon! God, is this what birthing a child feels like? It feels like your baby. Like I'm a proud uncle or something."

"I can make that your official title, if you want. Designer and Proud Enby Uncle, Bay Books."

"Perfect. Yes. Please."

"I am literally going to add it to the website right now."

"I'd be mad if you didn't."

"Anyway, actual pregnant people gestate for even longer than nine months and I've been here for three. Don't think it counts."

"Still long enough that Republican legislators would try to throw you in jail if you called it off."

"This metaphor is becoming very bleak."

"I know. Fuck, we live in bleak times. Thank Medusa you're opening a bookstore that's going to be full of joy and light."

Mae laughed.

"It's almost December on the coast. I'm already forgetting what light feels like."

"Exactly! That's why the world needs your store!"

"Ugh. Get here faster."

"Would if I could."

"I know."

"Maybe you should, I don't know, hire another employee to hold my space until I'm there. And to then continue holding my space after opening day. Just a wild idea. Throwing it out there."

"My my, look at the time. What do you know; I believe I have to go."

"Okay, bitch. I'll see you in two days. It's going to be incredible, you know."

"It'll be okay."

"*Incredible.*"

"I love you, Vik."

"Love you, too."

Mae stared out the front window after she'd placed her phone back on the counter.

She'd been doing that a lot, lately.

She knew she should be panicking about opening day being in three days, but the truth was, she'd had everything as ready as it was likely going to be a week ago. Any of the preparations, all of the spreadsheets she was crafting now merely verged on neurotic, moving things here or there, daydreaming about every possible thing she could keep track of in colored columns and rows. She ran home constantly to spend more time with the dogs, eventually drifting back to the store because she felt like she should. Because the store smelled less like Dell McCleary.

Mostly, these last few days, she spent her time staring.

She'd officially moved the pride flags last weekend. She found places for them elsewhere: behind the front door, on the wall by the end of the counter. She had never intended for them to obscure the view of the space forever. She wanted people to look, now, in the days leading up to opening. Wanted them to peer in and wonder. To see all she and Dell had done.

She'd stuck some stickers on the glass in their stead, in the corner closest to the door, next to a Black Lives Matter sticker, a small Palestinian flag. But she was still adjusting to it, the increased light, the view of the ocean behind Ginger's. It was a good spot for staring.

She knew Vik was right. It wasn't smart, for a number of reasons, for a store to only have one employee. Even Olive had several people on her staff, even if they weren't all full-time. Mae was grateful beyond measure that Vik would be there on opening day to help Mae through any rushes or hiccups.

But she had wanted to own something.

She had tried to be selfish.

Maybe it had worked too well.

Because now she didn't want to let it go.

It was possible nothing had ever been as much *hers* in her entire life as this little store, even if it had yet to open its doors to a single official customer. It was filled with all of her favorite books, with art and colors she loved, with pieces of this community, with things Dell and Vik had made for her.

Maybe she had only truly envisioned one other person behind the counter with her.

And that person had been so sure, at least for a time, that Mae would be the one to leave.

And while Mae knew he hadn't left because he wanted to, that there was nothing about this situation she had the right to feel upset about, it was still hard, sometimes, to swallow.

That she was still here.

And Dell was so very far away.

On the night before opening day, Mae stood in the center of the floor. Between the New Releases table and the table of local merchandise and gifts.

Vik and Jackson had gone to Dell's house to check on the dogs and wait on their pizza order. But Mae had wanted a little more time alone. A last hour when Bae Books was just hers.

She closed her eyes and remembered when the room was nothing but a bare floor and dust. When she'd danced, right here, all alone with Jesús's final playlist.

She remembered when she added the rug underneath her feet. When she and Dell had slept on it.

Her body had gotten stronger, these last three months. She spent a lot of time hunched over her keyboard, squinting at the computer screen, and maybe she'd never once used one of Dell's heavy duty tools, but she'd still become handy with a drill and a hammer. She'd done her fair share of heavy lifting.

Seriously. Boxes of books were fucking heavy.

She'd had her moments of doubt and soreness, but her body felt strong, just then.

She breathed in the last three months. Told herself to look at it all as it was, right now, one last time.

When she fluttered her lashes open again, a mote of dust danced in front of her eyes, highlighted by the rays of sun heading toward the horizon outside the window.

And like that, it all became clear.

She had wanted to own something. Something hers and hers alone.

But Dell had been there from the start. Telling her she couldn't.

And as she stood in this little shop, just one little space in this wide green Earth, she realized that even if Dell was gone—even if he maybe never came back—because she was starting to accept that he might not come back—he would still be in the bones of the place. She took a few steps to run a hand over the shelf closest to her. Crouched down to examine, again, the detail of the curving waves. Every time she touched them, it felt like touching the curve of his mouth, the rise of his cheek. The valleys at the corners of his eyes.

The more she looked, the more the others showed themselves, too: Vik's designs in every sticker and business card, in the sign above the front door. In the work of the Gutierrez boys, of Eli Zalasky and every other contractor who put in their time and skill. Mae couldn't walk across the rug without thinking of Olive and Cara.

Jesús was in every mote of dust that spun through the air.

Maybe this place wasn't hers and hers alone at all. Even if she was Bay Books's only ever employee.

Maybe nothing we ever tried—nothing good, anyway—was truly selfish, in the end.

On opening day of Bay Books, Mae woke slowly in Dell's bed, half-conscious and uneasy.

After the third snoozing of her phone's alarm, she made herself get out of bed.

She didn't want to.

She felt off, unlike herself, uncomfortable in her own skin. The opposite of how she wanted to feel on opening day. Vaguely, she recalled that she'd had some type of epiphany last night at the store, some great moment of peace, but whatever, that was still old naive Mae who hadn't *actually* opened a dumb small business yet.

Someone threw a *brick* through her *window.*

Mae brushed her teeth.

She'd had a steady job in Portland, a steady job where she helped people. She had her own apartment and good friends and a sense of safety.

She believed she could run a small business because, what? She liked stocking the shelves at Blockbuster when she was twenty years old?

She spit into the sink.

Oh god.

Mae let out the dogs, threw her hair in a bun. Checked that Vik and Jackson's car was still in the drive. They'd slept in the ADU, had actually insisted on it, even if that bed was definitely not big enough for both of them. Mae couldn't face them right now. She sent a quick text, a *going to the store early, join me whenever, seriously no rush*, and kicked her Kia into gear.

And the whole ride down to Main Street, she pictured hordes of angry middle-aged women walking into her store, picking up young adult novels with sex scenes and gay people, and screaming at her. Staring at the trans flag by the front counter and whispering to each other.

She parked in the alley, walked in through the back door. Put on the kettle for tea. Walking into the main room, she turned on the lights, booted up the computer. Retrieved the prepared cash till from the safe in the office, transferred it to the counter.

Mae knew she should be double-checking everything. Signage, displays, the security system, her scanners and POS system.

Mostly, she drank her tea and did a lot of staring. Vik had brought her a fresh bouquet of flowers: cosmos and coneflowers and yarrow. They sat next to the *pilea peperomioides*. The clock ticked away.

Fifteen minutes before open, a sense of overwhelming doom overtook her. Vik still hadn't arrived, which was fine, *good*; it was preferred to freak out alone.

The doom didn't have anything to do with Dell not

being here, with missing him, even if she kept checking her phone for a reassuring text from him—he'd been sending photos, lately, of the house where he grew up, of the town that looked rather gray and cold but still charming; she would kill for a picture from Michigan at this moment—but it was simply that this was all a *very bad idea.*

When time betrayed her, forcing her to move from her chair and flip the hand-painted sign she'd commissioned from Gemma to *Open*, Mae worried she might throw up.

Thirty seconds later, she'd barely returned to the counter when the door flew open with a jingle.

"Hi!" A middle-aged woman waved at her, dark blonde curls bouncing as she shook her body in a bit of a laugh. Three other women followed. "Sorry to be those weird people creeping at the end of the block waiting for the second you open!"

"We're just so excited," another one gushed. "We're in a book club, but we've never been able to buy books in our very own town."

"Oh, it's so good," a third gasped, staring around at the store. She hit the first woman in the side with the back of her hand. "I told you it'd be so good!"

"I know!"

"Well." Mae managed a wobbly smile. "Thank you for being Bay Books's very first official customers."

At that, all four women hooted, shaking their fists in the air. The sudden sound made Mae jump back a little.

"That was our goal!" The first one laughed. "Okay, ladies, before anyone else comes in!"

And they huddled in front of Mae's beautiful New Releases table, on her beautiful rug, between Dell's beautiful shelves, and took a selfie.

Mae blinked rapidly.

"I'm sorry," she said a moment later, finally getting a hold of herself and walking around the counter. "Can I get your names? I think I just fell in love with all of you."

And that was how Mae first met Robin, Carmen, Elizabeth, and Monroe.

"Sorry I'm late!" Vik called a few seconds later, rushing in from the office. "I cannot be*lieve* we slept in. I'm so sorry; that ADU is just—well, hello friends! Welcome to Bay Books!"

"Oh," Mae laughed. "I forgot to say that."

"That's all right, love." Vik kissed her on the cheek. "That's what I'm here for. Jackson's heading down to the IGA to buy all the pastries Liv has."

"Oh my god," Mae said. "Snacks. I was going to have snacks."

"That's what I just said, silly. Jackson's on top of it. What do you folks like to read?"

"Mae Kellerman!" Olive blustered through the door. "I was supposed to open my own shop ten minutes ago, but I just had to stop in first to see how you're doing. Oh, it looks *wonderful*." Olive squeezed Mae's arm, just above her elbow, so tight it almost hurt. "Robin! Doesn't this place look great? I *am* a little mad you stole this table from me at the flea." She frowned, running her fingers along its curved edge, shooting Mae a look in the New Jersey-honest way that Mae knew meant she *was* still a little mad. As she had been mad, at the flea, about every piece Mae found before her.

Mae felt her smile wobble again.

"Thank you for letting me steal it from you," she said. "Thank you for everything."

"Oh, no you don't!" Olive threw up a hand, blocking her face from Mae's view, waving at her cheeks with her other hand. "Not this early in the morning, Mae Kellerman. Oh! You have Francesca!" Still waving at her cheeks, Olive stepped toward the first shelf on the far wall. The first shelf Dell had installed. Local interest. Olive picked up the book of poetry from the writer who lived in Coos Bay. "Me and Robin saw her speak at the library in Newport last year! Oh, she's just *fabulous*."

"Excuse me, Small Businessperson of the Year!" Vik called from the counter. "I believe you have your first official sale, and the computer's gone sleepy."

Wiping her palms against her eyes, Mae shuffled herself behind the counter, tapping her POS system awake.

"Robin, right?" she confirmed. "What did we find today?"

Robin bought a thriller and a sticker and one of Kennedy Remington's candles and didn't stop talking the entire time Mae rung her up. Mae was definitely in love with her.

The book club ladies were just leaving when Gemma walked in. They held the hand of another person whom, with delight, Mae couldn't discern the gender of whatsoever.

"Wanted to show them my work," Gemma said.

"Of course." Mae stepped into the corner, lifted her arm toward Gemma's mural like Vanna White. "Vik, this is Gemma, my muralist."

"Oh, rad!" Vik pumped Gemma's hand up and down. "It's so great to meet you."

The door opened once more with a *whoosh*, and the waitress from The Bay Diner who had been nice to Mae once walked in. Followed by George and Aryanna, from her small business class in Newport.

"Oh—my gosh," Mae stuttered. "You guys didn't have to come all the way up here."

"You kidding?" George stuffed his hands in his pockets, the wrinkled brown skin of his face deepening as he smiled, eyes roaming the room. "You're an inspiration to us."

But then Mae noticed Gemma and their partner hovering by the front counter, and she didn't have time to chat.

"Let me know if you need anything," she said before hustling back to the till.

"This is cool," Gemma's partner said as Mae rang up their first item. They glanced again at the mural behind Mae, shot Gemma another grin. Glanced toward the trans flag at the end of the counter, and shot one at Mae. "This is really, really cool."

They were buying a stack of queer romance novels.

"Thanks," Mae said, her heart fluttering inside her chest.

She remembered, within that very first hour, what had been the best part, in the end, of every one of her previous jobs. Even if she often forgot.

Talking with strangers.

An act that had also been the hardest part of every job.

But sometimes, it was the most surprising form of art.

Liv's words had never truly left her, but she felt them in every heartbeat of today.

*You have to talk to people, Mae.*

*Say hi, sometimes.*

The next person to say hi back was a short white woman with feathery hair Mae hadn't even seen walk in. Mae greeted her with a smile and started ringing up her stack of picture books.

"My baby's gonna have a baby!" The woman declared

with the zeal of a grandparent-to-be. "I can't wait to read these to my grandbaby."

"Congratulations," Mae said. "Picture books are just the most beautiful things."

"Aren't they, though? I'm so glad you're still up and running here, even with that horrible incident with the window. I am *so* sorry about that, by the way."

Mae's smile faltered.

"Oh," she said. "Thanks."

The woman leaned in as she handed over her credit card.

"Say. Did they ever find who did that?"

For the first hour of Bay Books's opening, Mae hadn't thought once about that brick.

And she didn't want to now.

It wasn't the same thing as what had happened to Dell, wasn't near the same thing, but she understood his feelings about his attacker even more deeply now.

She didn't want to know who did it.

She just wanted to forget it had ever happened.

"No. I'm just focusing on the here and now." Mae forced a smile as she placed the woman's picture books in a paper bag, stamped with Vik's logo.

"That sounds like a good course of action. Thanks again!"

Mae focused on calming her pulse as she waved goodbye.

And not two seconds later, Jodi and Felix walked in.

She would *not* cry in front of her parents again. Why had that woman's comment affected her so much anyway? She was okay. Jodi and Felix were here.

"Oh, Mae." Jodi stopped short, a hand over her mouth.

Felix didn't stop for a second, heading immediately to the history section.

"Mom! Dad." Mae stepped out from behind the counter; Vik seamlessly took her place. She hugged her parents in turn. "How was the ride? Thanks for coming."

"We were careful. Drove the speed limit the whole way. Had a whole angry line of cars behind us. Oh, Mae, this is somehow exactly as I pictured it. It's so *you*. It's beautiful."

Mae would *not* cry in front of her parents again.

"Would you look at that." Felix's arm wrapped around Mae's shoulder. "It appears as if you bought every single one of my suggestions."

"Of course I did, Dad. I own a bookstore now. I need your nerd knowledge more than ever."

"You're going to get me choked up, here." He squeezed her shoulder, like he actually might get choked up. Except then he said, "And how have sales been going?"

"Dad. We've barely been open an hour."

"All right, all right."

"I'm going to look around, but we were thinking of making a day of it," Jodi said. "We'd love to see where you're staying up here, after you close up. Maybe celebrate with some dinner."

"Mom," Mae said. "I don't close for eight more hours."

"Mae," Jodi said. "We're retired. We have eight hours. Anyway, we won't be in your hair the whole time, and we won't stay long—"

"You'll leave before it gets dark? You really shouldn't be driving in the dark."

Jodi rolled her eyes. "Yes, Mae, we'll leave before it gets dark."

Mae's shoulders relaxed under her father's arm. "Yeah. Yeah, that sounds great."

"Can I check out the office? And the upstairs?" Felix asked, looking behind their shoulders, already analyzing every nook and cranny behind his glasses.

"Nothing's up there right now, but sure. Go wild, Mom and Dad."

"Mae Bae," Vik said two hours later, after Jodi and Felix had left, after another series of customers had rolled through. "Go take a break, okay? It's lunchtime."

"But—"

"Mae Kellerman." Vik used their serious-shit voice. "Go sit down."

So Mae grabbed a pastry, and she sat down. It was quieter in the office, but she could still hear Vik and Jackson out front, the din of the playlist she'd carefully curated for opening day, the murmur of customers.

Customers.

A wave of surrealness washed over her.

She brought out her phone, and bit her lip on a smile.

She swiveled in her chair to look out the back door as she opened the voicemail, to gaze at the raised beds and the place where she still hoped to see him, somehow, each morning she drove in.

"Mae."

It was followed by a short sigh of frustration, but as with every time Dell McCleary had ever said Mae's name, Mae shivered.

"Dammit, the time change keeps getting me, somehow. I must have just missed when you opened the doors, but... Mae, I wish I could be there." A pause. Mae imagined Dell's throat moving under his beard as he swallowed, a calloused hand running over his face. "But no matter how the day goes, you got this, okay? It's gonna be...it's gonna be fantastic, Mae. I'm so fucking proud of you."

Mae had been trying to keep her cool, let his voice breeze over her. But she almost gasped when he punched out the curse. He felt so present in that curse, so earnest and intense, like he was suddenly there again, next to her.

Except then he finished with, "I can't wait to hear how it goes. Talk to you soon," and when the line went silent in her ear, she tried, as she always tried, to not hear all the missing words he never said.

*I'll be back to see it soon.*

*Can't wait to see you again.*

"Hi," Mae said to a freckled woman with shiny red hair, when she returned to the floor. She forced a smile. "Welcome to Bay Books."

*Say hi, sometimes.*

"Oh my gosh, are you Mae?" The woman smiled in return, wide and toothy, holding out a hand. "Quinn. I've been following you online."

"Yeah? Do you live in Greyfin Bay?"

"I do, but I work remotely for an insurance company, so I rarely ever leave my house." She laughed, a bit self-deprecating. "But I've had your opening day on my calendar for weeks. Seriously, I need more reasons to make myself leave the house. Oh no, you have journals."

Quinn was beautiful, in that way people who were kind at heart always were.

"Of course I have journals. We all need pretty things to buy and then never use."

Quinn grinned. "Exactly."

A pair of goth teens stopped in next, who were first thrilled Mae had a graphic novel section at all and in the next breath, declared it "pretty mid." They gave her a list of titles she should buy for next time.

As the afternoon progressed, the locals who dropped in mixed more and more with weekend tourists, until at last, finally, Liv walked in.

She gusted out a breath, lifting up her baseball cap to rub at her forehead.

"Sorry I couldn't get here earlier, hon," she said. "One of my distributors—"

Mae cut her off with a hug.

Liv tapped her lightly on the back before pulling away.

"I'll allow it. This time. Anyway, how have things been going?"

"Good. Really good. Hey, actually, if you see Taylor Nguyen around, can you let her know I bought a bunch of Pokémon books for Lanh? I haven't seen them in a while." Seeing the goth girls had made Mae think of it. She wasn't sure, actually, if she'd seen either Taylor or Lanh since that first day in the IGA.

Liv's face fell.

"Mae." She shook her head, squeezed the brim of her baseball hat in her hands. "Taylor and Lanh are gone."

Mae's stomach dropped.

"Gone?"

"I mean—" Liv gestured emphatically, "they just moved. Sorry. They're okay. They're just not in Greyfin Bay anymore." She sighed. "Lanh's mom, Melody, is sick. That's why Taylor, Lanh's auntie, was always taking care of him. Melody needed better medical care, and Lanh needed more support, too, at school." Liv crossed her arms, looked out the window. "I mean, his setup here wasn't *so* bad; schools are still federally mandated to provide special education services, even in places like Greyfin Bay. But it'll get harder when he has to head to middle school, and Melody or Taylor would've had to travel farther to get him there, to attend all his meetings."

"Wait. Where *do* kids go to middle school? And high school?" Mae knew of the tiny elementary school in Greyfin Bay, further up on Klamath. But now that she thought on it, she had no idea where any other school was.

"There's a middle-high school county complex up north of Lincoln City," Liv said. "Or folks can petition for their kids to attend down in Newport."

Mae bit her lip, joining Liv in her stare out to Main Street. Distantly, Mae remembered that she herself had a bit of a drive to get to her high school, back in North Carolina. But it had felt normal at the time, because it was all she knew. Because Mae was able bodied and neurotypical.

She had forgotten, over her adulthood of living in cities with ample services. That it wasn't just matcha lattes that required extra effort, when you lived in a small town.

"Damn," Mae eventually said. "That's hard."

Liv sighed again.

"Yeah. I mean, it happens. Sometimes, folks have to leave. It's just...it hurts, you know. The more divided we become. When you lose another family that wasn't part of the majority. When you lose good people."

"Yeah." Mae's stomach sank even further.

"Anyway." Liv stuck her baseball cap back on her head and chucked Mae on the shoulder. "Sorry to be a bummer on your special day. There'll be more kids who want to buy your Pokémon books, believe me." Liv looked around the space with a smirk. "One day you'll be thinking this town's hit rock bottom, and then the next, some babe with pink hair will move in and open up a queer bookstore."

"Liv Gallagher." Mae beamed. "Did you just call me a *babe*?"

"Eh, don't let it go to your head. Listen, I gotta get back to the store. Just wanted to stop and say congratulations. So, congratulations, Mae. This really is a hell of a thing. Hope it stays around for a while."

"Yeah. Me too."

With another, softer chuck on Mae's arm, Liv was gone. Mae smiled at her retreating form until she was out of sight. And then the smile faded, as she thought about Lanh and Lanh's family.

She didn't have much time to dwell.

Because a few minutes later, the door burst open with Bay Books's loudest customers of the entire day.

"Honey!" Theo shouted. "We're home!"

And before Mae could even comprehend what was happening, Ben was wrapping her in a hug.

"Bay Books?" Theo continued. "More like *Gay Books*, am I right?"

"He's been practicing both of those lines for the last two days," Ozzy said.

"But—" Mae looked back at Vik and Jackson, who were smiling behind the counter, to Theo and Ozzy and Ben and Alexei. "But I didn't know—you didn't have to drive all this way!"

"And miss the opening of Bae Books? Bitch, please." Theo kissed her on the cheek. "And anyway, you know I love an excuse to start the weekend early."

"Yeah," Ben said. "Did you think only Vik and Jackson got to partake in the fun?"

"Well." Mae placed her hands on her hips. Let them drop. "Well. Thank you and I love you."

"Aw, it's even more special when you sound angry

about it," Ozzy said. And then he kissed her cheek, too. "Congratulations, Mae."

"Let's go buy some *books*!" Ben clapped his hands, and the group dispersed to look around. To browse with friends.

Except for Alexei. Who hung back by the window with Mae.

"Thank you," he said. He gave a long glance out the glass before looking back at her. "For giving us a reason to come back here. It feels like getting to visit them, you know?"

Mae nodded, throat thick.

"Yeah," she said. "I know."

"Lex! Mae!" Ben called. "You *did* connect with Emerson!"

Alexei and Mae exchanged a smile before turning to meet Ben at the table of local merchandise, including some salsa, jam, and other preserves from Short King Farms. Ben held a jar of pickles, mouth open in glee.

"Of course I did," Mae said.

"The pickles. Have you tried them? The pickles are so good, Mae."

"We already have a jar of Emerson's pickles at home," Alexei said.

"But we haven't purchased a jar of Emerson's pickles *from Mae*," Ben said. And Alexei shrugged, smiling at him helplessly.

"Where should we go to celebrate?" Theo asked after he'd made his purchases.

Mae almost opened her mouth to point out that there weren't necessarily a lot of places in Greyfin Bay to celebrate that were open past seven. That she felt comfortable enough in to be celebratory.

She'd contemplated maybe going to the brewery by

Lincoln City with Vik to celebrate, the one Liv had told her had a gay bartender. But she found, in her exhaustion, that she only wanted to be with the dogs.

"Jodi and Felix are here, too," she said. "Is just some takeout at the house okay? There's a Thai place that's pretty good."

"Sexy mountain man's house?" Ozzy asked, and Mae almost corrected him. She no longer thought of Dell as a mountain man, as a man at all. She only thought of him as Dell.

But not all things were hers to reveal.

"Yeah," she said. "At Dell's."

When her friends finally left to visit the beach, Mae pushed Vik and Jackson out the door to go with them.

When it came time to flip the sign on the door to *Closed*, to count her day's earnings for the first time, Bay Books was quiet.

Mae took out her phone.

*Went better than I even dreamed*, she texted.

And, after only a moment's hesitation, a statement equally as true: *I miss you*

And then she took a deep breath. And eventually, after the numbers were tallied, she locked the safe. Turned off the computers, the heat, the lights. Until she was ready to step through the back door and head home.

So it went in a small town, as in a city: some highs and some lows, until the day was done, and you tried again.

Jodi and Felix left before it was fully dark, as promised.

Vik and Jackson slept again in the ADU; Ben and Alexei took the guest room, previously only ever occupied by Liv.

Theo and Ozzy had a rental cottage reserved just south of town; they left at ten. “All these bitches assured me there’d be room in this place to sleep on the floor or whatever.” Theo kissed her cheek before they left. “But I’m too old for that shit.”

Love.

Even in Dell’s absence. Even in the forever absence of Jesús and Steve. Mae was surrounded by love.

No limits.

# twenty-nine

ON THE LAST Saturday of November, Georgia McCleary was released from the hospital.

She still had regular occupational therapy, a full schedule of appointments to follow through on. Dell installed a grab bar in her shower, helped move her bed from her upstairs bedroom to the living room, a temporary situation until the doctors signed off on Georgia navigating stairs on her own.

A temporary situation until Dell convinced her to move to Oregon.

"You know," he said as he put together, upon Georgia's request, the artificial Christmas tree she'd been using for years, "this could easily fit in the corner of the ADU. Although this one looks like it's seen better days anyway. We can get you a new one."

Georgia watched Dell fit it into its stand.

"More to the right," she instructed from the bed.

Georgia, for better or worse for Dell, had almost full speech capability again.

"Do you get yourself a tree?" she asked. "Out there in your new house. Do you put up decorations?"

Dell shrugged, adjusting some of the wire branches.

"I haven't gotten a tree the last few years. But I normally put up a few things. The things you've given me, mostly."

Georgia frowned.

"You should get yourself a tree, Dell. Don't they have lots of trees in Oregon? I bet you Mae loves a Christmas tree."

Before he could stop himself, Dell snorted. He could only imagine the kind of Christmas decorations Mae Kellerman loved most. Likely the ones most covered in glitter.

"When are you getting back to her?"

Dell's smile sank into a sigh. Georgia had started asking this with increasing frequency.

"You need someone with you, Mom. You might be out of the hospital, but you're still recovering."

"I do have friends, you know. Lots of 'em, in fact."

"I know." The fridge was entirely stocked with casseroles for the next six months. Dell's diet was now composed of pasta and cheese. If being back in the UP had taught Dell anything, it was that Georgia McCleary had friends. "But I'm your son."

Georgia sighed. "Oh, Dell."

Dell sat back on his haunches.

"I don't want to fight while we decorate the Christmas tree," he said, voice quiet.

"I don't want to, either," Georgia said, after a stretch of silence.

"Okay. Then let's not." Dell stood, hauling over the first box of ornaments. "Come on. Adaline said trying to put these on would be good fine motor practice. Up and at 'em, McCleary."

"You," Georgia grumbled as Dell handed her an ornament, "are a pain in my fine motor ass."

The next day, the first snow arrived.

And not even Christmas decorations could stave off the fight then.

Dell stared out the window at the sugar maple in the backyard, already fully covered in white, and worked his jaw back and forth.

"Mom," he said, voice quiet but firm. "Mom, you can't stay here."

Georgia turned from where she'd been working on a puzzle. Not one of the puzzles that still lived in the closet across from the laundry room, but a puzzle meant for children that Adaline had given them, with larger pieces, easier for Georgia's fingers to hold.

"Excuse me?"

Dell sighed.

"Mom, truly, no one should stay in the UP through the winter, but especially not someone recovering from a stroke."

"I have lived here my entire life, Dell," Georgia said, voice icy, "and snow hasn't stopped me yet."

"But maybe it should."

Georgia threw up a hand, turning back to the puzzle.

"I'm not having this conversation with you again."

Dell took a slow breath. He knew this particular iteration of the conversation had already gotten off to a rocky start, but he had to see it through.

"I'm sorry, Mom. But we *need* to have this conversation again. You shouldn't be alone. I know you'd still want your independence, which is why I built the ADU; it's your own private space. And I know you'd love—"

"Dell, I swear to god. I've tried to be kind about this in the past, but I am never moving into that damn ADU, as beautiful as it is."

"Mom." Dell held his head in his hands. "I miss you, okay? I want you closeby."

"And you don't think it breaks my heart?" Georgia suddenly shouted, a puzzle piece flying through the air. "To have you so far away? You're my entire world, kiddo. You always have been. My whole world. And I need you to stop reminding me, all the damn time, that you are thousands of miles away. Because I already know. I feel it every single day."

A horrible silence crackled through the living room. Dell thought his chest might cave in.

"I'm sorry, Mom," he whispered. "I'm so sorry."

"Ah, shit." Georgia's voice wobbled. Dell looked over to see her covering her own face with shaky hands. "*I'm* sorry, Dell. Please, forgive me. I didn't mean to say all that."

Dell wanted to go to her. Wanted to stop being angry at her.

Wanted to stop breaking her heart.

But it was still snowing, and she was still recovering from a stroke, and he didn't know what else to do.

He'd just opened his mouth to make another point when she dropped her hands and, with a tear-streaked face, looked right at him when she sang, "We ain't angry at you, love." A line to a song Dell wished she didn't know. He knew it had been a mistake, introducing Georgia to Noah Kahan.

He rubbed a hand over his face, turning back toward the window. Turning his back on his mom.

"You know the history of the McClearys," Georgia went on, as if she had not just caused Dell physical pain. Of course he knew the history of the McClearys, having heard Georgia's and his grandparents' stories many times before, having seen the photo albums and family trees. McCleary was his mother's name; he had changed it as soon as he was old enough to do so himself, leaving behind the name of his father, whom Dell didn't even remember. Dell had never once thought about that old name again.

"We came in through the island, like everyone else," Georgia said, repeating the story anyway, as Dell knew she would. And Dell couldn't help but turn back to her, to finally walk over to her and sit at her side, in gratitude that her speech and her memory had recovered enough for her to tell this story once more. "But the crowds of New York overwhelmed us. So we started the slow trek west, but the coal mines and steel factories of Pennsylvania and the Midwest suffocated us. So we started north instead, until your great-granddaddy came here. Where the trees were big, and the view was clear."

Georgia reached out a hand, no longer tremoring, and clasped it over his.

"You just needed to keep on goin', Dell," she whispered. "You went until you found even bigger trees. Ain't no McCleary who could get mad at you for that. Including me. Please believe me about that, honey."

Dell sighed.

"You would like those bigger trees, too," he said, stubbornly.

"Oh, Dell." Georgia sighed in return. "I'm sure I would.

But I've tried to tell you so many times. You know I'm a Yooper, through and through."

Dell had known, in some corner of his body, that every time she had, indeed, told him this before, she'd meant it. Even as he built an entire structure on his property in Oregon for her, that part of himself knew he was pursuing a useless dream.

But all the other corners of his body had needed to do it anyway.

"Mae's parents are from North Carolina," he said. "But they moved to the Oregon Coast, so they could be closer to their kid. So they could retire by the ocean instead of"—he gestured to the window, where the snow came down ever fiercer—"this."

He hated himself a little, as soon as he stopped talking. Didn't want to compare Georgia to Jodi and Felix, like some kind of parenting contest. He knew Jodi and Felix weren't better parents than Georgia.

Because Georgia was the best.

But he hadn't been able to stop thinking about Jodi and Felix, ever since he got on the plane to come out here. He'd spent so many minutes of recycled air in the middle of the sky being just so fucking angry about it.

"Well." Georgia shrugged. "I'm happy for them. But I'm not Mae's parents. I'm me. And this is who I am."

And something about the way Georgia said this, so matter-of-fact, made it finally, finally stick. Like a stitch in Dell's side, sharp and insistent, but with an inevitable dulling waiting in the future. Some folks were able to move easier. Some had deeper roots. Maybe there wasn't anything superior about either choice.

"I would like to meet Mae's parents, though," she said after a moment, voice turning thoughtful. "I know I can come out there and visit more, as easily as you could visit more here, too. I do apologize for that. You just know how I feel about planes." She waved a hand again. "Flying death traps. But I'll be better about that, now."

Except—dammit, couldn't she see she could barely complete a children's puzzle?—she *couldn't* visit just as easily as he could. He tried to picture her driving all the way to Green Bay or Great Rapids, sitting alone on a flying death trap, all the way to Oregon. What if another stroke struck her while she was driving? While she was sitting in the plane? What if the other passengers only thought she was sleeping? What if no one knew until it was too late?

Dell closed his eyes and took another deep breath.

No more fighting.

"You came when I needed you," he managed, after a moment. She had been there, at the hospital, after he'd been shot.

"I'll always be there when you need me," Georgia said. And then, tilting her head, as if remembering she had almost just died, "Well, I suppose as long as I can, physically. But the thing is, honey, we're both grown people. I love you, with my entire heart and soul, but I don't *need* you in the way you think I do. Just like I know you don't need me, either. I'm still always a phone call away when you experience a trigger, when you're having a rough day. You can get through the rest on your own. Sakes alive, Dell, you've been self-sufficient since you were fourteen."

And Dell couldn't help but laugh. And somewhere in the midst of it, he started crying.

Without a word, Georgia drew him in, wrapped a too-thin arm around his shoulder.

"Oh, hon," she said. "It's gonna be okay. Except," she added, "if you don't get the hell out of my house soon."

Dell couldn't summon a reply. Until later, when Georgia had completed the puzzle, and eaten some soup for lunch, and they both sat together in front of the TV while the snow continued to come down, rating the costumes on *Let's Make a Deal.*

"Make Rosemary come with you," he said during a commercial break. "Whenever you decide to come visit Greyfin Bay."

Georgia was silent.

"Or someone. Wait for me to come and fly out with you. Just...don't fly alone, okay? Please. I'll stop talking about the ADU. Promise. This is the only compromise I'll demand."

Another thirty-second commercial break later, Georgia patted Dell's knee.

"Okay, kid," she said. "Okay."

Time grew sticky as the air grew cold.

Some days passed fast, some dragged slow. Dell watched Georgia get better at some things, struggle with others. They bickered. He watched more TV than he had in years. They ate casseroles, the opposite of Dr. Collins's secondary prevention plan, but you couldn't stop the Midwest from being the Midwest. Couldn't let kindness, or cheese, go to waste. Georgia relayed stories he'd never heard before.

Dell worked on accepting it. That Georgia wouldn't join him in his After.

Some days, it felt like he'd been stuck here, in his oldest Before, for ages. He knew he should be communicating with Mae more, but he just felt so far away. From Mae, from the dogs, from Greyfin Bay. He could barely remember what it all smelled like.

Eventually, as the snow piled up, a new realization started to dawn.

Maybe he hadn't been working hard enough. At actually healing.

Maybe he needed to meld all of his Befores, all of his Afters.

Maybe he needed to stitch it all back together.

One morning while Georgia still slept, Dell opened his laptop. He logged in to MLS, the real estate database he'd used for the last twenty-five years of his life. He typed in his hometown.

A day later, through icy winds, Dell once more walked some property.

Some land he could borrow. A patch of the earth to conserve.

A new space to help him stitch himself together.

"Hey, Mom," Dell said one afternoon as he looked out the window of the living room. The sun was peeking through the clouds, slanting through bare trees. "Do you know what Michigan's state flower is?"

"You know, I don't believe I do," Georgia answered. "Or maybe I did one day, and my brain hasn't recaptured it. Google it for me, hon. That's a thing I'd like to know."

# *thirty*

MAE HIRED Karizma after Bay Books's opening weekend.

After the second weekend, she hired Zeke.

Both part-time, and she worried she wouldn't be able to sustain even those part-time hours after the holiday rush was over. But for now, they were a small team. For now, they helped Mae keep her head above water.

She spent more time in the office than she ever had before, as the days went by. Going over sales and inventory and budgets, schedules and payroll, each day after closing time.

As she had known it would, that day it happened, the desk always made her think of Dell.

She didn't always remember the details of that day specifically, but rather, the essence of Dell McCleary she missed most. Being alone in her office while the sky turned dark offered an opportunity to truly indulge in these things. His broad shoulders and his soft belly, the weight and reassurance of him. His stubbornness and determination: a person without pretense, a person who needed to get things *right*. Whether it was crafting bookshelves or trying on the idea of polyamory or taking care of his mother.

She hated how nostalgic and bittersweet it felt, those nights, thinking about Dell. Like he was a thing that had happened to her once, that she might not ever be able to see again.

Still, no matter how many nights went by, he was always there in the office, waiting for her.

That was the thing about love.

No matter how far away they sometimes felt, the ones that mattered never really left you.

Your body remembered the shit that was important.

In mid-December, Mae received a package from Michigan.

*Saw this at a bookstore in Marquette, when I was up visiting an old friend. Made me think of you.*

Mae let the note drop to the desk. Lifted the book it had been stuck to.

Tessa Dare. *Romancing the Duke.*

Jesús hugged her shoulders. *See?* he whispered. Jesús talked to her all the time, since Dell had been gone. Sometimes she wondered if he talked to her too much. If she was quietly losing her mind.

Maybe she did see. Maybe a mass market paperback always helped.

Maybe it was still hard.

She ran her finger over Dell's almost illegible handwriting before sliding the paper into the top drawer of the desk, next to her favorite pink pens, and returned to her profit and loss spreadsheet.

One day, Mae was reading an advanced reader copy of an upcoming release when an old white man walked in. He wore a faded baseball cap and a frown that looked vaguely familiar.

It wasn't until he brought up a book a short minute later, as if he'd known exactly what he was looking for and didn't have time to browse for anything else, that she recognized him. Remembered Liv's quiet laughter on her first full day in town.

Brooks, the writer with the secret pen name.

She examined the book he was purchasing, a new literary hardcover—*thank you for your service, Brooks*, she almost said—and tried to deduce if it was a clue. *Is this you?!* No, this book was definitely written by a Black man Mae had seen online a hundred times.

But still. It could be a clue.

She smiled politely, thanked him for visiting Bay Books.

And as soon as he left, she grabbed her phone, laughing as she brought up the group chat.

Until the door jingled again.

And Mae slowly put her phone back down.

He looked a touch different—older, scruffier—than he had in his profile picture. But Mae still recognized him all the same.

"Hi," she said. It was mid-morning on a Tuesday; there were no other customers to cushion them from each other. After a moment's hesitation, she added, "Luca."

"Hi," he said with an acknowledging nod. "Mae."

They exchanged small, awkward smiles. He turned toward a bookshelf.

"Let me know if you need anything," she said. And then she stared at her computer, heart thudding in her chest.

Until Luca brought a Martha Wells to the counter.

She didn't know how to process that he was just as hot as she'd imagined.

So she simply began ringing him up instead.

"Uh." He scratched his head, credit card clutched in his other hand. How strange, to feel so close to someone you'd never technically met before. "His mom's doing okay?" And then, before Mae could respond, "I overheard some people talking in the IGA."

At once, Mae's heart stopped thudding. She released a breath. She wanted to hug this man. To invite him out for a beer. They wouldn't even have to talk. They could just spend time, in that space of understanding, of missing Dell, together.

"Yeah," she eventually said, voice gentle. "It sounds like she's doing a lot better."

Luca nodded. Tucked the book under his arm.

"Hey Luca?" she said, when he was almost to the door. He half turned. "Keep coming in, okay? If you want to."

He gave her a small smile.

"It is nice, having a bookstore."

"I hoped it would be."

With another nod, he was gone.

A few days before Christmas, Dell called in the morning when Mae was still in bed, barely awake.

"Mae," he said, voice sounding more urgent than it normally did. Mae shot up from the pillows. *Georgia.* "I'm so sorry I didn't do this earlier. But Mae, the store should be yours."

Mae frowned, staring blurrily at Dell's bedside clock. Crosby stirred next to her.

"What?"

"12 Main Street. I want to sell it to you. I should have done that first thing, when we—it's yours anyway."

The words percolated through Mae's mind, much slower than she knew they should.

"But it hasn't been six months yet."

Dell released a quiet huff on the other end of the line. Mae thought she could hear his smile in it.

"It doesn't matter anymore," he said.

And Mae suddenly wanted to cry.

"I've never wanted to ask for details about Jesús's money, but is it enough to buy it outright?"

"No."

Why was he doing this to her now? Couldn't he at least have waited for her to be awake to break her heart?

"Okay. We can work out all the details over email, my bank and your bank and the title company and everything; we don't have to go over it all right now. But I can negotiate on price, if you don't have enough, after all the repairs and startup costs of the business and everything—"

"I have enough."

Mae didn't need to study her budgets; she'd been studying them for the last four and a half months. It would be disconcerting, giving away half of the rest of the money on a down payment, but to make a mortgage feasible, she knew that was what she had to do. She'd have to be more careful with each purchase, both for the store and for her own life, but maybe it would be good, having some discipline again.

It wasn't the money she was worried about.

"Okay. I'll send you some emails, okay? But go ahead and apply for a loan with your bank when you have time."

"Okay," she whispered.

"Oh god, it's still early there. I'm sorry, Mae. Go back to sleep. We'll talk about it more later, okay?"

Mae nodded, even though Dell couldn't see her.

"Tell Georgia"—tears filled her eyes—"I said hi."

"I will." Another smile in his words. And then, soft: "Good morning, Mae."

The line went quiet.

She knew this had been what she'd wanted. Back in the beginning. What she'd always wanted.

But it was hard, as she woke another morning in Dell's bed without Dell, to only see it as a severing.

She knew, on her hard days, that the dogs still tethered Dell to Greyfin Bay. That he'd eventually come back for the dogs, for his house.

But 12 Main Street was the thing that still tethered him to her.

Mae buried her face in Crosby's fur.

She was finally going to own something.

And she'd never hated anything more.

As happened with most things, Mae adjusted, inch by inch.

As she had adjusted to opening the store without Dell, as she had adjusted to continuing to run the store after her closest friends had gone back to Portland. As she had adjusted to life without Steve or Jesús. So too did she accept, eventually, her sole ownership of 12 Main.

And from the moment she filled out the loan application, she found herself spending more time upstairs, on the empty second floor, a spattering of her old furniture pushed against a wall. Her original thoughts for it—her own living space, a queer community center—no longer felt exactly right. But she didn't want it sitting empty anymore. She wanted it to be part of Bay Books.

She wanted it to honor Jesús.

She kept thinking about Robin and the book club ladies. The angsty teenagers who kept showing up in the afternoons, once school was out. She thought about Luca, writing his book.

And as winter turned dark and dreary, the sea beyond the sidewalks of Main Street gray and churning, Mae started a new project, to help find the light. A new space, to help stitch herself together.

# thirty-one

ON THE FIRST Monday of the new year, Mae heard a key turn in the lock as she shifted inventory past close, preparing for another week of new releases.

Somehow, she knew the moment she heard it. That someone wasn't picking the lock, that she wasn't being harmed. That it wasn't Vik, one of the only other people with a key, surprising her.

Her breath caught in her throat: half in hope, half in fear she was wrong. She stood frozen, trapped between the two.

Until she heard his heavy footsteps cross the threshold.

The book in her hands dropped to the shelf.

She had daydreamed about this moment, during the times she'd allowed herself to believe it would happen. How she'd sigh and smile, and slide her fingers between his, her other hand cupping his cheek. *Welcome home*, she'd say. And he'd smile back, and softly brush his nose against hers, and—

Mae burst into tears. Before she could even fully see

him, before she could take in his face. Loud, heaving, embarrassing tears; she covered her face with her hands.

"Hey there, Mae," Dell said, wrapping his arms around her. "Hey. It's okay."

It had been almost two months since she'd seen him.

And sometimes, during some years, two months felt like a very long time.

She was crying too hard to speak.

"I thought a surprise entrance would be romantic," he murmured into her hair. "But perhaps I misjudged."

And for a hot second, she was indeed filled with fury. That she hadn't known he'd been waiting in TSA lines, his big body cramped in airline seats; that he'd been walking through PDX, driving home over the Coastal Range. That she hadn't been able to worry. Hadn't been able to anticipate.

"Are you—" Oh god, he smelled so good, felt so good cocooning her, but she had to make sure. Maybe he just needed to get more things from his house to take back to the UP. "Are you actually back?"

"Yeah." He nuzzled his face into the side of her head. Mae could not believe he was here. "Well, there are some things I have to tell you. But yeah."

She must have frozen at *some things I have to tell you*, because he hugged her a bit tighter. "Mae, I'm back. I came straight here before I even went home," he said, voice softer. "Figured you'd still be here. Needed to see you before I even saw the dogs, if that helps."

It did.

She shoved her face into his neck. Rubbed her tears against his sweatshirt.

"Dell. I missed you so much." She clutched at the fabric. "I tried to tell myself I was holding it together, because I had the store, and it was selfish, needing you, because you had to be with your mom, but Dell—I missed you *so much*."

"Mae." Dell's voice turned his extra-special version of rough that made Mae's scalp tingle. "Mae, I missed you, too. I'm so sorry."

"You don't have to be sorry. I'm just—" Mae might pass out. "So glad to see you."

"Me too. You don't even know. Mae." Dell pulled back, taking hold of Mae's shoulders. Trying to look at her. But looking at Dell McCleary's face was still a little too much for Mae, so she scrunched her eyes closed and looked away. Just for a second. But Dell sighed. "Fuck. I've fucked up pretty bad, Mae, haven't I." He released her shoulders, running a hand through his hair. "I'm always fucking up with you."

"No. It's okay," Mae tried to unscrunch her eyes to say. To be brave enough to look at him and accept he was actually here. But Dell kept going before she was quite there.

"It was just—it was really hard, Mae, seeing Georgia sick, being back in Michigan, all of it, and...you're so...*Mae*, and I thought you'd be okay, busy with the store, and—" Dell sighed once more. "But those are all excuses. I know I could have communicated more. I know I disappeared, like I have a bad habit of doing. I'm so, so sorry."

"I *am* okay!" Mae shouted, wiping furiously at her face. Because fuck—she had to be clear about this. "I *am* busy with the store! Which is great, by the way!" Except *great* didn't even cover it. Mae loved her store. She loved it so much. She was so *happy*. She'd have to explain it to Dell better, when more oxygen reached her brain. "I know so many people now. I say hi *all the time.* Me and Liv have become great dog co-parents, too, I'll have you know. And my professor called my final project *impressive*, so! So. You texted, and you sent me that book, and I know you did what you could, and I'm *fine*; I'm good, I just—"

She couldn't explain it. That it felt like she was doing the best thing she'd ever done, living the best life she'd ever lived, while simultaneously floating in suspended animation, without him. She wasn't mad. She just—

She balled her hands into fists and stomped her foot.

"I just *missed* you!"

"Mae." Dell's mouth curved into that *damn* Dell smile as he stepped forward, cradling her cheeks in his palms. Mae shivered before she stepped away.

"No." She shook her head. "Tell me what those things are that you have to tell me, before you kiss me. I need to know what those things are before I climb you like a tree."

Because she couldn't float in suspended animation forever.

Dell stepped forward again. Until Mae's back just about hit the front counter.

"You sure it can't wait?" he asked, still smiling. "Because jumping to that climbing me like a tree part sounds better to me."

"I'm—" Mae struggled to take a breath. "I'm not sure of anything at this exact moment."

And somehow, that finally made Dell's eyes turn serious again.

"Okay," he said. And then, "I bought a house in the UP."

Mae's body turned to ice.

"But!" Dell held up his hands. "It's just a second, sometimes house. My home is still here, in the foothills, with you and the dogs. But Georgia's still getting older. Still has a chance of having another stroke, or a fall, or something else. And"—Dell took a breath—"I've finally accepted that she's staying there in that beautiful frozen tundra and there's nothing I can do about it. Except make myself drive to PDX and visit her more. So that's what I hope to do. I've been...ignoring a lot of my past, but I don't want to do that anymore. I want to..." His brow furrowed. His hands cupped the air, like he was holding the world in his hands. "Remember all of it. Hold onto all of it. Be here, and there, as much as I can."

Cautiously, his hands rested on her face again.

"A sometimes house," she said.

"Yeah," he whispered. "I'd love for you to go with me, sometimes, to that sometimes house. But I understand you have the store."

Mae swallowed.

"I have employees now."

"Yeah?" His eyes twinkled.

"Yeah. I mean, I'm definitely not ready to leave this place to Karizma and Zeke *quite* yet, and Karizma will have her baby, but—"

"Wait, Zeke who used to work at the bank?"

"Yeah. I guess he's bored with retirement. He's only here a day or two a week. But his wife sends me thank you emails like, all the time."

Dell's smile deepened. "Zeke's a good guy."

"Yeah. Dell, I would love to visit the UP with you."

His thumbs caressed her cheeks, eyes growing thoughtful.

"Can you help me get out of Greyfin Bay more in general? Not just when I need to visit Georgia, and...probably not back to Portland, at least not a lot. I might not ever be fully okay, going back there, but I'm going to work on it. I also can't guarantee I won't ever throw a mug at your head again, and I am so deeply sorry about that. But..."

Dell swallowed. Mae tracked the movement in his throat, forced herself to not lean forward and kiss it.

"Going to other places. Like maybe one day we could drive to the California border and back, just for the hell of it. Things like that. So I know I'm not hiding here. If that makes sense."

"Yeah," Mae whispered, eyes somehow refilling with tears. She was going to be so dehydrated. "Yeah, Dell. To all of it."

He smiled at her again. His eyes were calm. She tried, again, to take a full breath.

"Georgia's really okay?"

And Mae knew she was when Dell rolled his eyes.

"Yeah. For now anyway. Other than her threatening me with bodily harm daily if I didn't get out of her house and back to you."

Mae bit her lip. "I think I like this mom of yours."

"Yeah." Dell moved forward, shuffling Mae fully against the counter. Slotting their bodies fully against each other. "I actually would've been here earlier, if snowstorms didn't keep getting in my way."

Mae stared at Dell's mouth.

"Welcome back to the home of forever rain," she said.

"I have never been happier to be here."

And when he leaned in this time, she didn't stop him.

The feel of his lips, the scratch of his beard, the touch of his tongue. His belly against hers, his sweatshirt underneath her fingertips.

*I missed you*, she kissed him.

*Thank you for coming home,* she kissed him.

*Welcome to our store,* she kissed him.

And he kissed her back: an affirmation. An ember.

A full, settling breath.

She pulled away to say, "I have something I want to show you, too."

Taking him by the hand, she led him around the counter, into the office, and up the stairs. When they reached the second story, she released his hand to turn on all the lamps, the twinkle lights above the windows. Dell looked around at the couch, the chairs, the tables. The plants and the flowers, the framed postcards and art prints. The things she'd acquired from Olive over the last few weeks, combined with bits from her life in Portland, from her life in Madison. From her lives in Brooklyn and North Carolina. Her storage unit was empty; she'd turned in the keys and brought home the last of it after her Christmas visit to Vik and Jackson's. All of her bits were now here.

"What is this?"

"I...don't know, exactly, yet," Mae admitted. "But the more I talk to people, the longer I run the store...I don't have the spoons to run a queer community center, to do what I used to do. But I think Greyfin Bay needs a space. Where people can hold book clubs, or study, or start a writing group, or read, or...be still. A space to just be."

Mae tucked a stray strand of hair behind her ear.

"I also know it's a liability, having a free open space, so I had the security system extended up here, and I'd probably only have it open a few nights a week, or—"

"Mae." Dell stepped toward her. "I think it's lovely."

Her eyes flashed toward his. "Yeah? Lovely was...kind of what I was going for."

He glanced at the wall behind her.

"Gemma's work too, I presume?"

"Yeah. That's my favorite part."

She turned to look at it with him. The mural took up the entire length of the far wall, just completed by Gemma a few days before. A field of California poppies. An expanse of orange and green and blue sky.

"Poppies," Dell murmured.

"State flower of California," Mae explained. "Jesús, originally...was one of those damn Californians."

Dell, thankfully, grinned.

"I want it to feel like...how he always made people feel."

Dell stepped closer. Kissed her temple.

"It already does, Mae," he whispered. "But this reminds me." He reached into the pocket of his jeans. "I got you something."

He opened the tiny plastic bag and emptied the trinket into her palm. She brought it up to her face to examine.

"This is..."

"Apple blossom," Dell said. "State flower of Michigan."

Mae looked at him.

He lifted her gold chain from underneath her T-shirt.

"This okay?" he whispered. She nodded.

He had big hands, Dell McCleary, but he used them to make fine crafted, beautiful things. He didn't struggle at all with the clasp. With gliding the new pendant down to meet the others. And maybe Mae had believed him downstairs, when he'd said he was back. But maybe she *really* believed him when Michigan rested against her chest. Maybe she truly knew now that he'd still be with her, even when he had to leave again.

And maybe it was about time to get to that climbing like a tree part.

When she threw herself at him now, it wasn't at all gentle and kind like it had been downstairs.

"Dell," she said, yanking at his clothes, scratching at his neck. "*Please.*"

"Yes," he answered, ripping away her cardigan, her skirt with equal abandon. "Fuck yes."

And so her old coffee table was shoved to the side somewhat recklessly, the plant she'd placed on it almost crashing to the ground until Mae caught it at the last second. Jeans and leggings were hastily pushed off, shirts thrown to the side, until Mae and Dell were once more resting on a rug in 12 Main Street, making bad choices for their backs.

"On top," Dell breathed, grabbing Mae by the hips as they rolled into position. "I need you on top of me."

Dell's hands and mouth were everywhere—squeezing her ass, teeth grazing her skin, tongue swirling around her nipples, sucking, beard tickling. Mae moved against him, rubbed her clit against the length of him before he fumbled for a condom, before she placed him at her entrance; she was a breath away from screaming the entire time. "I'm so —I'm going to come in like five seconds." She sank onto him with a groan.

"Already," Dell breathed, "halfway there."

"I *missed* you," she panted, digging her fingers into his stomach, his breasts, his good shoulder.

"Fucking kiss me," Dell demanded. And so she did, swiftly too distracted by the heat of his mouth, her own sloppy desires to keep up any sort of respectable rhythm, but Dell took over without complaint, thrusting into her as their mouths clashed, as she emptied her cries onto his tongue.

"So good," she whispered, body no longer under her control. It had always been so good with Dell.

"So fucking good," he agreed, suddenly fisting a hand into her hair, fingers of his other hand sliding between their bodies, rubbing her just there, and—

*Oh god oh god*

She dropped her face to his shoulder, mouth open on his skin, all words knocked out of her. Distantly, she felt his fingers in her hair tighten, his body stutter beneath hers as they went still, tight tight tight and then loose, so fucking loose and hot and wet.

"Fuck." Dell's arms flopped to his sides. His chest moved underneath her mouth, a swelling inhale and release. "Mae. Fuck."

"Dell. Oh god I needed that so bad."

A rumble of laughter underneath her cheek.

"Me too." A kiss in her hair, before his head thudded back to the rug. "I'll do it more sensually next time."

"Mm," Mae mumbled. "Only if you really want to."

Another laugh, more relaxed.

Mae was never going to move again.

Except then Dell was nudging her shoulder.

"Mae," he whispered. "I have to pee."

Dell was truly the worst sometimes.

But she supposed she forgave him when he came back up the stairs a few minutes later, clad in a white T-shirt and black briefs, the roots of a tree spreading down his thigh, covering a scar he'd never deserved.

And he was still laughing.

"What's so funny?" she asked as she pulled on her leggings, only slightly grumpily, to go follow suit.

"The bathroom," he said. "I forgot about Jesús's bathroom."

She smiled then.

"It's gotten many compliments."

"I'm sure it has."

He kissed her on the mouth, short and sweet as she passed. The kind of short and sweet you shared when you had time. When you weren't worried about getting to do it again.

When she returned to his side five minutes later, wrapping an arm around his stomach, a leg around his thigh, her cheek nestled onto his shoulder, the last words she needed to say tumbled free.

"I was so sad when you sold me this building."

Dell jerked his head toward her so fast his beard almost scraped her corneas.

"What?"

"I—" She turned her face into his breast. "I know it was what I always wanted. But part of me had become convinced you might stay in Michigan permanently, to stay with your mom, so when you suddenly handed the building over to me, it felt like...you were ripping away the final Band-Aid that attached you to me. You know?"

"Mae." Dell exhaled, rubbing a hand over his face. "God, no. It's just—I should've sold it to you a long time ago, the first time we kissed, the first time I accepted I had feelings for you. I don't like power differentials in relationships, and me having ownership of your store when we were romantically involved felt wrong to me. I just kind of...forgot to do anything about it, in the hecticness of everything, and when I remembered, I had to make it right."

She shook her head.

"Of course you did," she said. *God*, she loved him.

"But I'm so sorry if it made you upset."

"No, it's okay." And then, giving his chest a kiss, "I had started to think of this place as *ours*, though."

A pause.

"Oh." Quiet, a bit surprised. "I didn't—" Dell swallowed. "That's kind of you, to think that, even though I really did just make some bookshelves."

"And paid for half of the repairs."

"Well—"

"And gave me a place to live. For free."

"I still don't exactly understand how that ended up happening, but I'm glad it did."

"And took me to the lumberyard. Listened to me, every day."

"If you—" Another uncertain pause. "I mean, we are still waiting on the title paperwork, I suppose, if you really want to change—"

"Oh no, I own this shit now. No take backs."

And Dell barked out a laugh that shook Mae's whole body.

"You are something else, Mae Kellerman."

Mae kissed the side of his breast again.

"I own this building," she said, "but it'll still always be a little bit yours."

Dell's laughter died down. His arm wrapped around her back, fingers dancing along her shoulder.

"That sounds good to me." A minute went by before he asked, "Did you really think I wasn't coming back?"

Mae could hear the troubled frown in his voice. She tried to not feel foolish.

"You just...never said, on the phone or over text. *Can't wait to come home. Can't wait to see you again.* You know? I got paranoid. Maybe a bit dramatic. I don't know."

Dell sighed.

"I was gone for two months, Mae," he said, voice quiet again, serious. "That's pretty dramatic. I just...I never want to lie to you. And I never knew when I'd be coming home. So I could never say it."

Mae closed her eyes.

“But I’ll be better, next time. At making sure you know I’ll always come back to you.”

“I know, Dell. I know.” And she did know. Not just that he would do better next time. Not just that he would always come back.

But that no matter what happened between them, Dell McCleary was a person who would never lie to her.

The trust she had in that—the trust she had in him—seeded through every part of her. It was a balm to overworked skin. It was the calcium in her bones.

They quieted as they listened to the creaks of the old building, the intermittent chatter of Main Street, the distant but ever present rush of the waves on Greyfin Beach. As they looked at the wall of Jesús’s poppies, brought to life by another queer person, another kind stranger, who lived in another small town along the coast.

“What was Jesús’s connection to Greyfin Bay?” Dell asked after a time, his hand running down Mae’s arm. “Why did he want his ashes spread here?”

“You know, I never actually knew until Alexei told me, that day we spread his ashes, when I first saw this building. Greyfin Bay was where Jesús and Steve had their first date.” Mae smiled into Dell’s skin. “They first met when they were out with mutual friends one night in Portland. Jesús thought Steve was hot but quiet, until late into the night, when marine life, of all things, came up in conversation. As weird stuff tends to come up in conversation when you’ve been at the bar too long. And Steve just...exploded, talking about how much he loved whales and sharks and rays and—”

Mae paused to smile again, picturing the memory she hadn’t actually witnessed.

“—how much he’d always wanted to go on a whale

watching tour. Steve was from Oregon but somehow had never been out here for one; when his family went on vacation they went to like...Paris and Venice and Saint Barts. Although I think it was Saint Barts where he first fell in love with marine life. Anyway, so Jesús invited him on a date to Greyfin Bay. He told Alexei that he fell in love with Steve the first moment he started talking about sharks at that bar, but it was when they came here, when he saw the look on Steve's face when he first saw a whale on that boat that he knew he was done for life."

They lapsed again into silence, staring at the poppies. Dell running that calloused hand up and down Mae's skin.

"Have you been on one of the whale watching tours?" Dell eventually asked. "You moved at the perfect time for one."

"No," Mae murmured. "I was too busy with the shop. Have you been on one?"

She wasn't surprised at all when Dell chuckled, a soft vibration against her cheek, and said, "No."

But then he added, "We should go, this year. In honor of them."

"Yeah." Mae smiled again. "In honor of them."

"We should probably go soon, in any case," Dell added, "before climate change drives whales away from Greyfin Bay for good."

"You are always full of pleasant thoughts, Dell McCleary."

"Always." And then, "I'm glad they brought Steve and Jesús together, though." A pause. "I'm glad they brought you to me."

"Yeah," Mae whispered. "I'm glad for that, too."

Another long moment passed.

"Hey Dell? When we go on that whale watching tour,

nine months or so from now. You won't judge me too harshly if Bay Books has shut down by then?"

Because Dell's predictions felt more realistic, now that she'd dwindled Steve and Jesús's savings in opening the shop. Now that she'd given half of what remained to the bank. Now that she'd seen, every day, how thin her profit margins were.

"It won't be shut down," Dell said automatically. Diplomatically. Kindly.

"It might," Mae countered. Dell's hand paused, for just a second, before returning to its ministrations.

"Then you'll figure something else out," Dell said. "And it'll still be incredible that you made Bay Books exist at all. As long as you're still with me, Mae? That's all I need."

Mae breathed in and out.

"But I know that whatever you do, even if it's not this," Dell added, voice so soft and affectionate Mae didn't know what to do with herself, "it'll be something good. Because that's who you are, Mae."

*Ohh,* Jesús whispered. *Mae. Never let this one go.*

"And you'll still be here," she said after a moment. "And Liv. And Olive, and Cara. Even if the whales go away."

"Even if the whales go away," Dell promised.

And that promise was good enough for her.

She had almost drifted to sleep when Dell spoke again.

"Hey. Mae. What was the last song on Jesús's death party playlist? The one you said was rude, that you never play."

Mae blinked awake.

"Can you reach my sweater? I think I'm ready to play it now."

Dell stretched to reach the cardigan. She fished her phone out of its pocket, navigated to Spotify.

She placed the phone on the floor next to them. Dell let out a breath as the opening strings of Judy Garland's "Over the Rainbow" swelled through the room.

"Oh," he said into her hair.

"Yeah," she agreed.

And she cried when Judy started singing, as one was wont to do when listening to this song. As one was wont to do when they'd been able to love very special people. When they'd been able to live through so many special seasons.

"I loved him," she said into Dell's chest. He rubbed her arm.

"I love you," he said after a moment.

It felt, for a second, as if he was saying it to make Mae feel better. As if to balance out the hurt.

But maybe he was just saying it because the moment felt right. Because he wanted to. Because he meant it.

Love wasn't a zero sum game. It wasn't something to balance, to even scores. Mae would always love Jesús.

And she would always love Dell.

"I love you, too," she replied.

And they lay on the floor of 12 Main Street, in the comfort of the other's warmth and the sound of the ocean beyond the glass, until the song was through.

# *acknowledgments*

Thank you, first and foremost, to romance novels and to the Oregon Coast. Thank you, too, to the small town that raised me and to the cities that have been my homes.

Thank you to Sawyer Cole and Chip Pons for sharing your experiences with me, for your encouragement and kindness, and for being such bright spots of positivity. Thank you to Corina Bair for your expertise, time, and affirming read-along comments (a writer's most favorite thing), and to Kali Hannon for your thoughtful, helpful feedback.

Thank you to Alicia Thompson and KT Hoffman for your friendship, epic emails of feedback and support, and for simply being you, always and every day.

Thank you to Chandra Fisher and Briana Miano for reading this book so quickly and understanding it so deeply. Thank you to the rest of The Writing Folks, always, but this time especially to Kat and Molly for teaching me what a hinge is.

Thank you to my agent, Kim Lionetti, for fixing the beginning of this book for me.

Thank you to every small business owner who hangs a trans flag on their walls and to every teacher who hangs one in their classrooms.

Thank you to the writing and reading community of Portland, Oregon, who have listened to me cry about Coast

Book for a long time, Alison Cochrun and Erin Connor in particular.

Thank you to KGW and Grant's Getaways, the most soothing local programming there ever was, the background to a lot of my daydreaming of Greyfin Bay.

Thank you to queer elders who have survived more than we'll ever be able to acknowledge. Thank you to everyone who works to make the world a kinder, more just place.

Finally, thank you to Manda Bednarik, for witnessing decades of my mess, and to Kathy, Fury, Angus, Tegan, and Tyson, even if Angus is too naughty to actually be trusted on the beach: visiting the coast with you all is my favorite thing.

# indie bookstores to support on the oregon coast

- Godfather's Books and Lucy's Books, Astoria
- Cannon Beach Book Company, Cannon Beach
- Beach Books, Seaside
- Cloud & Leaf Bookstore, Manzanita
- Bob's Beach Books and Robert's Bookshop, Lincoln City
- Nye Beach Book House, Newport
- Well-Read Books, Waldport
- Books by the Bay, North Bend
- WinterRiver Books, Bandon
- Sea Wolf Books, Port Orford
- Gold Beach Books, Gold Beach

# about the author

Originally from a small town in the Pocono Mountains of Pennsylvania, Anita Kelly now lives in the Pacific Northwest with their family. An educator by day, they write romance that celebrates queer love in all its infinite possibilities. Whenever not reading or writing, they're drinking too much tea, taking pictures, and dreaming of their next walk in the woods. They hope you get to pet a dog today.

# also by anita kelly

*Nashville Love*

Love & Other Disasters

Something Wild & Wonderful

How You Get the Girl

*Moonlighters*

Sing Anyway

Our Favorite Songs

Wherever Is Your Heart